Confession; or, The Blind Heart

Available from the Simms Initiatives and the University of South Carolina Press

The Army Correspondence of Colonel John Laurens, ed.

As Good as a Comedy and Paddy McGann

Beauchampe

Border Beagles

Carl Werner, 2 vols.

The Cassique of Kiawah

Castle Dismal

Charlemont

The Charleston Book, ed.

Confession

Count Julian

The Damsel of Darien, 2 vols.

Dramas: Norman Maurice, Michael Bonham, and Benedict Arnold

Egeria

Eutaw

The Forayers

The Geography of South Carolina

The Golden Christmas

Guy Rivers

Helen Halsey

Historical and Political Poems (*which includes* Monody, The Vision of Cortes, The Tri-Color, Donna Florida, and Charleston and Her Satirists)

The History of South Carolina

Joscelyn

Katharine Walton

The Letters of William Gilmore Simms, Vol. 1

The Letters of William Gilmore Simms, Vol. 2

The Letters of William Gilmore Simms, Vol. 3

The Letters of William Gilmore Simms, Vol. 4

The Letters of William Gilmore Simms, Vol. 5

The Letters of William Gilmore Simms, Vol. 6 (exp. ed.)

The Life of Captain John Smith

The Life of the Chevalier Bayard

The Life of Francis Marion

The Lily and the Totem

Marie de Berniere

Martin Faber and Other Tales, 2 vols.

Mellichampe

The Partisan

Pelayo, 2 vols.

Poems, Descriptive, Dramatic, Legendary, and Contemplative, 2 vols.

The Remains of Maynard Davis Richardson

Richard Hurdis

Sack and Destruction of the City of Columbia

The Scout

Selections from the Letters and Speeches of the Hon. James H. Hammond, ed.

Simms's Poems Areytos

Social and Political Prose: Slavery in America/Father Abbot

South Carolina in the Revolutionary War

Southward Ho!

Stories and Tales

A Supplement to the Plays of William Shakespeare

Vasconselos

Views and Reviews in American Literature, History and Fiction, 2 vols.

Voltmeier

War Poetry of the South

The Wigwam and the Cabin

Woodcraft

The Yemassee

Confession; or, The Blind Heart

A Domestic Story

William Gilmore Simms

Critical Introduction by Todd Hagstette

With a Biographical Overview by David Moltke-Hansen

The University of South Carolina Press

Cloth original published by Redfield, 1856
Paperback published by the University of South Carolina Press
Columbia, South Carolina 29208

www.sc.edu/uscpress

Manufactured in the United States of America

24 23 22 21 20 19 18 17 16 15
10 9 8 7 6 5 4 3 2 1

ISBN 978-1-61117-026-9 (pbk)

Published in cooperation with the Simms Initiatives, a project of the University of South Carolina Libraries with the generous support of the Watson-Brown Foundation.

William Gilmore Simms: A Biographical Overview

David Moltke-Hansen

Introduction

Harper's Weekly put it succinctly in its July 2, 1870, issue: "In the death of Mr. Simms, on the 11th of June, at Charleston, the country has lost one more of its time-honored band of authors, and the South the most consistent and devoted of her literary sons" (qtd. In Butterworth and Kibler 125–26). Indeed no mid-nineteenth-century writer and editor did more than William Gilmore Simms to frame white southern self-identity and nationalism, shape southern historical consciousness, or foster the South's participation and recognition in the broader American literary culture. No southern writer enjoyed more contemporary esteem and attention, at least after Edgar Allan Poe moved north. Among American romancers (or writers of prose epics), only New Yorker James Fenimore Cooper was as successful by the 1840s. In those same years, Simms was the South's most influential editor of cultural journals. He also was the region's most prolific cultural journalist and poet, publishing an average of one book review and one poem per week for forty-five years.

Before his death Simms saw his national reputation fall along with the Confederacy he had vigorously supported and with the slave regime that many in the North had come to despise. Nevertheless reprints of most of the twenty titles in the selected edition of his works, first published between 1853 and 1860, appeared up until World War I. Thereafter only *The Yemassee*, an early romance about an Indian war in South Carolina, continued in print. The tide began to turn in the 1950s, when five volumes of Simms's letters appeared and a growing number of his works were issued in new editions. Publication in 1992 of the first literary biography, by John C. Guilds, and establishment of the William Gilmore Simms Society and the *Simms Review* the next year at once reflected and fostered this revived interest. Yet not until the 2011 launch of the digital Simms edition of the South Caroliniana Library of the University of South Carolina did scholars of southern, American, and nineteenth-century culture have the prospect of ready access to all of Simms's separately published works. With the University of South Carolina Press's cooperation, readers also will have access to sixty works in paperback editions by the end of 2014. Simms himself never saw nearly so many of his works in print at one time.

Clearly the decline in the critical standing of, and historical attention to, Simms and his oeuvre in the century after his death has reversed in the years since. The last three decades of the twentieth century saw more published on Simms than the previous hundred years (Butterworth and Kibler 126–200; MLA International). The last decade of the twentieth and first decade of the twenty-first centuries saw more dissertations and theses on him (forty-one) than had appeared in all the years before. This is not to say that Simms is yet given the attention directed to some of his contemporaries. For the first decade of the twenty-first century, the Modern Language Association International Bibliography lists roughly four times as many scholarly publications on James Fenimore Cooper, more than ten times as many on Nathaniel Hawthorne, and sixteen times as many on Edgar Allan Poe. Not surprisingly, therefore, Simms is not yet included in most anthologies of American literature, although he is a subject or a source in an expanding and ever more diverse body of scholarship.

To prepare to read Simms, it is important to see his writings in multiple contexts. He rarely wrote about himself outside of his more personal poems and his letters (some fifteen hundred of the many thousands of which survive). Yet he systematically drew on his background, personal experience, and relationships in his work. He also shaped that work through a progressively developed poetics and philosophy of life, history, and art. He did so in the context of his very broad reading of both contemporary and earlier Western literature and in the midst of multiple professional engagements and responsibilities. The richness and variety of these writings and involvements make Simms a key figure for future understanding of the literary culture, issues, and networks in mid-nineteenth-century America.

Background

Simms's family history reflected the dynamics that fueled the spread southward and westward of the populations, plantation economy, and society of the South Atlantic states. Simms's ancestry also reflected the Scots-Irish and English roots of what became identified as southern culture by the 1830s, a generation after the end of most immigration to the region. Two of Simms's grandparents, William and Elisabeth Sims, were Scots-Irish and migrated to South Carolina from Ulster. One, John Singleton, was an American-born son of putatively English immigrants, who had come to South Carolina from Virginia. The fourth, Jane Miller, was daughter of two Scots-Irish and Irish descended people—John Miller, of North and then South Carolina, and Jane Ross. Ross's family also migrated to South Carolina from western Virginia, where members lived cheek by jowl with other Scots-Irish families, who migrated to the Carolinas (White, *Ross*). Simms's father and Uncle James migrated in 1808 from Charleston to Tennessee, then to Mississippi. This was after the bankruptcy of the elder William's business and the deaths of his wife and their other two sons. Following the last of these losses, the elder Simms's hair turned white in a week. To his anguished eyes, Charleston appeared "a place of tombs" (qtd. in Guilds 6, 12).

For the son, however, Charleston was home—so much so that he refused to leave his maternal grandmother and move to Mississippi when his uncle came to get him in 1816. Then the fifth largest and by far the wealthiest city, as well as one of the greatest ports, in America, Charleston was at the peak of its influence (Moltke-Hansen, "Expansion" 25–31; Rogers). Cotton culture on the sea islands to the south, begun in 1790, and rice culture in impounded lowcountry tidal marshes meant that the port was filled not only with sailors of many lands and languages, but also with enslaved people of many African and Creole cultures and speech ways (slaves continued to be imported legally in large numbers until 1808). This street life made vivid the transnational nature of plantation agriculture and the fact that the developing region's dramatically expanding borders "were not just geographic; they also were human, historical, and intellectual" (Moltke-Hansen, "Southern" 19).

Even more important for the future author, the expanding region's borders and nature were taking imaginative shape. The West of the senior William Gilmore Simms and the first Creek War in which he fought, the Revolutionary War of the young Simms's maternal grandfather, the backcountry of many related Scots-Irish settlers, all these became grist for a lonely, energetic boy, who spent as much time with books as he could (Simms, *Letters* 1:161). The possibilities of such settings, incidents, and characters were not confined to history alone. Simms reported that he "used to glow and shiver in turn over 'The Pilgrim's Progress,'" while "Moses' adventures in 'The Vicar of Wakefield' threw [him] into paroxysms of laughter" (Hayne 261–62). Sir Walter Scott's Border and medieval romances and James Fenimore Cooper's Leatherstocking tales also deeply colored his imagination (Simms, *Views* 1:248, and Moltke-Hansen, "Southern" 6–15). As affecting were the ghost stories and Revolutionary War tales of his grandmother and the verses sent, and tales told, by his father.

These diverse tales became reasons to explore—in books, but also on the ground. As a boy, Simms ranged through the city and along the banks of the Ashley River, which fed into Charleston Harbor. He did so in search of scenes of colonial and Revolutionary battles and incidents (*Letters* 1:lxii). He first heard his uncle's and father's many Irish and frontier stories when they visited in Charleston in 1816 and 1818, respectively. He heard more on his trips to Mississippi during the winter of 1824 through the spring of 1825 and again in 1826. The first trip took him through Georgia and Alabama, where he saw elements of the Creek and Cherokee nations. At the time, Simms later reported, he was a boy "cumbered with fragmentary materials of thought, . . . choked by the tangled vines of erroneous speculation, and haunted by passions, which, like so many wolves, lurked, in ready waiting, for their unsuspecting prey" (*Social* 6). When he first got to Mississippi, traveling partly by stage, partly by riverboat, and partly by horse, Simms learned that his father had just come back from "a trip of three hundred miles into the heart of the Indian country" (Trent 15). Later father and son "rode together on horseback to various settlements on the frontier of Alabama and Mississippi" (Guilds 10–11, 17–18). Simms recalled as well "having traveled 150 miles beyond the Mississippi" (Shillingsburg, "Literary Grist" 120). The next year he returned to the Southwest by ship. "During this [second] trip he carried a 'note book.'" There he jotted episodes, encounters, stories heard, characters seen, and descriptions of the landscapes unfolding around him. He also wrote "at least sixteen poems" (Kibler, "First"; Shillingsburg, "Literary Grist" 123).

Simms took a third western trip five years later, writing letters back to the newspaper that by then he was editing (*Letters* 1:10–38). Together these three trips provided materials for his writings over more than forty years. "The first . . . produced mainly short fiction; the second inspired much poetry; . . . the first and third . . . yielded three novels written in the 1830s" (Shillingsburg, "Literary Grist" 119). This was, in part, because of the trips' timing. Sixteen years after the first trip, Simms told students at the University of Alabama that in the interval their world had changed from a howling wilderness into a place of growing civilization (Simms, *Social* 5–6). Had he not gone when he did, he would have been too late to see the frontier. Later travels took him many other places and also provided much grist for his writing. Never again, however, did he experience the frontier firsthand. Furthermore, on these later trips Simms was a practiced professional writer, no longer that boy haunted by passions.

Personal Life

After the ten-year-old boy's momentous refusal to leave Charleston, his grandmother sent Simms for two years to the grammar school taught on the campus and by the faculty of the nearly moribund College of Charleston. By then he already was "versifying the events of the war [of 1812]," just concluded, publishing "doggerel" in the local papers, and learning to read in several languages (*Letters* 1:285). His trip west a decade later helped him decide to pursue both literature and a career in law, but back in Charleston—this despite his father's urging that he stay in Mississippi. Upon his return home, he began to read law and also launched a literary weekly, the *Album*, which ran for a year. He became engaged as well to Anna Malcolm Giles, daughter of a grocer and former state coroner.

A year later the young couple married. This was six months before Simms was admitted to the South Carolina bar, on his twenty-first birthday, not long before he was appointed as a city magistrate. Although living up the Ashley River in the more healthful, less expensive village of Summerville, Simms kept a law office in the city. Shortly after using his maternal inheritance to buy the *City Gazette* at the end of 1829 and moving down to Charleston Neck, just north of the city limits where he had lived as a boy, Simms lost both his father and his maternal grandmother. He also found himself attacked because of his Unionist stance in the Nullification crisis resulting from South Carolina's rejection of a federal tariff. Then, in early 1832, Simms's wife died. Soon after, he took his four-year-old daughter back to Summerville to live and determined to sell his newspaper and leave the state for a literary life in the North.

Fueling his ambition was the correspondence Simms had begun several years earlier with an accountant whom he had published in his *City Gazette* but not yet met—Scots immigrant James Lawson. At the time Lawson, seven years Simms's senior, edited a New York City newspaper and, in addition to writing plays and poetry, was a friend (and, later, informal literary agent) to a wide circle (McHaney, "An Early"). Simms's trip north in the summer of 1832 saw the two begin a lifelong friendship, cemented as they squired ladies about and interacted with Lawson's literary circle. In subsequent years Simms multiplied the number of his friendships, in both the North and the South, making them in some measure a replacement for the family that he had lost. Lawson remained the closest of his northern friends, while James Henry Hammond, a future governor and U.S. senator, became his closest friend in South Carolina.

Late in 1833, after his Summerville house burned, Simms wrote Lawson to say that he was enamored of "a certain fair one" (*Letters* 1:73). Seventeen-year-old Chevillette Eliza Roach was the daughter of "a literary-minded aristocrat of English descent" with two plantations on the banks of the Edisto River in Barnwell District (later County) (Guilds 70). The courtship was protracted, as Simms felt it necessary first to clear debts that friends had bought up on his behalf. He also was determined "to marry no woman" before he was "perfectly independent of her resources, and her friends" (*Letters* 1:78). Therefore he did not propose until the spring of 1836. The nuptials took place seven months later, and as a result, Simms came to call the four thousand acres of Woodlands Plantation, with its seventy slaves, home. It was twenty years, however, before he took over management of the plantation and, then, only in the wake of his father-in-law's final sickness and death. Five years after that, he lost his wife, the mother of fourteen of his fifteen children. Nine of the children Chevillette bore him had already died, devastating Simms repeatedly. Five were still living (three sons and two daughters), as was Simms's daughter by his first marriage, who helped raise the youngest of her siblings. Those remaining children—even Gilly, who fought in the Confederate army—all outlived their father. Gilly and a brother-in-law ran Woodlands after the war, when Simms, though dying of cancer, was earning what he could by writing again for publications in the North and editing one or another South Carolina newspaper.

Career

The trip north in 1832 did not result in Simms moving there. Except during the Civil War, however, he returned almost every year. This was because the contacts he made, and the exposure to literary culture that he enjoyed, helped him define his future as an author. Earlier he had written fiction and criticism as well as journalism, filling the pages of several short-lived cultural journals and his newspaper, but between the ages of nine and twenty-six Simms had focused his literary efforts primarily on poetry. Beginning with his first book of verse in 1825, he had published five small volumes in Charleston. A couple had received positive notice in New York, and in the fall of 1832, J. & J. Harper issued the sixth anonymously from there, *Atalantis: A Story of the Sea.* Coming back the following summer, Simms had in hand for the Harpers a gothic novella, *Martin Faber,* and after his return south, he also would send the manuscript of his first two-volume border romance, *Guy Rivers: A Tale of Georgia.*

The reception of these and the romances and short stories that followed quickly made Simms one of the nation's most successful fictionists. He continued to issue poetry as well—roughly a collection every three years over the thirty-seven years that he worked as a professional author. But this output was dwarfed by the fiction—on average a title every year (counting several serialized works but not counting the many revised editions). Then there were the two dozen separately published orations, histories, and biographies as well as edited collections of documents and dramas and a geography of South Carolina. Add to these the revised editions and the further printings and issues of his own works and it appears that Simms saw a title coming off the presses at the rate of one every three months or so. Making that figure all the more astounding is the fact that, during more than a dozen of those years (the early-to-mid 1840s, the late 1840s-to-early 1850s, and the mid-to-late 1860s), he also was editing a cultural journal or newspaper. Furthermore he contributed reams of reviews and poems, hundreds of op-ed pieces and columns, and dozens of short stories and public addresses, which were never collected and published in volume form.

His career mapped an arc. It ascended meteorically in the 1830s and peaked in the early-to-mid 1840s, before beginning to descend. One reason was the popularity of the historical fiction that Simms began to write. When he left behind the law, his first newspaper, and the Nullification controversy, as well as his sadness, historical fiction was all the rage. Sir Walter Scott had fueled the craze, beginning with the publication of his first Border romance in 1814. He died in September 1832. Seventeen years Simms's senior, James Fenimore Cooper, the closest America had to a Scott at the time, was at the peak of his reputation and success, having started publishing his romances in 1820. Thus the way had been prepared for a writer of Simms's historical imagination and preoccupations. Within five years of his first trip north, moreover, Lawson's (and now his) circle became loosely affiliated with a nationalistic and Democratic group, self-styled Young America, this after Young Italy and similar ethnic, nationalist, European, cultural and political movements (Moltke-Hansen, "Southern"). Edgar Allan Poe and other members gave Simms's first fictions positive, if not uncritical, attention.

By the end of the 1830s, paradoxically, Simms, like Cooper, found his success attracting unauthorized editions of his works because Britain and America did not have an international copyright agreement. Further, in the wake of the panic of 1837, Americans bought fewer books. Simms's response was to diversify his portfolio. He turned to biography and history, including his hugely successful *Life of Francis Marion* (1844). He also returned to the editor's chair, overseeing one and then another cultural journal. These were unlike the ones he had edited in the 1820s: they included contributions by numerous authors, not just those from Charleston, but from the region and also the North. The ambition motivating the journals was to connect and promote Charleston intellectually. Consequently the journals more closely resembled metropolitan quarterly reviews in their offerings.

The mid-1840s saw Simms involved in politics, even serving a term in the South Carolina legislature. By the middle of the Mexican-American War in 1847, he had concluded that the South needed to become an independent nation. Thereafter, although he maintained ties with many in the Young America circle, he no longer promoted his writings as fostering Americanism in literature (*Views*). Instead he increasingly emphasized the ways in which his three romance series—the colonial, the Revolutionary, and the border—were making tangible and meaningful the origins and development of the future southern nation and the sad but inevitable consequences for Native Americans (Watson, *From Nationalism*; compare Nakamura).

Sectional politics colored more and more of Simms's perceptions, speeches, and private communications. The rising tide of abolitionism had him aghast. It also fed his growing sense that his position in American letters was slipping. He returned to editing, and his poetry, which was more often explicitly about the South, became increasingly patriotic in tone. Although his first biographer, William Peterfield Trent, insisted that Simms's declining standing reflected the change in literary fashion from historical romances to realistic novels, Simms in fact wrote more and more as a social realist in the 1850s (Wimsatt, "Realism").

The Civil War consumed Simms. As he wrote Lawson, "Literature, especially poetry, is effectually overwhelmed by the drums, & the cavalry, and the shouting" (*Letters* 4:369–70). He did manage to editorialize often and to rework and finish things long on his desk, including poems, a novel, and a dramatic treatment of Benedict Arnold, the northern traitor in the Revolutionary War. Then, in the wake of the Confederacy's loss and the failure of his vision for the South, he found himself recording the loss in a new newspaper, dealing with the trauma in his poetry, and becoming more existential and psychological in his fictional treatments. Simms's old New York friends tried to help. He did edit and see through publication a volume of Confederate war poetry. Yet it is a measure of his reduced stature that the several new romances he published appeared only in serial form. In part this may have been because he was in a sense competing with himself. Publishers were beginning to reprint volumes out of the selected edition of his writings. Many of Simms's works were available in book form, just not new works.

Associations

As the *Letters* testify, Simms had complex, overlapping networks of friends and colleagues. As a boy and young man, he received the friendship, patronage, and commendation of a variety of well-placed people in Charleston, including Charles Rivers Carroll. It was Carroll with whom he read law, to whom he dedicated his first romance, and after whom he named a son. Both men were Unionists during the Nullification controversy. So were Hugh Swinton Legare (later U.S. attorney general) and the considerably older William Drayton, as well as lawyer and editor Richard Yeadon and Greenville, South Carolina, newspaper editor Benjamin Franklin Perry. Also considerably older was James Wright Simmons, who had joined with Simms to launch the *Southern Literary Gazette* in 1828, when Simms was twenty-two. Through him Simms had direct contact with such British literary figures as Leigh Hunt and Byron (Kibler, *Poetry* 15).

The next group of influential friends and collaborators that Simms acquired were members of the Lawson circle and included such figures as Edwin

Forrest, the Shakespearean actor, and Evert Duyckinck, who published several of Simms's volumes in Wiley and Putnam's series Library of American Books, which he edited. Among the many others were poets and editors William Cullen Bryant and Fitz-Greene Halleck. Simms also made nonliterary friends in New York and Philadelphia, such as John Jacob Bockee and William Hawkins Ferris, the cashier at the U.S. Treasury office in New York who, after the war, helped Simms, Henry Timrod (poet laureate of the Confederacy), and others.

As a Barnwell planter, Simms met a widening circle of South Carolina's leaders and literati. For instance his acquaintance with James Henry Hammond began in the late 1830s and deepened into a friendship in the early 1840s. It was in the early 1840s, too, when he again was editing cultural journals, that Simms became friends with many southern writers. He regarded several of them, including Virginians George Frederick Holmes, Edmund Ruffin, and Nathaniel Beverley Tucker as members, together with Hammond and himself, in a "sacred circle." Uniting the circle were members' devotion to the South and a shared sense of the marginal status and critical importance of the life of the mind in a largely rural and unintellectual region (Faust, *Sacred*). Others of Simms's wide connections in the region did not interact as much with each other, but Simms long corresponded with Maryland novelist and lawyer John Pendleton Kennedy, Irish-born Georgia poet Richard Henry Wilde, Alabama lawyer and writer Alexander Beaufort Meek, and Louisiana historian and assistant attorney general Charles Gayarré, among others. By the 1850s, when Simms once more returned to editing a cultural journal, many of the writers whom he recruited were members of a younger generation. Poets Paul Hamilton Hayne and Henry Timrod were two. Often they and a half dozen others of Simms's and their generations met in John Russell's Charleston Book Shop and adjourned to dinner at Simms's Smith Street home, "dubbed 'The Wigwam'" (*Letters* 1:cxxxvi). Shortly before his death fifteen or so years later, Simms wrote Hayne, "I am rapidly passing from the stage, where you young men are to succeed me" (*Letters* 5:287).

Thought

The welter of Simms's works disguises unities and dynamics of the thought underlying them. From early on Simms was convinced that art ennobles or transforms, as well as gives voice to individuals and societies; therefore it must be cultivated assiduously. Without the potential for high artistic attainment, he insisted, societies are not ready for the independence and regard of free peoples. This is where Simms the historian joined Simms the poet. Societies develop, he argued (using the stadialism of the Scottish historical school), from imitation through self-assertion to achievement and also from savagery through strife to settled agricultural communities and, ultimately, to a hierarchical civilization supporting a rich artistic life. It was the job of the artist to help envision the goal, inspire the pursuit, and inform the process. That process was at once progressive and dialectical. Order, without dynamism, stifled development, as did the obverse—the dominance by ungoverned impulses or uncontrolled license. This was true in the individual, but also in societies as a whole. War was necessary for civilization, but its success was measured in the securities of the home, the center of cultural production and reproduction.

Whether in the public or in the domestic arena, "the true governor, as [Thomas] Carlyle call[ed] him—the king man—" guided rather than impeded the forces of change and progress (Simms, "Guizot's" 122). There were few such men with the capacity to lead. The same was true of nations. Neither all people nor all peoples were equal in either capacity or attainment. That was why Native Americans were overrun and Africans had been enslaved by European peoples in the New World. Indeed, Simms argued, "slavery in all ages has been found the greatest and most admirable agent of Civilization," giving education and examples to less evolved peoples (*Letters* 3:174). The degree to which a people had evolved mattered. That was why, he held, Americans had won independence from the most powerful empire in the world. They had done so through their Revolution, led by an elite that felt correctly its time had come (Simms, "Ellet's" 328). By mid-1847 that also was Simms's judgment for the South: the region had evolved enough to become independent (*Letters* 2:332). The hope inspired and then failed him and the people he sought to lead.

While not all men could rise to the highest rank, they all had the same responsibility at home. There the father was patriarch, protector, and head, while the mother was nurturer, moral instructor, and heart. There, too, children's characters and minds were formed by age twelve ("Ellet's"). Children's upbringing was critical to citizenship, and it was through her sons and the support of her husband, father, and brothers that a woman shaped the public sphere. The culture and character instilled in the child expressed and informed not just the household, but the larger society—the people.

"The history of peoples and their embodiments in institutions, states, and artistic productions—these were the great subjects" in Simms's view (Moltke-Hansen, "Southern" 120). Yet "poets were the only class of philosophers who had recognized" this until his own day, when at last "we now read human histories. We now ask after the affections as well as the ceremonies of society" ("Ellet's" 319–20). Peoples or races—that is, ethnic groups—were not unchanging any more than were their politics and their cultures. They either advanced or were overrun by history. Further, new peoples emerged, and old identities were submerged. The Spanish conquistadors were the creation of centuries of conflict with the Moors: their motivation was the glory of conquest, not the routine of trade or the plow. On the other hand, the English settlements in North America reflected the impulse to transform the wilderness into verdant farms and build society (*Views* 64, 178–85; *Social* 8). The same impulse drove Americans westward in Simms's own day and gave Americans their Manifest Destiny.

To explore these facts of the South's settlement and its place in international conflicts, Simms wrote all together, between 1833 and 1863, two romances set in eighth-century Spain, two set during the Spanish exploration and conquest of the Americas and two during the later English colonization of South Carolina, seven set during the American Revolution, and—depending on how one counts—perhaps eight set on the borders of the nineteenth-century South. After the war he published one more Revolutionary romance and two more that, like it, were set beyond the boundaries of civilization. He also left two unfinished romances, also set beyond society's normal reach. These late works, however, no longer had as their framing justification the cultivation of the South's future and civilization.

White southerners had their independence foreclosed by the war. In his last works, therefore, Simms found himself exploring the psychological, philosophical, and historical impulses that led to the Confederacy's demise and what, in the aftermath, it meant to be a good man and to build for the future, however impoverished. On the first score, he argued that the impulse to idealism behind abolitionism ignored historical realities, becoming inhuman in its consequences. On the latter score, he affirmed responsibility for one's dependents and the virtues of stoicism, as well as a continued commitment to the beauty and truth of art and the impulses to the cultivated life and fields. Therefore, in the face of the burning of his Woodlands home and library in February 1865—during Sherman's march and in the midst of desperate circumstances—he insisted that home, or the ideals and past characterizing its potential, still was at the center of true civilization, but only if elevated by art (*Sense* 8, 17). It was wrong to measure civilization by the getting, spending, and mad dashing, or material progress and utilitarianism, characteristic of both a capitalistic North and also many southerners. These traits he often had attacked even before the war, insisting that "the work of the Imagination, which is the Genius of a race, is only begun when its material progress is supposed to be complete" (*Poetry* 12).

Writings

Simms expressed many of his ideas most personally in letters and most cogently in essays, speeches, and occasional introductions to his books. But he illustrated them most fully in his fiction and poetry. By the time he arrived in New

York in 1832, he had formed many of the core ideals and beliefs that would shape his work. His application of them, however, modified his understanding over time. Growing as a writer and growing in knowledge and experience, he also grew as a thinker.

In his hierarchy of values, poetry came first. It was a prophetic calling as well as evocative of the deeply felt (or, sometimes, the fleeting) and thus testimony to the perdurance and transcendence of the beautiful and the human spirit. Yet, as Simms often ruefully reflected, prose spoke to many more people. That was a principal reason why he turned to writing prose epics or romances. He gave his most concerted consideration of poetry's value and roles in three lectures in Charleston in 1854. Over the prior three years he had given portions of them in Augusta, Georgia, Washington, D.C., and Richmond and Petersburg, Virginia. Entitled *Poetry and the Practical,* they did not see print until 1996, as Simms never found the time to expand them as he wanted. On the other hand, his last address on the same themes, *The Sense of the Beautiful,* was issued soon after he delivered it, also in Charleston.

Many of his important reviews have not yet been gathered, but Simms collected some in 1845–46, and *Views and Reviews in American Literature, History and Fiction* came out in 1846 and 1847 in two "series." Beginning with a consideration of "Americanism" in literature, the first series explored the themes and periods of American history for treatment by the novelist. Simms argued there, and in forewords to several of his romances, that fiction rendered the past more truthfully, interestingly, and tellingly than histories and biographies could because fiction—like poetry—required imagination to look beyond what is not known or expressed. The second series examined additional American writers and what distinguished them, for instance, in their humor.

Despite their early success, Simms's romances, novellas, and stories provoked mixed reviews. Poe eventually concluded that Simms had become "the best novelist which this country has, on the whole, produced" but also insisted that "he should never have written 'The Partisan,' nor 'The Yemassee.'" This was in a review of *Confession.* That novel, like the gothic *Martin Faber,* demonstrated, Poe contended, that Simms's "genius [did] not lie in the outward so much as in the inner world." Yet he nevertheless wrote of Simms's short-story collection *The Wigwam and the Cabin* that "in invention, in vigor, in movement, in the power of exciting interest, and in the artistical management of his themes, he has surpassed, we think, any of his countrymen." Other critics, especially in the genteel and Whiggish Knickerbocker circle, joined Poe in condemning what they considered to be the excessively graphic and vulgar qualities of many characters and scenes, and Simms's prolixity and sententiousness, in his romances (Butterworth and Kibler 64, 50).

The violent realism and earthiness of the romances did not result in realistic novels. Although Simms received early praise for his characterizations (particularly of women), he used the romance formula, with its stereotypic heroes and heroines, predictable themes, and conventional polarities. People were on quests or had lost their way or were fighting long odds or were carrying forward the banner of (and modeling) civilization or were mired in the slough of despond or were resisting all the claims of civilized society and behavior or were pursuing love interests. Deceitfulness, selfishness, and greed opposed honor, high-mindedness, and honesty against the backdrop of the South's development from the earliest days of Spanish exploration to the westward movement in Simms's own youth.

It was only gradually that Simms married the psychological acuity of some of his portraits of the interior struggles of his gothic characters and fiction to the historical romance. Helping him think through how to do so were the biographies he wrote in the mid-1840s, but also the incidents on which he focused particular fictions, such as the murder in *Beauchampe; or, The Kentucky Tragedy* (1842). However incomplete the blending of realism and romanticism or of stereotypical and socially individuated renderings through the 1840s, by the 1850s Simms fundamentally had made the transition to social realism in such works as *Woodcraft* and *The Cassique of Kiawah.* Indeed some scholars have considered *Woodcraft* the first realistic novel in America (Bakker; Wimsatt, "Realism").

In some sense disguising the transition is the fact that Simms also increasingly wrote as a humorist and, in so doing, often rendered his late narratives fabulistically, when not writing social comedy or stories of manners. This dimension of Simms's work was largely hidden, however, until the 1974 publication of *Stories and Tales,* volume 5 in the Centennial Simms edition. There, for the first time, readers had access in print to "Bald-Head Bill Bauldy." There, too, for the first time one could read together that story, "Legend of the Hunter's Camp," and "How Sharp Snaffles Got His Capital and Wife," which was published posthumously in *Harper's Magazine* in October 1870. These and other stories and tales made it clear that Simms was a fecund contributor to southern and American humor.

Humor let Simms take up issues that he could not otherwise address in print and still expect to be well received. He did so both during and after the war. The war also pushed Simms past the emerging fashion of social realism. Having destroyed the familiar, the preoccupation of much realistic fiction, the war made the liminal central (Shillingsburg, "Cub"). While his romances and tales had often explored life on the edge or in extreme circumstances, whether in war or on the frontier or on the verge of madness or in fanciful realms, it had done so against a backdrop of, and with the goal of affirming, social norms and development. In the war's wake that goal seemed absurd. Mythologized memories of a healthy past might nurture a sense of the beautiful but could not help one deal with the present. Thus Simms's conclusion, in a March 1869 letter to Paul Hamilton Hayne: "Let us bury the Past lest it buries us!" (*Letters* 5:214). Fifteen months later he lay dead in the 13 Society Street, Charleston, home of his oldest daughter, with the shell holes in the walls of the bedroom he had shared with several children.

Posthumous Reputation

The twenty years after Simms's death saw him often respectfully treated, first in obituaries, later in memoirs and columns, and also in literary dictionaries and encyclopedias. Yet Charles Richardson's 1887 *American Literature: 1607–1885* proved a harbinger of a shift: Simms, Richardson observed, was "more respected than read," having "won considerable note because he was so sectional" and then having "lost it because he was not sectional enough," although he showed "silly contempt for his Northern betters" (qtd. in Butterworth and Kibler 130). Five years later Trent's biography of Simms appeared. It was the first full-length, scholarly treatment. Its central thesis was that Simms's environment frustrated his abilities: the South was inimical to art and the life of the mind, and Charleston high society's hauteur marginalized Simms despite his talent and character. Trent's second thesis was that Simms's commitment to the romance and his romanticism meant that his works had become largely unreadable in an age of literary realism. Although Vernon Parrington and later scholars recognized Simms's impulses to realism, the two theses long shaped Simms criticism and, indeed, also helped frame study of antebellum southern literature and intellectual life (Parrington 119–30).

A Virginian born in 1862, Trent was a progressive who wanted a New South radically different from the old. He saw his pioneering study of Simms as an opportunity to criticize what the Civil War had made untenable. From his perspective the Old South was not the expanding and rapidly developing environment, with a deep history, that Simms portrayed, but a place where slavery stultified and stunted the growth and progress displayed by the North. Southern—especially South Carolinian—writers occasionally challenged Trent's agenda and conclusions, but those critiques had little impact. Not until after publication of the Simms letters in the 1950s did scholars begin to consider the author in the historical and contemporary contexts that he had rendered in his poetry and fiction. And not until after the centennial of his death did a growing number of scholars, having concluded that southern intellectual history was not an oxymoron, begin to study in detail the culture in which Simms participated and to which he contributed so voluminously and variously.

Some of these scholars also have had agendas: they have wanted to see Simms included in the American literary canon, for instance, or they have wanted to defend the heritage that in their view Trent, and so many others, inappropriately belittled or ignorantly dismissed. More fruitfully, other scholars have begun to reframe the understanding of nineteenth-century American intellectual life by stripping away preconceptions that characterized earlier evaluations of Simms and his contemporaries. They are closely examining the historical record and transatlantic and other contemporary contexts and developments in the process. Although the pursuit of canonical status in a post-canonical age seems quixotic at this point, the explosion of the canon is leading to more varied fare being offered and may, therefore, mean that Simms, once his work is widely available, will be more often anthologized as well as studied. Defensiveness about Simms and the antebellum South may warm the hearts of like-minded people, just as critics of the Old South have been encouraged by shared presuppositions and disdain. Yet dueling cultural ideologies do not advance comity and may only reinforce mutual incomprehensions. Continued, deep research in original sources and the theoretical reframing that Atlantic history, the history of the book, and other perspectives offer—these approaches promise most for further study of Simms, his works, and his world.

Works Cited

For amplified readings by and on Simms and on his world, go to http://simms.library.sc.edu/bibliography.php.

Bakker, Jan. "Simms on the Literary Frontier; or, So Long Miss Ravenel and Hello Captain Porgy: *Woodcraft* Is the First 'Realistic' Novel in America." In *William Gilmore Simms and the American Frontier,* edited by John Caldwell Guilds and Caroline Collins, 64–78. Athens: University of Georgia Press, 1997.

Butterworth, Keen, and James E. Kibler Jr. *William Gilmore Simms: A Definitive Guide.* Boston: G. K. Hall, 1980.

Faust, Drew Gilpin. *A Sacred Circle: The Dilemma of the Intellectual in the Old South, 1840–1860.* Baltimore: Johns Hopkins University Press, 1977.

Guilds, John C. *Simms: A Literary Life.* Fayetteville: University of Arkansas Press, 1992.

Hayne, Paul Hamilton. "Ante-Bellum Charleston." *Southern Bivouac* 1 (October 1885): 257–68.

Kibler, James E. "The First Simms Letters: 'Letters from the West' (1826)." *Southern Literary Journal* 19 (Spring 1987): 81–91.

———. *The Poetry of William Gilmore Simms: An Introduction and Bibliography.* Columbia: Southern Studies Program, University of South Carolina, 1979.

McHaney, Thomas L. "An Early 19th-Century Literary Agent: James Lawson of New York." *Publications of the Bibliographical Society of America* 64 (Spring 1970): 177–92.

Moltke-Hansen, David. "The Expansion of Intellectual Life: A Prospectus." In *Intellectual Life in Antebellum Charleston,* edited by Michael O'Brien and David Moltke-Hansen, 3–44. Knoxville: University of Tennessee Press, 1986.

———. "Southern Literary Horizons in Young America: Imaginative Development of a Regional Geography." *Studies in the Literary Imagination* 42, no. 1 (2009): 1–31.

Nakamura, Masahiro. *Visions of Order in William Gilmore Simms: Southern Conservatism and the Other American Romance.* Columbia: University of South Carolina Press, 2009.

Parrington, Vernon L. *The Romantic Revolution in America, 1800–1860.* Vol. 2 of *Main Currents in American Thought.* New York: Harcourt, Brace and Company, 1927.

Rogers, George C., Jr. *Charleston in the Age of the Pinckneys.* Columbia: University South Carolina Press, 1980.

Shillingsburg, Miriam J. "The Cub of the Panther: A New Frontier." In *William Gilmore Simms and the American Frontier,* edited by John Caldwell Guilds and Caroline Collins, 221–36. Athens: University of Georgia Press, 1997.

———. "Literary Grist: Simms's Trips to Mississippi." *Southern Quarterly* 41, no. 2 (2003): 119–34.

Simms, William Gilmore. *Atalantis: A Story of the Sea: In Three Parts.* New York: J. & J. Harper, 1832.

———. *Beauchampe; or, The Kentucky Tragedy.* 2 vols. Philadelphia: Lea and Blanchard, 1842.

———. *The Cassique of Kiawah: A Colonial Romance.* New York: Redfield, 1859.

———. *Confession; or, The Blind Heart. A Domestic Story.* 2 vols. Philadelphia: Lea and Blanchard, 1841.

———. "Ellet's 'Women of the Revolution.'" *Southern Quarterly Review,* n.s. 1 (July 1850): 314–54.

———. "Guizot's Democracy in France." *Southern Quarterly Review* 15, no.29 (1849): 114–65.

———. *Guy Rivers: A Tale of Georgia.* 2 vols. New York: Harper & Brothers, 1834.

———. *The Letters of William Gilmore Simms.* Edited by Mary C. Simms Oliphant, Alfred Taylor Odell, and T. C. Duncan. 6 vols. Columbia: University of South Carolina Press, 1952–82.

———. *The Life of Francis Marion.* New York: Henry G. Langley, 1844.

———. *Martin Faber, the Story of a Criminal; and Other Tales.* 2 vols. New York: Harper & Brothers, 1837.

———. *Poetry and the Practical.* Edited by James E. Kibler. Fayetteville: University of Arkansas Press, 1996.

———. *The Sense of the Beautiful: An Address . . . before the Charleston County Agricultural and Horticultural Association, May 3, 1870.* Charleston: Charleston County Agricultural and Horticultural Association, 1870.

———. *The Social Principle: The Source of National Permanence. An Oration, Delivered before the Erosophic Society of the University of Alabama . . . December 13, 1842.* Tuscaloosa: Erosophic Society, University of Alabama, 1843.

———. *Stories and Tales.* Vol. 5 of *The Writings of William Gilmore Simms.* Centennial edition; introductions, explanatory notes, and texts established by John Caldwell Guilds. Columbia: University of South Carolina Press, 1974.

———. *Views and Reviews in American Literature, History and Fiction.* 2 vols. New York: Wiley and Putnam, 1845 (1846).

———. *The Wigwam and the Cabin.* 2 vols. New York: Wiley and Putnam, 1845–46.

———. *Woodcraft, or Hawks about the Dovecote: A Story of the South, at the Close of the Revolution.* New York: Redfield, 1854.

Trent, William Peterfield. *William Gilmore Simms.* Boston: Houghton, Mifflin, 1892.

Wakelyn, Jon L. *The Politics of a Literary Man: William Gilmore Simms.* Westport, Conn.: Greenwood Press, 1973.

Watson, Charles S. *From Nationalism to Secessionism: The Changing Fiction of William Gilmore Simms.* Westport, Conn.: Greenwood Press, 1993.

White, William B., Jr. *The Ross-Chesnut-Sutton Family of South Carolina.* Franklin, N.C.: Privately printed, 2002.

Wimsatt, Mary Ann. "Realism and Romance in Simms's Midcentury Fiction." *Southern Literary Journal* 12, no. 2 (1980): 29–48.

Critical Introduction

CONFESSION

Todd Hagstette

The grimness that attended William Gilmore Simms's literary imagination was frequently on display during key moments in his historical romances and short stories. He often was accused of sensationalism for his attachment to murder, licentiousness, and mayhem of every variety in crafting his literary panoply of American history. It was also undoubtedly this strain in his fiction that helped produce his success with the reading public. Marketing considerations aside, there was a darkness that lurked in Simms's mind and seemed to exorcise itself occasionally in print. Even his notoriously unsympathetic biographer William P. Trent was acute in perceiving the author's penchant for the macabre, noting that Simms's plantation "Woodlands was quiet and domestic enough, but whenever he shut himself up in his study he fell to talking with thieves and outlaws and brothers eager to kill one another" (121).

Despite this fascination in the author's mind, Simms only produced a handful of works wholly devoted to the gothic, the criminal, and the psychological. Of these, *Confession; or, The Blind Heart* is one of the most fully realized. In his study of the literary aesthetics of crime, John Cyril Barton notes that "novels didn't become a dominant form through which crime and criminal behavior were critically explored in the United States until Simms began writing them" (222). Though earlier writers, most notably Charles Brockden Brown, dramatized villainous behaviors in America, Simms helped to pioneer the contextualization of these acts as legal transgression, in addition to gothic sensationalism. *Confession* marks one of the earliest attempts in American fiction to trace the psychology of the criminal impulse through the unreliable first-person perspective of the murderer, who is unambiguously aware of the legal implications of his anticipated act.

Simms designed his novel to be experimental in its structure. In an introduction to the 1856 edition of the novel, from which this current volume is reprinted, Simms clarified his intentions for the work. His was a deeply psychological project, an attempt to "analyze the heart in some of its obliquities and perversities; to follow its toils, pursue its phases, and to trace, if possible, the secret of its self-deceptions, its self-baffling inconsistencies, its seemingly wilful [*sic*] warfare with reason and the sober experience." Ultimately, *Confession* was to be the declaration of "one single soul...put in bonds, put to the torture, and made to declare its dreary experience through its groans" (*Confession* 9-10). Simms hoped to demonstrate how the passions of man, specifically the monomaniacal exercise of a single passion, can unseat a person's otherwise healthy faculties. To make the experience tangible, he offered the reader direct access to the afflicted mind. This effort — to narrate a full novel through the limited first-person perspective of a character whose perceptions are increasingly unreliable as he is more and more corrupted by his own jealousy — was only partially successful. Some natural limitations with such a point-of-view trapped and stultified the narrative. Overall, Simms struggled with the task of retaining sympathy for a narrator whose judgments and mental processes, by necessity of the plot, were becoming increasingly erratic. Simms himself acknowledged the shortcomings of his style when, in his introduction, he apologized for the youthfulness of the novel's prose and for the sensationalism of its content. Nonetheless, for its successes and for its ambitious failings, *Confession* deserves recognition for its innovation.

Simms attempted a partial justification of the gratuity of the novel's plot with claims that some of the instances from the story were based on his own observations in the West. Coupled with his assertion that *Confession* originated in some of his earliest prose writing, Simms likely learned of the putative source material for his novel during visits he made to his father in Mississippi in the mid-1820s. What specific event inspired the novel, though, is unknown. More intriguing than the suggestion of a real-world analog to the plot is the possibility of an autobiographical component to the spirit of the story. Like his protagonist, Simms was functionally orphaned at an early age. His mother died in childbirth when the author was less than two years old, and his father in despondency left Charleston and his son to seek his fortunes in the West. Though Simms's upbringing in the care of his maternal grandmother was loving (unlike that of his fictional counterpart), "the sense of intolerable isolation from family ties was so intense with him that it haunted him almost to the point of obsession" (Salley lxii). The novel's focus on the redemptive potential of the frontier also emanates from this source.

Despite Simms's reluctance at age ten to live with his father in Mississippi, he took from the elder Simms's adventures the lesson that fresh starts, absolution, and opportunity lay in the West. Critics like Lewis M. Bush have gone so far as to identify individual referents for specific characters in the text (126-7). Many of these hard biographical associations are vaguely appropriate or somewhat inconclusive. Yet the potential for psychological touchstones is intriguing. In his 1856 introduction, Simms himself characterized the novel as "the natural progress of the author's mind to the solutions of his problems" (7). One has to wonder, then, at the turmoil and angst lurking within the author's mind. The gothic impulse, the psychological structure, and the autobiographical hints of the text all make *Confession; or, The Blind Heart* deserving of greater critical regard than it has thus far received.

The Work

In its experimental content and structure, *Confession* marks Simms's efforts to craft a psychologically realistic depiction of burgeoning madness. The specific lens through which he situates his exploration of the mind is the impact of childhood trauma on adult development and behavior. As such, the novel is the extended confession of Edward Clifford who is orphaned at an age when he is "just young enough to wonder why" his loving parents are gone (Simms, *Confession* 12). In this emotionally precarious state, he is sent to be reared by his aunt and uncle in Charleston, where his upbringing is marred by his foster parents' preference for their natural children. His siblings wear the finest new clothes, while he is garbed in hand-me-downs; they attend the city's best prep academy, and he is sent to the local charity school. This preference crosses into neglect and emotional abuse of young Clifford following the untimely death of his adoptive brother. He grows up with his cousin and foster-sister Julia as his only repository of familial affection.

Rising above the scorn of his adopted home and particularly his uncle's attempts to relegate him to a blue-collar vocation, Clifford becomes a lawyer and an increasingly prominent citizen. This triumph is effected through his own hard work and the patronage of the father of his boyhood companion William Edgerton. Eventually, Clifford elopes with Julia, much to her parents' chagrin. With a burgeoning career, a doting wife, and an optimistic financial outlook, Clifford has apparently succeeded in spite of his rearing. His turbulent childhood, though, leaves him emotionally scarred and suspicious of human relationships. When his wife develops a friendship with Edgerton based on their mutual artistic impulses, Clifford's jealousy silently erupts within him. Under the influence of his unfounded suspicions, the husband goes to great pains to orchestrate scenarios in which his wife and friend can be ostensibly alone, though under his scrutiny. He witnesses little in Julia's behavior that is directly damning but plenty that he can irrationally misconstrue. As Clifford remarks at one critical juncture: "Seen through the eyes of suspicion, there is no truth no virtue; the smile is that of the snake; the tear, that of the crocodile; the assurance, that of the traitor" (248).

Clifford attempts to obviate his growing impulse to kill Edgerton, primarily out of a sense of devotion to his patron, by moving his family west to Alabama.

In this endeavor, he follows his friend and confidant Frank Kingsley, a cavalier and candid bachelor. The move, though financially and socially regressive, placates Clifford and reinvigorates his relationship with Julia. This brief period of marital harmony is permanently disrupted, though, by an extended visit from Edgerton, traveling purportedly for his health. With a renewed effort to place the two assumed lovers into compromising situations, Clifford's monomania begins to consume him. Eventually, his corrupted perceptions convince him of infidelity, and Clifford poisons his wife and challenges Edgerton to a duel. Edgerton, however, commits suicide first. Thanks to posthumous letters from both Julia and Edgerton, Clifford realizes that though Edgerton did in fact pursue Julia, his advances were completely unwelcome. Edgerton had been tormented by his feelings, and Julia had been ever-hopeful of her husband's intercession. Anguished over the outcome of his mistaken assumptions, Clifford resolves on suicide. Yet, in the end, he is thwarted by Kingsley, who insists, "it is by living only that you can atone" (397). So, the end of the novel finds Clifford wandering farther west, into untamed Texas, in search of absolution.

Because most of the novel is psychological in its examinations, *Confession* is often considered a gothic narrative, even with its distinct absence of the supernatural. Simms himself implied as much when he suggested to Rufus Wilmot Griswold that the novel belonged in a group with some of his more readily recognized gothic works (*Letters* 2: 224). That said, placing *Confession* thematically within the author's canon is a difficult task. The novel exhibits characteristics of several of Simms's loose collections, but wholly belongs to none of them.

Some people have classed it among Simms's Border Romances, because of its plot's steady progression west; the most notable instance of this series assignment was in the 1856 Redfield edition of the novel, which grouped it under the series title "Border Novels and Romances of the South." In this group, *Confession* joined Simms's more clearly-defined novels of the southern frontier: *Beauchampe* (Redfield, 1856), *Border Beagles* (Redfield, 1859), *Charlemont* (Redfield, 1856), *Guy Rivers* (Redfield, 1860), and *Richard Hurdis* (Redfield, 1855). That these other works were crafted to dramatize the ethos of particular frontier states (*Beauchampe* and *Charlemont* for Kentucky, *Border Beagles* for Mississippi, *Guy Rivers* for Georgia, and *Richard Hurdis* for Alabama), whereas *Confession* was not, problematizes that text's inclusion.

Also in contradiction to this series assignment, Simms himself did not seem to have envisioned *Confession* as a Border Romance. In a 16 August 1841 letter to New York friend and informal literary agent James Lawson, Simms implied a distinction between the recently-completed *Confession* and the new novel he had underway (*Beauchampe*), for that latter work would "form one of the

'Hurdis' series" (*Letters* 1: 267). In other words, it was to be a tale of the border or frontier. On the other hand, Simms did not object to the designation in 1846 when Taylor, Wilde and Company in Baltimore proposed publishing *Confession* as part of a collection of his "Border Romances" (*Letters* 2: 132n). Financial concerns might have trumped artistic ones in this instance.

Though in his biography of Simms, John C. Guilds tacitly groups *Confession* with the Border Romances (168-9), elsewhere he explains why any such definition is fraught. After all, in categorizing his own fiction:

> Simms himself preferred to divide it into only two large groups: "domestic tales," or "tales of the South," by which he meant all those tales...dealing with regional themes and settings; and "tales of the imagination," by which he meant those stories under the influence of German Romanticism, usually with exotic settings and heavy philosophical or psychological undertones. (Introduction xxi)

The fact that Simms, himself, included books such as *Martin Faber*, *Confession*, and *The Wigwam and the Cabin* (featuring his ghost story "Grayling") in both groups, however, "reveals that he did not always clearly distinguish between his 'domestic' and his 'moral imaginative' tales"(Introduction xxii-xxiii). Yet this failure to distinguish, this melding of the two types, marks the very innovative spirit that characterizes Simms's experimental composition in *Confession*. Though the author once claimed that his novel was "marked chiefly by the characteristics of passion & imagination," he also gave it the subtitle *A Domestic Story* (*Letters* 2: 224). The gothic, the frontier, and the psychological all merge in this distinctive tale.

The Text

Building out of his early experiences with writing in the psychological gothic mode in such stories as *Martin Faber* (1833) and *Carl Werner* (1838) and anticipating his later work *Castle Dismal* (1844), William Gilmore Simms began to write the novel that would ultimately become *Confession; or, The Blind Heart* in late 1840 or early 1841. Though in his author's advertisement to the 1856 Redfield edition of the novel, he noted that the finished novel was constructed out of some of his earliest prose writings, to what material he was referring is uncertain. He first mentioned having begun the novel "in the winter" in a 24 February 1841 letter to James Lawson (*Letters* 1: 234). After composing approximately 150 pages, however, he ceased to make progress. This writer's block persisted at least into May 1841, where he cited vague "anxieties" as the reason for his inability to work. By August of that year, he finally managed to complete his text, and announced to Lawson on August 16 that the manuscript was now safely in the hands of the publishers (Guilds, *Simms* 104). The book was initially published in either October or November of 1841, by Lea and Blanchard of Philadelphia, as a two-volume work. Though not technically anonymous, the authorship of the first edition of *Confession* was left cryptic, which was not unusual at the time. Officially, the novel was attributed to "The Author of 'The Kinsmen,' 'The Yemassee,' 'Guy Rivers,' ETC." Later editions and printings were attributed to Simms by name, and the author freely discussed his writing of the book throughout his correspondence. The Redfield edition, which bore the name "W. Gilmore Simms, Esq." and was published as a one-volume work, was issued around 19 April 1856 (*Letters* 3: 385).

The first edition of *Confession*, issued by Lea & Blanchard, was unillustrated. The Redfield edition, beginning in 1856, featured two illustrations by F.O.C. Darley and engraved by Whitney & Jocelyn. Darley's choice of subject matter for his illustrations is somewhat intriguing. The first image presents Julia sitting beside a river engrossed in painting. Meanwhile, a young man stands to her side and observes her work from over her shoulder. He wears an approving and engaged expression. Because of Julia's calm demeanor and the scene's similarity to the Alabama respite period of the plot, the young man is surely Clifford (rather than Edgerton). Darley's goal here was obviously to depict a moment of tranquil marital bliss as a set-up and foil to the gothic action that concludes the story. Yet, Simms is very diligent to present Clifford as too left-brained and pragmatic to engage much in Julia's artistic impulses. Edgerton comes into their lives specifically as a compatriot for Julia in the exercise of her creative side. By locating Clifford and Julia's contentment in a scene from which the latter's fundamental estrangement can be inferred, Darley manifests a rather doomed portrait in the midst of potential success. The couple's position exacerbates this inference: Julia sits with her back to Clifford, and he scrutinizes her imaginative performance from the outside.

The second Darley illustration is equally interesting in its relationship to the action of the novel. Here we see a ruckus in a poker hall, with one man forcing another out an open window as onlookers stand by in evident astonishment. This is a clear depiction of Kingsley's outing of a cheater at the gambling hall. Darley's use of this character, in this rather tangential scene, as one of the hallmark images of the novel is a strange choice, at first glance. The oddity of its selection is mitigated by the psychological tenor of most to the work, this being one of the story's few action sequences. Nonetheless, Kingsley, while not exactly a minor character, is certainly peripheral to much of the novel's immediate drama. Yet, this image of manly action contrasts fittingly with the picture of pastoral respite in the accompanying illustration. Together, these two images dramatize one of the central conflicts of the novel, the consequences of feminine versus masculine action. Kingsley, as the man of action — the man's man — is Simms's voice of masculine resolve, particularly in its frontier expression. He disapproves of Edgerton, because he "wants manliness of character, and such a man always lacks sincerity" (*Confession* 319). Kingsley thus tries to spur Clifford. He criticizes him for allowing Edgerton into his marriage and for failing to play the man for his wife. When Julia is faced with Clifford's neglect and Edgerton's attention, "will she not become indifferent where she finds indifference — devoted where she finds devotion?" (*Confession* 320). The image of Kingsley's rough handling of the rounder at the poker table, then, is an analog for his recommended solution to Clifford's dilemma. Eject Edgerton. Face matters directly. The gothic unraveling of Clifford's sanity and betrothal is the result of his voyeuristic inaction, when simply throwing the man out of the window would suffice.

Also of interest in the front matter of the novel is the dedication. Simms initially dedicated *Confession* to one of his earliest and closest friends, James W[right] Simmons. Fifteen years older than Simms, Simmons had joined the younger man to launch and edit the *Southern Literary Gazette* in 1828. Yet Simmons's presence at the front of this novel was not due to literary kinship, but because he ultimately "became comptroller general and treasurer of the republic of Texas, and was connected with the Galveston *Banner*" (*Letters* 1: cxxxvii). In his dedication, Simms is clear to point out that Simmons is "now of Texas." The novel was composed and published during the brief existence of the Republic of Texas, in the aftermath of the Texas Revolution and in the gradual lead-up to the Mexican War. Furthermore, *Confession* features a plot progression that moves ever westward and self-consciously into the promise of renewal on the frontier. Simms's conclusion is heavy-handed in its conflation of manifest destiny with individual actualization. Clifford, in the last passages of the novel, notes his and Kingsley's odyssey concludes in "the rich empire of Texas — its plains, rich but barren — unstocked, wild running to waste with its tangled weeds needing, imploring the vigorous hand of cultivation. Even such, at that moment, was my heart! Rich in fertile affections, yet gone to waste; waiting, craving, praying for the hand of the cultivator!" (398).

The dedication to Simmons would seemingly foreground the aspects of *Confession* that place it within the context of Simms's Border series. And yet, interestingly, the dedication was removed for the publication of the Redfield edition of the novel, despite its designation in that edition as one of Simms's "Border Novels and Romances of the South." The reason for the removal of this dedication is uncertain. Simmons would live for another two years beyond this later edition of the book, so his death had nothing to do with the change. Other works in the Redfield series — such as *Katharine Walton* (1856), *Mellichampe*

(1854), and *Southward Ho!* (1854) — all bore new dedications with their publication, so house style or financial concerns over unnecessary pages were neither to blame. It could be that with the conclusion of the conflicts surrounding Texas years before, this dedication no longer held the gravity it enjoyed upon the novel's initial publication. Removing the Simmons dedication could also have been a subtle statement of Simms's reluctance to categorize his psychological experiment as another of his Border tales. After all, it is the gothic of *Confession* that marks its innovation.

The Context

Confession appeared at the front of what many critics consider to be the author's most productive period, the 1840s through the 1850s. The years following *Confession* saw the publication of the lion's share of Simms's Revolutionary War series, his most important short stories, the majority of his most well-regarded orations, all of his biographies, and his important two-volume essay collection *Views and Reviews*. This latter work would be cited as a fundamental text in the burgeoning Young American movement of the nineteenth century, "of which Simms was in effect the spokesman for the South" (Guilds, *Simms* 180-1). Young America's hyper-nationalistic aims were on display in the majority of Simms's works from this period. *Confession* is no exception. In both his emphasis on the southern borderlands and his efforts to Americanize the European gothic format, Simms sculpted *Confession* into a text *par excellence* of Young America ideology. Despite this position, the novel did not fare terribly well among critics.

Simms might have been justified in his introductory apology to the 1856 edition; the novel was not embraced by reviewers of the author's day, neither has it been since. A common tactic of the criticism is to brand the novel a poor imitation of the European psychological novel (helped in no small way by the epigraph from Goethe's *Faust* on the title page) or as a reinterpretation of William Shakespeare's *Othello*. Simms himself grouped the book "among the best of [his] performances" (*Letters* 2: 528), but was clearly aware of some of these potential complaints. In addition to the epigraph, which acknowledges the thematic origins of the work while, at the same time, implicitly suggesting the novel's subsequent development, Simms has his protagonist exclaim, "I am no Othello — I have no visitations of the moon!" (321).

Of those nineteenth-century critics who treated the novel outside the confines of discussion of its predecessors, those who were most sharply divided were Trent, Simms's initial biographer, and Edgar Allan Poe, the author's peer. Trent's 1892 biography is insistently regarded as biased and negative to its subject. This character to the study is nowhere more apparent than in its vitriolic assessment of *Confession*. Trent viewed the novel as a failed attempt "to rival Shakespeare in his greatest play [*Othello*]." He saw it as "made up of exaggerations and absurdities," and found in it "only a striking proof of the futility of attempting to write a novel in order to illustrate a pet theory, whether of psychology, or social science, or theology" (122-23). Poe, on the other hand, preferred Simms as a scribe of the ideological. In his 1841 review of *Confession*, he wrote of the author "He should never have written 'The Partisan,' nor 'The Yemassee'....His genius does not lie in the outward so much as in the inner world. 'Martin Faber' did him honor; and so do the present volumes....We welcome him home to his own proper field of exertion — the field of Godwin and Brown — the field of his own rich intellect and glowing *heart*" (306; Poe's emphasis alludes to *Confession*'s alternate title, *The Blind Heart*). Interestingly, both writers alluded to Simms's evocation of Godwin, yet assessed this inspiration quite differently.

The tenor of reviews subsequent to the novel's initial publication seems to have trended in a slightly more positive direction. An anonymous writer in 1845, in reviewing Simms's recently published *The Life of Francis Marion*, called *Confession* "extraordinary," and noted that the "genius and talents of Mr. Simms shine forth in their greatest splendor" in the novel's pages (qtd. in Butterworth and Kibler 59). Following its 1856 issue by Redfield, the novel was reviewed in *Godey's Lady's Book* as a "powerfully written tale" that "presents its author's genius in a novel light" (*Letters* 3: 385n). Simms's wrote to Thomas A Burke in August of that year to thank him for a kind review the editor had penned; Burke called *Confession* "one of the very best of all its author's productions," and doubted "if any reader of 'Confession' will care to put it a side [*sic*] until he has finished it" (*Letters* 3: 443n). These kinds of glowing reviews or, indeed, any reviews at all, were rather scarce, though. Some writers obviously found merit in the novel, but most readers and critics disparaged or ignored it.

The twentieth century has done little to remedy this neglect and improve the novel's fortunes. Donald Davidson, the most accomplished of Simms's reviewers, is a bit undecided in his estimation of the work. On the one hand, he criticizes *Confession* for seeming "too obviously worked up," that is to say too intently focused on being a literary production and not organic in its development. He censures the work for being "done with sheer literary muscle" without stemming, "like [Simms's] best work, from sources deeper than books and documents can supply." But, on the other hand, Davidson calls *Confession* the author's "strongest psychological novel," a work exhibiting "clear merit" (li). Negative or mixed critical assessments of the past might be changing, though. John C. Guilds declares that "*Confession* is a much better book than is generally acknowledged" (*Simms* 105), and Miriam Shillingsburg praises it as "one of the earliest convincing studies of domestic battery in American literature" (222). Simms is also increasingly being recognized as a forerunner of the southern gothic genre, and *Confession* factors heavily in that regard.

A close reading of the novel reveals a number of themes and motifs that scholars have yet to treat in any great detail. Many of these elements contribute to Simms's experimental style in the book, especially his efforts to craft a more American version of the gothic romance. For example, Edward Clifford, for all his psychological faults and behavioral foibles, is an expression of a quintessentially American character-type, the self-made man. His life is characterized by determination and success despite humble beginnings. Simms's treatment of this figure in *Confession* is complex and creative and marks his efforts at innovation. Not willing to allow his fictional rendering of the ideal American to be shallow and one-sided, though, Simms imbues his self-made man with duplicitous characteristics. Furthermore, though Simms ultimately celebrates this figure, he does so in a fashion that is subtle and ambiguous. His treatment of the self-made man gains depth also by his presentation of this character's antithesis in Edgerton. Indulged in childhood where Clifford was neglected, Edgerton lacks the discipline of his boyhood friend. Through the interaction of these contradictory figures, Simms offers a subtle portrait of the American character.

Clifford's ultimate rise in position from the feeblest and most tormented of beginnings draws on and reinforces the prototypical image of the American self-made man. Clifford is the epitome of this figure, not only because of his determination to succeed, but also because of his perseverance in the face of adversity. He survives the antagonism of his family, the lechery of his friend, and ultimately, the self-destructive nature of his own psyche. At the end of the novel, after the interplay of the gothic disasters, Clifford, unlike most gothic villains, lives through it. He is able to survive, persevere, and repent. His trouble begins, though, in the isolated nature of his upbringing, which renders it impossible for him to accept a natural love relationship with his wife or friends. Clifford, through his early education, has been taught that an untarnished companionship is a fantasy. Eventually, this influence brings about his apparently irrational jealousy of Julia and Edgerton's friendship. Referring to Clifford, Glenn M. Reed finds that Simms's "'self-made man' is so obsessed by the desire to have the unconditional love denied him by the death of his parents that he comes to scorn his social and material achievements and destroys the one thing he does prize, his wife"(xxi). So, though his origins have brought him to the full glory of the self-made man, they have also scarred him in such a way as to bring his downfall.

Despite the tragic end to which Clifford brings himself and his companions, Simms ultimately validates the character of the self-made man through a comparison with his rival. Though subtly portrayed throughout the novel, Edgerton is a perfect example of the indulged character type. He comes from a prominent Charleston family and enjoys all of the benefits of position that Clifford has had to do without. Though the hysterical and suspicious tone of Clifford's first-person narration initially makes the reader suspect Edgerton's innocence, Simms actually reveals his deuteragonist in the end to be far from a hapless victim of Clifford's antagonism. In the confessional letter that Edgerton addresses to Clifford he admits to desiring Julia. He further claims that, though he attempted in earnest to suppress his dishonorable urges, he could not: "My education did not fit me for such a struggle. The indulgence of fond parents had gratified all my wishes, and taught me to expect their gratification"(368). Therefore, not only does Edgerton reveal that Clifford's suspicion of him has been justified, but his reasons for his behavior look back to his childhood development.

This interplay of characters, combined with the fact that Edgerton commits suicide, helps to redeem Clifford's villainy. He is not wholly condemnable. This duality in characters and ambiguity of guilt forges the complex structure of Simms's version of the self-made man. Clifford is celebrated in his achievement, justified in his suspicions, and yet still partially condemned as the murderer of Julia. Yet, because of his perseverance, he is not wholly a monster. Bolstered by the positive facets of the self-made man, Clifford is able to live through the effects of the negative facets and hence is eligible for redemption.

One trait of Simms's novel that complicates the character types he establishes is the dual role Clifford is forced to play. As he begins to become his own nemesis, Clifford simultaneously portrays the protagonist and antagonist of the story's gothic conflict. Edgerton's influence on the plot fades as Clifford increasingly wars with himself. The formative influences that give him the perseverance of the self-made man also wound him psychologically. The cruel treatment by his aunt and uncle prohibits him from understanding true companionship, and this inability leads directly to the jealousy that destroys his marriage and his friend. As *Confession* is an experiment in psychological unraveling, the majority of its later pages are devoted to documenting the decline in Clifford's tormented psyche.

Though the jealousy that Clifford feels for his wife's friendship with Edgerton is uncomfortable, it is the pendulumatic shifts in his beliefs about his wife's fidelity that makes it tragic. Rather than confronting Julia, Clifford manipulates interactions between the two may-be lovers in order to spy on them. Even though encounter after encounter yields nothing incriminating in their behavior, Clifford, because of his wounded mind, remains unconvinced. In the face of no evidence, he begins to forge it out of Julia's seemingly harmless behavior. Bush remarks, "Clifford', insane with jealousy, his tortured mind twisting even the most innocent actions of Julia, continued to throw them together again and again in order to test her, and to bring his own 'damning doubts to a final trial'"(125). These engineered situations harry all three participants until they are all, in some way, destroyed by them. Julia from the seeming neglect of her husband, Edgerton from his unfruitioned love for Julia, and Clifford from his self-destructive monomania, all converge in a gothic implosion that leaves two dead and Clifford guilty, wounded, and alone. His own tormented psyche, in true gothic fashion, not only brings his own downfall but destroys all of those around him as well.

Yet, Clifford's story concludes with the possibility of expiation. Despite the hand-wringing efforts by readers to categorize Simms's novel as alternatively a border and a gothic romance, the conclusion of *Confession* suggests that these styles are fundamentally interlocked in American fiction. Clifford's progression towards the American frontier is necessitated by his destructive behavior but also suggestive of the possibility of redemption. In Simms's presentation here, manifest destiny is important to the thematic conclusion of the novel. His endorsement of America's westward expansion is an early and lucid dissertation on this very American article of faith. Clifford's wanderlust, inspired though it is by gothic dread, is a fictional realization of this policy. By leaving his hometown of Charleston for Montgomery, Alabama, he seeks escape from those elements that tax his frail psychology: the cuckolding impulses of Edgerton and the venomous ones of his aunt and uncle. The West, for Clifford, offers escape from his tangible and immediate problems. At the end of the novel, though, the West takes on almost mystical qualities, and the healing it promises is more holistic. Texas is the place where Clifford seeks not only the isolation of a sparsely peopled land, but also redemption for his crime. Moving westward, ultimately, cannot provide balm for those problems within himself that Clifford imports; but, the remove from civilization suggests at least a blank slate onto which one might inscribe a new beginning, a new life, and a new soul. With the true American mentality of manifest destiny, Clifford faces the next frontier seeking just such an inauguration. The journey, both literal and psychological will be a struggle, though. As Clifford notes, from the commission of his crimes and throughout his search for redemption, "evermore an echo arose from the bottom of my soul; and my lips repeated it to my own ears only; and but one word was spoken; and that word was — 'ATONEMENT!'" (*Confession* 398).

Works Cited

Barton, John Cyril. "William Gilmore Simms and the Literary Aesthetics of Crime and Capital Punishment." *Law & Literature* 22.2 (Summer 2010): 220-43.

Bush, Lewis M. "Werther on the Alabama Frontier: A Reinterpretation of Simms's *Confession.*" *Mississippi Quarterly* 21.2 (Spring 1968): 119-30.

Butterworth, Keen and James E. Kibler, Jr. *William Gilmore Simms: A Reference Guide.* Boston: G.K. Hall & Co., 1980.

Davidson, Donald. Introduction. *The Letters of William Gilmore Simms.* Ed. Mary C. Simms Oliphant, Alfred Taylor Odell, and T. C. Duncan Eaves. 6 vols. Columbia: U of South Carolina P, 1952-1982. xxxi-lviii.

Davis, David Brion. *Homicide in American Fiction, 1798 – 1860: A Study in Social Values.* Ithaca, NY: Cornell UP, 1957.

Desment, Christy. "*Confession; or, the Blind Heart*: An Antebellum *Othello.*" *Borrowers and Lenders* 1.1 (Spring 2005): 1-24.

Guilds, John Caldwell. Introduction. *The Writings of William Gilmore Simms: Stories and Tales.* Centennial Edition. Columbia: U of South Carolina P, 1974. xi-xxiv.

——. *"Long Years of Neglect": The Works and Reputation of William Gilmore Simms.* Fayetteville & London: The U of Arkansas P, 1988.

——. *Simms: A Literary Life.* Fayetteville: The U of Arkansas P, 1992.

Poe, Edgar Allan. Rev. of *Confession; or, The Blind Heart. A Domestic Story,* by William Gilmore Simms. *Graham's Magazine* 19.6 (December 1841): 306.

Reed, Glenn M. Introduction. *Martin Faber.* By William Gilmore Simms. Albany, NY: NCUP, 1990. i-xxi.

Salley, A.S. "William Gilmore Simms." *The Letters of William Gilmore Simms.* Ed. Mary C. Simms Oliphant, Alfred Taylor Odell, and T. C. Duncan Eaves. Vol. 1. Columbia: U of South Carolina P, 1952. lix-lxxxix.

Shillingsburg, Miriam. "The Battered Woman Syndrome in Simms's Fiction." *Studies in the Novel* 35.2 (Summer 2003): 219-30.

Simms, William Gilmore. *Confession; or, The Blind Heart. A Domestic Story.* New York: Redfield, 1856.

——. *The Letters of William Gilmore Simms.* Ed. Mary C. Simms Oliphant, Alfred Taylor Odell, and T. C. Duncan Eaves. 6 vols. Columbia: U of South Carolina P, 1952-1982.

Trent, William Peterfield. *William Gilmore Simms.* Boston: Houghton, Mifflin, 1892.

Confession.

CONFESSION

OR

THE BLIND HEART

A DOMESTIC STORY

By W. GILMORE SIMMS, Esq.

AUTHOR OF "GUY RIVERS"—"RICHARD HURDIS"—"BORDER BEAGLES"—"BEAUCHAMPE"—"KATHARINE WALTON"—"THE SCOUT," ETC.

WAGNER. But of the world—the heart, the mind of man
How happy could we know!
FAUST. What can we know?
Who dares bestow the infant his true name?
The few who felt and knew, but blindly gave
Their knowledge to the multitude—they fell!
Incapable to keep their full hearts in,
They, from the first of immemorial time,
Were crucified or burnt.
GOETHE'S FAUST, *MS. Version.*

NEW AND REVISED EDITION

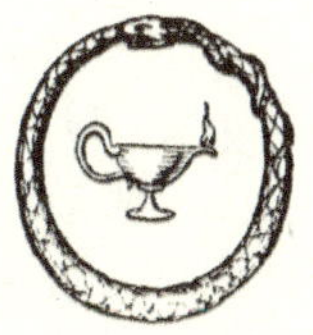

REDFIELD
34 BEEKMAN STREET, NEW YORK
1856

SAVAGE & McCREA, STEREOTYPERS,
13 Chambers Street, N. Y.

INTRODUCTION.

It is, no doubt, a departure from the general laws of Nature, when we exhibit, in a work of art, in fiction, the exercise of any one passion exclusively; when, as in the case of Miss Joanna Baillie, in her "Plays of the Passions," we endeavor to individualize a single passion to the exclusion of all the rest, and seek to build our interest entirely upon the exercise of the one feature, or quality of mind or heart, which we have thus established in this morbid ascendency. Nature does not usually work after this fashion. The passions dwell in groups and families, and there is perpetual play and co-operation between them. One of them may, indeed, exercise a predominating power; but the others are still visibly working, as tributaries—certainly a portion of them—and their presence is to be detected in the general agency; affording that sort of relief to the person in whose fortunes the chief interest lies, without which a passion resolves itself finally into madness. There is little question, indeed, that not only do most madnesses arise from such an absorbed condition of the mind, which thus subjugates all the energies to a single faculty, and compels them in a single direction, and keeps them intensely exercised and sorely straitened; but that all intensity, which throws a single passion into extreme superiority, for any length of time, so as to leave the rest wholly in abeyance, will so impair the intellectual strength as to render of questionable sanity all the performances of the party while in this condition. That this condition does and must exist occasionally, we know; for we have madness and monomania in the world: but, as it is the policy of neither moralist nor dramatist to select a madman for his hero, so it is false practice in art, and a great mistake, so to individualize a passion until it acts like madness—unless, where we make the character wholly subordinate to the fiction, and use it merely as a part of the inferior agency in bringing about results which are requisite for the large conditions of the story; and even this must be done very judiciously, and without making a too free use of the morbid agency.

I am not sure that I have not erred against my own rule in the tale which follows; but I am sure that I have had no purpose to violate it. Indeed, the form of monomania which I have here sought to delineate, I have endeavored to relieve by shows of other passions—nay, by the free exercise of other passions, and strong ones too—which would, under other circumstances, in the case of an individual trained by a more indulgent fortune, have fully availed to neutralize the one moral plague-spot, which, let to grow, and stimulated in its growth by external pressure, became finally, in the case of my hero, big enough, not only to cover the whole heart, but to impair the vigorous working of an otherwise noble brain. Self-esteem is, here, a passion; ambition, a passion; love, a passion: there are nice sensibilities, an honorable spirit, great gentleness, warm sympathies, and many talents. But the self-esteem, in an ambitious nature, goaded by continual wrong, grows into one of the most jealous of all passions; and, in the case of one equally endowed with a fine heart and noble faculties, it is apt to put on the most subtle as well as the most fiery form of jealousy. The jealousy of self-esteem, by-the-way, is of far greater intensity than that which springs from mortified affections alone; and this is the source of the diseased development which I here delineate.—Enough, perhaps, on this head, particularly as my object, throughout the tale, has been to make the hero lay bare the secret of his own disease, and, step by step, to exhibit its successive symptoms.

Portions of the following narrative were among the earliest prose-writings of the author. The materials are gathered from facts, in a domestic history, the sources of which he believes to be unquestionable. Some of the events occurred, indeed, under his own observation. Of this early manuscript he had almost lost all recollection, until he happened upon it while exploring the contents of a large mass of similar beginnings of his youth. The reperusal of the fragment possessed his mind so warmly with the subject, that he could not resist the desire to resume it. Attempting to arrange it for the press, he was led away by his own interest in the psychological history; and the work grew beneath his hands to a size far exceeding his original purpose, which contemplated nothing more than the construction of a rapid magazine article.

A work so growing, without design, may be strictly legitimate, as the natural progress of the author's mind to the solutions of his problems, yet fail in every essential, as a work of interest for the reader, or even of art. The mere logical array of facts, distribution and arrangement of the proper relations of parties and events—all these, however well done, may yet constitute no more claim to art than may be urged in behalf of a well-put law argument. The defect in design will most probably be a loss of warmth and color to the picture, to speak in the language of the studio. Such a process of gradual expansion, without heed to the design, is liable to many dangers and objections, in addition to the deficiency already mentioned; not the least of which, in the popular estimation, will be the absence of variety, and the lack of exciting action. To sit down, day by day, to the labors of the anatomist merely—to bare the nerves, and sinews, and tissues, and limbs, which we should prefer to clothe and color—is apt to become a somewhat dreary, even when an exciting, performance; and this is the danger always of one who, in fiction, works *under the surface*, rejecting those exhibitions of the moods *externally* which supply the performance with its incidents. We prefer the salient action to the contemplation of the silent agony; would rather behold the action than have it described to us; must see Richard writhing upon his couch, even while we listen to his dream; and are apt to feel it somewhat wearisome to trace the secret necessity of the soul, even though, in doing so, we are allowed to pierce its most hidden mysteries. We prefer to hear it cry aloud its agonies, rather than take upon ourselves the labor of seeking them where they lie concealed, and watching the secret struggles by which they are subdued.

To readers, therefore, who are simply in search of incident, and that sort of interest which appeals to the blood rather than the brain, it may be well, by way of caution, and to prevent unreasonable expectation, to say that this "Confession of the Blind Heart" offers very little encouragement. It partakes of few of the features of that school of Dumas, and Reynolds, and Ainsworth, in which the heart is made to roar out its hopes or sufferings, under incessant provocation and stimuli. It has its "disastrous chances;" but with few of those "moving accidents by flood and field"—those "hair-breadth 'scapes i' the imminent deadly breach"—which so richly garnish in general the tales of these popular writers.

Its interest is required to arise from other sources. It contemplates another class of readers. The trials and troubles of the hero are not only those of simple, domestic life, but they are of the sensibilities rather than the blood—diseased sensibilities, where the passions, exciting and erring, develop themselves in faults, vices, and weaknesses, rather than in crimes;

and where, even when crime occurs, it is motiveless as crime, not purposed as crime, but, under a blind judgment, as justice simply. The attempt is made to analyze the heart in some of its obliquities and perversities; to follow its toils, pursue its phases, and to trace, if possible, the secret of its self-deceptions, its self-baffling inconsistencies, its seemingly wilful warfare with reason and the sober experience. This is the simple design of the narrative, which, with great unity of plan and purpose, lacks all the usual varieties of art in prose fiction. It belongs, somewhat, to the class of works which the genius of Godwin has made to triumph in "Caleb Williams," even over a perverse system.

The writer reviews his work, now that it is finished (and now again when he revises its pages for the last time), with many misgivings. He is not blind to the difficulty of describing the struggles of a blind heart—taking that one heart up, almost alone, and making it narrate its own dreary consciousness of wrong-doing, of wrong-enduring, and of equal suffering in both conditions. Perhaps there can be no performance more difficult—none less likely to appeal to the merely popular reader—less likely to be successful, in common opinion, unless with a small and peculiarly-constituted circle. There is no relief to the picture—no background, or it is *all* background—gloomy even with its glare—an ominous shadow hanging like a cloud over the whole, and serving as the curtain which, half the time, conceals the sacrifice. Success, of a popular kind, is rarely possible in any work of fiction where events, which naturally speak for themselves, are mostly rejected from use; where the whole history depends for development upon the silent progress of the thoughts, and sentiments, and emotions—the passions themselves working as under-currents of moods and feelings—moods which look, but speak not, and feelings that boil for ever in fiery fountains, but are never suffered to overflow! A single soul is here selected from the rest, put in bonds, put to the torture, and made to declare its dreary experience through its groans. It is to suffer, not to act. It has no foil, no assistants; there is no chorus; no other actors are suffered on the scene. Its cry is necessarily a monotone. Its own intensity must supply the absence of exciting action. Can it make itself heard, felt—secure justice, compel sympathy—by this one cry of agony? That is the question. In degree with the intensity of its own agony, its own severe simplicity and truth, its own earnest feeling of sincerity, and the injustice of its suffering under the decree of an ingeniously perverse fate, will be the credence we accord to its appeal. It speaks, or not, to the purpose, as one giving evidence. Perhaps, like the frequent witness in other courts, it may speak some—nay, much—yet not the whole truth. The writer, however, has striven that such should not be the case. He has conducted the cross-examination with a searching scrutiny; and, if any matters of evidence are left unrevealed, the fault is rather in the lawyer than the witness. The courteous reader will be pleased to perceive this fault in neither. In neither—we answer for both—is it wilful.

W. G. S.

WOODLANDS, S. C., *March*, 1856.

CONFESSION,

OR

THE BLIND HEART.

CHAPTER I.

> "Who dares bestow the infant his true name?
> The few who felt and knew, but blindly gave
> Their knowledge to the multitude — they fell
> Incapable to keep their full hearts in,
> They, from the first of immemorial time,
> Were crucified or burnt."—GOETHE'S *Faust*.

THE pains and penalties of folly are not necessarily death. They were in old times, perhaps, according to the text, and he who kept not to himself the secrets of his silly heart was surely crucified or burnt. Though lacking in penalties extreme like these, the present is not without its own. All times, indeed, have their penalties for folly, much more certainly than for crime; and this fact furnishes one of the most human arguments in favor of the doctrine of rewards and punishments in the future state. But these penalties are not always mortifications and trials of the flesh. There are punishments of the soul; the spirit; the sensibilities; the intellect — which are most usually the consequences of one's own folly. There is a perversity of mood which is the worst of all such penalties. There are tortures which the foolish heart equally inflicts and endures. The passions riot on their own nature; and, feeding as they do upon that bosom from which they spring, and in which they flourish, may, not inaptly, be likened to that unnatural brood which gnaws into the heart of the mother-bird, and sustains its existence at the expense of hers. Meetly governed from the beginning, they are dutiful agents that bless themselves in their own obedience; but, pampered to excess, they are tyrants that never do justice, until at last, when they fitly conclude the work of destruction by their own.

The narrative which follows is intended to illustrate these opinions. It is the story of a blind heart—nay, of blind hearts—blind through their own perversity—blind to their own interests—their own joys, hopes, and proper sources of delight. In narrating my own fortunes, I depict theirs; and the old leaven of wilfulness, which belongs to our nature, has, in greater or less degree, a place in every human bosom.

I was the only one surviving of several sons. My parents died while I was yet an infant. I never knew them. I was left to the doubtful charge of relatives, who might as well have been strangers; and, from their treatment, I learned to doubt and to distrust among the first fatal lessons of my youth. I felt myself unloved—nay, as I fancied, disliked and despised. I was not merely an orphan. I was poor, and was felt as burdensome by those connections whom a dread of public opinion, rather than a sense of duty and affection, persuaded to take me to their homes. Here, then, when little more than three years old, I found myself—a lonely brat, whom servants might flout at pleasure, and whom superiors only regarded with a frown. I was just old enough to remember that I had once experienced very different treatment. I had felt the caresses of a fond mother—I had heard the cheering accents of a generous and a gentle father. The one had soothed my griefs and encouraged my hopes—the other had stimulated my energies and prompted my desires. Let no one fancy that, because I was a child, these lessons were premature. All education, to be valuable, must begin with the child's first efforts at discrimination. Suddenly, both of these fond parents disappeared, and I was just young enough to wonder why.

The change in my fortunes first touched my sensibilities, which it finally excited until they became diseased. Neglected, if not scorned, I habitually looked to encounter nothing but neglect or scorn. The sure result of this condition of mind was a look and feeling, on my part, of habitual defiance. I grew up with the mood of one who goes forth with a moral certainty that he must meet and provide against an enemy. But I am now premature.

The uncle and aunt with whom I found shelter were what is called in ordinary parlance, very good people. They attended the most popular church with most popular punctuality. They prayed with unction—subscribed to all the charities which had publicity and a fashionable list to recommend them—helped to send missionaries to Calcutta, Bombay, Owyhee, and other outlandish regions—paid their debts when they became due with commendable readiness—and were, in all out-of-door respects, the very sort of people who might congratulate themselves, and thank God that they were very far superior to their neighbors. My uncle had morning prayers at home, and my aunt thumbed Hannah More in the evening; though it must be admitted that the former could not always forbear, coming from church on the sabbath, to inquire into the last news of the Liverpool cotton market, and my aunt never failed, when they reached home, on the same blessed day, to make the house ring with another sort of eloquence than that to which she had listened with such sanctimonious devotion from the lips of the preacher. There were some other little offsets against the perfectly evangelical character of their religion. One of these—the first that attracted my infant consideration—was naturally one which more directly concerned myself. I soon discovered that, while I was sent to an ordinary charity school of the country, in threadbare breeches, made of the meanest material—their own son—a gentle and good, but puny boy, whom their indulgence injured, and, perhaps, finally destroyed—was despatched to a fashionable institution which taught all sorts of *ologies*—dressed in such choice broadcloth and costly habiliments, as to make him an object of envy and even odium among all his less fortunate school-fellows.

Poor little Edgar! His own good heart and correct natural understanding showed him the equal folly of that treatment to which he was subjected, and the injustice and unkindness which distinguished mine. He strove to make amends, so far as I was concerned, for the error of his parents. He was my playmate whenever he was permitted, but even this permission was qualified by some remark, some direction or counsel, from one or other of his parents, which was intended to let him know, and make me feel, that there was a monstrous difference between us.

The servants discovered this difference as quickly as did the objects of it; and though we were precisely of one age, and I was rather the largest of the two, yet, in addressing us, they paid him the deference which should only be shown to superior age, and treated me with the contumely only due to inferior merit. It was "Master Edgar," when he was spoken to—and "you," when I was the object of attention.

I do not speak of these things as of substantial evils affecting my condition. Perhaps, in one or more respects, they were benefits. They taught me humility in the first place, and made that humility independence, by showing me that the lesson was bestowed in wantonness, and not with the purpose of improvement. And, in proportion as my physical nature suffered their neglect, it acquired strength by the very roughening to which that neglect exposed it. In this I possessed a vast advantage over my little companion. His frame, naturally feeble, sunk under the oppressive tenderness to which the constant care of a vain father, a doting mother, and sycophantic friends and servants, subjected it. The attrition of boy with boy, in the half-manly sports of schoolboy life—its very strifes and scuffles—would have brought his blood into adequate circulation, and hardened his bones, and given elasticity to his sinews. But from all these influences, he was carefully preserved and protected. He was not allowed to run, for fear of being too much heated. He could not jump, lest he might break a blood-vessel. In the ball play, he might get an eye knocked out; and even tops and marbles were forbidden, lest he should soil his hands and wear out the knees of his green breeches. If he indulged in these sports it was only by stealth, and at the fearful cost of a falsehood on every such occasion. When will parents learn that entirely to crush and keep down the proper nature of the young, is to produce inevitable perversity, and stimulate the boyish ingenuity to crime?

With me the case was very different. If cuffing and kicking could have killed, I should have died many sudden and severe deaths in the rough school to which I was sent. If eyes were likely to be lost in the campus, corded balls of India-rubber, or still harder ones of wood, impelled by shinny (goff) sticks, would have obliterated all of mine though they had been numerous as those of Argus. My limbs and eyes escaped all injury; my frame grew tall and vigorous in consequence of neglect, even as the forest-tree, left to the conflict of all the winds of heaven; while my poor little friend, Edgar, grew daily more and more diminutive, just as some plant, which nursing and tendance within doors deprive of the wholesome sunshine and generous breezes of the sky. The paleness of his cheek increased, the languor of his frame, the meagerness of his form, the inability of his nature! He was pining rapidly away, in spite of that excessive care, which, perhaps, had been in the first instance, the unhappy source of all his feebleness.

He died—and I became an object of greater dislike than ever to his parents. They could not but contrast my strength with his feebleness—my improvement with his decline—and when they remembered how little had been their regard for me, and how much for him—without ascribing the difference of result to the true cause—they repined at the ways of Providence, and threw upon me the reproach of it. They gave me less heed and fewer smiles than ever. If I improved at school, it was well, perhaps; but they never inquired, and I could not help fancying that it was with a positive expression of vexation, that my aunt heard, on one occasion, from my teacher, in the presence of some guests, that I was likely to be an honor to the family.

"An honor to the family, indeed!" This was the clear expression in that Christian lady's eyes, as I saw them sink immediately after in a scornful examination of my rugged frame and coarse garments.

The family had its own sources of honor, was the calm opinion of both my patrons, as they turned their eyes upon their only remaining child—a little girl about five years old, who was playing around them on the carpet. This opinion was also mine, even then: and my eyes followed theirs in the same direction. Julia Clifford was one of the sweetest little fairies in the world. Tender-hearted, and just, and generous, like the dear little brother, whom she had only known to lose, she was yet as playful as a kitten. I was twice her age—just ten—at this period; and a sort of instinct led me to adopt the little creature, in place of poor Edgar, in the friendship of my boyish heart. I drew her in her little wagon—carried her over the brooklet—constructed her tiny playthings—and in consideration of my usefulness, in most generally keeping her in the best of humors, her mother was not unwilling that I should be her frequent playmate. Nay, at such times she could spare a gentle word even to me, as one throws a bone to the dog, who has jumped a pole, or plunged into the water, or worried some other dog, for his amusement. At no other period did my worthy aunt vouchsafe me such unlooked-for consideration.

But Julia Clifford was not my only friend. I had made another shortly before the death of Edgar; though, passingly it may be said, friendship-making was no easy business with a nature such as mine had now become. The inevitable result of such treatment as that to which my early years had been subjected, was fully realized. I was suspicious to the last degree of all new faces—jealous of the regards of the old; devoting myself where my affections were set and requiring devotion—rigid, exclusive devotion—from their object in return. There was a terrible earnestness in all my moods which made my very love a thing to be feared. I was no trifler—I could not suffer to be trifled with—and the ordinary friendships of man or boy can not long endure the exactions of such a disposition. The penalties are usually thought to be—and are—infinitely beyond the rewards and benefits.

My intimacies with William Edgerton were first formed under circumstances which, of all others, are most likely to establish them on a firm basis in our days of boyhood. He came to my rescue one evening, when, returning from school, I was beset by three other boys, who had resolved on drubbing me. My haughty deportment had vexed their self-esteem, and, as the same cause had left me with few sympathies, it was taken for granted that the unfairness of their assault would provoke no censure. They were mistaken. In the moment of my greatest difficulty, William Edgerton dashed in among them. My exigency rendered his assistance a very singular benefit. My nose was already broken — one of my eyes sealed up for a week's holyday; and I was suffering from small annoyances, of hip, heart, leg, and thigh, occasioned by the repeated cuffs, and the reckless kicks, which I was momently receiving from three points of the compass. It is true that my enemies had their hurts to complain of also; but the odds were too greatly against me for any conduct or strength of mine to neutralize or overcome; and it was only by Edgerton's interposition that I was saved from utter defeat and much worse usage. The beating I had already suffered. I was sore from head to foot for a week after; and my only consolation was that my enemies left the ground in a condition, if anything, something worse than my own.

But I had gained a friend, and that was a sweet recompense, sweeter to me, by far, than it is found or felt by schoolboys usually. None could know or comprehend the force of my attachment — my dependence upon the attachment of which I felt assured! — none but those who, with an earnest, impetuous nature like my own — doomed to denial from the first, and treated with injustice and unkindness — has felt the pang of a worse privation from the beginning; — the privation of that sustenance, which is the "very be all and end all" of its desire and its life — and the denial of which chills and repels its fervor — throws it back in despondency upon itself — fills it with suspicion, and racks it with a never-ceasing conflict between its apprehension and its hopes.

Edgerton supplied a vacuum which my bosom had long felt. He was, however, very unlike, in most respects, to myself. He was rather phlegmatic than ardent — slow in his fancies, and shy in his associations from very fastidiousness. He was too much governed by nice tastes, to be an active or performing youth; and too much restrained by them also, to be a popular one. This, perhaps, was the secret influence which brought us together. A mutual sense of isolation — no matter from what cause — awakened the sympathies between us. Our ties were formed, on my part, simply because I was assured that I should have no rival; and on his, possibly, because he perceived in my haughty reserve of character, a sufficient security that his fastidious sensibilities would not be likely to suffer outrage at my hands. In every other respect our moods and tempers were utterly unlike. I thought him dull, very frequently, when he was only balancing between jealous and sensitive tastes;—and ignorant of the actual, when, in fact, his ignorance simply arose from the decided preference which he gave to the foreign and abstract. He was contemplative—an idealist; I was impetuous and devoted to the real and living world around me, in which I was disposed to mingle with an eagerness which might have been fatal; but for that restraint to which my own distrust of all things and persons habitually subjected me.

CHAPTER II.

BOY PASSIONS—A PROFESSION CHOSEN.

BETWEEN William Edgerton and Julia Clifford my young life and best affections were divided, entirely, if not equally. I lived for no other—I cared to seek, to know, no other—and yet I often shrunk from both. Even at that boyish period, while the heavier cares and the more painful vexations of life were wanting to our annoyance, I had those of that gnawing nature, which seemed to be born of the tree whose evil growth "brought death into the world and all our wo." The pang of a nameless jealousy—a sleepless distrust—rose unbidden to my heart at seasons, when, in truth, there was no obvious cause. When Julia was most gentle—when William was most generous—even then, I had learned to repulse them with an indifference which I did not feel—a rudeness which brought to my heart a pain even greater than that which my wantonness inflicted upon theirs. I knew, even then, that I was perverse, unjust; and that there was a littleness in the vexatious mood in which I indulged, that was unjust to my own feelings, and unbecoming in a manly nature. But even though I felt all this, as thoroughly as I could ever feel it under any situation, I still could not succeed in overcoming that insane will which drove me to its indulgence.

Vainly have I striven to account for the blindness of heart—for such it is, in all such cases—which possessed me. Was there anything in my secret nature, born at my birth and growing with my growth—which impelled me to this wilfulness. I can scarcely believe so; but, after serious reflection, am compelled to think that it was the strict result of moods growing out of the particular treatment to which I had been subjected. It does not seem unnatural that an ardent temper of mind, willing to confide, looking to love and affection for the only aliment which it most and chiefly desires, and repelled in this search, frowned on by its superiors as if it were something base, will, in time, grow to be habitually wilful, even as the treatment which has schooled it. Had I been governed and guided by justice, I am sure that I should never have been unjust.

My waywardness in childhood did not often amount to rudeness, and never, I may safely say, where Julia was concerned. In her case, it was simply the exercise of a sullenness that repelled her approaches, even as its own approaches had been repelled by others. At such periods I went apart, communing sternly with myself, refusing the sympathy that I most yearned after, and resolving not to be comforted. Let me do the dear child the justice to say that the only effect which this conduct had upon her, was to increase her anxieties to soothe the repulsive spirit which should have offended her. Perhaps, to provoke this anxiety in one it loves, is the chief desire of such a spirit. It loves to behold the persevering devotion, which it yet perversely toils to discourage. It smiles within, with a bitter triumph, as it contemplates its own power, to impart the same sorrow which a similar perversity has already made it feel.

But, without seeking further to analyze and account for such a spirit, it is quite sufficient if I have described it. Perhaps, there are other hearts equally froward and wayward with my own. I know not if my story will amend—perhaps it may not even instruct or inform them—I feel that no story, however truthful, could have disarmed the humor of that particular mood of mind which shows itself in the blindness of the heart under which it was my lot to labor. I did not want knowledge of my own perversity. I knew—I felt it—as clearly as if I had seen it written in characters of light, on the walls of my chamber. But, until it had exhausted itself and passed away by its own processes, no effort of mine could have overcome or banished it. I stalked apart, under its influence, a gloomy savage—scornful and sad—stern, yet suffering—denying myself equally, in the perverse and wanton denial to which I condemned all others.

Perhaps something of this temper is derived from the yearnings of the mental nature. It may belong somewhat to the natural direction of a mind having a decided tendency to imaginative pursuits. There is a dim, vague, indefinite struggle, for ever going on in the nature of such a person, after an existence and relations very foreign to the world in which it lives; and equally far from, and hostile to that condition in which it thrives. The vague discontent of such a mind is one of the causes of its activity; and how far it may be stimulated into diseased intensity by injudicious treatment, is a question of large importance for the consideration of philosophers. The imaginative nature is one singularly sensitive in its conditions; quick, jealous, watchful, earnest, stirring, and perpetually breaking down the ordinary barriers of the actual, in its struggles to ascertain the extent of the possible. The tyranny which drives it from the ordinary resources and enjoyments of the young, by throwing it more completely on its own, impels into desperate activity that daring of the imaginative mood, which, at no time, is wanting in courage and audacity. My mind was one singularly imaginative in its structure; and my ardent temperament contributed largely to its activity. Solitude, into which I was forced by the repulsive and unkind treatment of my relatives, was also favorable to the exercise of this influence; and my heart may be said to have taken, in turn, every color and aspect which informed my eyes. It was a blind heart for this very reason, in respect to all those things for which it should have had a color of its own. Books and the woods—the voice of waters and of song—the dim mysteries of poetry, and the whispers of lonely forest-walks, which beguiled me into myself, and more remotely from my fellows, were all, so far as my social relations were concerned, evil influences! Influences which were only in part overcome by the communion of such gentle beings as William Edgerton and Julia Clifford.

With these friends, and these only, I grew up. As my years advanced, my intimacy with the former increased, and with the latter diminished. But this diminution of intimacy did not lessen the kindness of her feelings, or the ordinary devotedness of mine. She was still—when the perversity of heart made me not blind—the sweet creature to whom the task of ministering was a pleasure infinitely beyond any other which I knew. But, as she grew up to girlhood, other prospects opened upon her eyes, and other purposes upon those of her parents. At twelve she was carried by maternal vanity into company — sent to the dancing-school — provided with teachers in music and painting, and made to understand — so far as the actions, looks, and words of all around could teach — that she was the cynosure of all eyes, to whom the whole world was bound in deference.

Fortunately, in the case of Julia, the usual effects of maternal folly and indiscretion did not ensue. Nature interposed to protect her, and saved her in spite of them all. She was still the meek, modest child, solicitous of the happiness of all around her — unobtrusive, unassuming — kind to her inferiors, respectful to superiors, and courteous to, and considerate of all other persons. Her advancing years, which rendered these new acquisitions and accomplishments desirable, if not necessary, at the same time prompted her foolish mother to another step which betrayed the humiliating regard which she entertained for me. When I was seventeen, Julia was twelve, and when neither she nor myself had a solitary thought of love, the over-considerate mother began to think, on this subject, for us both. The result of her cogitations determined her that it was no longer fitting that Julia should be my companion. Our rambles in the woods together were forbidden; and Julia was gravely informed that I was a poor youth, though her cousin — an orphan whom her father's charity supported, and whom the public charity schooled. The poor child artlessly told me all this, in a vain effort to procure from me an explanation of the mystery (which her mother had either failed or neglected to explain) by which such circumstances were made to account for the new commands which had been given her. Well might she, in her simplicity of heart, wonder why it was, that because I was poor, she should be familiar with me no longer.

The circumstance opened my eyes to the fact that Julia was a tall girl, growing fast, already in her teens, and likely, under the rapidly-maturing influence of our summer sun, to be soon a woman. But just then — just when she first tasked me to solve the mystery of her mother's strange requisitions, I did not think of this. I was too much filled with indignation — the mortified self-esteem was too actively working in my bosom to suffer me to think of anything but the indignity with which I was treated. A brief portion of the dialogue between the child and myself, will give some glimpses of the blind heart by which I was afflicted.

"Oh, you do not understand it, Julia. You do not know, then, that you are the daughter of a rich merchant—the only daughter—that you have servants to wait on you, and a carriage at command—that you can wear fine silks, and have all things that money can buy, and a rich man's daughter desire. You don't know these things, Julia, eh?"

"Yes, Edward, I hear you say so now, and I hear mamma often say the same things; but still I don't see—"

"You don't see why that should make a difference between yourself and your poor cousin, eh? Well, but it does; and though you don't see it now, yet it will not be very long before you will see, and understand it, and act upon it, too, as promptly as the wisest among them. Don't you know that I am the object of your father's charity—that his bounty feeds me—and that it would not be seemly that the world should behold me on a familiar footing of equality or intimacy with the daughter of my benefactor—my patron—without whom I should probably starve, or be a common beggar upon the highway?"

"But father would not suffer that, Edward."

"Oh, no! no!—he would not suffer it, Julia, simply because his own pride and name would feel the shame and disgrace of such a thing. But though he would keep me from beggary and the highway, Julia, neither he nor your mother would spend a sixpence or make an effort to save my feelings from pain and misery. They protect me from the scorn of others, but they use me for their own."

The girl hung her head in silence.

"And you, too," I added—"the time will come when you, too, Julia, will shrink as promptly as themselves from being seen with your poor relation. You—"

"No! no! Edward—how can you think of such a thing?" she replied with girlish chiding.

"Think it!—I know it! The time will soon be here. But—obey your mother, Julia. Go! leave me now. Begin at once the lesson which, before many days, you will find it very easy to learn."

This was all very manly, so I fancied at the time; and then

blind with the perverse heart which boiled within me, I felt not the wantonness of my mood, and heeded not the bitter pain which I occasioned to her gentle bosom. Her little hand grasped mine, her warm tears fell upon it; but I flung away from her grasp, and left her to those childish meditations which I had made sufficiently mournful.

Subsequent reflection, while it showed me the brutality of my conduct to Julia, opened my eyes to the true meaning of her mother's interdiction; and increased the pang of those bitter feelings, which my conscious dependence had awakened in my breast. It was necessary that this dependence should be lessened; that, as I was now approaching manhood, I should cast about for the future, and adopt wisely and at once the means of my support hereafter. It was necessary that I should begin the business of life. On this head I had already reflected somewhat, and my thoughts had taken their direction from more than one conference which I had had with William Edgerton. His father was an eminent lawyer, and the law had been adopted for his profession also. I determined to make it mine; and to speak on this subject to my uncle. This I did. I chose an afternoon, the very week in which my conversation had taken place with Julia, and, while the dinner things were undergoing removal, with some formality requested a private interview with him. He looked round at me with a raised brow of inquiry—nodded his head—and shortly after rose from the table. My aunt stared with an air of supercilious wonder; while poor Julia, timid and trembling, barely ventured to give me a single look, which said—and that was enough for me—"I wish I dared say more."

My conference with my uncle was not of long duration. I told him it was my purpose—my desire—to begin as soon as possible to do something for myself. His answer signified that such was his opinion also. So far we were agreed; but when I told him that it was my wish to study the law, he answered with sufficient, and as I thought, scornful abruptness:—

"The law, indeed! What puts the law into your head? What preparations have you made to study the law? You know nothing of languages which every lawyer should know—Latin—"

I interrupted him to say that I had some slight knowledge of Latin—sufficient, I fancied, for all legal purposes.

"Ah! indeed! where did you get it?"

"A friend lent me a grammar and dictionary, and I studied myself."

"Oh, you are ambitious; but you deceive yourself. You were never made for a lawyer. Besides, how are you to live while prosecuting your studies? No, no! I have been thinking of something for you, Edward—and, just now, it happens fortunately that old Squire Farmer, the bricklayer, wants some apprentices—"

I could scarcely listen thus far.

"I thank you, sir, but I have no disposition to be a bricklayer."

"You must do something for yourself. You can not expect to eat the bread of idleness. I have done, and will do for you what I can—whatever is necessary;—but I have my own family to provide for. I can not rob my own child——"

"Nor do I expect it, Mr. Clifford," I replied hastily, and with some indignation. "It is my wish, sir, to draw as little as possible from your income and resources. I would not rob Julia Clifford of a single dollar. Nay, sir, I trust before many years to be able to refund you every copper which has been spent upon me from the moment I entered your household."

He said hastily:—

"I wish nothing of that, Edward;—but the law is a study of years, and is expensive and unpromising in every respect. Your clothes already call for a considerable sum, and such a profession requires, more than almost any other, that a student should be well dressed."

"I promise you, sir, that my dress shall be such as shall not trespass upon your income. I shall be governed by as much economy——"

He interrupted me to say, that

"His duty required that his brother's son should be dressed as well as his associates."

I replied, with tolerable composure:—

"I do not think, sir, that bricklaying will admit of very genteel clothing, nor do I think that the vocation will suit me. I have flattered myself, sir, that my talents——"

2

"Oh, you have talents, then, have you? Well, it is fortunate that the discovery has been made in season."

I bore with this, though my cheek was burning, and said—with an effort to preserve my voice and temper, in which, though the difficulty was great, I was tolerably successful—

"You have misunderstood me in some things, Mr. Clifford; and I will try now to explain myself clearly in others. Having resolved, sir, that the law shall be my profession——"

"Ha! resolved, say you?"

"Yes, sir."

"Well, go on—go on!"

"Having resolved to pursue the study of law, and seeing that I am burdensome and expensive to you—believing, too, that I can relieve you of the burden—I have simply requested permission of you to make the attempt."

"Why, how do you propose to do so?—how can you support yourself—that is relieve me of the burden of your expenses—and study the law at the same time?"

"Such things have been done, sir; and can be done again. I flatter myself I can do it. Industry will enable me to do so. I propose to apply for a clerkship in a mercantile establishment which I know stands in need of assistance, and while there will pursue my studies in such intervals of leisure as the business will afford me."

"You seem to have the matter ready cut and dry. Why do you come to me, then? Remember, I can make no advances."

"I need none, sir. My simple object with you, sir, was to declare my intention, and to request that I may be permitted to refer to you the merchants to whom I mean to apply, for a knowledge of my character and attainments."

"Oh, certainly, you may—for the character;—but as to the attainments"—with a sneering smile—"of them I can say nothing, and, perhaps, the less said the better. I've no doubt you'll do well enough with the merchants. It does not need much genius or attainment for such situations. But, if you'll take my counsel, you'll go to the bricklayer. We want bricklayers sadly. To be a tolerable lawyer, parts are necessary; and God knows the country is over-stocked with hosts of lawyers already, whose only parts lie in their impudence.

Better think a little while longer. Speak to old Farmer yourself."

I smiled bitterly—thanked him for his counsel, which was only a studied form of insult, and turned away from him without further speech, and with a proud swelling of indignation at my heart. Thus our conference ended. A week after, I was ensconced behind the counter of a wholesale dealer, and my hands at night were already busy in turning over the heavy folios of Chitty and Blackstone.

CHAPTER III.

ADMITTED AMONG THE LAWYERS.

BEHOLD me, then, merchandising by day, and conning by night the intricate mysteries of law. Books for the latter purpose were furnished by my old friend, William Edgerton, from his father's library. He himself was a student, beginning about the same time with myself; though with the superior privilege of devoting himself exclusively to this study. But if he had more time, I was more indefatigable. My pride was roused, and emulation soon enabled me to supply the want of leisure. My nights were surrendered, almost wholly, to my new pursuit. I toiled with all the earnestness which distinguished my temperament, stimulated to a yet higher degree by those feelings of pride and pique, which were resolved to convince my skeptical uncle that I was not entirely without those talents, the assertion of which had so promptly provoked his sneer. Besides, I had already learned that no such scheme as mine could be successfully prosecuted, unless by a stern resolution; and this implied the constant presence of a close, undeviating method in my studies. I tasked myself accordingly to read — understandingly, if possible — so many pages every night, making my notes, queries, doubts, &c., *en passant.* In order to do this, I prescribed to myself a rule, to pass directly from the toils of the day and the store to my chamber, suffering no stoppage by the way, and studiously denying myself the dangerous fascinations of that society which was everywhere at command, in the persons of young men about my own age and condition. The intensity of my character, and the suspiciousness which it induced, helped me in this determination. Perhaps, there is no greater danger to a young man's habits of study and business, than a chat at the street corner, with a merry and thoughtless group. A single half hour consumed in this manner, is almost always fatal to the remaining hours of the day. It breaks into the circle, and impairs the method without which the passage of the sun becomes a very weary and always an unprofitable progress. If you would be a student or anything, you must plunge headlong into it at the beginning — bury yourself in your business, and work your way out of your toils, by sheer, dogged industry.

My labors were so far successful that I could prosecute my studies with independence. I had left the dwelling of my uncle the moment I took employment in the mercantile house. My salary, though small, was ample; with my habits, it was particularly so. I had few of those vices in which young men are apt to indulge, and which, when they become habits, cease unhappily to be regarded as vices. I used tobacco in no shape, and no ardent spirits. I needed no stimulants, and, by the way, true industry never does. It is only indolence that needs drink; and indolence does need it; and the sooner drunkenness kills indolence by the use of drink, the better for society. The only objection to liquors as an agent for ridding the community of a nuisance, is, that it is rather too slow, and too offensive in its detailed operations; arsenic would be far less offensive, more summary, and is far more certain. You would seek vainly to cure drunkenness, unless you first cure the idleness which is its root and strength, and, while they last, its permanent support. But my object is not homily.

If I was free from vices such as these, however, I had vices of my own, which were only less odious as they were less obvious. That vexing, self-tormenting spirit of which I have spoken as the evil genius that dogged my footsteps — that moral perverseness which I have described as the "blind heart" — still afflicted me, though in a far less degree now than when I was the inmate of my uncle's dwelling, and exposed to all the caprices of himself, his wife and servants. I kept on good terms with my employers, for the very natural reason that they saw me attend to my business and theirs, with a hearty cheerfulness that went to work promptly in whatever was to be done, and executed its tasks with steady fortitude, neatness, and rapidity. But, even with them, I had my sulks — my humors — my stubborn fits of sullenness, that seemed anxious to provoke opposition, and awaken wrath. These, however, they considerately forgave in consideration of my real usefulness: and as they perceived that whatever might have been the unpleasantness occasioned by these specimens of spleen, they were never suffered to interfere with or retard the operations of business. "It's an ugly way he's got," was, probably, the utmost extent of what either of the partners said, and of what is commonly said on such occasions by most persons, who do not care to trouble themselves with a too close inquiry.

Well, at twenty-one, William Edgerton and myself were admitted to the practice of the law, and that too with considerable credit to ourselves. I had long since been carried by my friend into his family circle; and Mr. Edgerton, his father, had been pleased to distinguish me with sundry attentions, which were only grateful to me in consequence of the unusual deference with which his manner evinced his regard. His gentle inquiries and persuasive suggestions beguiled me into more freedom of speech than I had ever before been accustomed to; and his judicious management of my troubled spirit, for a time, stifled its contradictions, and suppressed its habitual tendencies. But it was with some jealousy, and an erectness of manner which was surely ungracious, though, perhaps, not offensive, that I endured and replied to his inquiries into my personal condition, my resources, and the nature of that dependence which I bore to the family of my uncle. When he learned—which he did not from me—in what manner I had pursued my studies—after what toils of the day, and at what late hours of the night—when he found from a close private examination, which he had given me, before my admission, that my knowledge of the law was quite as good as the greater number of those who apply for admission—he was pleased to express his astonishment at my perseverance, and delight at my success. When, too, in addition to this, he discovered, upon a minute inquiry from my employers and others, that I was abstemious, and indulged in no excesses of any kind, his interest in me increased, as I thought, who had been accustomed to nothing of the sort, beyond all reasonable measure—and I soon had occasion to perceive that it was no idle curiosity that prompted his consideration and inquiry.

Without my knowledge, he paid a visit to my uncle. This gentleman, I may be permitted here to say, had been quite as much surprised as anybody else, at my determined prosecution of my studies in spite of the difficulties by which I was surrounded. That I was pursuing them, while in the mercantile establishment to which I had gone, he did not believe; and very frequently when I was at his house—for I visited the family, and sometimes, though unfrequently, dined with them on a sabbath—he jeered me on my progress—the "wonderful progress," as he was pleased to term it—which he felt sure I was making with my Coke and Blackstone, while baling blankets, or bundling up plains and kerseys. This I bore patiently, sustained as I was by the proud, indomitable spirit within me, which assured me of the ultimate triumph which I felt positive would ensue. I enjoyed his surprise—a surprise that looked something like consternation—when the very day of my admission to the bar, and after that event, I encountered him in the street, and in answer to his usual sarcastic inquiry:—

"Well, Edward, how does the law come on? How is Sir William Blackstone, Sir Edward Coke, and the rest of the white heads?"

I simply put the parchment into his hands which declared my formal introduction to those venerable gentry.

"Why, you don't mean? Is it possible? So you really are admitted—a lawyer, eh?"

"You see, sir—and that, too, without any Greek."

"Well, and what good is it to do you? To have a profession, Edward, is one thing; to get business, another!"

"Yes, sir—but I take it, the profession must be had first. One step is gained. That much is sure. The other, I trust, will follow in due season."

"True, but I still think that the bricklayer would make the more money."

"Were money-making, sir, the only object of life, perhaps, then, that would be the most desirable business; but—"

"Oh, I forgot—the talents, the talents are to be considered."

And after the utterance of this sneer, our dialogue as may be supposed, did not much longer continue.

I did not know of the contemplated visit of Mr. Edgerton to

my worthy uncle, nor of its purpose, or I should, most assuredly, have put my veto upon the measure with all the tenacity of a resentful spirit; but this gentleman, who was a man of nice sensibility as well as strong good sense, readily comprehended a portion of my secret history from what was known to him. He easily conceived that my uncle was somewhat of a niggard from the manner in which I had employed myself during my preparation for the bar. He thought, however, that my uncle, though unwilling to expend money in the prosecution of a scheme which he did not approve—now that the scheme was so far successful as to afford every promise of a reasonable harvest, could not do less than come forward to the assistance of one who had shown such a determined disposition to assist himself.

He was mistaken. He little knew the man. His interview with my uncle was a short one. The parties were already acquainted, though not intimately. They knew each other as persons of standing in the same community, and this made the opening of Mr. Edgerton's business easy. I state the tenor of the interview as it came to my knowledge afterward.

"Mr. Clifford," he said, "you have a nephew—a young gentleman, who has been recently admitted to the bar—Mr. Edward Clifford."

The reply, with a look of wonder was necessarily affirmative.

"I have had much pleasure," continued the other, "in knowing him for some time. He is an intimate of my eldest son, and from what has met my eyes, sir, I should say, you are for tunate in having a nephew of so much promise."

"Why, yes, sir, I believe he is a clever youth enough," was the costive answer.

"He is more than that, sir. I regard him, indeed, as a most astonishing young man. The very manner in which he has pursued his studies while engaged in the harassing labors of a large wholesale business house of this city—alone establishes this fact."

The cheeks of my uncle reddened. The last sentence of Mr. Edgerton was unfortunate for his object. It conveyed a tacit reproof, which the niggardly conscience of Mr. Clifford readily appropriated and, perhaps, anticipated. He dreaded lest Mr. Edgerton knew all.

"You are probably aware, Mr. Edgerton," he replied with equal hesitancy and haste—"you have heard that Edward Clifford is an orphan—that he has nothing, and it was therefore necessary that he should learn to employ himself; though it was against my wish, sir, that he went into a mercantile house."

There was something suppressed in this—a mean evasion—for he could not easily have told Mr. Edgerton, without a blush, that, instead of the mercantile establishment, he would have made me a bricklayer's hodman. But this, it seems, Edgerton had found out for himself. His reply, however, was calculated to soothe the jealous apprehensions of Mr. Clifford. He had an object in view, which he thought too important to risk for the small pleasure of a passing sarcasm.

"Perhaps, it has happened for the best, Mr. Clifford. You were right in requiring the young man to do for himself. Were I worth millions, sir, I should still prefer that my son should learn that lesson—that he should work out his own deliverance with the sweat of his own brow."

"I agree with you, sir, perfectly," replied the other, with increased complacency. "A boy learns to value his money as he should, only when he has earned it for himself."

"Ah! it is not for this object simply," replied Mr. Edgerton, "that I would have him acquire habits of industry; it is for the moral results which such habits produce—the firmness, character, consistency—the strength and independence—temperance, justice—all of which arise, and almost only, from obedience to this law. But it is clear that one can not do everything by himself, and this young man, though he has gone on in a manner that might shame the best of us, is still not so thoroughly independent as he fancies himself. It will be some time before he will be able to realize anything from his profession, and he will need some small assistance in the meantime."

"I can not help him," exclaimed Mr. Clifford, abruptly—"I have not the means to spare. My own family need everything that I can give. He has himself only to blame. He chose his profession for himself. I warned him against it. He needn't send to me."

"Do not mistake me, Mr. Clifford," said Mr. Edgerton, calmly.

"Your nephew knows nothing of my present visit. I would be loath that he should know. It was the singular independence of his mind that led me to the conviction, that he would sooner die than ask assistance from anybody, that persuaded me to suggest to you in what manner you might afford him an almost necessary help, without offending his sensibility."

"Humph!" exclaimed the other, while a sneer mantled upon his lips. "You are very considerate, Mr. Edgerton; but the same sensibilities might prompt him to reject the assistance when tendered."

"No, sir," replied Edgerton, mildly —"I think I could manage that."

"I am sorry, sir, that I can not second your wishes in any material respect," was the answer of my uncle; — "but I will see Edward, and let him know that my house is open to him as it was from the time he was four years old; and he shall have a seat at my table until he can establish himself more to his satisfaction; but money, sir, in truth, I have not a cent to spare. My own necessities——"

"Enough, sir," said Mr. Edgerton, mildly; "I take it for granted, Mr. Clifford, that if you could contribute to the success of your brother's son, you certainly would neither refuse nor refrain to do so."

"Oh, surely — certainly not," replied the other, hastily. "Anything that I could do — anything in reason, sir, I should be very happy to do, but——"

And then followed the usual rigmarole about "his own family," and "hard times," and "diminished resources," and all those stereotype commonplaces which are for ever on the lips of stereotype insincere people. Mr. Clifford did not perceive the dry and somewhat scornful inuendo, which lay at the bottom of Mr. Edgerton's seemingly innocent assumption; and the latter took his leave, vexed with himself at having made the unsuccessful application — but still more angry with the meanness of character which he had encountered in my uncle.

CHAPTER IV.

——"She still soothed
The mock of others."

It is not improbable that, after a few hours given to calm reflection, my uncle perceived how obnoxious he might be made to public censure for his narrow treatment of my claims; and the next day he sent for me in order to tender me the freedom of his house—a tender which he had made the day before to Mr. Edgerton in my behalf. But his offer had been already anticipated by that excellent friend that very day. Coming warm and fresh from his interview with my uncle, he called upon me, and in a very plain, direct, business-like, but yet kind and considerate manner, informed me that he stood very much in need of an assistant who would prepare his papers—did me the honor to say that he fancied I would suit him better than anybody else he knew, and offered me six hundred dollars for my labors in that capacity for the first year of my service. My engagement to him, he said at the same time, did not imply such entire employment as would incapacitate me for the execution of any business which might be intrusted to my hands individually. I was permitted the use of a desk in his office, and was also permitted to hang out my own banner from his window I readily persuaded myself that I could be of service to Mr. Edgerton—such service as would, perhaps, leave my obligation a light one—and promptly acceded to his offer. He had scarcely departed when a servant brought a note from Mr. Clifford. Even while meditating what he fancied was a favor, he could not forbear the usual sneer. The following was his communication:

"Dear Edward: If you can spare a moment from your numerous clients, and are not in a great hurry to make your deposites, you will suffer me to see you at the office before two o'clock.

"Yours affectionately, "J. B. Clifford."

"Very affectionately!" I exclaimed. It might be nothing more than a pleasantry which he intended by the offensive passages in his note; but the whole tenor of his character and conduct forbade this conviction.

"No! no!" I muttered to myself, as the doubt suggested itself to my mind; "no! no! it is the old insolence — the insolence of pride, of conscious wealth — of power, as he thinks, to crush! But he is mistaken. He shall find defiance. Let him but repeat those sarcasms and that sneer which are but too frequent on his lips when he speaks to me, and I will answer him, for the first time, by a narration which shall sting him to the very soul, if he has one!"

This resolution was scarcely made when the image of Julia Clifford — the sweet child — a child now no longer — the sweet woman — interposed, and my temper was subdued of its resolve, though its bitterness remained unqualified.

And what of Julia Clifford? I have said but little of her for some time past, but she has not been forgotten. Far from it. She was still sufficiently the attraction that drew me to the dwelling of my selfish uncle. In the three years that I had been at the mercantile establishment, her progress, in mind and person, had been equally ravishing and rapid. She was no more the child, but the blooming girl — the delicate blossom swelling to the bud — the bud bursting into the flower — but the bloom, and the beauty, and the innocence — the rich tenderness, and the dewy sweet, still remained the same through all the stages of her progress from the infant to the woman. Wealth, and the arrogant example of those about her, had failed to change the naturally true and pure simplicity of her character. She was not to be beguiled by the one, nor misguided by the other, from the exquisite heart which was still worthy of Eden. When I was admitted to the bar at twenty-one, she was sixteen — the age in our southern country when a maiden looks her loveliest. But I had scarcely felt the changes in the last three years which had been going on in her. I beheld beauties added to beauties, charms to charms; and she seemed every day to be the possessor of fresh graces newly dropped from heaven; but there was no change. Increased perfection does not imply change, nor does it suffer it.

It was my custom, as the condescending wish of my uncle

expressed, that I should take my Sunday dinner with his family. I complied with this request, and it was no hard matter to do so. But it was a sense of delight, not of duty, that made me comply; and, but for Julia, I feel certain that I should never have darkened the doors, which opened to admit me only through a sense of duty. But the attraction — scarcely known to myself — drew me with singular punctuality; and I associated the privilege which had been accorded me with another. I escorted the ladies to church; sometimes, too, when the business of my employers permitted, I spent an evening during the week with the family; and beholding Julia I was not over-anxious to perceive the indifference with which I was treated by all others.

But let me retrace my steps. I subdued my choler so far as to go, with a tolerable appearance of calmness if not humility, to the interview which my uncle had been pleased to solicit. I need not repeat in detail what passed between us. It amounted simply to a supercilious offer, on his part, of lodging and board, until I should be sufficiently independent to open the oyster for myself. I thanked him with respect and civility, but, to his surprise, declined to accept his offer.

"Why, what do you propose to do?" he demanded.

"Do what I have been doing for the three past years; work for myself, and pay my board from the proceeds of my own labor."

"What, you go back to the merchants, do you? You are wiser than I thought. The law would not give you your bread here for twenty years in this city."

"You are mistaken, uncle," I said, good humoredly —"it is from the law that I propose to get my bread."

"Indeed! — You are even more sanguine than I thought you. But, pray, upon what do you base your expectations? — the talents, I suppose."

I felt the rankling of this well-known and offensive sneer, but replied simply to the point:—

"No, sir, upon assurances which you will probably think far more worthy of respect. I have already been employed by Mr. Edgerton as an attorney, at a salary of six hundred dollars."

"Ah, indeed! Well, you are a fortunate fellow, I must say, to get such a helping hand at the outset. But you may want some small amount to begin with—you can not draw upon Mr. Edgerton before services are rendered, and if fifty or a hundred dollars, Edward——"

"I thank you, sir;—so far from wanting money, I should be almost able to lend some. I have saved some two hundred from my mercantile salary"

I enjoyed the ghastly grin which rose to his features. It was evident that he was not pleased that I should be independent. He had set out with the conviction, when my father died, that my support and education would devolve upon him, and though they did not, yet it was plain enough to me that he was not unwilling that such should be the impression of the community. I had disarmed him entirely by the simplest process, and, mortified at being disappointed, he was disposed to hate the youth who had baffled him. It was the strangest thing in the world that such should be the feeling of any man, and that, too, in reference to so near a relation; but the case is nevertheless true. I saw it in his looks that moment—I felt it in his accents. I *knew* that such was the real feeling in his soul. There are motives which grow from vanities, piques, rivalries, and the miserable ostentations of a small spirit, which act more terribly upon the passions of man, than even the desire of gain or the love of woman. The heart of Mr. Clifford, was, after its particular fashion, a blind heart, like my own.

"Well, I am glad you are so well off. You will dine with us on Sunday, I suppose?"

My affirmative was a matter of course; and, on Sunday, the evident gratification of Julia when she saw me, amply atoned for all her father's asperities and injustice. She had heard of my success—and though in a sneer from the lips of her father it was not the less productive of an evident delight to her. She met me with the expression of this delight upon all her features.

"I am so glad, so very glad, and so surprised, too, Cousin Edward, at your success. And yet you kept it all to yourself. You might have told *me*, at least, that you were studying law. Why was it that I was never allowed to know of your intention?"

"Your father knew it, Julia."

"Yes, so he says now. He says you told him something

about it when you first went into a store; but he did not think you in earnest."

"Not in earnest! He little knew me, Julia."

"But your telling him, Edward, was not telling me. Why did you not tell me?"

"You might not have kept my secret, Julia. You know what naughty things are said of your sex, touching your inability to keep a secret."

"Naughty things, indeed—naughty and untrue! I'm sure, I should have kept your secret, if you desired it. But why should it be a secret?"

"Why, indeed!" I muttered, as the shadow of my perverseness passed deeply over my heart. "Why, unless to protect myself from the sneers which would stifle my ambition, and the sarcasm which would have stung my heart."

"But you have no fear of these from me, Cousin Edward," she said gently, and with dewy eyes, while her fingers slightly pressed upon my wrist.

"I know not that, Cousin Julia, I somehow suspect everything and everybody now. I feel very lonely in the world—as if there was a destiny at work to make my whole life one long conflict, which I must carry on without sympathy or succor."

"Oh, these are only notions, Edward."

"Notions!" I exclaimed, giving her a bitter smile as I spoke, while my thoughts reverted to the three years of unremitting and almost uncheered labor through which I had passed.

"Yes, notions only, Cousin Edward. You are full of such notions. You every now and then start up with a new one; and it makes you gloomy and discontented—"

"I make no complaints, Julia."

"No, that is the worst of it. You make no complaints, I think, because you do not wish to be cured of them. You prefer nursing your supposed cause of grief, with a sort of solitary pleasure—the gratification of a haughty spirit, that is too proud to seek for solace, and to find it."

Julia had in truth touched upon the true nature of my misanthropy—of that self-vexing and self-torturing spirit, which too effectually blinds the heart.

"But could I find it, Julia?" I asked, looking into her eyes with an expression which I began to feel was something very new to mine.

"Perhaps—I think—you could," was the half-tremulous answer, as she beheld the peculiar expression of my glance. The entrance of Mrs. Clifford, was, perhaps, for the first time, rather a relief to us both.

"And so you are a lawyer, Edward? Well, who would have thought of it? It must be a very easy thing to be made a lawyer."

Julia looked at me with eyes that reddened with vexation. I felt my gorge rising; but when I reflected upon the ignorance, and the unworthy nature of the speaker, I overcame the disposition to retort, and smilingly replied:—

"It's not such hard work as bricklaying, certainly."

"Ah," she answered, "if it were only half so profitable. But Mr. Clifford says that a lawyer now is only another name for a beggar—a sort of genteel beggar. The town's overrun with them—half of them live upon their friends."

"I trust I shall not add to the number of this class, Mrs. Clifford."

"Oh, no! I know *you* never will, Cousin Edward," exclaimed Julia, with a flush upon her cheeks at her own temerity.

"Really, Julia," said her mother, "you are very confident. How do you know anything about it?"

The sharp glances of rebuke which accompanied this speech daunted the damsel for a moment, and her eyes were suddenly cast in confusion upon the ground; but she raised them with boldness a moment after, as she replied:—

"We have every assurance, mother, for what I say, in the fact that Cousin Edward has been supporting himself at another business, while actually pursuing the study of law for these three years; and that very pride about which father spoke today, is another assurance—"

"Bless my stars, child, you have grown very pert on a sudden, to talk about guaranties and assurances, just as if you was a lawyer yourself. The next thing we hear, I suppose, will be that instead of being busy over the 'Seven Champions' and the last fashions, you, too, will be turning over the leaves of big law-books, and carrying on such studies in secret to surprise a body, as if there was any merit or good in doing such things secretly."

Julia felt that she had only made bad worse, and she hung her head in silence. For my part, though I suppressed my choler, the pang was only the more keenly felt for the effort to hide it. In my secret soul, I asked, "Will the day never come when I, too, will be able to strike and sting?" I blushed an instant after, at the small and mean appetite for revenge that such an inquiry implied. But I came to the support of Julia.

"Let me say, Mrs. Clifford, that I think—nay, I know—that Julia is right in her conjecture. The guaranty which I have given to my friends, by the pride and industry which I have shown, should be sufficient to convince them what my conduct shall be hereafter. I know that I shall never trespass upon their feelings or their pockets. They shall neither blush for nor lose by their relationship with Edward Clifford."

"Well said! well spoken! with good emphasis and proper action. Forrest himself could scarce have done it better!"

Such was the exclamation of Mr. Clifford, who entered the room at this moment. His mock applause was accompanied by a clamorous clapping of his hands. I felt my cheeks burn, and my blood boil. The truth is, I was not free from the consciousness that I had suffered some of the grandiloquent to appear in my manner while speaking the sentence which had provoked the ridicule of my uncle. The sarcasm acquired increase of sting in consequence of its being partially well-merited. I replied with some little show of temper, which the imploring glances of Julia did not altogether persuade me to suppress. The "blind heart" was growing stronger within me, from the increasing conviction of my own independence. In this sort of mimic warfare the day passed off as usual. I attended the family to church in the afternoon, took tea, and spent the evening with them—content to suffer the "stings and arrows"—however outrageous, of my exemplary and Christian aunt and uncle, if permitted to enjoy the presence and occasional smiles of the true angel, whose influence could still temper my feelings into a humane and patient toleration of influences which they yet burned to trample under foot.

CHAPTER V.

DEBUT.

A BRIEF interval now passed over, after my connection begun with Mr. Edgerton, in which time the world went on with me more smoothly, perhaps, than ever. My patron—for so this gentleman deserves to be called—was as indulgent as I could wish. He soon discerned the weaknesses in my character, and with the judgment of an old practitioner, he knew how to subdue and soften, without seeming to perceive them. I need not say that I was as diligent and industrious, and not less studious, while in his employ, than I had been in that of my mercantile acquaintance. The entire toils of the desk soon fell upon my shoulders, and I acquired the reputation among my small circle of acquaintance, of being a very good attorney for a young beginner. It is true, I was greatly helped by the continued perusal of an admirable collection of old precedents, which a long period of extensive practice had accumulated in the collection of my friend. But to be an attorney, simply, was not the bound of my ambition. I fancied that the forum was, before all others, my true field of exertion. The ardency of my temper, the fluency of my speech, the promptness of my thought, and the warmth of my imagination, all conspired in impressing on me the belief that I was particularly fitted for the arena of public disputation. This, I may add, was the opinion of Mr. Edgerton also; and I soon sought an occasion for the display of my powers.

It was the custom at our bar—and a custom full of danger—for young beginners to take their cases from the criminal docket. Their "'prentice han'," was usually exercised on some wretch from the stews, just as the young surgeon is permitted to hack the carcass of a tenant of the "Paupers' Field," the better to prepare him for practice on living and more worthy victims. Was there a rascal so notoriously given over to the gallows that no hope could possibly be entertained of his extrication from the toils of the evidence, and the deliberations of a jury, he was considered fair game for the young lawyers, who, on such cases, gathered about him with all the ghostly and keen propensities of vultures about the body of the horse cast out upon the commons.

The custom was evil, and is now, I believe, abandoned. It led to much irreverence among thoughtless young men—to an equal disregard of that solemnity which should naturally attach to the court of justice, and to the life of the prisoner arraigned before it. A thoughtless levity too frequently filled the mind of the young lawyer and his hearers, when it was known that the poor wretch on trial was simply regarded as an agent, through whose miserable necessity, the beginner was to try his strength and show his skill in the art of speech-making. It was my fortune, acting rather in compliance with the custom than my own preference, to select one of these victims and occasions for my debut. I could have done otherwise. Mr. Edgerton freely tendered to me any one of several cases of his own, on the civil docket, in which to make my appearance; but I was unwilling to try my hand upon a case in which the penalty of ill success might be a serious loss to my friend's client, and might operate to the injury of his business; and, another reason for my preference was to be found—though not expressed by me—in the secret belief which I entertained that I was peculiarly gifted with the art of appealing to the passions, and the sensibilities of my audience.

Having made my determination, I proceeded to prepare myself by a due consideration of the case at large; the history of the transaction, which involved the life of my client—(the allegation was for murder)—and of the testimony of the witnesses so far as it had been suggested in the *exparte* examination before the grand jury. I reviewed the several leading principles on the subject of the crime; its character, the sort of evidence essential to conviction, and certainly, to do myself all justice, as effectually prepared myself for the duties of the trial as probably any young man of the time and community was likely to have done. The case, I need not add, was hopelessly against me; the testimony conclusive; and I had nothing to do but to weigh its character with keen examination, pick out and expose its defects and inconsistencies, and suggest as plausible a presumption in favor of the accused, as could be reasonably made out from the possibilities and doubts by which all human occurrences are necessarily attended. Something, too, might be done by judicious appeals to the principle of mercy, assuming for the jury a discretion on this subject which, by the way, they have no right to exercise.

I was joined in the case by my friend, young Edgerton. So far our boyish fortunes had run together, and he was not unwilling, though against his father's counsel, to take the same occasion with me for entering the world in company. The term began; the case was one of the last on the criminal docket, and the five days which preceded that assigned for the trial, were days, I am constrained to confess, of a thrilling and terrible agitation to my mind. I can scarcely now recall the feelings of that week without undergoing a partial return of the same painful sensations. My soul was striving as with itself, and seeking an outlet for escape. I panted, as if for breath — my tongue was parched — my lips clammy — my voice, in the language of the poet, clove to the roof of my throat. Altogether, I have never felt such emotions either before or since.

I will not undertake to analyze them, or account for those conflicting sensations which make us shrink, with something like terror, from the very object which we desire. At length the day came, and the man; attended by his father, William Edgerton, and myself, took our places, and stood prepared for the issue. I looked round me with a dizzy feeling of uncertainty. Objects appeared to swim and tremble before my sight. My eyes were of as little service to me then as if they had been gazing to blindness upon the sun. Everything was confused and imperfect. I could see that the courthouse was filled to overflowing, and this increased my feebleness. The case was one that had occasioned considerable excitement in the community, It was one of no ordinary atrocity. This was a sufficient reason why the audience should be large. There was yet another. There were two new debutants. In a community where popular eloquence is, of all others, perhaps the most desirable talent, this circumstance was well calculated to bring many listeners. Besides, something was expected from both Edgerton and myself. We had not reached our present position without making for ourselves a little circle, in which we had friends to approve and exult, and enemies to depreciate, and condemn.

The proceedings were at length opened by the attorney-general, the witnesses examined, and turned over to us for cross-examination. This part of the duty was performed by my associate. The business fairly begun, my distraction was lessened. My mind, driven to a point, made a decisive stand; and the sound of Edgerton's voice, as he proposed his questions, served still more to dissipate my confusion. I furnished him with sundry questions, and our examination was admitted to be quite searching and acute. My friend went through his part of the labor with singular coolness. He was in little or no respect excited. He, perhaps, was deficient in enthusiasm. If there was no faltering in what he said, there was no fine phrensy. His remarks and utterance were subdued to the plainest demands of the subject. They were shrewd and sensible, not particularly ingenious, nor yet deficient in the proper analysis of the evidence. He acquitted himself creditably.

It was my part to reply to the prosecuting attorney; but when I rose, I was completely confounded. Never shall I forget the pang of that impotence which seemed to overspread my frame, and to paralyze every faculty of thought and speech. I was the victim to my own ardor. A terrible reaction of mind had taken place, and I was prostrated. The desire to achieve greatness — the belief that it was expected from me — the consciousness that hundreds of eyes were then looking into mine with hungering expectation, overwhelmed me! I felt that I could freely have yielded myself for burial beneath the floor on which I stood. My cheeks were burning, yet my hands were cold as ice, and my knees tottered as with an ague. I strove to speak, however; the eyes of the judge met mine, and they looked the language of encouragement — of pity. But this expression only increased my confusion. I stammered out nothing but broken syllables and incoherent sentences. What I was saying, I know not—how long I presented this melancholy spectacle of imbecility to the eyes of my audience, I know not. It may have been a few minutes only. To me it seemed an age; and I was just endued with a sufficient power of reflection to ask myself whether I had not better sit down at once in irreversible despair, when my wandering and hitherto vacant eyes caught a glance—a single glance—of a face opposite.

It was that of my uncle! He was perched on one of the loftiest benches, conspicuous among the crowd—his eyes keenly fixed upon mine, and his features actually brightened by a smile of triumphant malice and exultation.

That glance restored me. That single smile brought me strength. I was timid, and weak, and impotent no longer. Under the presence of habitual scorn, my habitual pride and independence returned to me. The tremors left my limbs. The clammy huskiness which had loaded my tongue, and made it cleave to the roof of my mouth, instantly departed; and my whole mind returned to my control as if beneath the command of some almighty voice. I now saw the judge distinctly—I could see the distinct features of every juryman; and with the pride of my restored consciousness, I retorted the smile upon my uncle's face with one of contempt, which was not without its bitterness.

Then I spoke, and spoke with an intenseness, a directness of purpose and aim—a stern deliberateness—a fire and a feeling—which certainly electrified my hearers with surprise, if with no more elevated emotions. That one look of hostility had done more for my mind than could have been effected in my behalf by all the kind looks and encouraging voices of all the friends in creation.

After a brief exordium, containing some general propositions on the subject of human testimony, which meant no more than to suggest the propriety of giving to the prisoner the benefit of what was doubtful and obscure in the testimony which had been taken against him—I proceeded to compare and contrast its several parts. There were some inconsistencies in the evidence which enable me to make something of a case. The character of the witnesses was something more than doubtful, and that, too, helped, in a slight degree, my argument. This was rapid, direct, closely wound together, and proved—such was the opinion freely expressed by others, afterward—that I had the capacity for consecutive arrangement of facts and inferences in a very remarkable degree. I closed with an appeal in favor of that erring nature, which, even in our own cases, led us hourly to the commission of sins and errors; and which, where the individual was poor, wretched, and a stranger, under the evil influences of destitution, vicious associations, and a lot in life, which, of necessity, must be low, might well persuade us to look with an eye of qualified rebuke upon his offences.

This was, of course, no argument, and was only to be considered the natural close of my labors. Before I was half through I saw my uncle rise from his seat, and hastily leave the court-room; and then I knew that I was successful—that I had triumphed, through that stimulating influence of his hate, over my own fears and feebleness. I felt sure that the speech must be grateful to the rest of my hearers, which *he* could not stay to hear; and in this conviction, the tone of my spirits became elevated—the thoughts gushed from me like rain, in a natural and unrestrainable torrent of language—my voice was clear and full, far more so than I had ever thought it could be made—and my action far more animated, perhaps, than either good taste or the occasion justified. The criminal was *not* acquitted; but both William Edgerton and myself were judged to have been eminently successful.

The result of my début, in other respects, was flattering far beyond my expectations. Business poured in upon me. My old employers, the merchants, were particularly encouraging and friendly. They congratulated me warmly on my success, assured me that they had always thought I was better calculated for the law than trade; and ended by putting into my hands all their accounts that needed a legal agency for collection. Mr. Edgerton was loud in his approbation, and that very week saw his son and myself united in co-partnership, with the prospect of an early withdrawal of the father from business in our favor. Indeed, the latter gave us to understand that his only purpose now was to see us fairly under way, with a sufficient knowledge of the practice, and assured of the confidence of his own friends, in order to give his years and enfeebled health a respite from the toils of the profession.

My worthy uncle, true to himself, played a very different part from these gentlemen. He hung back, forbore all words on the subject of my début, and of the promising auspices under which my career was begun, and actually placed certain matters of legal business into the hands of another lawyer. Of this, he himself gave me the first information in very nearly this language:—

"I have just had to sue Yardle & Fellows, and a few others, Edward, and I thought of employing you, but you are young, and there may be some legal difficulties in the way:—but when you get older, and arrive at some experience, we will see what can be done for you."

"You are perfectly right, sir," was my only answer, but the smile upon my lips said everything. I saw, then, that *he could not smile.* He was now exchanging the feeling of scorn which he formerly entertained for one of a darker quality. Hate was the necessary feeling which followed the conviction of his having done me wilful injustice—not to speak of the duties left undone, which were equally his shame.

There were several things to mortify him in my progress. His sagacity as a man of the world stood rebuked—his conduct as a gentleman—his blood as a relation, who had not striven for the welfare and good report of his kin, and who had suffered unworthy prejudices, the result of equal avarice and arrogance, to operate against him.

There is nothing which a base spirit remembers with so much malignant tenacity as your success in his despite. Even in the small matter just referred to, the appropriation of his law business, the observant fates gave me my revenge. By a singular coincidence of events, the very firm against which he had brought action the day before were clients of Mr. Edgerton. That gentleman was taken with a serious illness at the approach of the next court, and the business of their defence devolved upon his son and myself; and finally, when it was disposed of, which did not happen till near the close of that year, it so happened that I argued the case; and was successful.

Mr. Clifford was baffled, and you may judge the feeling with which he now regarded me. He had long since ceased to jest with me and at my expense. He was now very respectful, and I could see that his dislike grew daily in strict degree with his deference. But the deportment of Mr. Clifford — springing as it did from that devil, which each man is supposed to carry at times in his bosom, and of whose presence in mine at seasons I was far from unaware — gave me less annoyance than that of another of his household. Julia, too, had put on an aspect which, if not that of coldness, was at least, that of a very marked reserve. I ascribed this to the influence of her parents — perhaps, to her own sense of what was due to their obvious desires — to her own feeling of indifference — to any and every cause but the right one.

There were other circumstances to alarm me, in connection with this maiden. She was, as I have said, singularly beautiful; and, as I thought, until now, singularly meek and considerate. Her charms, about which there could be no two opinions, readily secured her numerous admirers, and when these were strengthened by the supposed fortune of which she was to be the heiress, the suitors were, some of them, almost as pressing, after the fashion of the world in which we lived, as those of Penelope. I now no longer secured her exclusive regard at the evening fireside or in our way to church. There were gallants on either hand — gay, dashing lads, with big whiskers, long locks, and smart ratans, upon whom madame, our lady-mother, looked with far more complacency than upon me. The course of Julia, herself, was, however, unexceptionable. She was singularly cautious in her deportment, and, if reserved to me, the most jealous scrutiny — after due reflection — never enabled me to discover that she was more lavish of her regards to any other. But the discovery of her position led me to another discovery which the reader will wonder, as I did myself, that I had not made before. This was the momentous discovery that my heart was irretrievably lost to her — that I loved her with all the intensity of a first passion, which, like every other passion in my heart, was absorbing during its prevalence. I could name my feelings to myself only when I perceived that such feelings were entertained by others; — only when I found that the prize, which I desired beyond all others, was likely to be borne away by strangers, did I know how much it was desirable to myself.

The discovery of this affection instantly produced its natural effects as well upon my deportment as upon my feelings; and that sleepless spirit of suspicion and doubt—that true creature and consequence of the habitual distrust which my treatment from boyhood had instilled into my mind—at once rose to strength and authority within me, and swayed me even as the blasts of November sway the bald tops of the slender trees which the gusts have already denuded of all foliage. The change in Julia's deportment, of which I have already spoken, increased the febrile fears and suspicions which filled my soul and overcame my judgment. She too—so I fancied—had learned to despise and dislike me, under the goading influences of her father's malice and her mother's silly prejudices. I jumped to the conclusion instantly, that I was bound to myself to assert my superiority, my pride and independence, in such a manner, as most effectually to satisfy all parties that their hate or love was equally a matter of indifference.

You may judge what my behavior was after this. For a time, at least, it was sufficiently unbecoming. The deportment of Julia grew more reserved than ever, and her looks more grave. There was a sadness evidently mingled with this gravity which, amid all the blindness of my heart, I could not help but see. She became sadder and thinner every day; and there was a wo-begone listlessness about her looks and movements which began to give me pain and apprehension. I discovered, too, after a while, that some apprehensions had also crept into the minds of her parents in respect to her health. Their looks were frequently addressed to her in evident anxiety. They restrained her exercises, watched the weather when she proposed to go abroad, strove in every way to keep her from fatigue and exposure; and, altogether, exhibited a degree of solicitude which at length had the effect of arousing mine.

Involuntarily, I approached her with more tenderness than my vexing spirit had recently permitted me to show; but I recoiled from the effects of my own attentions. I was vexed to perceive that my approaches occasioned a start, a flutter—a shrinking inward—as if my advance had been obtrusive, and my attempts at familiarity offensive.

I was then little schooled in the intricacies of the female heart. I little conjectured the origin of that seemingly paradoxical movement of the mind, which, in the case of one, sensitive and exquisitely delicate, prompts to flight from the very pursuit which it would yet invite; which dreads to be suspected of the secret which it yet most loves to cherish, and seeks to protect, by concealment, the feelings which it may not defend; even as the bird hides the little fledglings of its care from the hunter, whom it dare not attack.

Stupid, and worse than stupid, my blind heart saw nothing of this, and perverted what it saw. I construed the conduct of Julia into matter of offence, to be taken in high dudgeon and resolutely resented; and I drew myself up stiffly when she appeared, and by excess of ceremonious politeness only, avoided the reproach of brutality. Yet, even at such moments, I could see that there was a dewy reproach in her eyes, which should have humbled me, and made me penitent. But the effects of fifteen years of injudicious management were not to be dissipated in a few days even by the Ithuriel spells of love. My sense of independence and self-resource had been stimulated to a diseased excess, until, constantly on the *qui vive*, it became dogged and inflexible. It was a work of time to soften me and make me relent; and the labor then was one of my own secret thoughts, and unbiased private decision. The attempt to persuade or reason me into a conviction was sure to be a failure.

Months passed in this manner without effecting any serious change in Julia, or in bringing us a step nearer to one another. Meanwhile, the sphere of my observation and importance increased, as the circle of my acquaintance became extended. I was regarded as a rising young man, and one likely to be successful ultimately in my profession. The social privileges of my friends, the Edgertons, necessarily became mine; and it soon occurred that I encountered my uncle and his family in circles in which it was somewhat a matter of pride with him to be permitted to move. This, as it increased my importance in his sight, did not diminish his pains. But he treated me now with constant deference, though with the same unvarying coldness. When in the presence of others, he warmed a little. I was then "his nephew;" and he would affect to speak with great familiarity on the subject of my business, my interests, the last case in which I was engaged, and so forth—the object of which was to persuade third persons that our relations were precisely as they should be, and as people would naturally suppose them.

At all these places and periods, when it was my lot to meet with Julia, she was most usually the belle of the night. A dozen attendants followed in her train, solicitous of all her smiles, and only studious how to afford her pleasure. I, only, stood aloof—I, who loved her with a more intense fervor than all, simply because I had none, or few besides to love. The heart which has been evermore denied, will always burn with this intensity. Its passion, once enkindled, will be the all-absorbing flame. Devoted itself, it exacts the most religious devotion; and, unless it receives it, recoils upon its own resources, and shrouds itself in gloom, simply to hide its sufferings from detection.

I affected that indifference to the charms of this maiden, which no one of human sensibilities could have felt. Opinions might have differed in respect to her beauty; but there could be none on the score of her virtues and her amiability, and almost as few on the possessions of her mind. Julia Clifford, though singularly unobtrusive in society, very soon convinced all around her that she had an excellent understanding, which study had improved, and grace had adorned by all the most appropriate modes of cultivation. Her steps were always followed by a crowd—her seat invariably encircled by a group to itself. I looked on at a distance, wrapped up in the impenetrable folds of a pride, whose sleeves were momently plucked, as I watched, by the nervous fingers of jealousy and suspicion. Sometimes I caught a timid glance of her eye, addressed to the spot where I stood, full of inquiry, and, as I could not but believe, of apprehension;—and yet, at such moments, I turned perversely from the spot, nor suffered myself to steal another look at one, all of whose triumphs seemed made at my expense.

On one of these occasions we met—our eyes and hands, accidentally; and, though I, myself, could not help starting back with a cold chill at my heart, I yet fancied there was something monstrous insulting in the evident recoil of her person from the contact with mine, at the same moment. I was about to turn hurriedly away with a slight bow of acknowledgment, when the touching tenderness of her glance, so full of sweetness and sadness, made me shrink with shame from such a rudeness. Besides, she was so pale, so thin, and really looked so unwell, that my conscience, in spite of that blind heart whose perversity would still have kept me to my first intention, rebuked me, and drove me to my duty. I approached—I spoke to her—and my words, though few, under the better impulses of the moment, were gentle and solicitous, as they should have been. My tones, too, were softened:—wilfully as I still felt, I could not forbear the exercise of that better ministry of the affections which was disposed to make amends for previous misconduct. I do not know exactly what I said—I probably did nothing more than utter the ordinary phrases of social compliment;—but everything was obliterated from my mind in an instant, by the startling directness of what was said by her. Looking at me with a degree of intentness by which, alone, she was, perhaps, able to preserve her seeming calmness, she replied by an inquiry as remote from what my observation called for as possible, yet how applicable to me and my conduct!

"Why do you treat me thus, Edward? Why do you neglect me as you do—as if I were a stranger, or, at least, not a friend? What have I done to merit this usage from one who——"

She did not finish the sentence, but her reproachful eyes, full of a dewy suffusion that seemed very much like tears, appeared to conclude it thus—

"One who—used to love me!"

So different was this speech from any that I looked for—so different from what the usage of our conventional world would have seemed to justify—so strange for one so timid, so silent usually on the subject of her own griefs, as Julia Clifford—that I was absolutely confounded. Where had she got this courage? By what strong feeling had it been stimulated? Had I been at that time as well acquainted with the sex as I have grown since, I must have seen that nothing but a deep interest in my conduct and regard, could possibly have prompted the spirit of one so gentle and shrinking, to the utterance of so searching an appeal. And in what way could I answer it? How could I excuse myself? What say, to justify that cold, rude indifference to a relative, and one who had ever been gentle and kind and true to me. I had really nothing to complain of. The vexing jealousies of my own suspicious heart had alone informed it to its perversion; and there I stood — dumb, confused, stupid — speaking, when I did speak, some incoherent, meaningless sentences, which could no more have been understood by her than they can now be remembered by me. I recovered myself, however, sufficiently soon to say, before we were separated by the movements of the crowd :—

"I will come to you to-morrow, Julia. Will you suffer me to see you in the morning, say at twelve?"

"Yes, come!" was all her answer; and the next moment the harsh accents of her ever-watchful mother warned us to risk no more.

CHAPTER VI.

DENIAL AND DEFEAT.

MY sleep that night was anything but satisfactory. I had feverish dreams, unquiet slumbers, and woke at morning with an excruciating headache. I was in no mood for an explanation such as my promise necessarily implied, but I prepared my toilet with particular care—spent two hours at my office in a vain endeavor to divert myself, by a resort to business, from the conflicting and annoying sensations which afflicted me, and then proceeded to the dwelling of my uncle.

I was fortunate in seeing Julia without the presence of her mother. That good lady had become too fashionable to suffer herself to be seen at so early an hour. Her vanity, in this respect, baffled her vigilance, for she had her own apprehensions on the score of my influence upon her daughter. Julia was scarcely so composed in the morning as she had appeared on the preceding night. I was now fully conscious of a flutter in her manner, a flush upon her face, an ill-suppressed apprehension in her eyes, which betokened strong emotions actively at work. But my own agitation did not suffer me to know the full extent of hers. For the first time, on her appearance, did I ask myself the question—"For what did I seek this interview?" What had I to say—what hear? How explain my conduct—my coldness? On what imaginary and unsubstantial premises base the neglect in my deportment, amounting to rudeness, of which she had sufficient reason and a just right to complain? When I came to review my causes of vexation, how trivial did they seem. The reserve which had irritated me, on her part, now that I analyzed its sources, seemed a very natural reserve, such as was only maidenly and becoming. I now recollected that she was no longer a child—no longer the lively little fairy whom I could dandle on my knee and fling upon my shoulder, without a scruple or complaint. I stood like a trembling culprit in her presence. I was eloquent only through the force of a stricken conscience.

"Julia!" I exclaimed when we met, "I have come to make atonement. I feel how rude I have been, but that was only because I was very wretched."

"Wretched, Edward!" she exclaimed with some surprise. "What should make you wretched?"

"You—you have made me wretched."

"Me!" Her surprise naturally increased.

"Yes, you, dear Julia, and you only."

I took her hand in mine. Mine was burning—hers was colder than the icicles. Need I say more to those who comprehend the mysteries of the youthful heart. Need I say that the tongue once loosed, and the declaration of the soul must follow in a rush from the lips. I told her how much I loved her;—how unhappy it made me to think that others might bear away the prize; that, in this way, my rudeness arose from my wretchedness, and my wretchedness only from my love. I did not speak in vain. She confessed an equal feeling, and we were suffered a brief hour of unmitigated happiness together.

Surely there is no joy like that which the heart feels in the first moment when it gives utterance to its own, and hears the avowed passion of the desired object:—a pure flame, the child of sentiment, just blushing with the hues of passion, just budding with the breath and bloom of life. No sin has touched the sentiment;—no gross smokes have risen to involve and obscure the flame; the altar is tended by pure hands; white spirits; and there is no reptile beneath the fresh blossoming flowers which are laid thereon. The grosser passions sleep, like the fumes at the shrine of Apollo, beneath the spell of that master passion in whose presence they can only maintain a subordinate existence. I loved; I had told my love;—and I was loved in return. I trembled with the deep intoxication of that bewildering moment; and how I found my way back to my office—whom I saw on the way, or to whom I spoke, I know not. I loved;—I was beloved. He only can conceive the delirium of this sweet knowledge who has passed a life like mine — who has felt the frowns and the scorn, and the contempt of those who should have nurtured him with smiles — whose soul, ardent and sensitive, has been made to recoil cheerlessly back on itself — denied the sunshine of the affections, and almost forbade to hope. Suddenly, when I believed myself most destitute, I had awakened to fortune — to the realization of desires which were beyond my fondest dreams. I, whom no affection hitherto had blessed, had, in a moment, acquired that which seemed to me to comprise all others, and for which all others might have been profitably thrown away.

I fancied now that henceforth my sky was to be without a cloud. I did not — nor did Julia imagine for a moment that any opposition to our love could arise from her parents. What reason now could they have to oppose it? There was no inequality in our social positions. My blood had taken its rise from the same fountains with her own. In the world's estimation my rank was quite as respectable as that of any in my uncle's circle, and, for my condition, my resources, though small, were improving daily, and I had already attained such a place among my professional brethren, as to leave it no longer doubtful that it must continue to improve. My income, with economy — such economy as two simple, single-minded creatures, like Julia and myself, were willing to employ — would already yield us a decent support. In short, the idea of my uncle's opposition to the match never once entered my head. Yet he did oppose it. I was confounded with his blunt, and almost rugged refusal.

"Why, sir, what are your objections?"

He answered with sufficient coolness.

"I am sorry to refuse you, Edward, but I have already formed other arrangements for my daughter. I have designed her for another."

"Indeed, sir — may I ask with whom?"

"Young Roberts — his father and myself have had the matter for some time in deliberation. But do not speak of it, Edward — my confidence in you, alone, induces me to state this fact."

"I am very much obliged to you, sir; — but you do not surely mean to force young Roberts upon Julia, if she is unwilling?"

"Ah, she will not be unwilling. She's a dutiful child, who

will readily recognise the desires of her parents as the truest wisdom."

"But, Mr. Clifford—you forget that Julia has already admitted to me a preference——"

"So you tell me, Edward, and it is with regret that I feel myself compelled to say that I wholly disapprove of your seeking my daughter's consent, before you first thought proper to obtain mine. This seems to me very much like an abuse of confidence."

"Really, sir, you surprise me more than ever. Now that you force me to speak, let me say that, regarding myself as of blood scarcely inferior to that of my cousin, I can not see how the privilege of which I availed myself in proposing for her hand, can be construed into a breach of confidence. I trust, sir, that you have not contemplated your brother's son in any degrading or unbecoming attitude."

"No, no, surely not, Edward; but mere equality of birth does not constitute a just claim, by itself, to the affections of a lady."

"I trust the equality of birth, sir, is not impaired on my part by misconduct—by a want of industry, capacity—by inequalities in other respects—"

"And talents!"

He finished the sentence with the ancient sneer. But I was now a man—a strong one, and, at this moment particularly a stern one.

"Stop, sir," I retorted; "there must be an end to this. Whether you accede to my application or not, sir, there is nothing to justify you in an attempt to goad and mortify my feelings. I have proffered to you a respectful application for the hand of of your daughter, and though I were poorer, and humbler, and less worthy in all respects than I am, I should still be entitled to respectful treatment. At another time, with my sensibilities less deeply interested than they are, I should probably submit, as I have already frequently submitted, to the unkind and ungenerous sarcasms in which you have permitted yourself to indulge at my expense. But my regard for your daughter alone would prompt me to resent and repel them now. The object of my interview with you is quite too sacred—too solemnly invested

—to suffer me to stand silently under the scornful usage even of her father."

All this may have been deserved by Mr. Clifford, but it was scarcely discreet in me. It gave him the opportunity which, I do not doubt, he desired—the occasion which he had in view. It afforded him an excuse for anger, for a regular outbreak between us, which, in some sort, yielded him that justification for his refusal, without which he would have found it a very difficult matter to account for or excuse. We parted in mutual anger, the effect of which was to close his doors against me, and exclude me from all opportunities of interview with Julia, unless by stealth. Even then, these opportunities were secured by my artifice, without her privity. As dutiful as fond, she urged me against them; and, resolute to "honor her father and mother" in obedience to those holy laws without a compliance with which there is little hope and no happiness, she informed me with many tears that she was now forbidden to see me, and would therefore avoid every premeditated arrangement for our meeting. I did not do justice to her character, but reproached her with coldness—with a want of affection, sensibility, and feeling.

"Do not say so, Edward—do not—do not! I cold—I insensible—I wanting in affection for you! How, how can you think so?" And she threw herself on my bosom and sobbed until I began to fancy that convulsions would follow.

We separated, finally, with assurances of mutual fidelity—assurances which, I knew, from the exclusiveness of all my feelings, my concentrative singleness of character, and entire dependence upon the beloved object of those affections which were now the sole solace of my heart, would not be difficult for me to keep. But I doubted *her* strength—*her* resolution—against the pressing solicitations of parents whom she had never been accustomed to withstand. But she quieted me with that singular earnestness of look and manner which had once before impressed me previous to our mutual explanation. Like vulgar thinkers generally, I was apt to confound weakness of frame and delicacy of organization with a want of courage and moral resources of strength and consolation.

"Fear nothing for my truth, Edward. Though, in obedience

to my parents, I shall not marry against their will, be sure I shall never marry against my own."

"Ah, Julia, you think so, but—"

"I know so, Edward. Believe nothing that you hear against me or of me, which is unfavorable to my fidelity, until you hear it from my own lips."

"But you will meet me again—soon?"

"No, no, do not ask it, Edward. We must not meet in this manner. It is not right. It is criminal."

I had soon another proof of the decisive manner in which my uncle seemed disposed to carry on the war between us. Erring, like the greater number of our young men, in their ambitious desire to enter public life prematurely, I was easily persuaded to become a candidate for the general assembly. I was now just twenty-five—at a time when young men are not yet released from the bias of early associations, and the unavoidable influence of guides, who are generally blind guides. Until thirty, there are few men who think independently; and, until this habit is acquired—which, in too many cases, never is acquired—the individual is sadly out of place in the halls of legislation. It is this premature disposition to enter into public life, which is the sole origin of the numberless mistakes and miserable inconsistencies into which our statesmen fall; which cling to their progress for ever after, preventing their performances, and baffling them in all their hopes to secure the confidence of the people. They are broken-down political hacks in the prime of life, and just at the time when they should be first entering upon the duties of the public man. Seduced, like the rest, as well by my own vanity as the suggestions of favoring friends, I permitted my name to be announced, and engaged actively in the canvass. Perhaps the feverish state of my mind, in consequence of my relations with Julia Clifford and her parents, made me more willing to adopt a measure, about which, at any other time, I should have been singularly slow and cautious. As a man of proud, reserved, and suspicious temper, I had little or no confidence in my own strength with the people; and defeat would be more mortifying than success grateful to a person of my pride. I fancied, however, that popular life would somewhat subdue the consuming passions which were rioting within my bosom; and I threw myself into the thick of the struggle with all the ardor of a sanguine temperament.

To my surprise and increased vexation, I found my worthy uncle striving in every possible way, without actually declaring his purpose, in opposing my efforts and prospects. It is true he did not utter my name; but he had formed a complete ticket, in which my name was not; and he was toiling with all the industry of a thoroughgoing partisan in promoting its success. The cup which he had commended to my lips was overrunning with the gall of bitterness. *Hostility* to me seemed really to have been a sort of monomania with him from the first. How else was this wanton procedure to be accounted for? how, even with this belief, could it be excused? His conduct was certainly one of those mysteries of idiosyncracy upon which the moral philosopher may speculate to doomsday without being a jot the wiser.

If his desire was to baffle me, he was successful. I was defeated, after a close struggle, by a meagre majority of seven votes in some seventeen hundred; and the night after the election was declared, he gave a ball in honor of the successful candidates, in which his house was filled to overflowing. I passed the dwelling about midnight. Music rang from the illuminated parlor. The merry dance proceeded. All was life, gayety, and rich profusion. And Julia! even then she might have been whirling in the capricious movements of the dance with my happy rival—she as happy—unconscious of him who glided like some angry spectre beneath her windows, and almost within hearing of her thoughtless voice.

Such were my gloomy thoughts—such the dark and dismal subjects of my lonely meditations. I did the poor girl wrong. That night she neither sung nor danced; and when I saw her again, I was shocked at the visible alteration for the worse which her appearance exhibited. She was now grown thin, almost to meagreness; her cheeks were very wan, her lips whitened, and her beauty greatly faded in consequence of her suffering health.

Yet, will it be believed that, in that interview, though such was her obvious condition, my perverse spirit found the language of complaint and suspicion more easy than that of devotion and tenderness. I know that it would be easy, and feel that it would be natural, to account for and to excuse this brutality, by a reference to those provocations which I had received from her father. A warm temper, ardent and glowing, it is very safe to imagine, must reasonably become soured and perverse by bad treatment and continual injury. But this for me was no excuse. Julia was a victim also of the same treatment, and in far greater degree than myself, as she was far less able to endure it. Mine, however, was the perverseness of impetuous blood — unrestrained, unchecked — having a fearful will, an impetuous energy, and, gradually, with success and power, swelling to the assertion of its own unqualified dominion — the despotism of the blind heart.

Julia bore my reproaches until I was ashamed of them. Her submission stung me, and I loved then too ardently not to arrive in time at justice, and to make atonement. Would I had made it sooner! When I had finished all my reproaches and complainings, she answered all by telling me that the affair with young Roberts had been just closed, and she hoped finally, by her unqualified rejection of his suit, even though backed by all her father's solicitations, complaints, nay, threats and anger. How ungenerous and unmanly, after this statement had been made, appeared all the bitter chidings in which I had indulged! I need not say what efforts I made to atone for my precipitation and injustice; and how easily I found forgiveness from one who knew not how to harbor unkindness — and if she even had the feeling in her bosom, entertained it as one entertains his deadliest foe, and expelled it as soon as its real character was discovered.

CHAPTER VII.

TEMPTATION.

THUS stood the affair between my fair cousin and myself—a condition of things seriously and equally affecting her health and my temper—when an explosion took place, of a nature calculated to humble my uncle and myself, if not in equal degree, or to the same attitude, at least to a most mortifying extent in both cases. I have not stated before—indeed, it was not until the affair which I am now about to relate had actually exploded, that I was made acquainted with any of the facts which produced it—that, prior to my father's death, there had been some large business connections between himself and my uncle. In those days secret connections in business, however dangerous they might be in social, and more than equivocal in moral respects, were considered among the legitimate practices of tradesmen. What was the particular sort of relations existing between my father and uncle, I am not now prepared to state, nor is it absolutely necessary to my narrative. It is enough for me to say that an exposure of them took place, in part, in consequence of some discoveries made by my father's unsatisfied creditors, by which the obscure transactions of thirty years were brought to light, or required to be brought to light; and in the development of which, the fair business fame of my uncle was likely to be involved in a very serious degree—not to speak of the inevitable effects upon his resources of a discovery and proof of fraudulent concealment. The reputation of my father must have suffered seriously, had it not been generally known that he left nothing—a fact beyond dispute from the history of my own career, in which neither goods nor chattels, lands nor money, were suffered to enure to my advantage.

The business was brought to me. The merchant who brought it, and who had been busy for some years in tracing out the testimony, so far as it could be procured, gave me to understand that he had determined to place it in my hands for two reasons: firstly, to enable me to release the memory of my father from the imputation — under any circumstances discreditable — of bankruptcy, by compelling my uncle to disgorge the sums which he had appropriated, and which, as was alleged, would satisfy all my father's creditors; and, secondly, to give me an opportunity of revenging my own wrongs upon one, of whose course of conduct toward me the populace had already seen enough, during the last election, to have a tolerably correct idea.

I examined the papers, thanked my client for his friendly intentions, but declined taking charge of the case for two other reasons. My relations to the dead and to the living were either of them sufficient reasons for this determination. I communicated the grounds of action, in a respectful letter, to my uncle, and soon discovered, by the alarm which he displayed in consequence, that the cause of the complaint was in all probability good. The case belonged to the equity jurisdiction, and the relator soon filed his bill.

My uncle's tribulation may be conjectured from the fact that he called upon me, and seemed anxious enough to bury the hatchet. He wished me to take part in the proceedings — insisted, somewhat earnestly, and strove very hard to impress me with the conviction that my father's memory demanded that I should devote myself to the task of meeting and confounding the creditor who thus, as it were, had set to work to rake up the ashes of the dead; but I answered all this very briefly and very dryly:—

"If my father has participated in this fraud, he has reaped none of its pleasant fruits. He lived poor, and died poor. The public know that; and it will be difficult to persuade them, with a due knowledge of these facts, that he deliberately perpetrated such unprofitable villany. Besides, sir, you do not seem to remember that, if the claim of Banks, Tressell, & Sons, is good, it relieves my father's memory of the only imputation that now lies against it — that of being a bankrupt."

"Ay!" he cried hoarsely, "but it makes me one—me, your uncle."

"And what reason, sir, have I to remember or to heed this relationship?" I demanded sternly, with a glance beneath which he quailed.

"True, true, Edward, your reproach is a just one. I have not been the friend I should have been; but—let us be friends, now, and hereafter—we must be friends. Mrs. Clifford is very anxious that it should be so—and—and—Edward," solemnly, "you must help me out of this business. You must, by Heaven, you must—if you would not have me blow my brains out!"

The man was giving true utterance to his misery—the fruit of those pregnant fears which filled his mind.

"I would do for you, sir, whatever is proper for me to do, but can not meddle in this unless you are prepared to make restitution, which I should judge to be your best course."

"How can you advise me to beggar my child? This claim, if recognised, will sweep everything. The interest alone is a fortune. I can not think of allowing it. I would rather die!"

"This is mere madness, Mr. Clifford; your death would not lessen the difficulty. Hear me, sir, and face the matter manfully. You must do justice. If what I understand be true, you have most unfortunately suffered yourself to be blinded to the dishonor of the act which you have committed; you have appropriated wealth which did not belong to you, and, in thus doing, you have subjected the memory of my father to the reproach of injustice which he did not deserve. I will not add the reproach which I might with justice add, that, in thus wronging the father's memory, and making it cover your own improper gains, you have suffered his son to want those necessaries of education and sustenance, which—"

"Say no more, Edward, and it shall all be amended. Listen to me now; but stay—close that door for a moment—there! —Now, look you."

And, having taken these precautionary steps, the infatuated man proceeded to admit the dishonest practices of which he had been guilty. His object in making the confession, however, was not that he might make reparation. Far from it. It was rather to save from the clutch of his creditors, from the grasp of justice, his ill-gotten possessions. I have no patience in revealing the schemes by which this was to be effected; but, as a preliminary, I was to be made the proprietor of one half of the sum in question, and the possessor of his daughter's hand; in return for which I was simply to share with him in the performance of certain secret acts, which, without rendering his virtue any more conspicuous, would have most effectually eradicated all of mine.

"I have listened to you, Mr. Clifford, and with great difficulty. I now distinctly decline your proposals. Not even the bribe, so precious in my sight, as that which you have tendered in the person of your daughter, has power to tempt me into hesitation. I will have nothing to do with you in this matter. Restore the property to your creditors."

"But, Edward, you have not heard;—your share alone will be twenty odd thousand dollars, without naming the interest!"

"Mr. Clifford, I am sorry for you. Doubly sorry that you persist in seeing this thing in an improper light. Even were I disposed to second your designs, it is scarcely possible, sir, that you could be extricated. The discovery of those papers, and the extreme probability that Hansford, the partner of the English firm of Davis, Pierce, & Hansford, is surviving, and can be found, makes the probabilities strongly against you. My advice to you, is, that you make a merit of necessity;—that you endeavor to effect a compromise before the affair has gone too far. The creditors will make some concessions sooner than trust the uncertainties of a legal investigation, and whether you lose or gain, a legal investigation is what you should particularly desire to avoid. If you will adopt this counsel, I will act for you with Banks & Tressel: and if you will give me *carte blanche*, I think I can persuade them to a private arrangement by which they will receive the principal in liquidation of all demands. This may be considered a very fair basis for an arrangement, since the results of the speculation could only accrue from the business capacities of the speculator, and did not belong to a fund which the proprietor had resolved not to appropriate, and which must therefore, have been entirely unproductive. I do not promise you that they will accept, but it is not improbable. They are men of business—they need, at this moment, particularly, an active capital; and have had too much knowledge of the doubts and delays attending a prolonged suit in equity, not to listen to a proposition which yields them the entire principal of their claim."

I need not repeat the arguments and entreaties by which I succeeded in persuading my uncle to accede to the only arrangement which could possibly have rescued him from the public exposure which was impending; but he did consent, and, armed with his credentials, I proceeded to the office of Banks & Tressell, without loss of time.

Though resolved, if I could effect the matter, that my uncle should liquidate their claim to the uttermost farthing which they required, it was my duty to make the best bargain which I could, in reference to his unfortunate family. Accordingly, without suffering them to know that I had *carte blanche*, I simply communicated to them my wish to have the matter arranged without public investigation—that I was persuaded from a hasty review which I had given to the case, that there were good grounds for action;—but, at the same time, I dwelt upon the casualties of such a course—the possibility that the chief living witness—if he were living—might not be found, or might not survive long enough—as he was reputed to be very old—for the purposes of examination before the commission; —the long delays which belonged to a litigated suit, in which the details of a mixed foreign and domestic business of so many years was to be raked up, reviewed and explained; and the further chances, in the event of final success, of the property of the debtor being so covered, concealed, or made away with, as to baffle at last all the industry and labors of the creditor.

The merchants were men of good sense, and estimated the proverb—"a bird in hand is worth two in the bush"—at its true value. It did not require much argument to persuade them to receive a sum of over forty thousand dollars, and give a full discharge to the defendant; and I flattered myself that the matter was all satisfactorily arranged, and had just taken a seat at my table to write to Mr. Clifford to this effect, when, to my horror, I receive a note from that gentleman, informing me of his resolve to join issue with the claimants, and "maintain his *rights* (?) to the last moment." He thanked me, in very cold, consequential style, for my "*friendly* efforts"—the words italicised, as I have now written it;—but concluded with informing me that he had taken the opinion of older counsel, which, though it might be less correct than mine, was, perhaps, more full of promise for his interests.

This note justified me in calling upon the unfortunate gentleman. It is true I had not committed him to Banks & Tressell—the suggestions which I had made for the arrangement were all proposed as a something which I might be able to bring about in a future conference with him—but I was too anxious to save him from his lamentable folly—from that miserable love of money, which, overreaching itself in its blindness, as does every passion—was not only about to deliver him to shame but to destitution also.

I found him in Mrs. Clifford's presence. That simple and silly woman had evidently been made privy to the whole transaction, so far as my arguments had been connected with it;—for *all* the truth is not often to be got out of the man who means or has perpetrated a dishonesty. She had been alarmed at the immense loss of money, and consequently of importance, with which the family was threatened; and without looking into, or being able to comprehend the facts as they stood, she had taken ground against any measure which should involve such a sacrifice. Her influence over the weak man beside her, was never so clear to me as now; and in learning to despise his character more than ever, I discovered, at the same time, the true source of many of his errors and much of his misconduct. She did not often suffer him to reply for himself—yielded me the ultimatum from her own lips; and condescended to assure me that she could only ascribe the advice which I had given to her husband, to the hostile disposition which I had always entertained for herself and family. That I was "a wolf in sheep's clothing, *she* had long since been able to see, though all others unhappily seemed blind."

Here she scowled at her husband, who contented himself with walking to and fro, playing with his coatskirts, and feeling, no doubt, a portion of the shame which his miserable bondage to this silly woman necessarily incurred.

"Mr. Clifford has got a lawyer who can do for him what it

seems you can not," was her additional observation. "He promises to get him to dry land, and save him without so much as wetting his shoes, though his own blood relations, who are thought so smart, can not, it appears, do anything."

Of course I could have nothing to say to the worthy lady, but my expostulations were freely urged to Mr. Clifford.

"You, at least," said I, "should know the risks which you incur by this obstinacy. Mrs. Clifford can not be expected to know; and I now warn you, sir, that the case of Banks & Tressell is a very strong one, very well arranged, and so admirably hung together, in its several links of testimony, that, even the absence of old Hansford (the chief witness), should his answers never be obtained, would scarcely impair the integrity of the evidence. In a purely moral point of view, nothing can be more complete than it is now."

"Well, and who would it convict, Mr. Edward Clifford?" exclaimed the inveterate lady, anticipating her husband's answer with accustomed interference; "who would it convict, if not your own father? It was as much his business as my husband's; and if there's any shame, I'm sure his memory and his son will have to bear their share of it; and this makes it so much more wonderful to me that you should take sides against Mr. Clifford, instead of standing up in his defence."

"I would save him, madam, if you and he would let me," I exclaimed with some indignation. "Your reference to my father's share in this transaction does not affect me, as it is very evident that you are not altogether acquainted with the true part which he had in it. He had all the risk, all the loss, all the blame—and your husband all the profit, all the importance. He lived poor, and died so; without a knowledge of those profitable results to his brother of which the latter has made his own avails by leaving my father's memory to aspersion which he did not deserve, and his son to destitution and reproach which he merited as little. My father's memory is liable to no reproach when every creditor knows that he died in a state of poverty, in which his only son has ever lived. Neither he nor I ever shared any of the pleasant fruits, for which we are yet to be made accountable."

"And whose fault was it that you didn't get your share.

I'm sure Mr. Clifford made you as handsome an offer yesterday as any man could desire. Didn't he offer you half? But I suppose nothing short of the whole would satisfy so ambitious a person."

"Neither the half nor the whole will serve me, madam, in such a business. My respect for your husband and his family would, of itself, have been sufficient to prevent my acceptance of his offer."

"But there was Julia, too, Edward!" said Mr. Clifford, approaching me with a most insinuating smile.

"It is not yet too late," said Mrs. Clifford, unbending a little. "Take the offer of Mr. Clifford, Edward, and be one of us; and then this ugly business——"

"Yes, my dear Edward, even now, though I have spoken with young Perkins about the affair, and he tells me there's nothing so much to be afraid of, yet, for the look of the thing, I'd rather that you should be seen acting in the business. As it's so well known that your father had nothing, and you nothing, it'll then be easy for the people to believe that nothing was the gain of any of us; and—and——"

"Young Perkins may think and say what he pleases, and you are yourself capable of judging how much respect you may pay to his opinion. Mine, however, remains unchanged. You will have to pay this money—nay, this necessity will not come alone. The development of all the particulars connected with the transaction will disgrace you for ever, and drive you from the community. Even were I to take part with you, I do not see that it would change the aspect of affairs. So far from your sharing with me the reputation of being profitless in the affair, the public would more naturally suspect that I had shared with you—now, if not before—and the whole amount involved would not seduce me to incur this imputation."

"But my daughter—Julia——"

"Do not speak of her in this connection, I implore you, Mr. Clifford. Let her name remain pure, uncontaminated by any considerations, whether of mere gain or of the fraud which the gain is supposed to involve. Freely would I give the sum in question, were it mine, and all the wealth besides that I ever expect to acquire, to make Julia Clifford my wife;—but I can not suffer myself, in such a case as this, to accept her as a bribe, and to sanction crime. Nay, I am sure that she too would be the first to object."

"And so you really refuse? Well, the world's coming to a pretty pass. But I told Mr. Clifford, months ago, that you had quite forgot yourself, ever since you had grown so great with the Edgertons, and the Blakes, and Fortescues, and all them high-headed people. But I'm sure, Mr. Edward Clifford, my daughter needn't go a-begging to any man; and as for this business, whatever you may say against young Perkins, I'll take his opinion of the law against that of any other young lawyer in the country. He's as good as the best, I'm thinking."

"Your opinion is your own, Mrs. Clifford, but I beg to set you right on the subject of mine. I did not say anything against Mr. Perkins."

"Oh, I beg your pardon; I'm sure you did. You said he was nothing of a lawyer, and something more."

Was there ever a more perverse and evil and silly woman! I contented myself with assuring her that she was mistaken and had very much misunderstood me—took pains to repeat what I had really said, and then cut short an interview that had been painful and humbling to me on many grounds. I left the happy pair *tête-à-tête*, in their princely parlor together, little fancying that there was another argument which had been prepared to overthrow my feeble virtue. But all this had been arranged by the small cunning of this really witless couple. I was left to find my way down stairs as I might; and just when I was about to leave the dwelling—vexed to the heart at the desperate stolidity of the miserable man, whom avarice and weakness were about to expose to a loss which might be averted in part, and an exposure to infamy which might wholly be avoided—I was encountered by the attenuated form and wan countenance of his suffering but still lovely daughter.

CHAPTER VIII.

LOVE FINDS NO SMOOTH WATER IN THE SEA OF LAW.

"JULIA!" I exclaimed, with a start which betrayed, I am sure, quite as much surprise as pleasure. My mood was singularly inflexible. My character was not easily shaken, and, once wrought upon by any leading influence, my mind preserved the tone which it acquired beneath it, long after the cause of provocation had been withdrawn. This earnestness of character—amounting to intensity—gave me an habitual sternness of look and expression, and I found it hard to acquire, of a sudden, that command of muscle which would permit me to mould the stubborn lineaments, at pleasure, to suit the moment. Not even where my heart was most deeply interested—thus aroused—could I look the feelings of the lover, which, nevertheless, were most truly the predominant ones within my bosom.

"Julia," I exclaimed, "I did not think to see you."

"Ah, Edward, did you wish it?" she replied in very mournful accents, gently reproachful, as she suffered me to take her hand in mine, and lead her back to the parlor in the basement story. I seated her upon the sofa, and took a place at her side.

"Why should I not wish to see you, Julia? What should lead you to fancy now that I could wish otherwise?"

"Alas!" she replied, "I know not what to think—I scarcely know what I say. I am very miserable. What is this they tell me? Can it be true, Edward, that you are acting against my father—that you are trying to bring him to shame and poverty?"

I released her hand. I fixed my eyes keenly upon hers.

"Julia, you have your instructions what to say. You are sent here for this. They have set you in waiting to meet me here, and speak things which you do not understand, and assert things which I know you can not believe."

"Edward, I believe *you!*" she exclaimed with emphasis, but with downcast eyes; "but it does not matter whether I was sent here, or sought you of my own free will. They tell me other things—there is more—but I have not the heart to say it, and it needs not much."

"If you believe me, Julia, it certainly does not need that you should repeat to me what is said of me by enemies, equally unjust to me, and hostile to themselves. Yet I can readily conjecture some things which they have told you. Did they not tell you that your hand had been proffered me, and that I had refused it?"

She hung her head in silence.

"You do not answer."

"Spare me; ask me not."

"Nay, tell me, Julia, that I may see how far you hold me worthy of your love, your confidence. Speak to me—have they not told you some such story?"

"Something of this; but I did not heed it, Edward."

"Julia—nay!—did you not?"

"And if I did, Edward—"

"It surely was not to believe it?"

"No! no! no! I had no fears of you—have none, dear Edward! I knew that it was not, could not be true."

"Julia, it was true!"

"Ah!"

"True, indeed! There was more truth in *that* than in any other part of the story. Nay, more—had they told you all the truth, dearest Julia, that part, strange as it may appear, would have given you less pain than pleasure."

"How! Can it be so?"

"Your hand was proffered me by your father, and I refused it. Nay, look not from me, dearest—fear not for my affection—fear nothing. I should have no fear that you could suppose me false to you, though the whole world should come and tell you so. True love is always secured by a just confidence in the beloved object; and, without this confidence, the whole life is a series of long doubts, struggles, griefs, and apprehensions, which break down the strength, and lay the spirit in the dust. I will now tell you, in few words, what is the relation in which I stand to your father and his family. He, many years ago, committed an error in business, which the laws distinguish by a harsher name. By this error he became rich. Until recently, the proofs of this error were unknown. They have lately been discovered by certain claimants, who are demanding reparation. In the difficulty of your father, he came to me. I examined the business, and have given it as my opinion that he should stifle the legal process by endeavoring to make a private arrangement with the creditors."

"Could he do this?"

"He could. The creditors were willing, and at first he consented that I should arrange it with them. He now rejects the arrangement."

"But why?"

"Because it involves the surrender of the entire amount of property which they claim—a sum of forty thousand dollars."

"But, dear Edward, is it due?—does my father owe this money? If he does, surely he can not refuse. Perhaps he thinks that he owes nothing."

"Nay, Julia, unhappily he knows it, and the offer of your hand, and half of the sum mentioned, was made to me, on the express condition that I should exert my influence as a man, and my ingenuity as a lawyer, in baffling the creditors and stifling the claim."

The poor girl was silent and hung her head, her eyes fixed upon the carpet, and the big tears slowly gathering, dropping from them, one by one. Meanwhile, I explained, as tenderly as I could, the evil consequences which threatened Mr. Clifford in consequence of his contumacy.

"Alas!" she exclaimed, "it is not his fault. He would be willing—I heard him say as much last night—but mother—she will not consent. She refused positively the moment father said it would be necessary to sell out, and move to a cheaper house. Oh, Edward, is there no way that you can save us? Save my father from shame, though he gives up all the money."

"Would I not do this, Julia? Nay, were I owner of the necessary amount myself, believe me, it should not be withheld."

"I do believe you, Edward; but"—and here her voice sunk to a whisper—"you must try again, try again and again—for I think that father knows the danger, though mother does not; and I think—I hope—he will be firm enough, when you press him, and warn him of the danger, to do as you wish him."

"I am afraid not, Julia. Your mother—"

"Do not fear; hope—hope all, dear Edward; for, to confess to you, I *know* that they are anxious to have your support—they said as much. Nay, why should I hide anything from you? They sent me here to see—to speak with you, and—"

"To see what your charms could do to persuade me to be a villain. Julia! Julia! did you think to do this—to have me be the thing which they would make me?"

"No! no!—Heaven forbid, dear Edward, that you should fancy that any such desire had a place, even for a moment, in my mind. No! I knew not that the case involved any but mere money considerations. I knew not that—"

"Enough! Say no more, Julia! I do not think that you would counsel me to my own shame."

"No! no! You do me only justice. But, Edward, you will save my father! You will try—you will see him again—"

"What! to suffer again the open scorn, the declared doubts of my friendship and integrity, which is the constant language of your mother? Can it be that you would desire that I should do this—nay, seek it?"

"For my poor father's sake!" she cried, gaspingly.

But I shook my head sternly.

"For mine, then—for mine! for mine!"

She threw herself into my arms, and clung to me until I promised all that she required. And as I promised her, so I strove with her father. I used every argument, resorted to every mode of persuasion, but all was of no avail. Mr. Clifford was under the rigid, the iron government of his fate! His wife was one of those miserably silly women—born, according to Iago—

"To suckle fools and chronicle small beer"—

who, raised to the sudden control of unexpected wealth, becomes insane upon it, and is blind, deaf, and dumb, to all counsel or reason which suggests the possibility of its loss. From the very moment when Mr. Clifford spoke of selling out house, horses, and carriage, as the inevitable result which must follow his adoption of my recommendation, she declared herself against it at all hazards, particularly when her husband assured her that "the glorious uncertainties of the law" afforded a possibility of his escape with less loss. The loss of money was, with her, the item of most consideration; her mind was totally insensible to that of reputation. She was willing to make this compromise with me, as a sort of alternative, for, in that case, there would be no diminution of attendance and expense—no loss of rank and equipage. We should all live together—how harmoniously, one may imagine—but the grandeur and the state would still be intact and unimpaired. Even for this, however, she was not prepared, when she discovered that there was no certainty that my alliance would bring immunity to her husband. How this notion got even partially into his head, I know not; unless in consequence of a growing imbecility of intellect, which in a short time after betrayed itself more strikingly. But of this in its own place.

My attempts to convince my unfortunate uncle were all rendered unavailing, and shown to be so to Julia herself in a very short time afterward. The insolence of Mrs. Clifford, when I did seek an interview with her husband, was so offensive and unqualified, that Julia herself, with a degree of indignation which she could not entirely suppress, begged me to quit the house, and relieve myself from such undeserved insult and abuse. I did so, but with no unfriendly wishes for the wretched woman who presided over its destinies, and the no less wretched husband whom she helped to make so; and my place as consulting friend and counsellor was soon supplied by Mr. Perkins—one of those young barristers, to be found in every community, who regard the "penny fee" as the *sine qua non*, and obey implicitly the injunction of the scoundrel in the play: "Make money—honestly if you can, but—make money!" He was one of those creatures who set people at loggerheads, goad foolish and petulant clients into lawsuits, stir up commotions in little sets, and invariably comfort the suit-bringer with the most satisfactory assurances of success. It was the confident assurances of this person which had determined Mr. Clifford—his wife rather—to resist to the last the suit in question. Through the sheer force of impudence, this man had obtained a tolerable share of practice. His clients, as may be supposed, lay chiefly among such persons as, having no power or standard for judging, necessarily look upon him who is most bold and pushing as the most able and trustworthy. The bullies of the law—and, unhappily, the profession has quite too many—are very commanding persons among the multitude. Mr. Clifford knew this fellow's mental reputation very well, and was not deceived by the confidence of his assurances; nay, to the last, he showed a hankering desire to give me the entire control of the subject; but the hostility of Mrs. Clifford overruled his more prudent if not more honorable purposes; and, as he was compelled to seek a lawyer, the questionable moral standing of Perkins decided his choice. He wished one, in short, to do a certain piece of dirty work; and, as if in anticipation of the future, he dreaded to unfold the case to any of the veterans, the old-time gentlemen and worthies of the bar. I proposed this to him. I offered to make a supposititious relation of the facts for the opinion of Mr. Edgerton and others—nay, pledged myself to procure a confidential consultation—anything, sooner than that he should resort to a mode of extrication which, I assured him, would only the more deeply involve him in the meshes of disgrace and loss. But there was a fatality about this gentleman—a doom that would not be baffled, and could not be stayed. The wilful mind always precipitates itself down the abyss; and, whether acting by his own, or under the influence of another's judgment, such was, most certainly, the case with him. He was not to be saved. Mr. Perkins was regularly installed as his defender—his counsellor, private and public—and I was compelled, though with humiliating reluctance, to admit to the plaintiffs, Banks & Tressell, that there was no longer any hope of compromise. The issue on which hung equally his fortune and his reputation was insanely challenged by my uncle.

CHAPTER IX.

DUELLO.

BUT my share in the troubles of this affair was not to end, though I was no longer my uncle's counsellor. An event now took place which gave the proceedings a new and not less unpleasing aspect than they had worn before. Mrs. Clifford, it appears, in her communications to her husband's lawyer, did not confine herself to the mere business of the lawsuit. Her voluminous discourse involved her opinions of her neighbors, friends, and relatives; and, one day, a few weeks after, I was suddenly surprised by a visit from a gentleman—one of the members of the bar—who placed a letter in my hands from Mr. Perkins. I read this billet with no small astonishment. It briefly stated that certain reports had reached his ears, that I had expressed myself contemptuously of his abilities and character, and concluded with an explicit demand, not for an explanation, but an apology. My answer was immediate.

"You will do me the favor to say, Mr. Carter, that Mr. Perkins has been misinformed. I never uttered anything in my life which could disparage either his moral or legal reputation."

"I am sorry to say, Mr. Clifford," was the reply, "that denial is unnecessary, and can not be received. Mr. Perkins has his information from the lips of a lady; and, as a lady is not responsible, she can not be allowed to err. I am required, sir, to insist on an apology. I have already framed it, and it only needs your signature."

He drew a short, folded letter, from his pocket, and placed it before me. There was so much cool impertinence in this proceeding, and in the fellow's manner, that I could with difficulty refrain from flinging the paper in his face. He was one of the little and vulgar clique of which Perkins was a sort of centre.

The whole set were conscious enough of the low estimate which was put upon them by the gentlemen of the bar. Denied caste, they were disposed to force their way to recognition by the bully's process, and stung by some recent discouragements, Mr. Perkins was, perhaps, rather glad than otherwise, of the silly, and no less malicious than silly, tattle of Mrs. Clifford—for I did not doubt that the gross perversion of the truth which formed the basis of his note, had originated with her, which enabled him to single out a victim, who, as the times went, had suddenly risen to a comparative elevation which is not often accorded to a young beginner. I readily conjectured his object from his character and that of the man he sent. My own nature was passionate; and the rude school through which my boyhood had gone, had made me as tenacious of my position as the grave. That I should be chafed by reptiles such as these, stung me to vexation; and though I kept from any violence of action, my words did not lack of it.

"Mr. Perkins is, permit me to say, a very impertinent fellow; and, if you please, our conference will cease from this moment."

He was a little astounded—rose, and then recovering himself, proceeded to reply with the air of a veteran martinet.

"I am glad, sir, that you give me an opportunity of proceeding with this business without delay. My friend, Mr. Perkins, prepared me for some such answer. Oblige me, sir, by reading this paper." He handed me the challenge for which his preliminaries had prepared me.

"Accepted, sir; I will send my friend to you in the course of the morning."

As I uttered this reply, I bowed and waved him to the door. He did not answer, other than by a bow, and took his departure. The promptness which I had shown impressed him with respect. Baffled, in his first spring, the bully, like the tiger, is very apt to slink back to his jungle. His departure gave me a brief opportunity for reflection, in which I slightly turned over in my mind the arguments for and against duelling. But these were now too late—even were they to decide me against the practice—to affect the present transaction; and I sallied out to seek a friend—a friend!

Here was the first difficulty. I had precious little choice among friends. My temper was not one calculated to make or keep friends. My earnestness of character, and intensity of mood, made me dictatorial; and where self-esteem is a large and active development, as it must be in an old aristocratic community, such qualities are continually provoking popular hostility. My friends, too, were not of the kind to whom such scrapes as the present were congenial. I was unwilling to go to young Edgerton, as I did not wish to annoy his parents by my novel anxieties. But where else could I turn? To him I went. When he heard my story, he began by endeavoring to dissuade me from the meeting.

"I am pledged to it, William," was my only answer.

"But, Edward, I am opposed to duelling myself, and should not promote or encourage, in another, a practice which I would not be willing myself to adopt."

"A good and sufficient reason, William. You certainly should not. I will go to Frank Kingsley."

"He will serve you, I know; but, Edward, this duelling is a bad business. It does no sort of good. Kill Perkins, and it does not prove to him, even if he were then able to hear, that Mrs. Clifford spoke a falsehood; and if he kills you, you are even still farther from convincing him.

"I have no such desire, William; and your argument, by the way, is one of those beggings of the question which the opponents of duelling continually fall into when discussing the subject. The object of the man, who, in a case like mine, fights a duel, is not to prove his truth, but to protect himself from persecution. Perkins seeks to bully and drive me out of the community. Public opinion here approves of this mode of protecting one's self;—nay, if I do not avail myself of its agency, the same public opinion would assist my assailant in my expulsion. I fight on the same ground that a nation fights when it goes to war. It is the most obvious and easy mode to protect myself from injury and insult. So long as I submit, Perkins will insult and bully, and the city will encourage him. If I resist, I silence this fellow, and perhaps protect other young beginners. I have not the most distant idea of convincing him of my truth by fighting him—nay, the idea of giving him satisfaction is an idea that never entered my brain. I simply take a popular mode of securing myself from outrage and persecution."

"But, do you secure yourself? Has duelling this result?"

"Not invariably, perhaps; simply because the condition of humanity does not recognise invariable results. If it is shown to be the probable, the frequent result, it is all that can be expected of any human agency or law."

"But, is it probable—frequent?"

"Yes, almost certain, almost invariable. Look at the general manners, the deportment, the forbearance, of all communities where duelling is recognised as an agent of society. See the superior deference paid to females, the unfrequency of bullying, the absence of blackguarding, the higher tone of the public press, and of society in general, from which the public press takes its tone, and which it represents in our country, but does not often inform. Even seduction is a rare offence, and a matter of general exclamation, where this extra-judicial agent is recognised."

And so forth. It is not necessary to repeat our discussion of this vexed question, of its uses and abuses. I did not succeed in convincing him, and, under existing circumstances, it is not reasonable to imagine that his arguments had any influence over me. To Frank Kingsley I went, and found him in better mood to take up the cudgels, and even make my cause his own. He was one of those ardent bloods, who liked nothing better than the excitement of such an affair; whether as principal or assistant, it mattered little. To him I expressed my wish that his arrangements should bring the matter to an issue, if possible, within the next twenty-four hours.

"Prime!" he exclaimed, rubbing his hands. "That's what I like. If you shoot as quickly now, and as much to the point, you may count any button on Perkins's coat."

He proceeded to confer with the friend of my opponent, while, with a meditative mind, I went to my office, necessarily oppressed with the strange feelings belonging to my situation. In less than two hours after Kingsley brought me the *carte*, by which I found that the meeting was to take place two miles out of town, by sunrise the day after the one ensuing — the weapons, pistols — distance, as customary, ten paces!

"You are a shot, of course?" said Kingsley.

My answer, in the negative, astonished him.

"Why, you will have little or no time for practice."

"I do not intend it. My object is not to kill this man; but to make him and all others see that the dread of what may be done, either by him or them, will never reconcile me to submit to injury or insult. I shall as effectually secure this object by going out, as I do, without preparation, as if I were the best shot in America. He does not know that I am not; and a pistol is always a source of danger when in the grasp of a determined man."

"You are a queer fellow in your notions, Clifford, and I can not say that I altogether understand you; but you must certainly ride out with me this afternoon, and bark a tree. It will do no hurt to a determined man to be a skilful one also."

"I see no use in it."

"Why — what if you should wish to wing him?"

"I think I can do it without practice. But I have no such desire."

"Really you are unnecessarily magnanimous. You may be put to it, however. Should the first shot be ineffectual and he should demand a second, would you throw away that also?"

"No! I should then try to shoot him. As my simple aim is to secure myself from persecution, which is usually the most effectual mode of destroying a young man in this country, I should resort only to such a course as would be likely to yield me this security. That failing, I should employ stronger measures; precisely as a nation would do in a similar conflict with another nation. One must not suffer himself to be destroyed or driven into exile. This is the first law of nature — this of self-preservation. In maintaining this law, a man must do any or all things which in his deliberate judgment, will be effectual for the end proposed. Were I fighting with savages, for example, and knew that they regarded their scalps with more reverence than their lives, I should certainly scalp as well as slay."

"They would call that barbarous?"

"Ay, no doubt; particularly in those countries where they paid from five to fifty, and even one hundred pounds to one Indian for the scalp of his brother, until they rid themselves of both. But see you not that the scalping process, as it produces the most terror aud annoyance, is decidedly the most merciful, as being most likely to discourage and deter from war. If the scalp could be taken from the head of every Seminole shot down, be sure the survivors never after would have come within range of rifle-shot."

But these discussions gave way to the business before me. Kingsley left me to myself, and though sad and serious with oppressive thoughts, I still had enough of the old habits, dominant with me, to go to my daily concerns, and arrange my papers with considerable industry and customary method. My professional business was set in order, and Edgerton duly initiated in the knowledge of all such portions as needed explanation. This done, I sat down and wrote a long farewell letter to Julia, and one, more brief, but renewing the counsel I had previously given to her father, in respect to the suit against him. These letters were so disposed as to be sent in the event of my falling in the fight. The interval which followed was not so easy to be borne. Conscience and reflection were equally busy, and unpleasantly so. I longed for the time of action which should silence these unpleasant monitors.

The brief space of twenty-four hours was soon overpassed, and my anxieties ceased as the moment for the meeting with my enemy, drew nigh. My friend called at my lodgings a good hour before daylight—it was a point of credit with him that we should not delay the opposite party the sixtieth part of a second. We drove out into the country in a close carriage, taking a surgeon—who was a friend of Kingsley—along with us. We were on the ground in due season, and some little time before our customers. But they did not fail or delay us. They were there with sufficient promptitude.

Perkins was a man of coolness and courage. He took his position with admirable *nonchalance;* but I observed, when his eyes met mine, that they were darkened with a scowl of anger. His brows were contracted, and his face which was ordinarily red, had an increased flush upon it which betrayed unusual excitement. He evidently regarded me with feelings of bitter animosity. Perhaps this was natural enough, if he believed the story of Mrs. Clifford—and my scornful answer to his friend, Mr. Carter, was not calculated to lessen the soreness. For my part, I am free to declare, I had not the smallest sentiment of unkindness toward the fellow. I thought little of him, but did not hate—I could not have hated him. I had no wish to do him hurt; and, as already stated, only went out to put a stop to the further annoyances of insolents and bullies, by the only effectual mode—precisely as I should have used a bludgeon over his head, in the event of a personal assault upon me. Of course, I had no purpose to do him any injury, unless with the view to my own safety. I resolved secretly to throw away my fire. Kingsley suspected me of some such intention, and earnestly protested against it.

"I should not place you at all," he said, "if I fancied you could do a thing so d——d foolish. The fellow intends to shoot you if he can. Help him to a share of the same sauce."

I nodded as he proceeded to his arrangements. Here some conference ensued between the seconds:—

"Mr. Carter was very sorry that such a business must proceed. Was it yet too late to rectify mistakes? Might not the matter be adjusted?"

Kingsley, on such occasions, the very prince of punctilio, agreed that the matter was a very lamentable one—to be regretted, and so forth—but of the necessity of the thing, he, Mr. Carter, for his principal, must be the only judge.

"Mr. Carter could answer for his friend, Mr. Perkins, that he was always accessible to reason."

"Mr. Kingsley never knew a man more so than *his* principal."

"May we not reconcile the parties?" demanded Mr. Carter.

"Does Mr. Perkins withdraw his message?" answered Kingsley by another question.

"He would do so, readily, were there any prospect of adjusting the matter upon an honorable footing."

"Mr. Carter will be pleased to name the basis for what he esteems an honorable adjustment."

"Mr. Perkins withdraws his challenge."

"We have no objection to that."

"He substitutes a courteous requisition upon Mr. Clifford for an explanation of certain language, supposed to be offensive, made to a lady."

"Mr. Clifford denies, without qualification, the employment of any such language."

"This throws us back on our old ground," said Carter—"there is a lady in question—"

"Who can not certainly be brought into the controversy," said Kingsley—"I see no other remedy, Mr. Carter, but that we should place the parties. We are here to answer to your final summons."

"Very good, sir; this matter, and what happens, must lie at your door. You are peremptory. I trust you have provided a surgeon."

"His services are at your need, sir," replied Kingsley with military courtesy.

"I thank you, sir—my remark had reference to your own necessity. Shall we toss up for the word?"

These preliminaries were soon adjusted. The word fell to Carter, and thus gave an advantage to Perkins, as his ear was more familiar than mine with the accents of his friend. We were placed, and the pistol put into my hands, without my uttering a sentence.

"Coolly now, my dear fellow," said Kingsley in a whisper, as he withdrew from my side;—"wing him at least—but don't burn powder for nothing."

Scarcely the lapse of a moment followed, when I heard the words "one," "two," "three," in tolerably rapid succession, and, at the utterance of the last, I pulled trigger. My antagonist had done so at the first. His eye was fixed upon mine with deliberate malignity—*that* I clearly saw—but it did not affect my shot. This, I purposely threw away. The skill of my enemy did not correspondend with his evident desires. I was hurt, but very slightly. His bullet merely raised the skin upon the fleshy part of my right thigh. We kept our places while a conference ensued between the two seconds. Mr. Perkins, through his friend, declared himself unsatisfied unless I apologized, or—in less unpleasant language—explained. This demand was answered by Kingsley with cavalier indifference. He came to me with a second pistol. His good-humored visage was now slightly ruffled.

"Clifford!" said he, as he put the weapon into my hand, "you must trifle no longer. This fellow abuses your generosity. He knows, as well as I, that you threw away your fire; and he will play the same game with you, on the same terms, for a month together, Sundays not excepted. I am not willing to stand by and see you risk your life in this manner; and, unless you tell me that you will give him as good as he sends, I leave you on the spot. Will you take aim this time?"

"I will!"

"You promise me then?"

"I do!"

I was conscious of the increased activity of my organ of destructiveness as I said these words. I smiled with a feeling of pleasant bitterness—that spicy sort of malice which you may sometimes rouse in the bosom of the best-natured man in the world, by an attempt to do him injustice. The wound I had received, though very trifling, had no little to do with this determination. It was not unlike such a wound as would be made by a smart stroke of a whip, and the effect upon my blood was pretty much as if it had been inflicted by some such instrument. I was stung and irritated by it, and the pertinacity of my enemy, particularly as he must have seen that my shot was thrown away, decided me to punish him if I could. I did so! I was not conscious that I was hurt myself, until I saw him falling!—I then felt a heavy and numbing sensation in the same thigh which had been touched before. A faintness relieved me from present sensibility, and when I became conscious, I found myself in the carriage, supported by Kingsley and the surgeon, on my way to my lodgings. My wound was a flesh wound only; the ball was soon extracted, and in a few weeks after, I was enabled to move about with scarcely a feeling of inconvenience. My opponent suffered a much heavier penalty. The bone of his leg was fractured, and it was several months before he was considered perfectly safe. The lesson he got made him a sorer and shorter—a wiser, if not a better man; but as I do not now, and did not then, charge myself with the task of bringing about his moral improvement, it is not incumbent upon me to say anything further on this subject. We will leave him to get better as he may.

CHAPTER X.

HEAD WINDS.

THE hurts of Perkins did not, unhappily, delay the progress of my uncle to that destruction to which his silly wife and knavish lawyer had destined him. His business was brought before the court by the claimants, Messrs. Banks & Tressell; and a brief period only was left him for putting in his answer. When I thought of Julia, I resolved, in spite of all previous difficulties—the sneers of the father, and the more direct, coarse insults of the mother—to make one more effort to rescue him from the fate which threatened him. I felt sure that, for the reasons already given, the merchants would still be willing to effect a compromise which would secure them the principal of their claim, without incurring the delay and risk of litigation. Accordingly, I penned a note to Mr. Clifford, requesting permission to wait upon him at home, at a stated hour. To this I received a cold, brief answer, covering the permission which I sought. I went, but might as well have spared myself the labor and annoyance of this visit. Mrs. Clifford was still in the ascendant—still deaf to reason, and utterly blind to the base position into which her meddlesome interference in the business threw her husband. She had her answer ready; and did not merely content herself with rejecting my overtures, but proceeded to speak in the language of one who really regarded me as busily seeking, by covert ways, to effect the ruin of her family. Her looks and language equally expressed the indignation of a mind perfectly convinced of the fraudulent and evil purposes of the person she addressed. Those of my uncle were scarcely less offensive. A grin of malicious self-gratulation mantled his lips as he thanked me for my counsel, which, he yet remarked, "however wise and good, and well-intended, he did not think it advisable to adopt. He had every confidence in the judgment of Mr. Perkins, who, though without the great legal knowledge of some of his youthful neighbors, had enough for his purposes; and had persuaded him to see the matter in a very different point of view from that in which I was pleased to regard it."

There was no doing anything with or for these people. The fiat for their overthrow had evidently been issued. The fatuity which leads to self-destruction was fixed upon them; and, with a feeling rather of commiseration than anger, I prepared to leave the house. In this interview, I made a discovery, which tended still more to lessen the hostility I might otherwise have felt toward my uncle. I was constrained to perceive that he labored under an intellectual feebleness and incertitude which disconcerted his expression, left his thoughts seemingly without purpose, and altogether convinced me that, if not positively imbecile in mind and memory, there were yet some ugly symptoms of incapacity growing upon him which might one day result in the loss of both. I had always known him to be a weak-minded man, disposed to vanity and caprice, but the weakness had expanded very much in a brief period, and now presented itself to my view in sundry very salient aspects. It was easy now to divert his attention from the business which he had in hand—a single casual remark of courtesy or observation would have this effect—and then his mind wandered from the subject with all the levity and caprice of a thoughtless damsel. He seemed to entertain now no sort of apprehension of his legal difficulties, and spoke of them as topics already adjusted. Nay, for that matter, he seemed to have no serious sense of any subject, whatever might be its personal or general interest; but, passing from point to point, exhibited that instability of mental vision which may not inaptly be compared to that wandering glance which is usually supposed to distinguish and denote, in the physical eye, the presence of insanity. It was not often now that he indulged, while speaking to me, in that manner of hostility—those sneers and sarcastic remarks—which had been his common habit. This was another proof of the change which his mental man had undergone. It was not that he was more prudent or more tolerant than before. He was quite as little disposed to be generous toward me. But he now appeared wholly incapable of that degree of intellectual concentration which could enable him to examine a subject to its close. He would begin to talk with me seriously enough, and with a due solemnity, about the suit against him; but, in a tangent, he would dart off to the consideration of some trifle, some household matter, or petty affair, of which, at any other time, he must have known that his hearers had no wish to hear. Poor Julia confirmed the conjectures which I entertained, but did not utter, by telling me that her father had changed very much in his ways ever since this business had been begun.

"Mother does not see it, but he is no longer the same man. Oh, Edward, I sometimes think he's even growing childish."

The fear was a well-founded one. Before the case was tried, Mr. Clifford was generally regarded, among those who knew him intimately, as little better than an imbecile; and so rapid was the progress of his infirmity, that when the judgment was given, as it was, against him, he was wholly unable to understand or fear its import. His own sense of guilt had anticipated its effects, and his intense vanity was saved from public shame only by the substitution of public pity. The decree of the court gave all that was asked; and the handsome competence of the Cliffords was exchanged for a miserable pittance, which enabled the family to live only in the very humblest manner.

It will readily be conjectured, from what I have stated in respect to myself, that mine was not the disposition to seek revenge, or find cause for exultation in these deplorable events. I had no hostility against my unhappy uncle; I should have scorned myself if I had. If such a feeling ever filled my bosom, it would have been most effectually disarmed by the sight of the wretched old man, a grinning, gibbering idiot, half-dancing and half-shivering from the cold, over the remnants of a miserable and scant fire in the severest evening in November. It was when the affair was all over; when the property of the family was all in the hands of the sheriff; when the mischievous counsel of such a person as Jonathan Perkins, Esquire, could do no more harm even to so foolish a person as my uncle's wife; and when his presence, naturally enough withdrawn from a family from which he could derive no further profit, and which he had helped to ruin, was no longer likely to offend mine by meeting him there—that I proceeded to renew my direct intercourse with the unfortunate people whom I was not suffered to save.

The reader is not to suppose that I had kept myself entirely aloof from the family until these disasters had happened. I sought Julia when occasion offered, and, though she refused it, tendered my services and my means whenever they might be bestowed with hope of good. And now, when all was over, and I met her at the door, and she sank upon my bosom, and wept in my embrace, still less than ever was I disposed to show to her mother the natural triumph of a sagacity which had shown itself at the expense of hers. I forgot, in the first glance of my uncle, all his folly and unkindness. He was now a shadow, and the mental wreck was one of the most deplorable, as it was one of the most rapid and complete, that could be imagined. In less than seven months, a strong man—strong in health—strong, as supposed, in intellect—singularly acute in his dealings among tradesmen—regarded by them as one of the most shrewd in the fraternity—vain of his parts, of his family, and of his fortune—solicitous of display, and constant in its indulgence!—that such a man should be stricken down to imbecility and idiotism—a meagre skeleton in form—pale, puny, timid—crouching by the fireplace—grinning with stealthy looks, momently cast around him—and playing—his most constant employment—with the bellows-strings that hung beside him, or the little kitten, that, delighted with new consideration, had learned to take her place constantly at his feet! What a wreck!

But the moral man had been wrecked before, or this could not have been. It was only because of his guilt—of its exposure rather—that he sunk. In striving to shake off the oppressive burden, he shook off the intellect which had been compelled chiefly to endure it. The sense of shame, the conviction of loss, and, possibly, other causes of conscience which lay yet deeper—for the progeny of crime is most frequently a litter as numerous as a whelp's puppies—helped to crush the mind which was neither strong enough to resist temptation at first, nor to bear exposure at last. I turned away with a tear, which I could not suppress, from the wretched spectacle. But I could have borne with more patience to behold this ruin, than to subdue the rising reproach which I felt as I turned to encounter Mrs. Clifford.

This weak woman, still weak, received me coldly, and I could see in her looks that she regarded me as one whom it was natural to suppose would feel some exultation at beholding their downfall. I saw this, but determined to say nothing, in the attempt to undo these impressions. I knew that time was the best teacher in all such matters, and resolved that my deportment should gradually make her wiser on the subject of that nature which she had so frequently abused, and which, I well knew, she could never understand. But this hope I soon discovered to be unavailing. Her disaster had only soured, not subdued her; and, with the natural tendency of the vulgar mind, she seemed to regard me as the person to whom she should ascribe all her misfortunes. As, to her narrow intellect, it seemed natural that I should exult in the accomplishment of my predictions, so it was a process equally natural that she should couple me with their occurrence; and, indeed, I was too nearly connected with the event, through the medium of my unconscious father, not to feel some portion of the affliction on his account also; though neither his memory nor my reputation suffered from the development of the affair in the community where we lived.

Mrs. Clifford did not openly, or in words, betray the feelings which were striving in her soul; but the general restraint which she put upon herself in my presence, the acerbity of her tone, manner, and language, to poor Julia, and the unvaried querulousness of her remarks, were sufficient to apprize me of the spite which she would have willingly bestowed upon myself, had she any tolerable occasion for doing so. A few weeks served still further to humble the conceit and insolence of the unfortunate woman. The affair turned out much more seriously than I expected. A sudden fall in the value of real and personal estate, just about the time when the sheriff's sale took place, rendered necessary a second levy, which swept the miserable remnant of Mr. Clifford's fortune, leaving nothing to my uncle but a small estate which had been secured by settlement to Mrs. Clifford and her daughter, and which the sheriff could not legally lay hands on.

I came forward at this juncture, and, having allowed them to remove into the small tenement to which, in their reduced condition they found it prudent to retire, I requested a private interview with Mrs. Clifford, and readily obtained it.

I was received by the good lady in apparent state. All the little furniture which she could save from the former, was transferred very inappropriately to the present dwelling-house. The one was quite unsuited to the other. The massive damask curtains accorded badly with the little windows over which they were now suspended, and the sofa, ten feet in length, occupied an unreasonable share of an apartment twelve by sixteen. The *dais* of piled cushions, on which so many fashionable groups had lounged in better times, now seemed a mountain, which begot ideas of labor, difficulty, and up-hill employment, rather than ease, as the eye beheld it cumbering two thirds of the miserable area into which it was so untastefully compressed. These, and other articles of splendor and luxury, if sold, would have yielded her the means to buy furniture more suitable to her circumstances and situation, and left her with some additional resources to meet the daily and sometimes pressing exigencies of life.

The appearance of this parlor argued little in behalf of the salutary effect which such reverses might be expected to produce in a mind even tolerably sensible. They argued, I fancied, as unfavorably for my suit as for the humility of the lady whom I was about to meet. If the parlor of Mrs. Clifford bore such sufficient tokens of her weakness of intellect, her own costume betrayed still more. She had made her person a sort of frame or rack upon which she hung every particle of that ostentatious drapery which she was in the habit of wearing at her fashionable evenings. A year's income was paraded upon her back, and the trumpery jewels of three generations found a place on every part of her person where it is usual for fashionable folly to display such gewgaws. She sailed into the room in a style that brought to my mind instantly the description which Milton gives of the approach of Delilah to Samson, after the first days of his blind captivity :—

"But who is this, what thing of sea or land?—
Female of sex it seems—
That so bedecked, ornate and gay,
Comes this way sailing, like a stately ship
Of Tarsus, bound for the isles
Of Javan or Gadire,
With all her bravery on and tackle trim,
Sails filled, and streamers waving,
Courted by all the winds that hold their play,
An amber scent of odorous perfume
Her harbinger!"

No description could have been more just and literal in the case of Mrs. Clifford. I could scarce believe my eyes; and when forced to do so, I could scarcely suppose that this bravery was intended for my eyes only. Nor was it;—but let me not anticipate. This spectacle, I need not say, sobered me entirely, if anything was necessary to produce this effect, and increased the grave apprehensions which were already at my heart. The next consequence was to make the manner of my communication serious even to severity. A smile, which was of that doubtful sort which is always sinister and offensive, overspread her lips as she motioned me to resume the seat from which I had risen at her entrance; while she threw herself with an air of studied negligence upon one part of the sofa. I felt the awkwardness of my position duly increased, as her house, dress, and manner, convinced me that she was not yet subdued to hers; but a conscious rectitude of intention carried me forward, and lightened the task to my feelings.

"Mrs. Clifford," I said, without circumlocution, "I have presumed to ask your attention this morning to a brief communication which materially affects my happiness, and which I trust may not diminish, if it does not actually promote, yours. Before I make this communication, however, I hope I may persuade myself that the little misunderstandings which have occurred between us are no longer to be considered barriers to our mutual peace and happiness——"

"Misunderstandings, Mr. Clifford?—I don't know what misunderstandings you mean. I'm sure I've never misunderstood you."

I could not misunderstand the insolent tenor of this speech, but I availed myself of the equivoque which it involved to express my gratification that such was the case.

"My path will then be more easy, Mrs. Clifford—my purpose more easily explained."

"I am glad you think so, sir," she answered coolly, smoothing down certain folds of her frock, and crossing her hands upon her lap, while she assumed the attitude of a patient listener. There was something very repulsive in all this; but I saw that the only way to lessen the unpleasantness of the scene, and to get on with her, would be to make the interview as short as possible, and come at once to my object. This I did.

"It is now more than a year, Mrs. Clifford, since I had the honor to say to my uncle, that I entertained for my cousin Julia such a degree of affection as to make it no longer doubtful to me that I should best consult my own happiness by seeking to make her my wife. I had the pleasure at the same time to inform him, which I believed to be true, that Julia herself was not unwilling that such should be the nearer tie between us——"

"Yes, yes, Mr. Clifford, I know all this; but my husband and myself thought better of it, and——" she said with fidgetty impatience.

"And my application was refused," I said calmly; thus finishing the sentence where she had paused.

"Well, sir, and what then?"

"At that time, madam, my uncle gave as a reason that he had other arrangements in view."

"Yes, sir, so we had; and this reminds me that those arrangements were broken off entirely in consequence of the perversity which you taught my daughter. I know it all, sir; there's no more need to tell me of it, than there is to deny it. You put my daughter up to refusing young Roberts, who would have jumped at her, as his father did—and he one of the best families and best fortunes in the city. I'm sure I don't know, sir, what object you can have in reminding me of these things."

Here was ingenious perversity. I bore with it as well as I could, and strove to preserve my consideration and calmness.

"You do your daughter injustice, Mrs. Clifford, and me no less, in this opinion. But I do not seek to remind you of misunderstandings and mistakes, the memory of which can do no good.

My purpose now is to renew the offer to you which I originally made to Mr. Clifford. My attachment to your daughter remains unaltered, and I am happy to say that fortune has favored me so far as to enable me to place her in a situation of comparative comfort and independence which I could not offer then——"

"Which is as much as to say that she don't enjoy comfort and independence where she is; and if she does not, sir, to whom is it all owing, sir, but to you and your father? By your means it is that we are reduced to poverty; but you shall see, sir, that we are not entirely wanting in independence. My answer, sir, is just the same as Mr. Clifford's was. I am very much obliged to you for *the honor* you intend my family, but we must decline it. As for the comfort and independence which you proffer to my daughter, I am happy to inform you that she can receive it at any moment from a source perhaps far more able than yourself to afford both, if her perversity does not stand in the way, as it did when young Roberts made his offers. Mr. Perkins, sir, the excellent young man that you tried to murder, is to be here, sir, this very morning, to see my daughter. Here's his letter, sir, which you may read, that you may be under no apprehensions that my daughter will ever suffer from a want of comfort and independence."

She flung a letter down on the sofa beside her, but I simply bowed, and declined looking at it. I did not, however, yield the contest in this manner. I urged all that might properly be urged on the subject, and with as much earnestness as could be permitted in an interview with a lady—and such a lady!—but, as the reader may suppose, my toils were taken in vain: all that I could suggest, either in the shape of reason or expostulation, only served to make her more and more dogged, and to increase her tone of insolence; and sore, stung with vexation, disappointed, and something more than bewildered, I dashed almost headlong out of the house, without seeing either Julia or her father, precisely at the moment when Mr. Perkins was about to enter.

CHAPTER XI.

CRISIS.

THE result of this interview of my rival with the mother of Julia, was afforded me by the latter. The mother had already given her consent to his suit—that of Julia alone was to be obtained; and to this end the arts of the suitor and the mother were equally devoted. Her refusal only brought with it new forms of persecution. Her steps were haunted by the swain, to whom Mrs. Clifford gave secret notice of all her daughter's intentions. He was her invariable attendant at church, where I had the pain constantly to behold them, in such close proximity, that I at length abandoned the customary house of worship, and found my pew in another, where I could be enabled to endure the forms of service without being oppresssd by foreign and distracting thoughts and fancies.

Of the progress of the suit I had occasional intelligence from Julia herself, whom I had, very reluctantly on her part, persuaded to meet me at the house of a female relative and friend, who favored our desires and managed our interviews. Brief were these stolen moments, but oh, how blissful! The pleasures they afforded, however, were almost wholly mine. The clandestine character of our meetings served to deprive her of the joy which they otherwise might have yielded; and the fear that she was not doing right, humbled her spirit and made her tremble with frequent apprehensions.

At length Mrs. Clifford suspected our interviews, and detected them. We had a most stormy scene on one occasion, when the sudden entrance of this lady surprised us together, at the house of our friend. The consequence of this was, a rupture between the ladies, which resulted in Julia's being forbidden to visit the house of her relative again. This measure was followed by others of such precaution, that at length I could no longer communicate with her, or even seek her, unless when she was on her way to church. Her appearance then was such as to awaken all my apprehensions. Her form, always slender, was become more so. The change was striking in a single week. Her face, usually pale and delicate, was now haggard. Her walk was feeble, and without elasticity. Her whole appearance was wo-begone and utterly spiritless. Days and weeks passed, and my heart was filled with hourly-increasing apprehensions. I returned to the familiar church, but here I suffered a new alarm. That sabbath the family pew was unoccupied. While I trembled lest something serious had befallen her, I was called on by the family physician. This gentleman had been always friendly. He had been my father's physician, and had been his friend and frequent guest; he knew my history, and sympathized with my fortunes. He now knew the history of Julia's affections. She had made him her confidante so far. and he brought me a letter from her. She was sick, as I expected. This letter was of startling tenor:—

"Save me, Edward, if you can. I am now willing to do as you proposed. I can no longer endure these annoyances—these cruel persecutions! My mother tells me that I must submit and marry this man, if we would save ourselves from ruin. It seems he has a claim against the estate for professional services; and as we have no other means of payment, without the sale of all that is left, he is base enough to insist upon my hand as the condition of his forbearance. He uses threats now, since entreaties have failed him. Oh, Edward, if you can save me, come!—for, of a certainty, I can not bear this persecution much longer and live. I am now willing to consent to do what Aunt Sophy recommended. Do not think me bold to say so, dear Edward—if I am bold, it is despair which makes me so."

I read this letter with mingled feelings of indignation and delight—indignation, because of the cruelties to which the worthless mother and the base suitor subjected one so dear and innocent; delight, since the consent which she now yielded placed the means of saving her at my control. The consent was to a flight and clandestine marriage, to which I had, with

5

the assistance of our mutual friend, endeavored to persuade her, in several instances, before.

The question now was, how to effect this object, since we had no opportunities for communication; but, before I took any steps in the matter, I made it a point of duty to deprive the infamous attorney, Perkins, of his means of power over the unhappy family. I determined to pay his legal charges; and William Edgerton, at my request, readily undertook this part of the business. They were found to be extortionate, and far beyond anything either warranted by the practice or the fee-bill. Edgerton counselled me to resist the claim; but the subject was too delicate in all its relations, and my own affair with Perkins would have made my active opposition seem somewhat the consequence of malice and inveterate hostility. I preferred to pay the excess, which was done by Edgerton, rather than have any further dispute or difficulty with one whom I so much despised. Complete satisfaction was entered upon the records of the court, and a certified discharge, under the hand of Perkins himself—which he gave with a reluctance full of mortification—was sent in a blank envelope to Mrs. Clifford. She was thus deprived of the only excuse—if, indeed, such a woman ever needs an excuse for wilfulness—for persecuting her unhappy daughter on the score of the attorney.

But the possession of this document effected no sort of change in her conduct. She pursued her victim with the same old tenacity. It was not to favor Perkins that she strove for this object: it was to baffle *me*. That blind heart, which misguides all of us in turn, was predominant in her, and rendered her totally incapable of seeing the cruel consequences to her daughter which her perseverance threatened. Julia was now so feeble as scarcely to leave her chamber; the physician was daily in attendance; and, though I could not propose to make use of his services in promoting a design which would subject him to the reproach of the grossest treachery, yet, without counsel, he took it upon him plainly to assure the mother that the disorder of her daughter arose solely from her mental afflictions. He went farther. Mrs. Clifford, whose garrulity was as notorious as her vanity and folly, herself took occasion, when this was told her, to ascribe the effect to me; and, with her own coloring, she continued, by going into a long history of our "course of wooing." The doctor availed himself of these statements to suggest the necessity of a compromise, assuring Mrs. Clifford that I was really a more deserving person than she thought me, and, in short, that some concessions must be made, if it was her hope to save her daughter's life.

"She is naturally feeble of frame, nervous and sensitive, and these excitements, pressing upon her, will break down her constitution and her spirits together. Let me warn you, Mrs. Clifford, while yet in season. Dismiss your prejudices against this young man, whether well or ill founded, and permit your daughter to marry him. Suffer me to assure you, Mrs. Clifford, that such an event will do more toward her recovery than all my medicine."

"What, and see him the master of my house—he, the poor beggar-boy that my husband fed in charity, and who turned from him with ingratitude in his moment of difficulty, and left him to be despoiled by his enemies? Never! never! Daughter of mine shall never be wife of his! The serpent! to sting the hand of his benefactor!"

"My dear Mrs. Clifford, this prejudice of yours, besides being totally unfounded, amounts to monomania. Now, I know something of all these matters, as you should be aware; and I should be sorry to counsel anything to you or to your family which would be either disgraceful or injurious. So far from this young man being ungrateful, neglectful, or suffering your husband to be preyed on by enemies, I am of opinion that, if his counsel had been taken in this late unhappy business, you would probably have been spared all of the misery and nearly one half of the loss which has been incurred by the refusal to do so."

"And so you, too, are against us, doctor? You, too, believe everything that this young man tells you?"

"No, madam; I assure you, honestly, that I never heard a single word from his lips in regard to this subject. It is spoken of by everybody but himself."

"Ay! ay! the whole town knows it, and from who else but him, I wonder? But you needn't to talk, doctor, on the subject. My mind's made up. Edward Clifford, while I have breath to say 'No,' and a hand to turn the lock of the door against him, shall never again darken these doors!"

The physician was a man of too much experience to waste labor upon a case so decidedly hopeless. He knew that no art within his compass could cure so thorough a case of heart-blindness, and he gave her up; but he did not give up Julia. He whispered words of consolation into her ears, which, though vague, were yet far more useful than physic.

"Cheer up, my daughter; be of good heart and faith. *I am sure* that there will be some remedy provided for you, before long, which will do you good. I have given the letter to your aunt, and she promises to do as you wish."

It may be said, *en passant*, that the billet sent to me had been covered in another to my female friend and Julia's relative; and that the doctor, though not unconscious of the agency of this lady between us, was yet guilty of no violation of the faith which is always implied between the family and the physician. He might *suspect*, but he did not *know;* and whatever might have been his suspicions, he certainly did not have the most distant idea of that concession which Julia had made, and of the course of conduct for which her mother's persecutions had now prepared her mind.

Mr. Perkins, though deprived of his lien upon Mrs. Clifford, by reason of his claim, did not in the least forego his intentions. His complaints and threatenings necessarily ceased—his tone was something lowered; but he possessed a hold upon this silly woman's prejudices which was far superior to any which he might before have had upon her fears. His hostility to me was grateful to the hate which she also entertained, and which seemed to be more thoroughly infixed in her after her downfall—which, as it has been seen, she ascribed to me; chiefly because of my predictions that such would be the case. In due proportion to her hate for me, was her desire to baffle my wishes, even though it might be at the expense of her own daughter's life. But a vain mother has no affections—none, at least, worthy of the name, and none which she is not prepared to discard at the first requisition of her dearer self. Her hate of me was so extreme as to render her blind to everything besides—her daughter's sickness, the counsel of the physician, the otherwise obvious vulgarity and meanness of Perkins, and that gross injustice which I had suffered at her hands from the beginning, and which, to many minds, might have amply justified in me the hostile feelings which she laid to my charge. In this blindness she precipitated events, and by her cruelty justified extremities in self-defence. The moment that Julia exhibited some slight improvement, she was summoned to an interview with Perkins, and in this interview her mother solemnly swore that she should marry him. The base-minded suitor stood by in silence, beheld the loathing of the maiden, heard her distinct refusal, yet clung to his victim, and permitted the violence of the mother, without rebuke — that rebuke which the true gentleman might have administered in such a case, and which, to forbear, was the foulest shame — the rebuke of his own decided refusal to participate in such a sacrifice. But he was not capable of this; and Julia, stunned and terrified, was shocked to hear Mrs. Clifford appoint the night of the following Thursday for the forced nuptials.

"She will consent — she shall consent, Mr. Perkins," were the vehement assurances of the mother, as the craven-spirited suitor prepared to take his leave. "I know her better than you do, and she knows me. Do you fear nothing, but bring Mr. ——" (the divine) "along with you. We shall put an end to this folly."

"Oh, do not, do not, mother, if you would not drive me mad!" was the exclamation of the destined victim, as she threw herself at the feet of her unnatural parent. "You will kill me to wed this man! I can not marry him — I can not love him. Why would you force this matter upon me—why! why!"

"Why will you resist me, Julia? why will you provoke your mother to this degree? You have only to consent willingly, and you know how kind I am."

"I can not consent!" was the gasping decision of the maiden.

"You shall! you must! you will!"

"Never! never! On my knees I say it, mother. God will witness what you refuse to believe. I will die before I consent to marry where I do not give my heart."

"Oh, you talk of dying, as if it was a very easy matter. But you won't die. It's more easy to say than do. Do you come,

Mr. Perkins. Don't you mind—don't you believe in these denials, and oaths, and promises. It's the way with all young ladies. They all make a mighty fuss when they're going to be married; but they're all mighty willing, if the truth was known. I ought to know something about it. I did just the same as she when I was going to marry Mr. Clifford; yet nobody was more willing than I was to get a husband. Do you come and bring the parson; she'll sing a different tune when she stands up before him, I warrant you."

"That shall never be, Mr. Perkins!" said the maiden solemnly, and somewhat approaching the person whom she addressed. "I have already more than once declined the honor you propose to do me. I now repeat to you that I will sooner marry the grave and the winding-sheet than be your wife! My mother mistakes me and all my feelings. For your own sake, if not for mine, I beg that *you* will not mistake them; for, if the strength is left me for speech, I will declare aloud to the reverend man whom you are told to bring, the nature of those persecutions to which you have been privy. I will tell him of the cruelty which I have been compelled to endure, and which you have beheld and encouraged with your silence."

Perkins looked aghast, muttered his unwillingness to prosecute his suit under such circumstances, and prepared to take his leave. His mutterings and apologies were all swallowed up in that furious storm of abuse and denunciation which now poured from the lips of the exemplary mother. These we need not repeat. Suffice it that the deep feelings of Julia—her sense of propriety and good taste—prevailed to keep her silent, while her mother, still raving, renewed her assurances to the pettifogger that he should certainly receive his wife at her hands on the evening of the ensuing Thursday. The unmanly suitor accepted her assurances—and took leave of mother and daughter, with the expression of a simpering hope, intended chiefly for the latter, that her objections would resolve themselves into the usual maidenly scruples when the appointed time should arrive. Julia mustered strength enough to reply in language which brought down another storm from her mother upon her devoted head.

"Do not deceive yourself, Mr. Perkins—do not let the assurances of my mother deceive you. She does not know me. I can not and will not marry you. I will sooner marry the grave —the winding-sheet—the worm!"

Her strength failed her the moment he left the apartment. She sank in a fainting-fit upon the floor, and was thus saved from hearing the bitter abuse which her miserable and misguided parent continued to lavish upon her, even while undertaking the task of her restoration. The evident exhaustion of her frame, her increasing feebleness, the agony of her mind, and the possibly fatal termination of her indisposition, did not in the least serve to modify the violent and vexing mood of this most unnatural woman!

CHAPTER XII.

"GONE TO BE MARRIED."

THESE proceedings, the tenor of which was briefly communicated to me in a hurried note from Julia, despatched by the hands of the physician, under a cover, to the friendly aunt, rendered it imperatively necessary that, whatever we proposed to do should be done quickly, if we entertained any hope to save her. The tone of her epistle alarmed me exceedingly in one respect, as it evidently showed that she could not much longer save herself. Her courage was sinking with her spirits, which were yielding rapidly beneath the continued presence of that persecution which had so long been acting upon her. She began now to distrust her own strength—her very powers of utterance to declare her aversion to the proposed marriage, if ever the trial was brought to the threatened issue before the holy man.

"What am I to do—what say—" demanded her trembling epistle, "should they go so far? Am I to declare the truth?—can I tell to strange ears that it is my mother who forces this cruel sacrifice upon me? I dread I can not. I fear that my soul and voice will equally fail me. I tremble, dear Edward, when I think that the awful moment may find me speechless, and my consent may be assumed from my silence. Save me from this trial, dearest Edward; for I fear everything now—and fear myself—my unhappy weakness of nerve and spirit—more than all. Do not leave me to this trial of my strength—for I have none. Save me if you can!"

It may be readily believed that I needed little soliciting to exertion after this. The words of this letter occasioned an alarm in my mind, little less—though of a different kind—than that which prevailed in hers. I knew the weakness of hers—I knew hers—and felt the apprehension that she might fail at the proper moment, even more vividly than she expressed it.

This letter did not take me by surprise. Before it was received, and soon after the first with which she had favored me, by the hands of the friendly physician, I had begun my preparations with the view to our clandestine marriage. I was only now required to quicken them. The obstacle, on the face of it, was, comparatively, a small one. To get her from a dwelling, in which, though her steps were watched, she was not exactly a prisoner, was scarcely a difficulty, where the lover and the lady are equally willing.

Our mode of operations was simple. There was a favorite servant—a negro—who had been raised in the family, had been a playmate with my poor deceased cousin and myself, and had always been held in particular regard by both of us. He was not what is called a house-servant, but was employed in the yard in doing various offices, such as cutting wood, tending the garden, going of messages, and so forth. This was in the better days of the Clifford family. Since its downfall he had been instructed to look an owner, and, opportunely, at this moment, when I was deliberating upon the process I should adopt for the extrication of his young mistress, he came to me to request that I would buy him. The presence of this servant suggested to me that he could assist me materially in my plans. Without suffering him to know the intention which I had formed, I listened to his garrulous harangue. A negro is usually very copious, where he has an auditor; and though, from his situation, he could directly see nothing of the proceedings in the house of his owner, yet, from his fellow-servants he had contrived to gather, perhaps, a very correct account of the general condition of things. It appeared from his story that the attachment of Miss Julia to myself was very commonly understood. The effort of the mother to persuade her to marry Perkins was also known to him; but of the arrangement that the marriage should take place at the early day mentioned in her note, he told me nothing, and, in all probability, this part of her proceedings was kept a close secret by the wily dame Peter—the name of the negro—went on to add, that, loving

5*

me, and loving his young mistress, and knowing that we loved one another, and believing that we should one day be married, he was anxious to have me for his future owner.

"I will buy you, Peter, on one condition."

"Wha's dat, Mas' Ned?"

"That you serve me faithfully on trial, for five days, without letting anybody know who you serve—that you carry my messages without letting anybody hear them except that person to whom you are sent—and, if I give you a note to carry, that you carry it safely, not only without suffering anybody to see the note but the one to whom I send it, but without suffering anybody to know or suspect that you've got such a thing as a note about you."

The fellow was all promises; and I penned a billet to Julia which, in few words, briefly prepared her to expect my attendance at her house at three in the afternoon of the very day when her nuptials were contemplated. I then proceeded to a friend—Kingsley—the friend who had served me in the meeting with Perkins; a bold, dashing, frank fellow, who loved nothing better than a frolic which worried one of the parties; and who, I well knew, would relish nothing more than to baffle Perkins in a love affair, as we had already done in one of strife. To him I unfolded my plan and craved his assistance, which was promised instantly. My female friend, the relative of Julia, whose assistance had been already given us, and whose quarrel with Mrs. Clifford in consequence, had spiced her determination to annoy her still further whenever occasion offered, was advised of our plans; and William Edgerton readily undertook what seemed to be the most innocent part of all, to procure a priest to officiate for us, at the house of the lady in question, and at the appointed time.

My new retainer, Peter, brought me due intelligence of the delivery of the note, in secret, to Julia, and a verbal answer from her made me sanguine of success. The day came, and the hour; and in obedience to our plan, my friend, Kingsley, proceeded boldly to the dwelling of Mrs. Clifford, just as that lady had taken her seat at the dinner-table, requesting to see and speak with her on business of importance. The interview was vouchsafed him, though not until the worthy lady had instructed the servant to say that she was just then at the dinner-table, and would be glad if the gentleman would call again.

But the gentleman regretted that he could not call again. He was from Kentucky, desirous of buying slaves, and must leave town the next morning for the west. The mention of his occupation, as Mrs. Clifford had slaves to sell, was sufficient to persuade her to lay down the knife and fork with promptness; and the servant was bade to show the Kentucky gentleman into the parlor. Our arrangement was, that, with the departure of the lady from the table, Julia should leave it also—descend the stairs, and meet me at the entrance.

Trembling almost to fainting, the poor girl came to me, and I received her into my arms, with something of a tremor also. I felt the prize would be one that I should be very loath to lose; and joy led to anxiety, and my anxiety rendered me nervous to a womanly degree. But I did not lose my composure and when I had taken her into my arms, I thought it would be only a prudent precaution to turn the key in the outer door, and leave it somewhere along the highway. This I did, absolutely forgetting, that, in thus securing myself against any sudden pursuit, I had also locked up my friend, the Kentucky trader.

Fortune favored our movements. Our preparations had been properly laid, and Edgerton had the divine in waiting. In less than half an hour after leaving the house of her parents, Julia and myself stood up to be married. Pale, feeble, sad—the poor girl, though she felt no reluctance, and suffered not the most momentary remorse for the steps she had taken, and was about to take, was yet necessarily and naturally impressed with the solemnity and the doubts which hung over the event. Young, timid, artless, apprehensive, she was unsupported by those whom nature had appointed to watch over and protect her; and though they had neglected, and would have betrayed their trust, she yet could not but feel that there was an incompleteness about the affair, which, not even the solemn accents of the priest, the deep requisitions of those pledges which she was called upon to make, and the evident conviction which she now entertained, that what had been done was necessary to be done, for her happiness, and even her life—could entirely remove. There was an awful but sweet earnestness in the sad, intense glance of entreaty, with which she regarded me when I made the final response. Her large black eye dilated, even under the dewy suffusion of its tears, as it seemed to say:—

"It is to you now—to you alone—that I look for that protection, that happiness which was denied where I had best right to look for it. Ah! let me not look, let me not yield myself to you in vain!"

How imploring, yet how resigned was that glance of tears—love in tears, yet love that trusted without fear! It was the embodiment of innocence, struggling between hope and doubt, and only strengthened for the future by the pure, sweet faith which grew out of their conflict. I look back upon that scene, I recall that glance, with a sinking of the heart which is full of terror and terrible reproach. Ah! then, then, I had no fear, no thought, that I should see that look, and others, more sad, more imploring still, and see them without a corresponding faith and love! I little knew, in that brief, blessed hour, how rapidly the blindness of the heart comes on, even as the scale over the eyes—but such a scale as no surgeon's knife can cut away.

CHAPTER XIII.

BAFFLED FURY.

In the first gush of my happiness — the ceremony being completed, and the possession of my treasure certain — I had entirely forgotten my Kentucky friend, whom I had locked up, in confidential *tête-à-tête* with madam, my exemplary mother-in-law. He was a fellow with a strong dash of humor, and could not resist the impulse to amuse himself at the expense of the lady, by making an admirable scene of the proceeding. He began the business by stating that he had heard she had several negroes whom she wished to sell — that he was anxious to buy — he did not care how many, and would give the very best prices of any trader in the market. At his desire, all were summoned in attendance — some three or four in number, that she had to dispose of — all but the worthy Peter, who, under existing circumstances, was quite too necessary to my proceedings to be dispensed with. These were all carefully examined by the trader. They were asked their ages, their names, their qualities; whether they were willing to go to Kentucky, the paradise of the western Indian, and so forth — all those questions which, in ordinary cases, it is the custom of the purchaser to ask. They were then dismissed, and the Kentuckian next discussed with the lady the subject of prices. But let the worthy fellow speak for himself:—

"I was so cursed anxious," he said, "to know whether you had got off and in safety, for I was beginning to get monstrous tired of the old cat, that I jumped up every now and then to take a peep out of the front window. I made an excuse to spit on such occasions — though sometimes I forgot to do so — and then I would go back and begin again, with something about the bargain and the terms, and whether the negroes were honest, and sound, and all that. Well, though I looked out as often as I well could with civility, I saw nothing of you, and began to fear that something had happened to unsettle the whole plan; but, after a while, I saw Peter, with his mouth drawn back and hooked up into his ears, with his white teeth glimmering like so many slips of moonshine in a dark night, and I then concluded that all was as it should be. But seeing me look out so earnestly and often, the good lady at length said:—

"'I suppose, sir, your horses are in waiting. Perhaps you'd like to have a servant to mind them.'

"'No, ma'am, I'm obliged to you; but I left the hotel on foot.'

"'Yes, sir,' said she, 'but I thought it might be your horses, seeing you so often look out.'

"I could scarcely keep in my laughter. It did burst out into a sort of chuckle; and, as you were then safe—I knew *that* from Peter's jaws—I determined to have my own fun out of the old woman. So I said—pretty much in this sort of fashion, for I longed to worry her, and knew just how it could be done handsomest—I said:—

"'The truth is, ma'am—pardon me for the slight—but really I was quite interested—struck, as I may say, by a very suspicious transaction that met my eyes a while ago, when I first got up to spit from the window.'

"'Ah, indeed, sir! and pray, if I may ask, what was it you saw?'

"'Really very curious; but getting up to spit, and looking out before I did so—necessary caution, ma'am—some persons might be just under the window, you know—'

"'Yes, sir, yes.' The old creature began to look and talk mighty eager.

"'An ugly habit, ma'am—that of spitting. We Kentuckians carry it to great excess. Foreigners, I'm told, count it monstrous vulgar—effect of tobacco-chewing, ma'am—a deuced bad habit, I grant you, but 'tis a habit, and there's no leaving it off, even if we would. I don't think Kentuckians, as a people, a bit more vulgar than English, or French, or Turks, or any other respectable people of other countries.'

"'No, sir, certainly not; but the transaction—what you saw.'

"'Ah, yes! beg pardon; but, as I was saying, something really quite suspicious! Just as I was about to spit, when I went to the window, some ten minutes ago—perhaps you did not observe, but I did not spit. Good reason for it, ma'am—might have done mischief.'

"'How, sir?'

"'Ah, that brings me to the question I want to ask: any handsome young ladies living about here, ma'am?—here, in your neighborhood?'

"'Why, yes, sir,' answered the old tabby, with something like surprise; 'there's several—there's the Masons, just opposite; the Bagbys, next door to them below, and Mr. Wilford's daughter: all of them would be considered pretty by some persons. On the same side with us, there's Mrs. Freeman and her two daughters, but the widow is accounted by many the youngest looking and prettiest of the whole, though, to my thinking, that's saying precious little for any. Next door to us is a Mr. and Mrs. Gibbs, who have a daughter, and she *is* rather pretty, but I don't know much about them. It might be a mother's vanity, sir, but I think I may be proud of having a daughter myself, who is about as pretty as any of the best among them; and that's saying a great deal less for her than might be said.'

"'Ah, indeed—you a daughter, ma'am? But she is not grown-up, of course—a mere child?'

"'Oh, I beg your pardon, sir,' said the old creăture, tickled up to the eyes, and looking at me with the sweetest smiles; 'though it may surprise you very much, she is not only no child, but a woman grown; and, what's more, I think she will be made a wife this very night.'

"'Egad, then I suspect she's not the only one that's about to be made a wife of. I suspect some one of these young ladies, your neighbors, will be very soon in the same condition.'

"'Indeed, sir—pray, who?—how do you know?' and the old tabby edged herself along the sofa until she almost got jam up beside me.

"'Well,' said I, 'I don't *know* exactly, but I'm deucedly suspicious of it, and, more than that, there's some underhand work going on.'

"This made her more curious than ever; and her hands and

feet, and indeed her whole body, got such a fidgeting, that I fancied she began to think of getting St. Vitus for a bedfellow. Her eagerness made her ask me two or three times what made me think so; and, seeing her anxiety, I purposely delayed in order to worry her. I wished to see how far I could run her up. When I did begin to explain, I went to work in a round-about way enough — something thus, old Kentuck — as I began: 'Well, ma'am, this tobacco-chewing, as I said before, carried me, as you witnessed, constantly to the window. I don't know that I chew more than many others, but I know I chew too much for my good, and for decency, too, ma'am.'

" 'Yes, sir, yes; but the young lady, and—'

" 'Ah, yes, ma'am. Well, then, going to the window once, twice, or thrice, I could not help but see a young man standing beneath it, evidently in waiting — very earnest, very watchful — seemingly very much interested and anxious, as if waiting for somebody.'

" 'Is it possible?' whispered the tabby, full of expectation.

" 'Yes, very possible, ma'am — very true. There he stood; I could even hear his deep-drawn sighs — deep, long, as if from the very bottom of his heart.'

" 'Was he so *very* near, sir?'

" 'Just under the window — going to and fro — very anxious. I was almost afraid I had spit on him, he looked up so hard — so—'

" 'What, sir, up at you? at — at *my* windows, sir?'

" 'Not exactly, ma'am, that was only my notion, for I thought I might have spit upon him, and so wakened his anger; but, indeed, he looked all about him, as, indeed, it was natural that he should, you know, if he meditated anything that wa'n't exactly right. There was a carriage in waiting — a close carriage — not a hundred yards below, and—'

" 'Ah, sir, do tell me what sort of a looking young gentleman was it — eh?'

" 'Good-looking fellow enough, ma'am — rather tall, slenderish, but not so slender — wore a black frock.' By this time the old creature was up at the window — her long, skinny neck stretched out as far as it could go.

" 'Ah!' said I, 'ma'am, you're quite too late, if you expect to see the sport. They're off; I saw the last of them when I took my last spit from the window. They were then—'

"'But, sir, did he—did you say that this person—the person you spit on—carried a young lady away with him?'

"'You mistake me, ma'am—'

"'Ah!'—she drew a mighty long breath as if relieved.

"'I did *not* spit upon him; I only came near doing it once or twice. If I hadn't looked, I should very probably have divided my quid pretty equally between both of them.'

"'Both! both!' she almost screamed. 'Did she go with him, then?—was there in truth a young woman?'

"You never saw a creature in such a tearing fidget. Her long nose was nearly stuck into my face, and both her hands, all claws extended, seemed ready for my cheeks. I felt a little ticklish, I assure you; but I kept up my courage, determined to see the game out, and answered very deliberately, after I had put a fresh quid into my jaws:—

"'Ay, that she did, ma'am, and seemed deuced glad to go, as was natural enough. A mighty pretty girl she was, too; rather thin, but pretty enough to tempt a clever fellow to do anything. I reckon they're nigh on to being man and wife by this time, let the old people say what they will.'

"But the old put didn't wait to hear me say all this. Before the words were well out of my mouth, she gave a bounce, to the bell-rope first—I thought she'd ha' jerked it to pieces—and then to the head of the stairs.

"'Excuse me for a moment, sir, if you please,' she said, in a considerable fidget.

"'Certainly, ma'am,' says I, with a great Kentucky sort of bow and natural civility; and then I could hear her squalling from the head of the stairs, and at the top of her voice, 'Julia! Julia! Julia!'—but there was no answer from Julia. Then came the servants; then came the outcry; then she bounced back into the parlor, and blazed out at me for not telling her at once that it was her daughter who had been carried off, without making so long a story of it, and putting in so much talk about tobacco.

"'Lord bless you, my dear woman!' says I, innocent enough, 'was that pretty girl your daughter? That accounts for the fellow looking up at the window so often; and I to fancy that it was all because I might have given him a quid!'

"'You must have seen her *then!*'

"'Well, ma'am,' said I, 'I must come again about the negroes. I see you've got your hands full.'

"And, with that, I pushed down stairs, while she blazed out at her husband, whom she called an old fool; and me, whom she called a young one; and the negroes, whom she ordered to fly in a hundred ways in the same breath; and, to make matters worse, she seized her hat and shawl, and bounced down the steps after me. Here we were in a fix again, that made her a hundred times more furious. The street-door was locked on the outside, and the key gone, and I fastened up with the old mad tabby. I tried to stand it while the servants were belaboring to break open, but the storm was too heavy, and, raising a sash, I went through: and, in good faith, I believe she bounced through after me; for, when I got fairly into the street and looked round, there she went, bounce, flounce, pell-mell, all in a rage, steam up, puffing like a porpoise—though, thank Jupiter! she took another course from myself. I was glad to get out of her clutches, I assure you."

Such was Kingsley's account of his expedition, told in his particular manner; and endued with the dramatic vitality which he was well able to give it, it was inimitable. It needs but a few words to finish it. Mrs. Clifford, with unerring instinct, made her way to the house of that friendly lady who had assisted our proceedings. But she came too late for anything but abuse. Julia was irrevocably mine. Bitter was the clamor which, in our chamber, assailed us from below.

"Oh, Edward, how shall I meet her?" was the convulsive speech of Julia, as she heard the fearful sounds of her mother's voice—a voice never very musical, and which now, stimulated by unmeasured rage—the rage of a baffled and wicked woman—poured forth a torrent of screams rather than of human accents. We soon heard the rush of the torrent up stairs, and in the direction of our chamber.

"Fear nothing, Julia; her power over you is now at an end. You are now mine—mine only—mine irrevocably!"

"Ah, she is still my mother!" gasped the lovely trembler in

my arms. A moment more, and the old lady was battering at the door. I had locked it within. Her voice, husky but subdued, now called to her daughter—

"Julia! Julia! Julia!—come out!"

"Who is there? what do you want?" I demanded. I was disposed to keep her out, but Julia implored me to open the door. She had really no strength to reply to the summons of the enraged woman; and her entreaty to me was expressed in a whisper which scarcely filled my own ears. She was weak almost to fainting. I trembled lest her weakness, coupled with her fears, and the stormy scene that I felt might be reasonably anticipated, would be too much for her powers of endurance. I hesitated. She put her hand on my wrist.

"For my sake, Edward, let her in. Let her see me. We will have to meet her, and better now—now, when I feel all the solemnity of my new position, and while the pledges I have just made are most present to my thoughts. Do not fear for me. I am weak and very feeble, but I am resolute. I feel that I am not wrong."

She could scarcely gasp out these brief sentences. I urged her not to risk her strength in the interview.

"As you love me, do as I beg you," she replied, with entreating earnestness. "It does not become me to keep my mother, under any circumstances, thus waiting at the door, and asking entrance."

Meanwhile, the clamors of Mrs. Clifford were continued. Julia's aunt was there also, and the controversy was hot and heavy between them. Annoyed as I was, and apprehensive for Julia, I yet could not forbear laughing at the ludicrousness of my position and the whole scene. I began to think, from the equal violence of the two ancient dames without, that they might finally get to blows. This was also the fear of Julia, and another reason why we should throw open the door. I at length did so; and soon had the doubtful satisfaction of transferring to myself all the wrath of the disappointed mother. She rushed in, the moment the door turned upon its hinges, almost upsetting me in the violence of her onset. Bounding into the apartment with a fury that was utterly beyond her own control, I was led to fear that she might absolutely inflict violence upon her daughter, who by this time had sunk, in equal terror and exhaustion, upon a sofa in the remotest corner of the room. I hastily placed myself between them, and did not scruple, with extended hands, to maintain a safe interval of space between the two. I will not attempt to describe the tigress rage or the shrieking violence which ensued on the part of this veteran termagant. It was only closed at length, when, Julia having fainted under the storm, dead to all appearance, I picked up the assailant *vi et armis*, and, in defiance of screams and scratches—for she did not spare the use of her talons—resolutely transported her from the chamber.

CHAPTER XIV.

ONE DEBT PAID.

STAGGERING forward under this burden — a burden equally active and heavy — who should I encounter at the head of the stairs, but the liege lord of the lady — my poor imbecile uncle. As soon as she beheld him — foaming and almost unintelligible in her rage — she screamed for succor — cried "murder" "rape," "robbery," and heaven knows what besides. A moment before, though she scratched and scuffled to the utmost, she had not employed her lungs. A momentary imprecation alone had broken from her, as it were, perforce and unavoidably. Now, nothing could exceed the stentorian tumult which her tongue maintained. She called upon her husband to put me to death — to tear me in pieces — to do anything and everything for the punishing of so dreadful an offender as myself. In thus commanding him, she did not forbear uttering her own unmeasured opinion of the demerits of the man whose performances she required.

"If you had the spirit of a man, Clifford — if you were not a poor shoat — you'd never have submitted so long as you have to this viper's insolence. And there you stand, doing nothing — absolutely still as a stock, though you see him beating your wife. Ah! you monster! — you coward! — that I should ever have married a man that wasn't able to protect me."

This is a sufficient sample of her style, and not the worst. I am constrained to confess that some portions of the good lady's language would better have suited the modes of speech common enough among the Grecian housekeepers at the celebration of the Eleusinian mysteries. I have omitted not a few of the bad words, and forborne the repetition of that voluminous eloquence poured out, after the Billingsgate fashion, equally upon myself, her daughter, and husband. During the vituperation she still kicked and scuffled; my face suffered, and my eyes narrowly escaped. But I grasped her firmly; and when her husband, my worthy uncle, in obedience to her orders, sprang upon me, with the bludgeon which he now habitually carried, I confronted him with the lusty person of his spouse, and regret to say, that the first thwack intended for my shoulders, descended with some considerable emphasis upon hers. This increased her fury, and redoubled her screams. But it did not lessen my determination, or make me change my mode of proceeding. I resolutely pushed her before me. The husband stood at the head of the stairs and my object was to carry her down to the lower story. The stairs were narrow, and by keeping up a good watch, I contrived to force him to give ground, using his spouse as a sort of battering-*ram* — not to perpetrate a pun at the expense of the genders — which, I happened to know, had always been successful in making him give ground on all previous occasions. His habitual deference for the dame, assisted me in my purpose. Step by step, however, he disputed my advance; but I was finally successful; without any injury beyond that which had been inflicted by the talons of the fair lady, and perhaps a single and slight stroke upon the shoulder from the club of her husband, I succeeded in landing her upon the lower flat in safety. Beyond a squeeze or two, which the exigency of the case made something more affectionate than any I should have been otherwise pleased to bestow upon her, she suffered no hurt at my hands.

But, though willing to release her, she was not so willing herself to be released. When I set her free, she flew at me with cat-like intrepidity; and I found her a much more difficult customer than her husband. Him I soon baffled. A moment sufficed to grapple with him and wrench the stick from his hands, and then, with a moderate exercise of agility, I contrived to spring up the stairway which I had just descended, regain the chamber, and secure the door, before they could overtake or annoy me with their further movements. My wife's aunt, meanwhile, had been busy with her restoratives. Julia was now recovering from the fainting fit; and I had the satisfaction of hearing from one of the servants that the baffled enemy had gone off in a fury that made their departure seem a flight rather than a mere retreat.

I should have treated the whole event with indifference — their rage and their regard equally — but for my suffering and sensitive wife. Wronged as she had been, and so persecuted as to render all her subsequent conduct justifiable, she yet forgot none of her filial obligations; and, in compliance with her earnest entreaties, I had already, the very day after this conflict, prepared an elaborate and respectful epistle to both father and mother, when an event took place of startling solemnity, which was calculated to subdue my anger, and make the feelings of my wife, if possible, more accessible than ever to the influences of fear and sorrow. Only three days from our marriage had elapsed, when her father was stricken speechless in the street. He was carried home for dead. I have already hinted that, months before, and just after the threatened discovery of those fraudulent measures by which he lost his fortune, his mind had become singularly enfeebled; his memory failing, and all his faculties of judgment — never very strong — growing capricious, or else obtuse and unobserving. These were the symptoms of a rapid physical change, the catastrophe of which was at hand. How far the excitement growing out of his daughter's flight and marriage may have precipitated this result, is problematical. It may be said, in this place, that my wife's mother charged it all to my account. I was pronounced the murderer of her husband. On this head I did not reproach myself. It was necessary, however, that a reconciliation should take place between the father and his child. To this I had, of course, no sort of objection. But it will scarce be believed that the miserable woman, her mother, opposed herself to their meeting with the utmost violence of her character. Nothing but the outcry of the family and all its friends — including the excellent physician whose secret services had contributed so much toward my happiness — compelled her to give way, though still ungraciously, to the earnest entreaty of her daughter for permission to see her father before he died! and even then, by the deathbed of the unhappy and almost unconscious man, she recommenced the scene of abuse and bitter reproach, which, however ample the reader and hearer may have already found it, it appears she had left unfinished. It was in the midst of a furious tirade, directed against myself, chiefly, and Julia, in part, that the spasms of death, unperceived by the mother, passed over the contracted muscles of the father's face. The bitter speech of the blind woman — blind of heart — was actually finished after death had given the final blow to the victim. Of this she had no suspicion, until instructed by the piercing shrieks of her daughter, who fell swooning upon the corse before her.

CHAPTER XV.

HONEYMOON PERIOD.

It was supposed by Julia and certain of her friends that an event so solemn, so impressive, and so unexpected, as the death of Mr. Clifford, would reasonably affect the mind of his widow; and the concessions which I had meditated to address to herself and her late husband were now so varied as to apply solely to herself. I took considerable pains in preparing my letter, with the view to soften her prejudices and asperities, as well as to convince her reason. There was one suggestion which Julia was disposed to insist on, to which, however, I was singularly averse. In the destitution of Mrs. Clifford, her diminished and still diminishing resources, not to speak of her loneliness, she thought that I ought to tender her a home with us. Had she been any other than the captious, cross-grained creature that she was—had her misfortunes produced only in part their legitimate and desirable effects of subduing her perversity—I should have had no sort of objection. But I knew her imperious and unreasonable nature; and I may here add, that, by this time, I knew something of my own: I was a man of despotic character. The constant conflicts which I had had from boyhood, resulting as they had done in my frequent successes and final triumph, had, naturally enough, made me dictatorial. Sanguine in temperament, earnest in character, resolute in impulse, I was necessarily arbitrary in mood. It was not likely that Mrs. Clifford would forget her waywardnesses, and it was just as unreasonable that I should submit to her insolences. Besides, one's home ought to be a very sacred place. It is necessary that the peace there should compensate and console for the strifes without. To hope for this in any household where there is more than one master, would be worse than idle. Nay, even if there were peace, the chances are still great that there would be some lack of propriety. Domestic regulations would become inutile. Children and servants would equally fail of duty and improvement under conflicting authorities; and all the sweet social harmonies of family would be jarred away by misunderstandings if not bickerings, leading to coldness, suspicion, and irremediable jealousies. These things seemed to threaten me from the first moment when Julia submitted to me her desire that her mother should be invited to take up her abode with us. I reasoned with her against it; suggested all the grounds of objection which I really felt; and reviewed at length the long history of our connection from my childhood up, which had been distinguished by her constant hostility and hate. "How," I asked, "can it be hoped that there will be any change for the better now? She is the same woman, I the same man! It is not reasonable to think that the result of our reunion will be other than it has been." But Julia implored.

"I know what you say is reasonable—is just; but, dear Edward, she is my mother, and she is alone."

I yielded to her wishes. Could I else? My letter to her mother concluded with a respectful entreaty that she would take apartments in our dwelling, and a chair at our table, and lessen, to this extent, the expenses of her own establishment.

"What!" exclaimed the frenzied woman to Julia's aunt, to whom the charge of presenting the communication was committed—"what! eat the bread of that insolent and ungrateful wretch? Never! never!"

She flung the epistle from her with disdain; and, to confess a truth, though, on Julia's account, I should have wished a reconciliation, I was by no means sorry, on my own, that such was her ultimatum. I gave myself little further concern about this foolish person, and was happy to see that in a short time my wife appeared to recover from the sadness and stupor which the death of her father and the temper of her mother had naturally induced. The truth is, she had, for so long a period previously to her marriage, suffered from the persecutions of the latter, and moaned over the shame and imbecility of the former, that her present situation was one of great relief, and, for a while, of comparative happiness.

We lived in a pleasant cottage in the suburbs. A broad and

placid lake spread out before our dwelling; and its tiny billows, under the pressure of the sweet southwestern breezes, beat almost against our very doors. Green and shady groves environed us on three sides, and sheltered us from the intrusive gaze of the highway; and never was a brighter collection of flowers and blossoms clustered around any habitation of hope and happiness before. I rented the cottage on moderate terms, and furnished it neatly, but simply, as became my resources. All things considered, the prospect was fair and promising before us. Julia had few toils, and ample leisure for painting and music, for both of which she had considerable taste; for the former art, in particular, she possessed no small talent.

Our city, indeed, seemed one peculiarly calculated for these arts. Our sky was blue—deeply, beautifully blue; our climate mild and delightful. Our people were singularly endowed with the genius for graceful and felicitous performances. Music was an ordinary attribute of the great mass; and in no community under the sun was there such an overflow of talent in painting and sculpture. It was the grand error of our wise heads to fancy that our city could be made one of great trade; and, in a vain struggle to give it some commercial superiority over its neighbor communities, the wealth of the people was thrown away upon projects that yielded nothing; and the arts were left neglected in a region which might have been made—and might still be made—if not exclusively, at least pre-eminently their own. The ordinary look of the women was beauty, the ordinary accent was sweetness. The soft moonlight evenings were rendered doubly harmonious by the tender tinkling of the wandering guitar, or the tones of the plaintive flute; while, from every third dwelling, rose the more stately but scarcely sweeter melodies stricken by pliant fingers from the yielding soul of the divine piano. The tastes even of the mechanic were refined by this language, the purest in which passion ever speaks; and an ambition—the result of the highest tone of aristocratic influence upon society—prompted his desires to purposes and a position to which in other regions he is not often permitted to aspire. These influences were assisted by the peculiar location of our city—by its suburban freedom from all closeness; its innumerable gardens, the appanage of every household; its piazzas, verandahs, porches; its broad and minstrel-wooing rivers; and the majestic and evergreen forests, which grew and gathered around us on every hand. If ever there was a city intended by nature more particularly than another for the abodes and the offices of art, it was ours. It will become so yet: the mean, money-loving soul of trade can not always keep it from its destinies. We may never see it in our day; but so surely as we live, and as it shall live, will it become an Athens in our land—a city of empire by the sea, renowned for genius and taste—and the chosen retreat of muses, younger and more vigorous, and not less lovely, than the old!

Julia was in a very high degree impregnated with the taste and desire for art which seemed so generally the characteristic of our people. I speak not now of the degree of skill which she possessed. Her teacher was a foreigner, and a mere mechanic; but, while he taught her only the ordinary laws of painting, her natural endowment wrought more actively in favor of her performances. She soon discovered how much she could learn from the little which her teacher knew; and when she made this discovery, she ceased to have any use for his assistance. Books, the study of the old masters, and such of the new as were available to her, served her infinitely more in the prosecution of her efforts; and these I stimulated by all means in my power: for I esteemed her natural endowments to be very high, and very well knew how usual it is for young ladies, after marriage, to give up those tastes and accomplishments which had distinguished and heightened their previous charms. It was quite enough that I admired the art, and tasked her to its pursuit, to make her cling to it with alacrity and love. We wandered together early in the morning and at the coming on of evening, over all the sweet, enticing scenes which were frequent in our suburbs. Environed by two rivers, wide and clear, with deep forests beyond—a broad bay opening upon the sea in front—lovely islands of gleaming sand, strewn at pleasant intervals, seeming, beneath the transparent moonlight, the chosen places of retreat for naiads from the deep and fairies from the grove—there was no lack of objects to delight the eye and woo the pencil to its performances. Besides, never was blue sky, and gold-and-purple sunset, more frequent, more rich, more shifting in its shapes and colors, from beauty to superior beauty, than in our latitude. The eye naturally turned up to it with a sense of hunger; the mind naturally felt the wish to record such hues and aspects for the use of venerating love; and the eager spirit, beginning to fancy the vision wrought according to its own involuntary wish, seemed spontaneously to cry aloud, in the language of the artist, on whom the consciousness of genius was breaking with a sun-burst for the first time, "I, too, am a painter!"

Julia's studio was soon full of beginnings. Fragmentary landscapes were all about her. Like most southrons, she did not like to finish. There is an impatience of toil—of its duration at least—in the southern mind, which leaves it too frequently unperforming. This is a natural characteristic of an excitable people. People easily moved are always easily diverted from their objects. People of very vivid fancy are also very capricious. There is yet another cause for the non-performance of the southern mind—its fastidiousness. In a high state of social refinement, the standards of taste become so very exacting, that the mind prefers not to attempt, rather than to offend that critical judgment which it feels to be equally active in its analysis and rigid in its requisitions. Genius and ambition must be independent of such restraints. "Be bold, be bold, be bold!" is the language of encouragement in Spenser; and when he says, at the end, "Be not too bold," we are to consider the qualification as simply a quiet caution not to allow proper courage to rush into rashness and insane license. The *genius* that suffers itself to be fettered by the *precise*, will perhaps learn how to polish marble, but will never make it live, and will certainly never live very long itself!

With books and music, painting and flowers, we passed the happy moments of the honeymoon. I yielded as little of myself and my mind to my office and clients, in that period, as I possibly could. My cottage was my paradise. My habits, as might be inferred from my history, were singularly domestic. Doomed, as I had been, from my earliest years, to know neither friends nor parents; isolated, in my infancy, from all those tender ties which impress upon the heart, for all succeeding years, tokens of the most endearing affection; denied the smiles of those who yet filled my constant sight—my life was a long yearning for things of love—for things to love! While the struggle continued between Julia's parents and myself, though confiding in her love, I had yet no confidence in my own hope to realize and to secure it. Now that it was mine—mine, at last—I grew uxorious in its contemplation. Like the miser, I had my treasure at home, and I hastened home to survey it with precisely the same doubts, and hopes, and fears, which the disease of avarice prompts in the unhappy heart of its victim. To this disease, in chief, I have to attribute all my future sorrows; but the time is not yet for that. It is my joys now that I have to contemplate and describe. How I dwelt, and how I dreamed! how I seemed to tread on air, in the unaccustomed fullness of my spirit! how my whole soul, given up to the one pursuit, I fondly fancied had secured its object! I fancied—nay, for the time, I was happy! Surely, I was happy!

CHAPTER XVI.

THE HAPPY SEASON.

SURELY, I then was happy! I can not deceive myself as to the character of those brief Eden moments of security and peace. Even now, lone as I appear in the sight of others—degraded as I feel myself—even now I look back on our low white cottage, by the shores of that placid lake—its little palings gleaming sweetly through its dense green foliage—recall those happy, halcyon days, and feel that we both, for the time, had attained the secret—the secret worth all the rest—of an enjoyment actually felt, and quite as full, flush, and satisfactory, as it had seemed in the perspective. Possession had taken nothing of the *gusto* from hope. Truth had not impaired a single beauty of the ideal. I looked in Julia's face at morning when I awakened, and her loveliness did not fade. My lips, that drank sweetness from hers, did not cease to believe the sweetness to be there—as pure, as warm, as full of richness, as when I had only dreamed of their perfections. Our days and nights were pure, and gentle, and fond. One twenty-four hours shall speak for all.

When we rose at morning, we prepared for a ramble, either into the woods, or along the banks of the lovely river that lay west of, and at a short distance only from, our dwelling. There, wandering, as the sun rose, we imparted to each other's eyes the several objects of beauty which his rising glance betrayed. Sometimes we sat beneath a tree, while she hurriedly sketched a clump of woods, the winding turn of the shore, its occasional crescent form or abrupt headland, as they severally appeared in a new light, and at a happy moment of time, beneath our vision. The songs of pleasant birds allured us on; the sweet scent of pines and myrtle refreshed us; and a gay, wholesome, hearty spirit was awakened in our mutual bosoms, as thus, day after day, while, like the day, our hearts were in their first youth, we resorted to the ever-fresh mansions of the sovereign Nature. This habit produces purity of feeling, and continues the habit in its earliest simplicity. The childlike laws which it encourages and strengthens are those which virtue most loves, and which strained forms of society are the first to overthrow. The pure tastes of youth are those which are always most dear to humanity; and love is easy of access, and peace not often a stranger to the mind, where these tastes preserve their ascendency.

My profession was something at variance with these tastes and feelings. The very idea of law, which presupposes the frequent occurrence of injustice, engenders, by its practice, a habit of suspicion. To throw doubt upon the fact, and defeat and prevent convictions of the probable, are habits which lawyers soon acquire. This is natural from the daily encounter with bad and striving men — men who employ the law as an instrument by which to evade right, or inflict wrong; and, this apart, the acute mind loves, for its own sake, the very exercise of doubt, by which ingenuity is put in practice, and an adroit discrimination kept constantly at work.

I was saved, however, from something of this danger. The injustice which I had been subjected to, in my own boyhood, had filled me with the keenest love for the right. The idea of injustice aroused my sternest feelings of resistance. I had adopted the law as a profession with something of a patriotic feeling. I felt that I could make it an instrument for putting down the oppressor, the wrong-doer — for asserting right, and maintaining innocence! I had my admiration, too, at that period, of that logical astuteness, that wonderful tenacity of hold and pursuit, and discrimination of attribute and subject, which distinguish this profession beyond all others, and seem to confirm the assumption made in its behalf, by which it has been declared the perfection of human reason. It will not be subtracting anything from this estimate, if I express my conviction, founded upon my own experience, that, though such may be the character of the law as an abstract science, it deserves no such encomium as it is ordinarily practised. Lawyers are too commonly profound only in the technicalities of the profession; and a very keen study and acquaintance with these —certainly a too great reliance upon them, and upon the dicta of other lawyers—leads to a dreadful departure from elementary principles, and a most woful disregard, if not ignorance, of those profounder sources of knowledge without which laws multiply at the expense of reason, and not in support of it; and lawyers may be compared to those ignorant captains to whom good ships are intrusted, who rely upon continual sounding to grope their way along the accustomed shores. Let them once leave the shores, and get beyond the reach of their plummets, and the good ship must owe its safety to fortune and the favor of the winds, for further skill is none.

I did not find the practice of the law affect my taste for domestic pleasures; on the contrary, it stimulated and preserved them. After toiling a whole morning in the courts, it was a sweet reprieve to be allowed to hurry off to my quiet cottage, and hear the one dear voice of my household, and examine the quiet pictures. These never stunned me with clamors; I was never pestered by them to determine the *meum et tuum* between noisy disputants, neither of whom is exactly right. There, my eye could repose on the sweetest scenes—scenes of beauty and freshness—the shady verdure of the woods, the rich variety of flowers, and pure, calm, transparent waters, hallowed by the meek glances of the matron moon. No creature could have been more gentle than my wife. She met me with a composed smile, equally bright and meek. I never heard a complaint from her lips. The evils of which other men complain —the complaints about servants, scoldings about delay or dinner—never reached my ears. The kindest solicitude that, in my fatigue, or amid the toils of a business of which wives can know little, and for which they make too little allowance, there should be nothing at home to make me irritable or give me disquiet, distinguished equally her sense and her affection. If it became her duty to communicate any unpleasant intelligence— any tidings which might awaken anger or impatience—she carefully waited for the proper time, when the excitement of my blood was overcome, and repose of blood and brain had naturally brought about a kindred composure of mind.

Our afternoons were usually spent in the shade of the garden or piazza. Sometimes, I sat by her while she was sketching. At others, she helped me to dress and train my garden-vines. Now and then we renewed our rambles of the morning, heedfully observing the different aspects of the same scenes and objects, which had then delighted us, under the mellowing smiles of the sun at its decline. With books, music, and chess, our evenings passed away without our consciousness; and day melted into night, and night departed and gave place to the new-born day, as quietly as if life had, in truth, become to us a great instrument of harmony, which bore us over the smooth seas of Time, to the gentle beating of fairy and unseen minstrelsy. Truly, then, we were two happy children. The older children of this world, stimulated by stronger tastes and more lofty indulgences, may smile at the infantile simplicity of such resources and modes of enjoyment. They were childish, but perhaps not the less wise for that. Infancy lies very near to heaven. Childhood is a not unfit study for angels; and happy were it for us could we maintain the hearts and the hopes of that innocent period for a longer day within our bosoms. In our world we grow too fast, too presumptuously. We live on too rich food, moral and intellectual. The artifices of our tastes prove most fatally the decline of our reason. But, for us—we two linked hearts, so segregated from all beside—we certainly lived the lives of children for a while. But we were not to live thus always. In some worldly respects, *I* was still a child: I cared little for its pomps, its small honors, its puny efforts, its tinselly displays. But I had vices of mind—vices of my own—sufficient to embitter the social world where all seems now so sweet—where all, in truth, *was* sweet, and pure, and worthy—and which might, under other circumstances, have been kept so to the last. I am now to describe a change!

CHAPTER XVII.

THE EVIL PRINCIPLE.

HERETOFORE, I have spoken of the blind hearts of others—of Mr. Clifford and his wilful wife—I have yet said little to show the blindness of my own. This task is now before me, and, with whatever reluctance, the exhibition shall resolutely be made. I have described a couple newly wed—eminently happy—blessed with tolerable independence—resources from without and within—dwelling in the smiles of Heaven, and not uncheered by the friendly countenance of man. I am to display the cloud, which hangs small at first, a mere speck, but which is to grow to a gloomy tempest that is to swallow up the loveliness of the sky, and blacken with gloom and sorrow the fairest aspects of the earth. I am to show the worm in the bud which is to bring blight—the serpent in the garden which is to spoil the Eden. Wo, beyond all other woes, that this serpent should be engendered in one's own heart, producing its blindness, and finally working its bane! Yet, so it is! The story is a painful one to tell; the task is one of self-humiliation. But the truth may inform others—may warn, may strengthen, may save—before their hearts shall be utterly given up to that blindness which must end in utter desperation and irretrievable overthrow.

If the reader has not been utterly unmindful of certain moral suggestions which have been thrown out passingly in my previous narrative, he will have seen that, constitutionally, I am of an ardent, impetuous temper—an active mind, ready, earnest, impatient of control—seeking the difficult for its own sake, and delighting in the conquest which is unexpected by others.

Such a nature is usually frank and generous. It believes in

the affections — it depends upon them. It freely gives its own, but challenges the equally free and spontaneous gift of yours in return. It has little faith in the things which fill the hearts of the mere worldlings. Worldly honors may delight it, but not worldly toys. It has no veneration for gewgaws. The shows of furniture and of dress it despises. The gorgeous equipage is an encumbrance to it; the imposing jewel it would not wear, lest it might subtract something from that homage which it prefers should be paid to the wearer. It is all selfish — thoroughly selfish — but not after the world's fashion of selfishness. It hoards nothing, and gives quite as much as it asks. What does it ask? What? It asks for love — devoted attachment; the homage of the loved one and the friends; the implicit confidence of all around it! Ah! can anything be more exacting? Cruelly exacting, if it be not worthy of that it asks!

Imagine such a nature, denied from the beginning! The parents of its youth are gone! — the brother and the sister — the father and the friend! It is destitute, utterly, of these! It is also destitute of those resources of fortune which are supposed to be sufficient to command them. It is thrown upon the protection, the charge of strangers. Not strangers — no! From strangers, perhaps, but little could be expected. It is thrown upon the care of relatives — a father's brother! Could the tie be nearer? Not well! But it had been better if strangers had been its guardians. Then it might have learned to endure more patiently. At least, it would have felt less keenly the pangs inflicted by neglect, contumely, injustice. In this situation it grows up, like some sapling torn from its parent forest, its branches hacked off, its limbs lacerated! It grows up in a stranger-soil. The sharp winds assail it from every quarter. But still it lives — it grows. It grows wildly, rudely, ungracefully; but it is strong and tough, in consequence of its exposure and its trials. Its vitality increases with every collision which shakes and rends it; until, in the pathetic language of relatives unhappily burdened with such encumbrances, "it seems impossible to kill it!"

I will not say that mine tried to kill me, but I do say that they took precious little care that I was not killed. The effect upon my body was good, however — the effect of their indifference. This roughening process is a part of physical training which very few parents understand. It is essential—should be insisted on—but it must not be accompanied with a moral roughening, which forces upon the mind of the pupil the conviction that the ordeal is meant for his destruction rather than for his good. There will be a recoil of the heart—a cruel recoil from the humanities—if such a conviction once fills the mind. It was this recoil which I felt! With warm affections seeking for objects of love—with feelings of hope and veneration, imploring for altars to which to attach themselves—I was commanded to go alone. The wilderness alone was open to me: what wonder if my heart grew wild and capricious even as that of the savage who dwells only amid their cheerless recesses? With a smile judiciously bestowed—with a kind word, a gentle tone, an occasional voice of earnest encouragement—my uncle and aunt might have fashioned my heart at their pleasure. I should have been as clay in the hands of the potter—a pliant willow in the grasp of the careful trainer. A nature constituted like mine is, of all others, the most flexible; but it is also, of all others, the most resisting and incorrigible. Approach it with a judicious regard to its affections, and you do with it what you please. Let it but fancy that it is the victim of your injustice, however slight, and the war is an interminable one between you!

Thus did I learn the first lessons of suspiciousness. They attended me to the schoolhouse; they governed and made me watchful there. The schoolhouse, the play-places—the very regions of earnest faith and unlimited confidence—produced no such effects in me. They might have done so, had I ceased, on going to school, to see my relatives any longer. But the daily presence of my uncle and aunt, with their system of continued injustice, at length rendered my suspicious moods habitual. I became shy. I approached nobody, or approached them with doubt and watchfulness. I learned, at the earliest period, to look into character, to analyze conduct, to pry into the mysterious involutions of the working minds around me. I traced, or fancied that I traced, the performance to the unexpressed and secret motive in which it had its origin. I discovered, or believed that I discovered, that the world was divided into banditti and hypocrites. At that day I made little allowance for the existence of that larger class than all, who happen to be the victims. Unless this were the larger class, the other two must very much and very rapidly diminish. My infant philosophy did not carry me very deeply into the recesses of my own heart. It was enough that I felt some of its dearest rights to be outraged — I did not care to inquire whether it was altogether right itself.

At length, there was a glimpse of dawn amid all this darkness. The world was not altogether evil. All hearts were not shut against me; and in the sweet smiles of Julia Clifford, in her kind attentions, soothing assurances, and fond entreaties, there was opportunity, at last, for my feelings to overflow. Like a mountain-stream long pent up, which at length breaks through its confinements, my affections rushed into the grateful channel which her pliant heart afforded me. They were wild, and strong, and devoted, in proportion to their long denial and restraint. Was it not natural enough that I should love with no ordinary attachment — that my love should be an impetuous torrent — all-devoted — struggling, striving — rushing only in the one direction — believing, in truth, that there was none other in the world in which to run?

This was a natural consequence of the long sophistication of my feelings. I knew nothing of the world — of society. I had shared in none of its trusts; I had only felt its exactions. Like some country-boy, or country-girl, for the first time brought into the great world, I surrendered myself wholly to the first gratified impulse. I made no conditions, no qualifications. I set all my hopes of heart upon a single cast of the die, and did not ask what might be the consequences if the throw was unfortunate.

One of the good effects of a free communication of the young with society is, to lessen the exacting nature of the affections. People who live too much to themselves — in their own centre, and for their own single objects — become fastidious to disease. They ask too much from their neighbors. Willing to surrender their *own* affections at a glance, they fancy the world wanting in sensibility when they find that their readiness in this respect fails to produce a corresponding readiness in others. This is the natural history of that enthusiasm which is thrown back upon itself and is chilled by denial. The complaint of coldness and selfishness against the world is very common among very young or very inexperienced men. The world gets a bad character, simply because it refuses to lavish its affections along the highways—simply because it is cautious in giving its trusts, and expects proofs of service and actual sympathy rather than professions. Men like myself, of a warm, impetuous nature, complain of the heartlessness of mankind. They fancy themselves peculiarly the victims of an unkind destiny in this respect; and finally cut their throats in a moment of frenzy, or degenerate into a cynicism that delights in contradictions, in sarcasms, in self-torture, and the bitterest hostility to their neighbors.

Society itself is the only and best corrective of this unhappy disposition. The first gift to the young, therefore, should be the gift of society. By this word society, however, I do not mean a set, a clique, a pitiable little circle. Let the sphere of movement be sufficiently extended—as large as possible—that the means of observation and thought may be sufficiently comprehensive, and no influences from one man or one family shall be suffered to give the bias to the immature mind and inexperienced judgment. In society like this, the errors, prejudices, weaknesses, of one man, are corrected by a totally opposite form of character in another. The mind of the youth hesitates. Hesitation brings circumspection, watchfulness; watchfulness, discrimination; discrimination, choice; and a capacity to choose implies the attainment of a certain degree of deliberateness and judgment with which the youth may be permitted to go upon his way, supposed to be provided for in the difficult respect of being able henceforward to take care of himself.

I had no society—knew nothing of society—saw it at a distance, under suspicious circumstances, and was myself an object of its suspicion. Its attractions were desirable to me, but seemed unattainable. It required some sacrifices to obtain its *entrée*, and these sacrifices were the very ones which my independence would not allow me to make. My independence was my treasure, duly valued in proportion to the constant strife by which it was assailed. I had that! *That* could not be taken from me. *That* kept me from sinking into the slave, the tool, the sycophant, perhaps the brute; *that* prompted me to hard study in secret places; *that* strengthened my heart, when, desolate and striving against necessity, I saw nothing of the smiles of society, and felt nothing of the bounties of life. Then came my final emancipation—my success—my triumph! My independence was assailed no longer. My talents were no longer doubted or denied. My reluctant neighbors sent in their adhesion. My uncle forbore his sneers. Lastly, and now—Julia was mine! My heart's desires were all gratified as completely as my mind's ambition!

Was I happy? The inconsiderate mind will suppose this very probable—will say, I should be. But evil seeds that are planted in the young heart grow up with years—not so rapidly or openly as to offend—and grow to be poisonous weeds with maturity. My feelings were too devoted, too concentrative, too all-absorbing, to leave me happy, even when they seemed gratified. The man who has but a single jewel in the world, is very apt to labor under a constant apprehension of its loss. He who knows but one object of attachment—whose heart's devotion turns evermore but to one star of all the countless thousands in the heavens—wo is he, if that star be shrouded from his gaze in the sudden overflow of storms!—still more wo is he, when that star withdraws, or seems to withdraw, its corresponding gaze, or turns it elsewhere upon another worshipper! See you not the danger which threatened me? See you not that, never having been beloved before—never having loved but the one—I loved that one with all my heart, with all my soul, with all my strength; and required from that one the equal love of heart, soul, strength? See you not that my love—linked with impatient mind, imperious blood, impetuous enthusiasm, and suspicious fear—was a devotion exacting as the grave—searching as fever—as jealous of the thing whose worship it demands as God is said to be of ours?

Mine was eminently a jealous heart! On this subject of jealousy, men rarely judge correctly. They speak of Othello as jealous—Othello, one of the least jealous of all human natures! Jealousy is a quality that needs no cause. It makes its own cause. It will find or make occasion for its exercise, in the most innocent circumstances. The *proofs* that made

Othello wretched and revengeful, were sufficient to have deceived any jury under the sun. He had proofs. He had a strong ease to go upon. It would have influenced any judgment. He did not seek or find these proofs for himself. He did not wish to find them. He was slow to see them. His was not jealousy. His error was that of pride and self-esteem. He was outraged in both. His mistake was in being too prompt of action in a case which admitted of deliberation. This was the error of a proud man, a soldier, prompt to decide, prompt to act, and to punish if necessary. But never was human character less marked by a jealous mood than that of Othello. His great self-esteem was, of itself, a sufficient security against jealousy. Mine might have been, had it not been so terribly diseased by ill-training.

CHAPTER XVIII.

PRESENTIMENTS.

WITHOUT apprehending the extent of my own weakness, the forms that it would take, or the tyrannies that it would inflict, I was still not totally uninformed on the subject of my peculiar character; and, fearing then rather that I might pain my wife by some of its wanton demonstrations, than that she would ever furnish me with an occasion for them, I took an opportunity, a few evenings after our marriage, to suggest to her the necessity of regarding my outbreaks with an indulgent eye.

My heart had been singularly softened by the most touching associations. We sat together in our piazza, beneath a flood of the richest and balmiest moonlight, screened only from its silvery blaze by interposing masses of the woodbine, mingled with shoots of oleander, arbor-vitæ, and other shrub-trees. The mild breath of evening sufficed only to lift quiveringly their green leaves and glowing blossoms, to stir the hair upon our cheeks, and give to the atmosphere that wooing freshness which seems so necessary a concomitant of the moonlight. The hand of Julia was in mine. There were few words spoken between us; love has its own sufficing language, and is content with that consciousness that all is right which implores no other assurances. Julia had just risen from the piano: we had both been touched with a deeper sense of the thousand harmonies in nature, by listening to those of Rossini; and now, gazing upon some transparent, fleecy, white clouds that were slowly pressing forward in the path of the moonlight, as if in duteous attendance upon some maiden queen, our mutual minds were busied in framing pictures from the fine yet fantastic forms that glowed, gathering on our gaze. I felt the hand of Julia trembling in my own. Her head sank upon my shoulder; I felt a warm drop fall from her eyes upon my hand, and exclaimed—

"Julia, you weep! wherefore do you weep, dear wife?"

"With joy, my husband! My heart is full of joy. I am so happy, I can only weep. Ah! tears alone speak for the true happiness."

"Ah! would it last, Julia—would it last!"

"Oh, doubt not that it will last. Why should it not? What have we to fear?"

Mine was a serious nature. I answered sadly, if not gloomily:—

"Because it is a joy of life that we feel, and it must share the vicissitudes of life."

"True, true, but love is a joy of eternal life as well as of this."

There was a beautiful and consoling truth in this one little sentence, which my self-absorption was too great, at the time, to suffer me to see. Perhaps even she herself was not fully conscious of the glorious and pregnant truth which lay at the bottom of what she said. Love is, indeed, not merely *a* joy of eternal life: it is *the* joy of eternal life!—its particular joy—a dim shadow of which we sometimes feel in this—pure, lasting, comparatively perfect, the more it approaches, in its performances and its desires, the divine essence, of which it is so poor a likeness. We should so live, so love, as to make the one run into the other, even as a small river runs down, through a customary channel, into the great deeps of the sea. Death should be to the affections a mere channel through which they pass into a natural, a necessary condition, where their streams flow with more freedom, and over which, harmoniously controlling, as powerful, the spirit of love broods ever with "dovelike wings outspread." I answered, still gloomily, in the customary world commonplaces:—

"We must expect the storm. It will not be moonlight always. We must look for the cloud. Age, sickness, death!—ah! do these not follow on our footsteps, ever unerring, certain always, but so often rapid? Soon, how soon, they haunt us in the happiest moments—they meet us at every corner! They never altogether leave us."

"Enough, dear husband. Dwell not upon these gloomy thoughts. Ah! why should you—*now?*'

"I will not; but there are others, Julia."

"What others? Evils?"

"Sadder evils yet than these."

"Oh, no!—I hope not."

"Coldness of the once warm heart. The chill of affection in the loved one. Estrangement—indifference!—ah, Julia!"

"Impossible, Edward! This can not, *must* not be, with us. You do not think that I could be cold to you; and you—ah! surely *you* will never cease to love me?"

"Never, I trust, never!"

"No! you must not—*shall* not. Oh, Edward, let me die first before such a fear should fill my breast. You I love, as none was loved before. Without your love, I am nothing. If I can not hang upon you, where can I hang?"

And she clung to me with a grasp as if life and death depended on it, while her sobs, as from a full heart, were insuppressible in spite of all her efforts.

"Fear nothing, dearest Julia: do you not believe that I love you?"

"Ah! if I did not, Edward—"

"It is with you always to make me love you. You are as completely the mistress of my whole heart as if it had acknowledged no laws but yours from the beginning."

"What am I to do, dear Edward?"

"Forbear—be indulgent—pity me and spare me!"

"What mean you, Edward?"

"That heart which is all and only yours, Julia, is yet, I am assured, a wilful and an erring heart! I feel that it is strange, wayward, sometimes unjust to others, frequently to itself. It is a cross-grained, capricious heart; you will find its exactions irksome."

"Oh, I know it better. You wrong yourself."

"No! In the solemn sweetness of this hour, dear Julia—now, while all things are sweet to our eyes, all things dear to our affections—I feel a chill of doubt and apprehension come over me. I am so happy—so unusually happy—that I can not feel sure that I am so—that my happiness will continue long. I will try, on my own part, to do nothing by which to risk its loss. But I feel that I am too wilful, at times, to be strong in keeping a resolution which is so very necessary to our mutual happiness. You must help—you must strengthen me, Julia."

"Oh, yes! but how? I will do anything—be anything."

"I am capricious, wayward; at times, full of injustice. Love me not less that I am so—that I sometimes show this waywardness to you—that I sometimes do injustice to your love. Bear with me till the dark mood passes from my heart. I have these moods, or have had them, frequently. It may be—I trust it will be—that, blessed with your love, and secure in its possession, there will be no room in my heart for such ugly feelings. But I know not. They sometimes take supreme possession of me. They seize upon me in all places. They wrap my spirit as in a cloud. I sit apart. I scowl upon those around me. I feel moved to say bitter things—to shoot darts in defiance at every glance—to envenom every sentence which I speak. These are cruel moods. I have striven vainly to shake them off. They have grown up with my growth—have shared in whatever strength I have; and, while they embitter my own thoughts and happiness, I dread that they will fling their shadow upon yours!"

She replied with gayety, with playfulness, but there was an effort in it.

"Oh, you make the matter worse than it is. I suppose all that troubles you is the blues. But you will never have them again. When I see them coming on I will sit by you and sing to you. We will come out here and watch the evening; or you shall read to me, or we will ramble in the garden—or—a thousand things which shall make you forget that there was ever such a thing in the world as sorrow."

"Dear Julia—will you do this?"

"More—everything to make you happy." And she drew me closer in her embrace, and her lips with a tremulous, almost convulsive sweetness, were pressed upon my forehead; and clinging there, oh! how sweetly did she weep!

"You will tire of my waywardness—of my exactions. Ah! I shall force you from my side by my caprice."

"You can not, Edward, if you would," she replied, in mournful accents like my own, "I have no remedy against you! I have nobody now to whom to turn. Have *I* not driven all from my side—all but you?"

It was my task to soothe her now.

"Nay, Julia, be not you sorrowful. You must continue glad and blest, that you may conquer my sullen moods, my dark presentiments. When I tell you of the evils of my temper, I tell you of occasional clouds only. Heaven forbid that they should give an enduring aspect to our heavens!"

She responded fervently to my ejaculation. I continued:—

"I have only sought to prepare you for the management of my arbitrary nature, to keep you from suffering too much, and sinking beneath its exactions. You will bear with me patiently. Forgive me for my evil hours. Wait till the storm has overblown; and find me your own, then, as much as before; and let me feel that you are still mine—that the tempest has not separated our little vessels."

"Will I not? Ah! do not fear for me, Edward. It is a happiness for me to weep here—here, in your arms. When you are sad and moody, I will come as now."

"What if I repulse you?"

"You will not—no, no!—you will not."

"But if I do? Suppose——"

"Ah! it is hard to suppose that. But I will not heed it. I will come again."

"And again?"

"And again!"

"Then you will conquer, Julia. I feel that you will conquer! You will drive out the devils. Surely, then, I shall be incorrigible no longer."

Such was my conviction then. I little knew myself.

CHAPTER XIX.

DISTRUST.

I LITTLE knew myself! This knowledge of one's self is the most important knowledge, which very few of us acquire. We seldom look into our own hearts for other objects than those which will administer to their petty vanities and passing triumphs. Could we only look there sometimes for the truth! But we are blind—blind all! In some respects I was one of the blindest!

I have given a brief glimpse of our honeymoon. Perhaps, as the world goes, the picture is by no means an attractive one. Quiet felicity forms but a small item in the sources of happiness, now-a-days, among young couples. Mine was sufficiently quiet and sufficiently humble. One would suppose that he who builds so lowly should have no reason to apprehend the hurricane. Social ambition was clearly no object with either of us. We sighed neither for the glitter nor the regards of fashionable life. Neither upon fine houses, jewels, or equipages, did we set our hearts. For the pleasures of the table I had no passion, and never was young woman so thoroughly regardless of display as Julia Clifford. To be let alone—to be suffered to escape in our own way, unharming, unharmed, through the dim avenues of life—was assuredly all that we asked from man. Perhaps—I say it without cant—this, perhaps, was all that we possibly asked from heaven. This was all that *I* asked, at least, and this was much. It was asking what had never yet been accorded to humanity. In the vain assumption of my heart I thought that my demands were moderate.

Let no man console himself with the idea that his chances of success are multiplied in degree with the insignificance, or seeming insignificance, of his aims. Perhaps the very reverse of this is the truth. He who seeks for many objects of enjoyment—whose tastes are diversified—has probably the very best prospect that some of them may be gratified. He is like the merchant whose ventures on the sea are divided among many vessels. He may lose one or more, yet preserve the main bulk of his fortune from the wreck. But he who has only a single bark—one freightage, however costly—whose whole estate is invested in the one venture—let him lose that, and all is lost. It does not matter that his loss, speaking relatively, is but little. Suppose his shipment, in general estimation, to be of small value. The loss to him is so much the greater. It was the dearer to him because of its insignificance, and being all that he had; is quite as conclusive of his ruin, as would be the foundering of every vessel which the rich merchant sent to sea.

I was one of these petty traders. I invested my whole capital of the affections in one precious jewel. Did I lose it, or simply fear its loss? Time must show. But, of a truth, I felt as the miser feels with his hoarded treasure. While I watched its richness and beauty, doubts and dread beset me. Was it safe? Everything depended upon its security. Thieves might break in and steal. Enough, for the present, to say, that much of my security, and of the security of all who, like me, possess a dear treasure, depends upon our convictions of security. He who apprehends loss, is already robbed. The reality is scarcely worse than the hourly anticipation of it.

My friends naturally became the visiters of my family. Certain of the late Mrs. Clifford's friends were also ours. Our circle was sufficiently large for those who already knew how to distinguish between the safe pleasures of a small set, and the horse-play and heartless enjoyments of fashionable jams. Were we permitted in this world to live only for ourselves, we should have been perfectly gratified had this been even less. We should have been very well content to have gone on from day to day without ever beholding the shadow of a stranger upon our threshold.

This was not permitted, however. We had a round of congratulatory visits. Among those who came, the first were the old, long-tried friends to whom I owed so much—the Edgertons. No family could have been more truly amiable than this; and

William Edgerton was the most amiable of the family. I have already said enough to persuade the reader that he was a very worthy man. He was more. He was a principled one. Not very highly endowed, perhaps, he was yet an intelligent gentleman. None could be more modest in expression—none less obtrusive in deportment—none more generous in service. The defects in his character were organic—not moral. He had no vices—no vulgarities. But his temperament was an inactive one. He was apt to be sluggish, and when excited was nervous. He was not irritable, but easily discomposed. His tastes were active at the expense of his genius. With ability, he was yet unperforming. His standards were morbidly fastidious. Fearing to fall below them, he desisted until the moment of action was passed for ever; and the feeling of his own weakness, in this respect, made him often sad, but to do him justice, never querulous.

With a person so constituted, the delicate tastes and sensibilities are like to be indulged in a very high degree. William Edgerton loved music and all the quiet arts. Painting was his particular delight. He himself sketched with great spirit. He had the happy eye for the *tout ensemble* in a fine landscape. He knew exactly how much to take in and what to leave out, in the delineation of a lovely scene. This is a happy talent for discrimination which the ordinary artist does not possess. It is the capacity which, in the case of orators and poets, informs them of the precise moment when they should stop. It is the happiest sort of judgment, since, though the artist may be neither very excellent in drawing, nor very felicitous in color, it enables him always to bestow a certain propriety on his picture which compensates, to a certain degree, for inferiority in other respects. To know how to grasp objects with spirit, and bestow them with a due regard to mutual dependence, is one of the most exquisite faculties of the landscape-painter.

William Edgerton, had he been forced by necessity to have made the art of painting his profession would have made for himself a reputation of no inferior kind. But amateur art, like amateur literature, rarely produces any admirable fruits. Complete success only attends the devotee to the muse. The worship must be exclusive at her altar; the attendance constant and unremitting. There must be no partial, no divided homage. She is a jealous mistress, like all the rest. The lover of her charms, if he would secure her smiles, must be a *professor* at her shrine. He can not come and go at pleasure. She resents such impertinence by neglect. In plain terms, the fine arts must be made a business by those who desire their favor. Like law, divinity, physic, they constitute a profession of their own; require the same diligent endeavor, close study, fond pursuit! William Edgerton loved painting, but his business was the law. He loved painting too much to love his profession. He gave too much of his time to the law to be a successful painter—too much time to painting to be a lawyer. He was nothing! At the bar he never rose a step after the first day, when, together, we appeared in our mutual maiden case; and contenting himself with the occasional execution of a landscape, sketchy and bold, but without finish, he remained in that nether-land of public consideration, unable to grasp the certainties of either pursuit at which he nevertheless was constantly striving; striving, however, with that qualified degree of effort, which, if it never could secure the prize, never could fatigue him much with the endeavor to do so.

He was perfectly delighted when he first saw some of the sketches of my wife. He had none of that little jealousy which so frequently impairs the temper and the worth of amateurs. He could admire without prejudice, and praise without reserve. He praised them. He evidently admired them. He sought every occasion to see them, and omitted none in which to declare his opinion of their merits. This, in the first pleasant season of my marriage—when the leaves were yet green and fresh upon the tree of love—was grateful to my feelings. I felt happy to discover that my judgment had not erred in the selection of my wife. I stimulated her industry that I might listen to my friend's eulogy. I suggested subjects for her pencil. I fitted up an apartment especially as a studio for her use. I bought her some fine studies, lay figures, heads in marble and plaster; and lavished, in this way, the small surplus fund which had heretofore accrued from my professional industry, and that personal frugality with which it was accompanied.

William Edgerton was now for ever at our house. He

brought his own pictures for the inspection of my wife. He sometimes painted in her studio. He devised rural and aquatic parties with sole reference to landscape scenery and delineation; and indifferent to the law always, he now abandoned himself almost entirely to those tastes which seemed to have acquired of a sudden, the strangest and the strongest impulse.

In this—at least for a considerable space of time—I saw nothing very remarkable. I knew his tastes previously. I had seen how little disposed he was to grapple earnestly with the duties of his profession; and did not conceive it surprising, that, with family resources sufficient to yield him pecuniary independence, he should surrender himself up to the luxurious influence of tastes which were equally lovely in themselves, and natural to the first desires of his mind. But when for days he was missed from his office—when the very hours of morning which are most religiously devoted by the profession to its ostensible if not earnest pursuit, were yielded up to the easel—and when, overlooking the boundaries which, according to the conventional usage, made such a course improper, he passed many of these mornings at my house, during my absence, I began to entertain feelings of disquietude.

For these I had then no name. The feelings were vague and indefinable, but not the less unpleasant. I did not fancy for a moment that I was wronged, or likely to be wronged, but I felt that he was doing wrong. Then, too, I had my misgivings of what the world would think! I did not fancy that he had any design to wrong me; but there seemed to me a cruel want of consideration in his conduct. But what annoyed me most was, that Julia should receive him at such periods. He was thoughtless, enthusiastic in art, and thoughtless, perhaps, in consequence of his enthusiasm. But I expected that she should think for both of us in such a case. Women, alone, can be the true guardians of appearances where they themselves are concerned; and it was matter of painful surprise to me that she should not have asked herself the question: "What will the neighbors think, during my husband's absence, to see a stranger, a young man, coming to visit me with periodical regularity, morning after morning?"

That she did not ask herself this question should have been a very strong argument to show me that her thoughts were all innocent. But there is a terrible truth in what Cæsar said of his wife's reputation: "She must be free from suspicion." She must not only do nothing wrong, but she must not suffer or do anything which might incur the suspicion of wrong-doing. There is nothing half so sensible to the breath of calumny, as female reputation, particularly in regions of high civilization, where women are raised to an artificial rank of respect, which obviates, in most part, the obligations of their dependence upon man, but increases, in due proportion, some of their responsibilities to him. Poor Julia had no circumspection, because she had no feeling of evil. I believe she was purity itself; I equally believe that William Edgerton was quite incapable of evil design. But when I came from my office, the first morning that he had thus passed at my house in my absence, and she told me that he had been there, and how the time had been spent, I felt a pang, like a sharp arrow, suddenly rush into my brain. Julia had no reserve in telling me this fact. It was a subject she seemed pleased to dwell upon. She narrated with the earnest, unseeing spirit of a self-satisfied child, the sort of conversation which had taken place between them—praised Edgerton's taste, his delicacy, his subdued, persuasive manners, and showed herself as utterly unsophisticated as any Swiss mountain-girl who voluntarily yields the traveller a kiss, and tells her mother of it afterward. I listened with chilled manners and a troubled mind.

"You are unwell, Edward," she remarked tenderly, approaching and throwing her arms around my neck, as she perceived the gradual gathering of that cloud upon my brows.

"Why do you think so, Julia?"

"Oh, you look so sad—almost severe, Edward, and your words are so few and cold. Have I offended you, dear Edward?"

I was confused at this direct question. I felt annoyed, ashamed. I pleaded headache in justification of my manner—it did ache, and my heart, too, but not with the ordinary pang; and I felt a warm blush suffuse my cheek, as I yielded to the first suggestion which prompted me to deceive my wife.

A large leading step was thus taken, and progress was easy afterward.

Oh! sweet spirit of confidence, thou only true saint, more needful than all, to bind the ties of kindred and affection! why art thou so prompt to fly at the approach of thy cold, dark enemy, distrust? Why dost thou yield the field with so little struggle? Why, when the things, dearest to thee of all in the world's gift—its most valued treasure, its purest, sweetest, and proudest trophies—why, when these are the stake which is to reward thy courage, thy adherence, to compensate thee for trial, to console thee for loss and outrage—why is it that thou art so ready to despond of the cause so dear to thee, and forfeit the conquest by which alone thy whole existence is made sweet. This is the very suicide of self. Fearful of loss, we forsake the prize, which we have won; and hearkening to the counsel of a natural enemy, eat of that bitter fruit which banishes for ever from our lips the sweet savor which we knew before, and without which, no savor that is left is sweet.

CHAPTER XX.

PROGRESS OF THE EVIL SPIRIT.

If I felt so deeply annoyed at the first morning visit which William Edgerton paid to my wife, what was my annoyance when these visits became habitual. I was miserable but could not complain. I was ashamed of the language of complaint on such a subject. There is something very ridiculous in the idea of a jealous husband—it has always provoked the laughter of the world; and I was one of those men who shrunk from ridicule with a more than mortal dread. Besides, I really felt no alarm. I had the utmost confidence in my wife's virtue. I had not the less confidence in that of Edgerton. But I was jealous of her deference—of her regard—for another. She was, in my eyes, as something sacred, set apart—a treasure exclusively my own! Should it be that another should come to divide her veneration with me? I was vexed that she should derive satisfaction from another source than myself. This satisfaction she derived from the visits of Edgerton. She freely avowed it.

"How amiable—how pleasant he is," she would say, in the perfect innocence of her heart; "and really, Edward, he has so much talent!"

These praises annoyed me. They were as so much wormwood to my spirit. It must be remembered that I was not myself what the world calls an amiable man. I doubt if any, even of my best friends, would describe me as a pleasant one. I was a man of too direct and earnest a temperament to establish a claim, in reasonable degree, to either of these characteristics. I was, accordingly, something blunt in my address—the tones of my voice were loud—my manner was all *empressement,* except when I was actually angry, and then it was cold, hard, dry, inflexible. I was the last person in the world to pass for an amiable. Now, Julia, on the other hand, was quiet, subdued, timorous—the tones of a strong, decided voice startled her—she shrunk from controversy—yielded always with a happy grace in anticipation of the conflict, and showed, in all respects, that nice, almost nervous organization which attaches the value of principles and morals to mere manners, and would be as much shocked, perhaps, at the expression of a rudeness, as at the commission of a sin. Not that such persons would hold a sin to be less criminal or innocuous than would we ourselves; but that they regard mere conduct as of so much more importance.

When, therefore, she praised William Edgerton for those qualities which I well knew I did not possess, I could not resist the annoyance. My self-esteem—continually active—stimulated as it had been by the constant moral strife, to which it had been subjected from boyhood—was continually apprehending disparagement. Of the purity of Julia's heart, and the chastity of her conduct, the very freedom of her utterance was conclusive. Had she felt one single improper emotion toward William Edgerton, her lips would never have voluntarily uttered his name, and never in the language of applause. On this head I had not then the slightest apprehension. It was not jealousy so much as *egoïsme* that was preying upon me. Whatever it was, however, it could not be repressed as I listened to the eulogistic language of my wife. I strove, but could not subdue, altogether, the evil spirit which was fast becoming predominant within me. Yet, though speaking under its immediate influence, I was very far from betraying its true nature. My *egoïsme* had not yet made such advances as to become reckless and incautious. I surprised her by my answer to her eulogies.

"I have no doubt he is amiable—he is amiable—but that is not enough for a man. He must be something more than amiable, if he would escape the imputation of being feeble—something more if he would be anything!"

Julia looked at me with eyes of profound and dilating astonishment. Having got thus far, it was easy to advance. The first step is half the journey in all such cases.

"William Edgerton is a little too amiable, perhaps, for his own good. It makes him listless and worthless. He will do nothing at pictures, wasting his time only when he should be at his business."

"But did I not understand you, Edward, that he was a man of fortune, and independent of his profession?" she answered timidly.

"Even that will not justify a man in becoming a trifler. No man should waste his time in painting, unless he makes a trade of it."

"But his leisure, Edward," suggested Julia, with a look of increasing timidity.

"His leisure, indeed, Julia;—but he has been here all day—day after day. If painting is such a passion with him, let him abandon law and take to it. But he should not pursue one art while professing another. It is as if a man hankered after that which he yet lacked the courage to challenge and pursue openly.'

"I don't think you love pictures as you used to, Edward," she remarked to me, after a little interval passed in unusual silence.

"Perhaps it is because I have matters of more consequence to attend to. *You* seem sufficiently devoted to them now to excuse my indifference."

"Surely, dear Edward, something I have done vexes you. Tell me, husband. Do not spare me. Say, in what have I offended?"

I had not the courage to be ingenuous. Ah! if I had!

"Nay, you have not offended," I answered hastily—"I am only worried with some unmanageable thoughts. The law, you know, is full of provoking, exciting, irritating necessities."

She looked at me with a kind but searching glance. My soul seemed to shrink from that scrutiny. My eyes sunk beneath her gaze.

"I wish I knew how to console you, Edward: to make you entirely happy. I pray for it, Edward. I thought we were always to be so happy. Did you not promise me that you would always leave your cares at your office—that our cottage should be sacred to love and peace only?"

She put her arms about my neck, and looked into my face with such a sweet, strange, persuasive smile—half mirth, half sadness—that the evil spirit was subdued within me. I clasped her fervently in my embrace, with all my old feelings of confidence and joy renewed. At this moment the servant announced Mr. Edgerton, and with a start—a movement—scarcely as gentle as it should have been, I put the fond and still beloved woman from my embrace!

CHAPTER XXI.

CHANGES OF HOME.

FROM this time my intercourse with William Edgerton was, on my part, one of the most painful and difficult constraint. I had nothing to reproach him with; no grounds whatever for quarrel; and could not, in his case—regarding the long intimacy which I had maintained with himself and father, and the obligations which were due from me to both—adopt such a manner of reserve and distance as to produce the result of indifference and estrangement which I now anxiously desired. I was still compelled to meet him—meet him, too, with an affectation of good feeling and good humor, which I soon found it, of all things in the world, the most difficult even to pretend. How much would I have given could he only have provoked me to anger on any ground—could he have given me an occasion for difference of any sort or to any degree—anything which could have justified a mutual falling off from the old intimacy! But William Edgerton was meekness and kindness itself. His confidence in me was of the most unobservant, suspicionless character; either that, or I succeeded better than I thought in the effort to maintain the external aspects of old friendship. He saw nothing of change in my deportment. He *seemed* not to see it, at least; and came as usual, or more frequently than usual, to my house, until, at length, the studio of my wife was quite as much his as hers—nay, more; for, after a brief space, whether it was that Julia saw what troubled me, or felt herself the imprudence of Edgerton's conduct, she almost entirely surrendered it to him. She was not now so often to be seen in it.

This proceeding alarmed me. I dreaded lest my secret should be discovered. I was shocked lest my wife should suppose me jealous. The feeling is one which carries with it a sufficiently severe commentary, in the fact that most men are heartily ashamed to be thought to suffer from it. But, if it vexed me to think that she should know or suspect the truth, how much more was I troubled lest it should be seen or suspected by others! This fear led to new circumspection. I now affected levities of demeanor and remark; studiously absented myself from home of an evening, leaving my wife with Edgerton, or any other friend who happened to be present; and, though I began no practices of profligacy, such as are common to young scapegraces in all times, I yet, to some moderate extent, affected them.

A tone of sadness now marked the features of my wife. There was an expression of anxiety in her countenance, which, amid all her previous sufferings, I had never seen there before. She did not complain; but sometimes, when we sat alone together, I reading, perhaps, and she sewing, she would drop her work in her lap, and sigh suddenly and deeply, as if the first shadows of the upgathering gloom were beginning to cloud her young and innocent spirit, and force her apprehensions into utterance. This did not escape me, but I read its signification, as witches are said to read the Bible, backward. A gloomier fancy filled my brain as I heard her unconscious sigh.

"It is the language of regret. She laments our marriage. She could have found another, surely, who could have made her happier. Perhaps, had Edgerton and herself known each other intimately before!—"

Dark, perverse imagining! It crushed me. I felt, I can not tell, what bitterness. Let no one suppose that I endured less misery than I inflicted. The miseries of the damned could not have exceeded mine in some of the moments when these cruel conjectures filled my mind. Then followed some such proofs as as these of the presence of the Evil One:—

"You sigh, Julia. You are unhappy."

"Unhappy? no, dear Edward, not unhappy! What makes you think so?"

"What makes you sigh, then?"

"I do not know. I am certainly not unhappy. Did I sigh, Edward?"

"Yes, and seemingly from the very bottom of your heart. I

fear, Julia, that you are not happy; nay, I am sure you are not! I feel that I am not the man to make you happy. I am a perverse—"

"Nay, Edward, now you speak so strangely, and your brow is stern, and your tones tremble! What can it be afflicts you? You are angry at something, dear Edward. Surely, it can not be with me."

"And if it were, Julia, I am afraid it would give you little concern."

"Now, Edward, you are cruel. You do me wrong. You do yourself wrong. Why should you suppose that it would give me little concern to see you angry? So far from this, I should regard it as the greatest misery which I had to suffer. Do not speak so, dearest Edward—do not fancy such things. Believe me, my husband, when I tell you that I know nothing half so dear to me as your love—nothing that I would not sacrifice with a pleasure, to secure, to preserve *that!*"

"Ah! would you give up painting?"

"Painting! that were a small sacrifice! I worked at it only because you used to like it."

"What, you think I do not like it now?"

"I *know* you do not."

"But you paint still?"

"No! I have not handled brush or pencil for a week. Mr. Edgerton was reproaching me only yesterday for my neglect."

"Ah, indeed! Well, you promised him to resume, did you not? He is a rare persuader! He is so amiable, so mild—you could not well resist."

It was from her face that I formed a rational conjecture of the expression that must have appeared in mine. Her eyes dilated with a look of timid wonder, not unmixed with apprehension. She actually shrunk back a space; then, approaching, laid her hand upon my wrist, as she exclaimed:—

"God of heaven, Edward, what strange thought is in your bosom? what is the meaning of that look? Look not so again, if you would not kill me!"

I averted my face from hers, but without speaking. She threw her arms around my neck.

"Do not turn away from me, Edward. Do not, do not, I

entreat you! You must not—no! not till you tell me what is troubling you—not till I soothe you, and make you love me again as much as you did at first."

When I turned to her again, the tears—hot, scalding tears—were already streaming down my cheeks.

"Julia, God knows I love you! Never woman yet was more devotedly loved by man! I love you too much—too deeply—too entirely! Alas, I love nothing else!"

"Say not that you love me too much—that can not be! Do I not love you—you only, you altogether? Should I not have your whole love in return?"

"Ah, Julia! but my love is a convulsive eagerness of soul—a passion that knows no limit! It is not that my heart is entirely yours: it is that it is yours with a frenzied desperation. There is a fanaticism in love as in religion. My love is that fanaticism. It burns—it commands—where yours would but soothe and solicit."

"But is mine the less true—the less valuable for this, dear Edward?"

"No, perhaps not! It may be even more true, more valuable; it may be only less intense. But fanaticism, you know, is exacting—nothing more so. It permits no half-passion, no moderate zeal. It insists upon devotion like its own. Ah, Julia, could you but love as I do!"

"I love you all, Edward, all that I can, and as it belongs to my nature to love. But I am a woman, and a timid one, you know. I am not capable of that wild passion which you feel. Were I to indulge it, it would most certainly destroy me. Even as it sometimes appears in you, it terrifies and unnerves me. You are so impetuous!"

"Ah, you would have only the meek, the amiable!"

And thus, with an implied sarcasm, our conversation ended. Julia turned on me a look of imploring, which was naturally one of reproach. It did not have its proper influence upon me. I seized my hat, and hurried from the house. I rushed, rather than walked, through the streets; and, before I knew where I was, I found myself on the banks of the river, under the shade of trees, with the soft evening breeze blowing upon me, and the placid moon sailing quietly above. I threw myself down upon the grass, and delivered myself up to gloomy thoughts. Here was I, then, scarcely twenty-five years old; young, vigorous; with a probable chance of fortune before me; a young and lovely wife, the very creature of my first and only choice, one whom I tenderly loved, whom, if to seek again, I should again, and again, and only, seek! Yet I was miserable—miserable in the very possession of my first hopes, my best joys—the very treasure that had always seemed the dearest in my sight. Miserable blind heart! miserable indeed! For what was there to make me miserable? Absolutely nothing—nothing that the outer world could give—nothing that it could ever take away. But what fool is it that fancies there must be a reason for one's wretchedness? The reason is in our own hearts; in the perverseness which can make of its own heaven a hell! not often fashion a heaven out of hell!

Brooding, I lay upon the sward, meditating unutterable things, and as far as ever from any conclusion. Of one thing alone I was satisfied—that I was unutterably miserable; that my destiny was written in sable; that I was a man foredoomed to wo! Were my speculations strange or unnatural! Unnatural indeed! There is a class of surface-skimming persons, who pronounce all things unnatural which, to a cool, unprovoked, and perhaps unprovokable mind, appear unreasonable: as if a vexed nature and exacting passions were not the most unreasonable yet most natural of all moral agents. My woes may have been groundless, but it was surely not unnatural that *I* felt and entertained them.

Thus, with bitter mood, growing more bitter with every moment of its unrestrained indulgence, I gloomed in loneliness beside the banks of that silvery and smooth-flowing river. Certainly the natural world around me lent no color to my fancies. While all was dark within, all was bright without. A fiend was tugging at my heart; while from a little white cottage, a few hundred yards below, which grew flush with the margin of the stream, there stole forth the tender, tinkling strains of a guitar, probably touched by fair fingers of a fair maiden, with some enamored boy, blind and doting, hovering beside her. I, too, had stood thus and hearkened thus, and where am I—what am I!

I started to my feet. I found something offensive in the music. It came linked with a song which I had heard Julia sing a hundred times; and when I thought of those hours of confidence, and felt myself where I was, alone—and how lone!—bitterer than ever were the wayward pangs which were preying upon the tenderest fibres of my heart.

In the next moment I ceased to be alone. I was met and jostled by another person as I bounded forward, much too rapidly, in an effort to bury myself in the deeper shadow of some neighboring trees. The stranger was nearly overthrown in the collision, which extorted a hasty exclamation from his lips, not unmingled with a famous oath or two. In the voice I recognised that of my friend Kingsley—the well-known pseudo-Kentucky gentleman, who had acted a part so important in extricating my wife from her mother's custody. I made myself known to him in apologizing for my rudeness.

"You here!" said he; "I did not expect to meet you. I have just been to your house, where I found your wife, and where I intended to stop a while and wait for you. But Bill Edgerton, in the meanwhile, popped in, and after that I could hear nothing but pictures and paintings, Madonnas, Ecce Homos, and the like; till I began to fancy that I smelt nothing but paint and varnish. So I popped out, with a pretty blunt excuse, leaving the two amateurs to talk in oil and water-colors, and settle the principles of art as they please. Like you, I fancy a real landscape, here, by the water, and under the green trees, in preference to a thousand of their painted pictures."

It may be supposed that my mood underwent precious little improvement after this communication. Dark conceits, darker than ever, came across my mind. I longed to get away, and return to that home from which I had banished confidence!—ah, only too happy if there still lingered hope! But my friend, blunt, good-humored, and thoughtless creature as he was, took for granted that I had come to look at the landscape, to admire water-views by moonlight, and drink fresh draughts of sea-breeze from the southwest; and, thrusting his arm through mine, he dragged me on, down, almost to the threshold of the cottage, whence still issued the tinkle, tinkle, of the guitar which had first driven me away.

"That girl sings well. Do you know her—Miss Davison? She's soon to be married, *they* say (d—n 'they say,' however—the greatest scandal-monger, if not mischief-maker and liar, in the world!)—she is soon to be married to young Trescott—a clever lad who sniffles, plays on the flute, wears whisker and imperial on the most cream-colored and effeminate face you ever saw! A good fellow, nevertheless, but a silly! She is a good fellow, too, rather the cleverest of the twain, and perhaps the oldest. The match, if match it really is to be, none of the wisest for that very reason. The damsel, now-a-days, who marries a lad younger than herself, is laying up a large stock of pother, which is to bother her when she becomes thirty—for even young ladies, you know, after forty, may become thirty. A sort of dispensation of nature. She sings well, nevertheless."

I said something—it matters not what. Dark images of home were in my eyes. I heard no song—saw no landscape. The voice of Kingsley was a sort of buzzing in my ears.

"You are dull to-night, but that song ought to soothe you. What a cheery, light-hearted wench it is! Her voice does seem so to rise in air, shaking its wings, and crying tira-la! tira-la! with an enthusiasm which is catching! I almost feel prompted to kick up my heels, throw a summerset, and, while turning on my axis, give her an echo of tira-la! tira-la! tira-la! after her own fashion."

"You are certainly a happy, mad fellow, Kingsley!" was my faint, cheerless commentary upon a gayety of heart which I could not share, and the unreserved expression of which, at that moment, only vexed me.

"And you no glad one, Clifford. That song, which almost prompts me to dance, makes no impression on you! By-the-way, your wife used to sing so well, and now I never hear her. That d——d painting, if you don't mind, will make her give up everything else! As for Bill Edgerton, he cares for nothing else but his varnish, trees, and umber-hills, and streaky water. You shouldn't let him fill your wife's mind with this oil-and-varnish spirit—giving up the piano, the guitar, and that sweeter instrument than all, her own voice. D—n the paintings!—his long talk on the subject almost makes me sick of everything like a picture. I now look upon a beautiful landscape like this, as a thing that is shortly to be desecrated—taken in vain—scratched out of shape and proportion upon a deal-board, and colored after such a fashion as never before was seen in the natural world, upon, or under, or about this solid earth. D—n the pictures, I say again!—but, for God's sake, Clifford, don't let your wife give up the music! Make her play, even if she don't like it. She likes the painting best, but I wouldn't allow it! A wife is a sort of person that we set to do those things that we wish done and can't do for ourselves. That's my definition of a wife. Now, if I were in your place, with my present love for music and dislike of pictures, I'd put her at the piano, and put the paint-saucers, and the oil, and the smutted canvass, out of the window; and then—unless he came to his senses like other people—I'd thrust Bill Edgerton out after them! I'd never let the best friend in the world spoil my wife."

The effect of this random chatter of my good-natured friend upon my mind may well be imagined. It was fortunate that he was quite too much occupied in what he was saying to note my annoyance. In vain, anxious to be let off, was I restrained in utterance—cold, unpliable. The good fellow took for granted that it was an act of friendship to try to amuse; and thus, yearning with a nameless discontent and apprehension to get home, I was marched to and fro along the river-bank, from one scene to another—he, meanwhile, utterly heedless of time, and as actively bent on perpetual motion as if his sinews were of steel and his flesh iron. Meanwhile, the guitar ceased, and the song in the cottage of Miss Davison; the lights went out in that and all the other dwellings in sight; the moon waned; and it was not till the clock from a distant steeple tolled out the hour of eleven with startling solemnity, that Kingsley exclaimed:—

"Well, *mon ami*, we have had a ramble, and I trust I have somewhat dissipated your gloomy fit. And now to bed—what say you?—with what appetite we may!"

With what appetite, indeed! We separated. I rushed homeward, the moment he was out of sight—once more stood before my own dwelling. There the lights remained unextinguished, and William Edgerton was still a tenant of my parlor!

CHAPTER XXII.

SELF-HUMILIATION.

I HAD not the courage to enter my own dwelling! My heart sank within me. It was as if the whole hope of a long life, an intense desire, a keen unremitting pursuit, had suddenly been for ever baffled. Let no one who has not been in my situation; who has not been governed by like moral and social influences from the beginning; who knows not my sensibilities, and the organization—singular and strange it may be—of my mind and body; let no such person jump to the conclusion that there was any thing unnatural, however unreasonable and unreasoning, in the wild passion which possessed me. I look back upon it with some surprise myself. The fears which I felt, the sufferings I endured, however unreasonable, were yet true to my training. That training made me selfish; how selfish let my blindness show! In the blindness of self I could see nothing but the thing I feared, the one phantom—phantom though it were—which was sufficient to quell and crush all the better part of man within me, banish all the real blessings which were at command around me. I gave but a single second glance through the windows of my habitation, and then darted desperately away from the entrance! I bounded, without a consciousness, through the now still and dreary streets, and found myself, without intending it, once more beside the river, whose constant melancholy chidings, seemed the echoes—though in the faintest possible degree—of the deep waters of some apprehensive sorrow then rolling through all the channels of my soul.

What was it that I feared? What was it that I sought? Was it love? Can it be that the strange passion which we call by this name, was the source of that sad frenzy which filled and afflicted my heart? And was I not successful in my love? Had

I not found the sought?—won the withheld? What was denied to me that I desired? I asked of myself these questions. I asked them in vain. I could not answer them. I believe that I can answer now. It was sincerity, earnestness, devotion from her, all speaking through an intensity like that which I felt within my own soul.

Now, Julia lacked this earnestness, this intensity. Accustomed to submission, her manner was habitually subdued. Her strongest utterance was a tear, and that was most frequently hidden. She did not respond to me in the language in which my affections were wont to speak. Sincerity she did not lack—far from it—she was truth itself! It is the keener pang to my conscience now, that I am compelled to admit this conviction. Her modes of utterance were not less true than mine. They were not less significant of truth; but they were after a different fashion. In a moment of calm and reason, I might have believed this truth; nay, I knew it, even at those moments when I was most unjust. It was not the truth that I required so much as the presence of an attachment which could equal mine in its degree and strength. This was not in her nature. She was one taught to subdue her nature, to repress the tendencies of her heart, to submit in silence and in meekness. She had invariably done so until the insane urgency of her mother made her desperate. But for this desperation she had still submitted, perhaps, had never been my wife. In the fervent intensity of my own love, I fancied, from the beginning, that there was something too temperate in the tone of hers. Were I to be examined now, on this point, I should say that her deportment was one which declared the nicest union of sensibility and maidenly propriety. But, compared with mine, her passions were feeble, frigid. Mine were equally intense and exacting. Perhaps, had she even responded to my impetuosity with a like fervor, I should have recoiled from her with a feeling of disgust much more rapid and much more legitimate, than was that of my present frenzy.

Frenzy it was! and it led me to the performance of those things of which I shame to speak. But the truth, and its honest utterance now, must be one of those forms of atonement with which I may hope, perhaps vainly, to lessen, in the sight of Heaven, some of my human offences. I had scarcely reached the water-side before a new impulse drove me back. You will scarcely believe me when I tell you that I descended to the base character of the spy upon my household. The blush is red on my cheek while I record the shameful error. I entered the garden, stole like a felon to the lattice of the apartment in which my wife sat with her guest, and looked in with a greedy fear, upon the features of the two!

What were my own features then? What the expression of my eyes? It was well that I could not see them; I felt that they must be frightful. But what did I expect to see in this espionage? As I live, honestly now, and with what degree of honesty I then possessed, I may truly declare that when I *thought* upon the subject at all, I had no more suspicion that my wife would be guilty of any gross crime, than I had of the guilt of the Deity himself. Far from it. Such a fancy never troubled me. But, what was it to me, loving as I did, exclusive, and selfish, and exacting as I was—what was it to me if, forbearing all crime of conduct, she yet regarded another with eyes of idolatry—if her mind was yielded up to him in deference and regard; and thoughts, disparaging to me, filled her brain with his superior worth, manners, merits? He had tastes, perhaps talents, which I had not. In the forum, in all the more energetic, more imposing performances of life, William Edgerton, I knew, could take no rank in competition with myself. But I was no ladies' man. I had no arts of society. My manners were even rude. My address was direct almost to bluntness. I had no discriminating graces, and could make no sacrifice, in that school of polish, where the delicacy is too apt to become false, and the performances trifling. It is idle to dwell on this; still more idle to speculate upon probable causes. It may be that there are persons in the world of both sexes, and governed by like influences, who have been guilty of like follies; to them my revelations may be of service. My discoveries, if I have made any, were quite too late to be of much help to me.

To resume, I prowled like a guilty phantom around my own habitation. I scanned closely, with the keenest eyes of jealousy, every feature, every movement of the two within. In the eyes of Edgerton, I beheld—I did not deceive myself in this—I beheld the speaking soul, devoted, rapt, full of love for the object of his survey. That he loved her was to me sufficiently clear. His words were few, faintly spoken, timid. His eyes did not encounter hers; but when hers were averted, they riveted their fixed glances upon her face with the adherence of the yearning steel for the magnet! Bitterly did I gnash my teeth—bitterly did my spirit rise in rebellion, as I noted these characteristics. But, vainly, with all my perversity of feeling and judgment, did I examine the air, the look, the action, the expression, the tones, the words of my wife, to make a like discovery. All was passionless, all seeming pure, in her whole conduct. She was gentle in her manner, kind in her words, considerate in her attentions; but so entirely at ease, so evidently unconscious, as well of improper thoughts in herself as of an improper tendency in him, that, though still resolute to be wilful and unhappy, I yet could see nothing of which I could reasonably complain. Nay, I fancied that there was a touch of listlessness, amounting to indifference, in her air, as if she really wished him to be gone; and, for a moment, my heart beat with a returning flood of tenderness, that almost prompted me to rush suddenly into the apartment and clasp her to my arms.

At length, Edgerton departed. When he rose to do so, I felt the awkwardness of my situation—the meanness of which I had been guilty—the disgrace which would follow detection. The shame I already felt; but, though sickening beneath it, the passion which drove me into the commission of so slavish an act, was still superior to all others, and could not then be overcome. I hurried from the window and from the premises while he was taking his leave. My mind was still in a frenzy. I rambled off, unconsciously, to the most secluded places along the suburbs, endeavoring to lose the thoughts that troubled me. I had now a new cause for vexation. I was haunted by a conviction of my own shame. How could I look Julia in the face—how meet and speak to her, and hear the accents of her voice and my own after the unworthy espionage which I had instituted upon her? Would not my eyes betray me—my faltering accents, my abashed looks, my flushed and burning cheeks? I felt that it was impossible for me to escape detection. I was sure that every look, every tone, would sufficiently betray my secret. Perhaps I should not have felt this fear, had I possessed the courage to resolve against the repetition of my error. Could I have declared this resolution to myself, to forego the miserable proceeding which I had that night begun, I feel that I should then have taken one large step toward my own deliverance from that formidable fiend which was then raging unmastered in my soul. But I lacked the courage for this. Fatal deficiency! I felt impressed with the necessity of keeping a strict watch upon Edgerton. I had seen, with eyes that could not be deceived, the feeling which had been expressed in his. I saw that he loved her, perhaps, without a consciousness himself of the unhappy truth. I hurried to the conclusion, accordingly, that he must be looked after. I did not so immediately perceive that in looking after him, I was, in truth, looking after Julia; for what was my watch upon Edgerton but a watch upon her? I had not the confidence in her to leave her to herself. That was my error. The true reasoning by which a man in my situation should be governed, is comprised in a nutshell. Either the wife is virtuous or she is not. If she is virtuous, she is safe without my espionage. If she is not, all the watching in the world will not suffice to make her so. As for the discovery of her falsehood, he will make that fast enough. The security of the husband lies in his wife's purity, not in his own eyes. It must be added to this argument that the most virtuous among us, man or woman, is still very weak; and neither wife, nor daughter, nor son, should be exposed to unnecessary temptation. Do we not daily implore in our own prayers, to be saved from temptation?

I need not strive to declare what were my thoughts and feelings as I wandered off from my dwelling and place of espionage that night. No language of which I am possessed could embody to the idea of the reader the thousandth part of what I suffered. An insane and morbid resentment filled my heart. A close, heavy, hot stupor, pressed upon my brain. My limbs seemed feeble as those of a child. I tottered in the streets. The stars, bright mysterious watchers, seemed peering down into my face with looks of smiling inquiry. The sudden bark of a watch-dog startled and unnerved me. I felt with the consciousness of a mean action, all the humiliating weakness which belongs to it.

It took me a goodly hour before I could muster up courage to return home, and it was then midnight. Julia had retired to her chamber, but not yet to her couch. She flew to me on my entrance—to my arms. I shrunk from her embraces; but she grasped me with greater firmness. I had never witnessed so much warmth in her before. It surprised me, but the solution of it was easy. My long stay had made her apprehensive. It was so unusual. My coldness, when she embraced me, was as startling to her, as her sudden warmth was surprising to me. She pushed me from her—still, however, holding me in her grasp, while she surveyed me. Then she started, and with newer apprehensions.

Well she might. My looks alarmed her. My hair was dishevelled and moist with the night-dews. My cheeks were very pale. There was a quick, agitated, and dilating fullness of my eyes, which rolled hastily about the apartment, never even resting upon her. They dared not. I caught a hasty glance of myself in the mirror, and scarcely knew my own features. It was natural enough that she should be alarmed. She clung to me with increased fervency. She spoke hurriedly, but clearly, with an increased and novel power of utterance, the due result of her excitement. Could that excitement be occasioned by love for me—by a suspicion of the truth, namely, that I had been watching her? I shuddered as this last conjecture passed into my mind. That, indeed, would be a humiliation—worse, more degrading, by far, than all.

"Oh, why have you left me—so long, so very long? where have you been? what has happened?"

"Nothing—nothing."

"Ah, but there is something, Edward. Speak! what is it, dear husband? I see it in your eyes, your looks! Why do you turn from me? Look on me! tell me! You are very pale, and your eyes are so wild, so strange! You are sick, dear Edward; you are surely sick: tell me, what has happened?"

Wild and hurried as they were, never did tones of more touching sweetness fall from any lips. They unmanned—nay, I use the wrong word—they *manned* me for the time. They brought me back to my senses, to a conviction of her truth, to a momentary conviction of my own folly. My words fell from me without effort—few, hurried, husky—but it was a sudden heart-gush, which was unrestrainable.

"Ask me not, Julia — ask me nothing; but love me, only love me, and all will be well — all is well."

"Do I not — ah! do I not love you, Edward?"

"I believe you — God be praised, I *do* believe you!"

"Oh, surely, Edward, you never doubted this."

"No, no! — never!"

Such was the fervent ejaculation of my lips; such, in spite of its seeming inconsistency, was the real belief within my soul. What was it, then, that I did doubt? wherefore, then, the misery, the suspense, the suspicion, which grew and gathered, corroding in my heart, the parent of a thousand unnamed anxieties? It will be difficult to answer. The heart of man is one of those strange creations, so various in its moods, so infinite in its ramifications, so subtle and sudden in its transitions, as to defy investigation as certainly as it refuses remedy and relief. It is enough to say that, with one schooled as mine had been, injuriously, and with injustice, there is little certainty in any of its movements. It becomes habitually capricious, feeds upon passions intensely, without seeming detriment; and, after a season, prefers the unwholesome nutriment which it has made vital, to those purer natural sources of strength and succor, without which, though it may still enjoy life, it can never know happiness.

CHAPTER XXIII.

PROGRESS OF PASSION.

"BUT, do not leave me another time—not so long, Edward. Do not leave me alone. Your business is one thing. *That* you must, of course, attend to; but hours—not of business—hours in which you do no business—hours of leisure—your evenings, Edward—these you must share with me—you must give to me entirely. Ah! will you not? will you not promise me?"

These were among the last words which she spoke to me ere we slept that night. The next morning, almost at awaking, she resumed the same language. I could not help perceiving that she spoke in tones of greater earnestness than usual—an earnestness expressive of anxiety for which I felt at some loss to account. Still, the tenor of what she said, at the time, gave me pleasure—a satisfaction which I did not seek to conceal, and which, while it lasted, was the sweetest of all pleasures to my soul. But the busy devil in my heart made his suggestions also, which were of a kind to produce any other but satisfying emotions. While I stood in my wife's presence—in the hearing of her angel-voice, and beholding the pure spirit speaking out from her eyes—he lay dormant, rebuked, within his prison-house, crouching in quiet, waiting a more auspicious moment for activity. Nor was he long in waiting; and then his cold, insinuating doubts—his inquiries—begot and startled mine!

"Very good—all very good!" Such was the tone of his suggestions. "She may well compound for the evenings with you, since she gives her whole mornings to your rival."

Archimedes asked but little for the propulsion of a world. The jealous spirit—a spirit jealous like mine—asks still less for the moving of that little but densely-populous world, the human heart. I forgot the sweet tones of my wife's words—

the pure-souled words themselves—tones and words which, while their sounds yet lingered in my ears, I could not have questioned—I did not dare to question. The tempter grew in the ascendant the moment I had passed out of her sight; and when I met William Edgerton the next day, he acquired greatly-increased power over my understanding.

William Edgerton had evidently undergone a change. He no longer met my glances boldly with his own. Perhaps, had he done so, my eyes would have been the first to shrink from the encounter. He looked down, or looked aside, when he spoke to me; his words were few, timorous, hesitating, but studiously conciliatory; and he lingered no longer in my presence than was absolutely unavoidable. Was there not a consciousness in this? and what consciousness? The devil at my heart answered, and answered with truth, "He loves your wife." It would have been well, perhaps, had the cruel fiend said nothing farther. Alas! I would have pardoned, nay, pitied William Edgerton, had the same chuckling spirit not assured me that she also was not insensible to him. I was continually reminded of the words, "Your business must, of course, be attended to!"—"What a considerate wife!" said the tempter; "how very unusual with young wives, with whom business is commonly the very last consideration!"

That very day, I found, on reaching home, that William Edgerton had been there—had gone there almost the moment after he had left me at the office; and that he had remained there, obviously at work in the studio, until the time drew nigh for my return to dinner. My feelings forbade any inquiries. These facts were all related by my wife herself. I did not ask to hear them. I asked for nothing more than she told. The dread that my jealousy should be suspected made me put on a sturdy aspect of indifference; and that exquisite sense of delicacy, which governed every movement of my wife's heart and conduct, forbade her to say—what yet she certainly desired I should know—that, in all that time, she had not seen him, nor he her. She had studiously kept aloof in her chamber so long as he remained. Meanwhile, I brooded over their supposed long and secret interviews. These I took for granted. The happiness they felt—the mutual smile they witnessed—

the unconscious sighs they uttered! Such a picture of their supposed felicity as my morbid imagination conjured up would have roused a doubly damned and damning fiend in the heart of any mortal.

What a task was mine, struggling with these images, these convictions!—my pride struggling to conceal, my feelings struggling to endure. Then, there were other conflicts. What friends had the Edgertons been to me—father, mother—nay, that son himself, once so fondly esteemed, once so fondly esteeming! Of course, no ties such as these could have made me patient under wrong. But they were such as to render it necessary that the wrong should be real, unquestionable, beyond doubt, beyond excuse. This I felt, this I resolved.

"I will wait! I will be patient! I will endure, though the vulture gnaws incessant at my heart! I will do nothing precipitate. No, no: I must beware of that! But let me prove them treacherous—let them once falter, and go aside from the straight path, and then—oh, then!"

Such, as in spoken words, was the unspoken resolution of my soul; and this resolution required, first of all, that I should carry out the base purpose which, without a purpose, I had already begun. I must be a spy upon their interviews. They must be followed, watched—eyes, looks, hands! Miserable necessity! but, under my present feelings and determination, not the less a necessity. And I, alone, must do it; I, alone, must peer busily into these mysteries, the revelation of which can result only in my own ruin—seeking still, with an earnest diligence, to discover that which I should rather have prayed for eternal and unmitigated blindness, that I might not see! Mine was, indeed, the philosophy of the madman.

I persevered in it like one. I yielded all opportunities for the meeting of the parties—all opportunities which, in yielding, did not expose me to the suspicion of having any sinister object. If, for example, I found, or could conjecture, that William Edgerton was likely to be at my house this or that evening, I studiously intimated, beforehand, some necessity for being myself absent. This carried me frequently from home—lone, wandering, vexing myself with the most hideous conjectures, the most self-torturing apprehensions. I sped away, obviously, into the city — to alleged meetings with friends or clients — or on some pretence or other which seemed ordinary and natural. But my course was to return, and, under cover of night, to prowl around my own premises, like some guilty ghost, doomed to haunt the scene of former happiness, in its wantonness rendered a scene of ever-during misery. Certainly, no guilty ghost ever suffered in his penal tortures a torture worse than mine at these humiliating moments. It was torture enough to me that I was sensible of all the unhappy meanness of my conduct. On this head, though I strove to excuse myself on the score of a supposed necessity, I could not deceive myself — no! — not for the smallest moment.

Weeks passed in this manner — weeks to me of misery — of annoyance and secret suffering to my wife. In this time, my espionage resulted in nothing but what has been already shown — in what was already sufficiently obvious to me. William Edgerton continued his insane attentions: he sought my dwelling with studious perseverance — sought it particularly at those periods when he fancied I was absent — when he knew it — though such were not his exclusive periods of visitation. He came at times when I was at home. His passion for my wife was sufficiently evident to me, though her deportment was such as to persuade me that she did not see it. All that I beheld of her conduct was irreproachable. There was a singular and sweet dignity in her air and manner, when they were together, that seemed one of the most insuperable barriers to any rash or presumptuous approach. While there was no constraint about her carriage, there was no familiarity — nothing to encourage or invite familiarity. While she answered freely, responding to all the needs of a suggested subject, she herself never seemed to broach one; and, after hours of nightly watch, which ran through a period of weeks, in which I strove at the shameful occupation of the espial, I was compelled to admit that all her part was as purely unexceptionable as the most jealous husband could have wished it.

But not so with the conduct of William Edgerton. His attentions were increasing. His passion was assuming some of the forms of that delirium to which, under encouragement, it is usually driven in the end. He now passionately watched my wife's countenance, and no longer averted his glance when it suddenly encountered hers. His eyes, naturally tender in expression, now assumed a look of irrepressible ardency, from which, I now fancied—pleased to fancy—that hers recoiled! He would linger long in silence, silently watching her, and seemingly unconscious, the while, equally of his scrutiny and his silence. At such times, I could perceive that Julia would turn aside, or her own eyes would be marked by an expression of the coldest vacancy, which, but for other circumstances, or in any other condition of my mind, would have seemed to me conclusive of her indignation or dislike. But, when such became my thought, it was soon expelled by some suggestion from the busy devil of my imagination:—

"They may well put on this appearance now; but are such their looks when they meet, sometimes for a whole morning, in the painting-room?" Even here, the fiend was silenced by a fact which was revealed to me in one of my nocturnal watches.

"Clifford not at home?" said Edgerton one evening as he entered, addressing my wife, and looking indifferently around the room. "I wished to tell him about some pictures which are to be seen at ——'s room—really a lovely Guido—an infant Savior—and something, said to be by Carlo Dolce, though I doubt. You must see them. Shall I call for you to-morrow morning?"

"I thank you, but have an engagement for the morning."

"Well, the next day. They will remain but a few days longer in the city."

"I am sorry, but I shall not be able to go even the next day, I am so busy."

"Busy? ah! that reminds me to ask if you have given up the pencil altogether? Have you wholly abandoned the studio? I never see you now at work in the morning. I had no thought that you had so much of the fashionable taste for morning calls, shopping, and the like."

"Nor have I," was the quiet answer. "I seldom leave home in the morning."

"Indeed!" with some doubtfulness of countenance, almost amounting to chagrin—"indeed! how is it that I so seldom see you, then?"

"The cares of a household, I suppose, might be my sufficient excuse. While my liege lord works abroad, I find my duties sufficiently urgent to task all my time at home."

"Really—but you do not propose to abandon the atelier entirely? Clifford himself, with his great fondness for the art, will scarcely be satisfied that you should, even on a pretence of work."

"I do not know. I do not think that *my husband*"—the last two words certainly emphasized—"cares much about it. I suspect that music and painting, however much they delighted and employed our girlhood, form but a very insignificant part of our duties and enjoyments when we get married."

"But you do not mean to say that a fine landscape, or an exquisite head, gives you less satisfaction than before your marriage?"

"I confess they do. Life is a very different thing before and after marriage. It seems far more serious—it appears to me a possession now, and time a sort of property which has to be economized and doled out almost as cautiously as money. I have not touched a brush this fortnight. I doubt if I have been in the painting-room more than once in all this time."

This conversation, which evidently discomfited William Edgerton, was productive to me of no small satisfaction. After a brief interval, consumed in silence, he resumed it:—

"But I must certainly get you to see these pictures. Nay, I must also—since you keep at home—persuade you to look into the studio to-morrow, if it be only to flatter my vanity by looking at a sketch which I have amused myself upon the last three mornings. By-the-way, why may we not look at it to-night?"

"We shall not be able to examine it carefully by night," was the answer, as I fancied, spoken with unwonted coldness and deliberation.

"So much the better for me," he replied, with an ineffectual attempt to laugh; "you will be less able to discern its defects."

"The same difficulty will endanger its beauties," Julia answered, without offering to rise.

"Well, at least, you must arrange for seeing the pictures at ——'s. They are to remain but a few days, and I would not have you miss seeing them for the world. Suppose you say Saturday morning?"

"If nothing happens to prevent," she said; "and I will endeavor to persuade Mr. Clifford to look at them with us."

"Oh, he is so full of his law and clients, that you will hardly succeed."

This was spoken with evident dissatisfaction. The arrangement, which included me, seemed unnecessary. I need not say that I was better pleased with my wife than I had been for some time previous; but here the juggling fiend interposed again, to suggest the painful suspicion that she knew of my whereabouts, of my jealousy, of my espionage; that her words were rather meant for my ears than for those of Edgerton; or, if this were not the case, her manner to Edgerton was simply adopted, as she had now become conscious of her own feelings —feelings of peril—feelings which would not permit her to trust herself. Ah! she feared herself: she had discovered the passion of William Edgerton, and it had taught her the character and tendency of her own. Was there ever more self-destroying malice than was mine? I settled down upon this last conviction. My wife's coldness was only assumed to prevent Edgerton from seeing her weakness; and, for Edgerton himself, I now trembled with the conviction that I should have to shed his blood.

CHAPTER XXIV.

A GROUP.

THIS conviction now began to haunt my mind with all the punctuality of a shadow. It came to me unconsciously, uncalled for; mingled with other thoughts and disturbed them all. Whether at my desk, or in the courts; among men in the crowded mart, or in places simply where the idle and the thoughtless congregate, it was still my companion. It was, however, still a shadow only; a dull, intangible, half-formed image of the mind; the crude creature of a fear rather than a desire; for, of a truth, nothing could be more really terrible to me than the apparent necessity of taking the life of one so dear to me once, and still so dear to the only friends I had ever known. I need not say how silently I strove to banish this conviction. My struggles on this subject were precisely those which are felt by nervous men suddenly approaching a precipice, and, though secure, flinging themselves off, in the extremity of their apprehensions of that danger which has assumed in their imaginations an aspect so absorbing. With such persons, the extreme anxiety to avoid the deed, whether of evil or of mere danger, frequently provokes its commission. I felt that this risk encountered me. I well knew that an act often contemplated may be already considered half-performed; and though I could not rid myself of the impression that I was destined to do the deed the very idea of which made me shudder, I yet determined, with all the remaining resolution of my virtue, to dismiss it from my thought, as I resolved to escape from its performance if I could.

It would have been easy enough for me to have kept this resolution as it was enough for me to make it, had it not clashed with a superior passion in my mind; but that blindness of heart under which I labored, impaired my judgment, enfeebled my resolution, baffled my prudence, defeated all my faculties of self-preservation. I was, in fact, a monomaniac. On one subject, I was incapable of thought, of sane reasoning, of fixed purpose. I am unwilling to distinguish this madness by the word "jealousy." In the ordinary sense of the term it was not jealousy. Phrenologists would call it an undue development of self-esteem, diseased by frequent provocation into an irritable suspiciousness, which influenced all the offices of thought. It was certain, to myself, that in instituting the watch which I did over the conduct of my wife and William Edgerton, I did not expect to discover the commission of any gross act which, in the vulgar acceptation of the world, constitutes the crime of infidelity. The pang would not have been less to my mind, though every such act was forborne, if I perceived that her eyes yearned for his coming, and her looks of despondency took note of his absence. If I could see that she hearkened to his words with the ears of one who deferred even to devotedness, and found that pleasure in his accents which should only have been accorded to mine. It is the low nature, alone, which seeks for developments beyond these, to constitute the sin of faithlessness. Of looks, words, consideration, habitual deference, and eager attention, I was quite as uxorious as I should have been of the warm kiss, or the yielding, fond embrace. They were the same in my eyes. It was for the momentary glance, the passing word, the forgetful sigh, that I looked and listened, while I pursued the unhappy espionage upon my wife and her lover. That he was her lover, was sufficiently evident—how far she was pleased with his devotion was the question to be asked and—answered!

The self-esteem which produced these developments of jealousy, in my own home, was not unexercised abroad. The same exacting nature was busy among my friends and mere acquaintance. Of these I had but few; to these I could be devoted; for these I could toil; for these I could freely have perished! But I demanded nothing less from them. Of their consideration and regard I was equally uxorious as I was of the affections of my wife. I was an *intensifier* in all my relations, and was not willing to divide or share my sympathies. I became suspicious when I found any of my acquaintance forming new intimacies, and sunk into reserves which necessarily produced a severance of the old ties between us. It naturally followed that my few friends became fewer, and I finally stood alone. But enough of self-analysis, which, in truth, owes its origin to the very same mental quality which I have been discussing—the presence and prevalence of *egoïsme*. Let us hurry our progress.

My wife advised me of the visit which William Edgerton had proposed to the picture collection.

"I will go," she said, "if you will."

"You must go without me."

"Ah, why? Surely, you can go one morning?"

"Impossible. The morning is the time for business. *That* must be attended to, you know."

"But you needn't slave yourself at it because it is business, Edward. But that I know that you are not a money-loving man, I should suppose, sometimes, from the continual plea of business, that you were a miser, and delighted in filling old stockings to hide away in holes and chinks of the wall. Come, now, Saturday is not usually a busy day with you lawyers; steal it this once and go with us. I lose half the pleasure of the sight always, when you are not with me, and when I know that you are engaged in working for me elsewhere."

"Ah, you mistake, Julia. You shall not flatter me into such a faith. You lose precious little by my absence."

"But, Edward, I do; believe me—it is true."

"Impossible! No, no, Julia, when you look on the Carlo Dolce and the Guido, you will forget not only the toils of the husband, but that you have one at all. You will forget my harsh features in the contemplation of softer ones."

"Your features are not harsh ones, Edward."

"Nay, you shall not persuade me that I am not an Orson—a very wild man of the woods. I know I am. I know that I have harsh features; nay, I fancy you know it too, by this time, Julia."

"I admit the sternness at times, Edward, but I deny the harshness. Besides, sternness, you know, is perfectly compatible with the possession of the highest human beauty. I am not sure that a certain portion of sternness is not absolutely necessary to manly beauty. It seems to me that I have never yet seen what I call a handsome man, whose features had not a certain sweet gravity, a sort of melancholy defiance, in them which neutralized the effect of any effeminacy which mere beauty must have had; and imparted to them a degree of character which compelled you to turn again and look, and made you remember them, even when they had disappeared from sight. Now, it may be the vanity of a wife, Edward, but it seems to me that this is the very sort of face which you possess."

"Ah! you are very vain of me, I know—very!"

"Proud, fond—not vain!"

"You deceive yourself still, I suspect, even with your distinctions. But you must forego the pleasure of displaying my 'stern beauties,' as your particular possession, at the gallery. You must content yourself with others not so stern, though perhaps not less beautiful, and certainly more amiable. Edgerton will be your sufficient chaperon."

"Yes, but I do not wish to be troubling Mr. Edgerton so frequently; and, indeed, I would rather forego the pleasure of seeing the pictures altogether, than trespass in this way upon his attention and leisure."

"Indeed, but I am very sure you do not trespass upon either. He is an idle, good fellow, relishes anything better than business, and you know has such a passion for painting and pictures that its indulgence seems to justify anything to his mind. He will forget everything in their pursuit."

All this was said with a studious indifference of manner. I was singularly successful in concealing the expression of that agony which was gnawing all the while upon my heart. I could smile, too, while I was speaking—while I was suffering! Look calmly into her face and smile, with a composure, a strength, the very consciousness of which was a source of terrible overthrow to me at last. I was surprised to perceive an air of chagrin upon Julia's countenance, which was certainly unstudied. She was one of those who do not well conceal or cloak their real sentiments. The faculty of doing so is usually much more strongly possessed by women than by men—much more easily commanded—but *she* had little of it. Why should she wear this expression of disappointment—chagrin! Was she really anxious that I should attend her? I began to think so—began to relent, and think of promising that I would go with her, when she somewhat abruptly laid her hand upon my arm.

"Edward, you leave me too frequently. You stay from me too long, particularly at evening. Do not forget, dear husband, how few female friends I have; how few friends of any sort—how small is my social circle. Besides, it is expected of all young people, newly married, that they will be frequently together; and when it is seen that they are often separate—that the wife goes abroad alone, or goes in the company of persons not of the family, it begets a suspicion that all is not well—that there is no peace, no love, in the family so divided. Do not think, Edward, that I mean this reproachfully—that I mean complaint—that I apprehend the loss of your love: oh no! I dread too greatly any such loss to venture upon its suspicion lightly, but I would guard against the conjectures of others——"

"So, then, it is not that you really wish my company. It is because you would simply maintain appearances."

"I would do both, Edward. God knows I care as little for mere appearances, so long as the substances are good, as you do; but I confess I would not have the neighbors speak of me as the neglected wife; I would not have you the subject of vulgar reproach."

"To what does all this tend?" I demanded impatiently.

"To nothing, Edward, if by speaking it I make you angry."

"Do not speak it, then!" was my stern reply.

"I will not; do not turn away—do not be angry:" here she sobbed once, convulsively; but with an effort of which I had not thought her capable, she stifled the painful utterance, and continued grasping my wrist as she spoke with both her hands, and speaking in a whisper—

"You are not going to leave me in anger. Oh, no! Do not! Kiss me, dear husband, and forgive me. If I have vexed you, it was only because I was so selfishly anxious to keep you more with me—to be more certain that you are all my own!"

I escaped from this scene with some difficulty. I should be doing my own heart, blind and wilful as it was, a very gross injustice, if I did not confess that the sincere and natural deportment of Julia had rendered me largely doubtful of the good sense or the good feeling of the course I was pursuing. But the effects of it were temporary only. The very feeling, thus forced upon me, that I was, and had been, doing wrong, was a humiliating one; and calculated rather to sustain my self-esteem, even though it lessened the amount of justification which my jealousy may have supposed itself possessed of. The disease had been growing too long within my bosom. It had taken too deep root—had spread its fibres into a region too rank and stimulating not to baffle any ordinary diligence on the part of the extirpator, even if he had been industrious and sincere. It had been growing with my growth, had shared my strength from the beginning, was a part of my very existence! Still, though not with that hearty fondness which her feeling demanded, I returned her caresses, folded her to my bosom, kissed the tears from her cheek, and half promised myself, though I said nothing of this to her, that I would attend her to the picture exhibition.

But I did not. Half an hour before the appointed time I resolved to do so; but the evil spirit grew uppermost in that brief interval, and suggested to me a course more in unison with its previous counsellings. Under this mean prompting I prepared to go to the gallery, but not till my wife had already gone there under Edgerton's escort. The object of this afterthought was to surprise them there—to enter at the unguarded moment, and read the language of their mutual eyes, when they least apprehended such scrutiny.

Pitiful as was this design, I yet pursued it. I entered the picture room at a moment which was sufficiently auspicious for my objects. They were the only occupants of the apartment. I learned this fact before I ascended the stairs from the keeper of the gallery, who sat in a lower room. The stairs were carpeted. I wore light thin pumps, which were noiseless. I may add, as a singular moral contradiction, that I not only did not move stealthily, but that I set down my feet with greater emphasis than was usual with me, as if I sought, in this way to lessen somewhat the meanness of my proceeding. My approach, however, was entirely unheard; and I stood for a few seconds in the doorway, gazing upon the parties without making them conscious of my intrusion.

Julia was sitting, gazing, with hand lifted above her eyes, at a Murillo—a ragged Spanish boy, true equally to the life and to the peculiar characteristics of that artist—dark groundwork, keen, arch expression, great vivacity, with an air of pregnant humor which speaks of more than is shown, and makes you fancy that other pictures are to follow in which the same boy must appear in different phases of feeling and of fortune.

I need not say that the pictures, however, called for a momentary glance only from me. My glances were following my thoughts, and they were piercing through the only possible avenues, the cheeks, the lips, the tell-tale eyes, deep down into the very hearts of the suspected parties. They were so placed that, standing at the door, and half-hidden from sight by a screen, I could see with tolerable distinctness the true expression in each countenance, though I saw but half the face. Julia was gazing upon the pictures, but Edgerton was gazing upon her! He had no eyes for any other object; and I fancied, from the abstracted and almost vacant expression of his looks, that I might have advanced and placed myself broadly before him without startling him from his dream. In his features, speaking, even in their obliviousness of all without, was one sole, absorbing sentiment of devotion. His eyes were riveted with a strenuous sort of gaze upon her, and her only. He stood partly on one side, but still behind her, so that, without changing her position, she could scarcely have beheld his countenance. I looked in vain, in the brief space of time which I employed in surveying them, but she never once turned her head; nor did he once withdraw his glance from her neck and cheek, a part only of which could have been visible to him where he stood. Her features, meanwhile, were subdued and placid. There was nothing which could make me dissatisfied with her, had I not been predisposed to this dissatisfaction; and when the tones of my voice were heard, she started up to meet me with a sudden flash of pleasure in her eyes which illuminated her whole countenance.

"Ah! you are come, then. I am so glad!"

She little knew why I had come. I blushed involuntarily with the conviction of the base motive which had brought me. She immediately grasped my arm, drew me to the contemplation of those pictures which had more particularly pleased herself, absolutely seeming to forget that there was a third person in the room. William Edgerton turned away and busied himself, for the first time no doubt, in the examination of a landscape on the opposite wall. I followed his movement with my glance for a single instant, but his face was studiously averted.

CHAPTER XXV.

THE OLD GOOSE FINDS A YOUNG GANDER.

WE will suppose some months to have elapsed in this manner—months, to me, of prolonged torture and suspicion. Circumstances, like petty billows of the sea, kept chafing upon the low places of my heart, keeping alive the feverish irritation which had already done so much toward destroying my peace, and overthrowing the guardian outposts of my pride and honor. How long the strife was to be continued before the ocean-torrents should be let in—before the wild passions should quite overwhelm my reason—was a subject of doubt, but not the less a subject of present and of exceeding fear. In these matters, I need not say that there was substantially very little change in the character of events that marked the progress of my domestic life. William Edgerton still continued the course which he had so unwittingly begun. He still sought every opportunity to see my wife, and, if possible, to see her alone. He avoided me as much as possible; seldom came to the office; absolutely gave up his business altogether; and, when we met, though his words and manner were solicitously kind, there was a close restraint upon the latter, a hesitancy about the former, a timid apprehensiveness in his eye, and a generally-shown reluctance to approach me, which I could not but see, and could not but perceive, at the same time, that he endeavored with ineffectual effort to conceal. He was evidently conscious that he was doing wrong. It was equally clear to me that he lacked the manly courage to do right. What was all this to end in? The question became momently more and more serious. Suppose that he possessed no sort of influence over my wife? Even suppose his advances to stop where they were at present—his course already, so far, was a humiliating indignity, allowing that it became perceptible to the eyes of others. That revelation once made, there could be no more proper forbearance on the part of the husband. The customs of our society, the tone of public opinion—nay, outraged humanity itself—demanded then the interposition of the avenger. And that revelation was at hand.

Meanwhile, the keenest eyes of suspicion could behold nothing in the conduct of Julia which was not entirely unexceptionable. If William Edgerton was still persevering in his pursuit, Julia seemed insensible to his endeavors. Of course, they met frequently when it was not in my power to see them. It was my error to suppose that they met more frequently still—that he saw her invariably in his morning visits to the studio, which was not often the case—and, when they did meet, that she derived quite as much satisfaction from the interview as himself. Of their meetings, except at night, when I was engaged in my miserable watch upon them, I could say nothing. Failing to note anything evil at such periods, my jealous imagination jumped to the conclusion that this was because my espionage was suspected, and that their interviews at other periods were distinguished by less prudence and reserve. And yet, could I have reasoned rightly at this period, I must have seen that, if such were the case, there would have been no such display of *empressement* as William Edgerton made at these evening visits. Did he expend his ardor in the day, did he apprehend my scrutiny at night, he would surely have suppressed the eagerness of his glance—the profound, all-forgetting adoration which marked his whole air, gaze, and manner. Nor should I have been so wretchedly blind to what was the obvious feeling of discontent and disquiet in her bosom. Never did evenings seem to pass with more downright dullness to any one party in the world. If Edgerton spoke to her, which he did not frequently, his address was marked by a trepidation and hesitancy akin to fear—a manner which certainly indicated anything but a foregone conclusion between them; while her answers, on the other hand, were singularly cold, merely replying, and calculated invariably to discourage everything like a protracted conversation. What was said by Edgerton was sufficiently harmless—nor harmless merely. It was most commonly mere ordinary commonplace, the feeble effort of one who feels the necessity of speech, yet dares not speak the voluminous passions which alone could furnish him with energetic and manly utterance. Had the scales not been abundantly thick and callous above my eyes, how easily might these clandestine scrutinies have brought me back equally to happiness and my senses! But though I thus beheld the parties, and saw the truth as I now relate it, there was always then some little trifling circumstance that would rise up, congenial to suspicion, and cloud my conclusions, and throw me back upon old doubts and cruel jealousies. Edgerton's tone may, at moments, have been more faltering and more tender than usual; Julia's glance might sometimes encounter his, and then they both might seem to fall, in mutual confusion, to the ground. Perhaps she sung some little ditty at his instance—some ditty that she had often sung for me. Nay, at his departure, she might have attended him to the entrance, and he may have taken her hand and retained his grasp upon it rather longer than was absolutely necessary for his farewell. How was I to know the degree of pressure which he gave to the hand within his own? That single grasp, not unfrequently, undid all the better impressions of a whole evening consumed in these unworthy scrutinies. I will not seek further to account for or to defend this unhappy weakness. Has not the great poet of humanity said—

> "Trifles, light as air,
> Are, to the jealous, confirmations strong
> As proofs of Holy Writ"?

Medical men tell us of a predisposing condition of the system for the inception of epidemic. It needs, after this, but the smallest atmospheric changes, and the contagion spreads, and blackens, and taints the entire body of society, even unto death. The history of the moral constitution is not unanalogous to this. The disease, the damning doubt, once in the mind, and the rest is easy. It may sleep and be silent for a season, for years, unprovoked by stimulating circumstances; but let the moral atmosphere once receive its color from the suddenly-passing cloud, and the dark spot dilates within the heart, grows active, and rapidly sends its poisonous and poisoning tendrils through all the avenues of mind. Its bitter secretions in my soul affected all the objects of my sight, even as the jaundiced man lives only in a saffron element. Perhaps no course of conduct on the part of my wife could have seemed to me entirely innocent. Certainly none could have been entirely satisfactory, or have seemed entirely proper. Even her words, when she spoke to me alone, were of a kind to feed my prevailing passion. Yet, regarded under just moods, they should have been the most conclusive, not simply of her innocence, but of the devotedness of her heart to the requisitions of her duty. Her love and her sense of right seemed harmoniously to keep together. Gentlest reproaches chided me for leaving her, when she sought for none but myself. Sweetest endearments encountered my return, and fondest entreaties would have delayed the hour of my departure. Her earnestness, when she implored me not to leave her so frequently at night, almost reached intensity, and had a meaning, equally expressive of her delicacy and apprehensions, which I was unhappily too slow to understand.

Six months had probably elapsed from the time of Mr. Clifford's death, when, returning from my office one day, who should I encounter in my wife's company but her mother? Of this good lady I had been permitted to see but precious little since my marriage. Not that she had kept aloof from our dwelling entirely. Julia had always conceived it a duty to seek her mother at frequent periods without regarding the ill treament which she received; and the latter, becoming gradually reconciled to what she could no longer prevent, had at length so far put on the garments of Christian charity as to make a visit to her daughter in return. Of course, though I did not encourage it, I objected nothing to this renewed intercourse; which continued to increase until, as in the present instance, I sometimes encountered this good lady on my return from my office. On these occasions I treated her with becoming respect, though without familiarity. I inquired after her health, expressed myself pleased to see her, and joined my wife in requesting her to stay to dinner. Until now, she usually declined to do so; and her manner to myself hitherto was that of a spoiled child indulging in his sulks. But, this day, to my great consternation, she was all smiles and good humor.

A change so sudden portended danger. I looked to my wife, whose grave countenance afforded me no explanation. I looked to the lady herself, my own countenance no doubt sufficiently expressive of the wonder which I felt, but there was little to be read in that quarter which could give me any clue to the mystery. Yet she chattered like a magpie; her conversation running on certain styles of dress, various purchases of silks, and satins, and other stuffs, which she had been buying—a budget of which, I afterward discovered, she had brought with her, in order to display to her daughter. Then she spoke of her teeth, newly filed and plugged, and grinned with frequent effort, that their improved condition might be made apparent. Her chatter was peculiarly that of a flippant and conceited girl-child of sixteen, whose head has been turned by premature bringing out, and the tuition of some vain, silly, wriggling mother. I could see, by my wife's looks, that there was a cause for all this, and waited, with considerable apprehension, for the moment when we should be alone, in order to receive from her an explanation. But little of Mrs. Clifford's conversation was addressed to me, though that little was evidently meant to be particularly civil. But, a little before she took her departure, which was soon after dinner, she asked me with some abruptness, though with a considerable smirk of meaning in her face, if I "knew a Mr. Patrick Delaney." I frankly admitted that I had not this pleasure; and with a still more significant smirk, ending in a very affected simper, meant to be very pleasant, she informed me, as she took her leave, that Julia would make me wiser. I looked to Julia when she was gone, and, with some chagrin, and with few words, she unravelled the difficulty. Her mother—the old fool—was about to be married, and to a Mr. Patrick Delaney, an Irish gentleman, fresh from the green island, who had only been some eighteen months in America.

"You seem annoyed by this affair, Julia; but how does it affect you?"

"Oh, such a match can not turn out well. This Mr. Delaney is a young man, only twenty-five, and what can he see in mother to induce him to marry her? It can only be for the little pittance of property which she possesses."

I shrugged my shoulders while replying:—

"There must be some consideration in every marriage-contract."

"Ah! but, Edward, what sort of a man can it be to whom money is the consideration for marrying a woman old enough to be his mother?"

"And so little money, too. But, Julia, perhaps he marries her as a mother. He is a modest youth, who knows his juvenility, and seeks becoming guardianship. But the thing does not concern us at all."

"She is my mother, Edward."

"True; but still I do not see that the matter should concern us. You do not apprehend that Mr. Patrick Delaney will seek to exercise the authority of a father over either of us?"

"No! but I fear she will repent."

"Why should that be a subject of fear which should be a subject of gratulation? For my part, I hope she may repent. We are told she can not be saved else."

Julia was silent. I continued:—

"But what brings her here, and makes her so suddenly affable with me? That is certainly a matter which looks threatening. Does she explain this to you, Julia?"

"Not otherwise than by declaring she is sorry for former differences."

"Ah, indeed! but her sorrow comes too late, and I very much suspect has some motive. What more? the shaft is not yet shot."

"You guess rightly; she invites us to the wedding, and insists that we must come, as a proof that we harbor no malice."

"Is that all?"

"All, I believe."

"She is more considerate than I expected. Well, you promised her?"

"No; I told her I could say nothing without consulting you."

"And would you wish to go, Julia?"

"Oh, surely, dear husband."

"We will both go, then."

A week afterward the affair took place, and we were among the spectators.

CHAPTER XXXVI.

THE HEART-FIEND FINDS AN ECHO FROM THE FIEND WITHOUT.

AND a spectacle it was! Mrs. Clifford, about to become Mrs. Delaney, was determined that the change in her situation should be distinguished by becoming eclât. Always a silly woman, fond of extravagance and show, she prepared to celebrate an occasion of the greatest folly in a style of greater extravagance than ever. She accordingly collected as many of her former numerous acquaintances as were still willing to appear within a circle in which wealth was no longer to be found. Her house was small, but, as has been elsewhere stated in this narrative, she had made it smaller by stuffing it with the massive and costly furniture which had been less out of place in her former splendid mansion, and had there much better accorded with her fortunes. She now still further stuffed it with her guests. Of course, many of those present, came only to make merry at her expense. Her husband was almost entirely unknown to any of them; and it was enough to settle his pretensions in every mind, that, in the vigor of his youth, a really fine-looking, well-made person of twenty-five, he was about to connect himself, in marriage, with a haggard old woman of fifty, whose personal charms, never very great, were nearly all gone; and whose mind and manners, the grace of youth being no more, were so very deficient in all those qualities which might commend one to a husband. So far as externals went, Mr. Delancy was a very proper man. He behaved with sufficient decorum, and unexpected modesty; and went through the ordeal as composedly as if the occurrence had been frequently before familiar; as indeed we shall discover in the sequel, was certainly the case. But this does not concern us here.

Three rooms were thrown open to the company. We had refreshments in abundance and great variety, and at a certain hour, we were astounded by the clamor of tamborine and fiddle giving due notice to the dancers. Among my few social accomplishments, this of dancing had never been included. Naturally, I should, perhaps, be considered an awkward man. I was conscious of this awkwardness at all times when not excited by action or some earnest motive. I was incapable of that graceful loitering, that flexibleness of mind and body, which excludes the idea of intensity, of every sort, and which constitutes one of the great essentials for success in a ball-room. It was in this very respect that my *friend*, William Edgerton, may be said to have excelled most young men of our acquaintance. He was what, in common speech, is called an accomplished man. Of very graceful person, without much earnestness of character, he had acquired a certain fastidiousness of taste on the subjects of costume and manners, which, without Brummellizing, he yet carried to an extent which betrayed a considerable degree of mental feebleness. This somewhat assimilated him to the fashionable dandy. He walked with an air equally graceful, noble, and unaffected. He was never on stilts, yet he was always *en règle.* He had as little *mauvais honte* as *mauvais ton.* In short, whatever might have been his deficiencies, he was confessedly a very neat specimen of the fine gentleman in its most commendable social sense.

William Edgerton was among the guests of Mrs. Clifford. There had been no previous intimacy between the Edgerton and Clifford families, yet he had been specially invited. Mrs. C. could have had but a single motive for inviting him — so I thought — that of making her evening a jam. She had just that ambition of the lady of small fashion, who regards the number rather than the quality of her guests, and would prefer a saloon full of Esquimaux or Kanzas, and would partake of their sea-blubber, rather than lose the triumph of making more noise than her rival neighbors, the Sprigginses or Wigginses.

William Edgerton did not seek me; but, when I left the side of my wife to pay my respects to some ladies at the opposite end of the room, he approached her. A keen pang that rendered me unconscious of everything I was saying — nay, even of the persons to whom I was addressing myself—shot through my heart, as I beheld him crossing the floor to the place that I had left. Involuntarily, the gracefulness of his person and carriage provoked in my mind a contrast most unfavorable to me, between him and myself. It was no satisfaction to me at that time to reflect that I was less graceful only because I was more earnest, more sincere. This is usually the case, and is reasonably accounted for. Intensity and great earnestness of character, are wholly inconsistent with a nice attention to forms, carriage, demeanor. But what does a lady care for such distinction? Does she even suspect it? Not often. If she could only fancy for a moment that the well-made but awkward man who traverses the room before her, carried in his breast a soul of such ardency and volume that it subjected his very motion arbitrarily to its own excitements, its own convulsions; that the very awkwardness which offended her was the result of the most deep and passionate feelings—feelings which, like the buried flame in the mountain, are continually boiling up for utterance—convulsing the prison-house which retained them—shaking the solid earth with their pent throes, that will not always be pent! Ah! these things do not move ladies' fancies. There are very few endowed with that thoughtful pride which disdains surfaces. Julia Clifford was one of these few! But I little knew it then.

The approach of William Edgerton to my wife was a signal for my torture all that evening. From that moment my mind was wandering. I knew little what I said, or looked, or did. My chat with those around me became, on a sudden, bald and disjointed; and when I beheld the pair, both nobly formed—he tall, graceful, manly—she, beautiful and bending as a lily—a purity beaming, amid all their brightness, from her eyes—a purity which, I had taught myself to believe, was no longer in her heart—when I beheld them advance into the floor, conspicuous over all the rest, in most eyes, as they certainly were in mine—I can not describe—you may conjecture—the cold, fainting sickness which overcame my soul. I could have lain myself down upon the lone, midnight rocks, and surrendered myself to solitude and storm for ever.

They entered the stately measures of the Spanish dance.

But the grace of movement which won the murmuring applause of all around me, only increased the agony of my afflictions. I saw their linked arms—the compliant, willing movements of their mutual forms—and dark were the images of guilt and hateful suspicion which entered my brain and grew to vivid forms, in action before me. I fancied the fierce, passionate yearnings in the heart of Edgerton; I trembled when I conjectured what fancies filled the heart of Julia. I can not linger over the torturing influence of those moments—moments which seemed ages! Enough that I was maddened with the delirium, now almost as its height, which had been for months preying upon my brain like some corroding serpent.

The dance closed. Edgerton conducted her to a seat and placed himself beside her. I kept aloof. I watched them from a distance; and in sustaining this watch, I was compelled to recall my senses with a stern degree of resolution which should save my feelings from the detection of those inquisitive glances which I fancied were all around me. If I was weakest among men, in the disease which destroyed my peace, Heaven knows I was among the strongest of men in concealing its expression at the very moment when every pulsation of my heart was an especial agony. I affected indifference, threw myself into the midst of a group of such people as talk of their neighbor's bonnets or breeches, the rise of stocks, or the fall of rain; and how Mrs. Jenkins has set up her carriage, and Mr. Higgins has been compelled to set down, and to sell out his. Interesting details, perhaps, without which the nine in ten might as well be tongueless or tongue-tied for ever. This stuff I had to hear, and requite in like currency, while my brain was boiling, and dim, but terrible images of strife, and storm, and agony, were rushing through it with howling and hisses. There I sat, thus seemingly engaged, but with an eye ever glancing covertly to the two, who, at that moment, absorbed every thought of my mind, every feeling of my heart, and filled them both with the bitterest commotion. The glances of their mutual eyes, the expression of lip and cheek, I watched with the keenest analysis of suspicion. In Julia, I saw sweetness mixed with a delicate reserve. She seemed to speak but little. Her eyes wandered from her companion—frequently to where I sat—

but I gave myself due credit, at such moments, for the ability with which I conducted my own espionage. My inference—equally unjust and unnatural—that her timid glances to myself denoted in her bosom a consciousness of wrong—seemed to me the most natural and inevitable inference. And when I noted the ardency of Edgerton's gaze, his close, unrelaxing attentions, the seeming forgetfulness of all around which he manifested, I hurried to the conclusion that his words were of a character to suit his looks, and betray in more emphatic utterance, the passion which they also betrayed.

The signal, after a short respite, devoted to fruits, ices, &c., was made for the dancers, and William Edgerton rose. I noted his bow to my wife, saw that he spoke, and necessarily concluded, that he again solicited her to dance. Her lips moved—she bowed slightly—and he again took his seat beside her. I inferred from this that she declined to dance a second time. She was certainly more prudent than himself. I assigned to prudence—to policy—on her part, what might well have been placed to a nobler motive. I went further.

"She will not dance with him," said the busy fiend at my shoulder, "for the very reason that she prefers a quiet seat beside him. In the dance they mingle with others; they can not speak with so much ease and safety. Now she has him all to herself."

I dashed away, forgetful, gloomily, from the knot by which I had been encompassed. I passed into the adjoining room, which was connected by folding doors, with that I left. The crowd necessarily grouped itself around the dancers, and against a window-jamb, I stood absolutely forgetting where I was—alone among the many—with my eye stretching over the heads of the flying masses, to the remote spot where my wife still sat with Edgerton. I was aroused from my hateful dream by a slight touch upon my arm. I started with a painful sense of my own weakness—with a natural dread that the secret misery under which I labored was no longer a secret. I writhed under the conviction that the cold, the sneering, and the worthless, were making merry with my afflictions. I met the gaze of the bride—the mistress of ceremonies—my wife's mother, Mrs. Delaney, late Clifford. I shuddered as I beheld her glance. I could not mistake the volume of meaning in her smile — that wretched smile of her thin, withered lips, brimful of malignant cunning, which said emphatically as such smile could say :—

"I see you on the rack; I know that you are writhing; and I enjoy your tortures."

I started, as if to leave her, with a look of fell defiance, roused, ready to burst forth into utterance, upon my own face. But she gently detained my arm.

"You are troubled."

"No."

"Ah! but you are. Stop awhile. You will feel better."

"Thank you; but I feel very well."

"No, no, you do not. You can not deceive me. I know where the shoe pinches; but what did you expect? Were you simple enough to imagine that a woman would be true to her husband, who was false to her own mother?"

"Fiend!" I muttered in her ear.

"Ha! ha! ha!" was the unmeasured response of the beldame, loud enough for the whole house to hear. I darted from her grasp, which would have detained me still, made my way — how I know not — out of the house, and found myself almost gasping for breath, in the open air of the street.

She, at least, had been sagacious enough to find out my secret!

CHAPTER XXVII.

KINGSLEY.

THE fiendish suggestion of the mother, against the purity of her own child, almost divested me, for the moment, of my own rancor—almost deprived me of my suspicions! Could anything have been more thoroughly horrible and atrocious! It certainly betrayed how deep was the malignant hatred which she had ever borne to myself, and of which her daughter was now required to bear a portion. What a volume of human depravity was opened on my sight, by that single utterance of this wretched mother. Guilt and sin! ye are, indeed, the masters everywhere! How universal is your dominion! How ye rage—how ye riot among souls, and minds, and fancies—never utterly overthrown anywhere—busy always—everywhere—sovereign in how many hapless regions of the heart! Who is pure among men? Who can be sure of himself for a day—an hour? Precious few! None, certainly, who do not distrust their own strength with a humility only to be won from prayer—prayer coupled with moderate desires, and the presence of a constant thought, which teaches that time is a mere agent of eternity, and he who works for the one only, will not even be secure of peace during the period for which he works. Truly, he who lives not for the future is the very last who may reasonably hope to enjoy the blessings of the present.

But this was not the season, nor was mine the mood, for moral reflections of any sort. My secret was known! That was everything. When the conduct of William Edgerton had become such, as to awaken the notice of third persons, I was justified in exacting from him the heavy responsibility he had incurred. The vague, indistinct conviction had long floated before my mind, that I would be required to take his life. The period which was to render this task necessary, was that which had now arrived—when it had been seen by others—not interested like myself—that he had passed the bounds of propriety. Of course, I was arguing in a circle, from which I should have found it impossible to extricate myself. Thousands might have seen that I was jealous, without being able to see any just cause for my jealousy. It was, however, quite enough for a proud spirit like my own, that its secret fear should be revealed. It did not much matter, after this, whether my suspicions were, or were not causeless. It was enough that they were known—that busy, meddling women, and men about town, should distinguish me with a finger—should say: "His wife is very pretty and—very charitable!"

"Ha! ha! ha!"

I, too, could laugh, under such musings, and in the spirit of Mrs. Delaney—late Clifford.

"Ha! ha! ha!" The street echoed, beneath the windows of that reputable lady, with my involuntary, fiendish laughter. I stood there—and the music rang through my senses like the cries of exulting demons. She was there—of my wife the thoughts ran thus, she was there, whirling, perchance, in the mazes of that voluptuous dance, then recently become fashionable among us; his arm about her waist—her form inclining to his, as if seeking support and succor—and both of them forgetting all things but the mutual intoxication which swallowed up all things and thoughts in the absorbing sensuality of one! Or, perhaps, still apart, they sat to themselves—her ear fastened upon his lips—her consciousness given wholly to his discourse; and that discourse!—"Ha! ha! ha!"—I laughed again, as I hurried away from the spot, with gigantic strides, taking the direction which led to my own lonely dwelling.

All was stillness there, but there was no peace. I entered the piazza, threw myself into a chair, and gazed out upon the leaves and waters, trying to collect my scattered thoughts—trying to subdue my blood, that my thoughts might meet in deliberation upon the desolating prospect which was then spread before me. But I struggled for this in vain. But one thought was mine at that hour. But one fearful image gathered in completeness and strength before my mind; and that was one calculated to banish all others and baffle all their deliberations.

"The blood of William Edgerton must be shed, and by these hands! My disgrace is known! There is no help for it!"

I had repeatedly resolved this gloomy conviction in my mind. It was now to receive shape and substance. It was a thing no longer to be thought upon. It was a thing to be done! This necessity staggered me. The kindness of the father, the kindness and long true friendship of the son himself, how could I requite this after such a fashion? How penetrate the peaceful home of that fond family with an arm of such violence, as to rend their proudest offspring from the parental tree, and, perhaps, in destroying it, blight for ever the venerable trunk upon which it was borne? Let it not be fancied that these feelings were without effect. Let it not be supposed that I weakly, willingly, yielded to the conviction of this cruel necessity—that I determined, without a struggle, upon this seemingly necessary measure! Verily, I then, in that dreary house and hour, wrestled like a strong man with the unbidden prompter, who counselled me to the deed of blood. I wrestled with him as the desperate man, knowing the supernatural strength of his enemy, wrestles with a demon. The strife was a fearful one. I could not suppress my groans of agony; and the cold sweat gathered and stood upon my forehead in thick, clammy drops.

But the struggle was vain to effect my resolution. It had been too long present as a distinct image before my imagination. I had already become too familiar with its aspects. It had the look of a fate to my mind. I fancied myself—as probably most men will do, whose self-esteem is very active—the victim of a fate. My whole life tended to confirm this notion. I was chosen out from the beginning for a certain work, in which, myself a victim, I was to carry out the designs of destiny in the case of other victims. I had struggled long not to believe this—not to do this work. But the struggle was at last at an end. I was convinced, finally. I was ready for the work. I was resigned to my fate. But oh! how grateful once had one of these victims seemed in my eyes! How beautiful, and still how dear was the other!

I rose from my seat and struggle, with the air of one strengthened by thoughtful resolution for any act. Prayer could not have strengthened me more. I felt a singular degree of strength. I can well understand that of fanaticism from my own feelings. Nothing, in the shape of danger, could have deterred me from the deed. I positively had no remaining fear. But, how was it to be done? With this inquiry in my mind, still unanswered, I took a light, went into my study, and drew from my escritoir the few small weapons which I had in possession. These are soon named. One was a neat little dirk—broad in blade, double-edged, short—sufficient for all my purposes. I examined my pistols and loaded them—a small, neat pair, the present of Edgerton himself. This fact determined me not to use them. I restored them to the escritoir; put the dagger between the folds of my vest, and prepared to leave the house.

At this moment a heavy knocking was heard at the gate. I resumed my seat in the piazza until the servant should report the nature of the interruption. He was followed in by my friend Kingsley.

"I am glad to find you home," said he abruptly, grasping my hand; "home, and not a-bed. The hour is late, I know, but the devil never keeps ordinary hours, and men, driven by his satanic majesty, have some excuse for following his example."

This exordium promised something unusual. The manner of Kingsley betrayed excitement. Nay, it was soon evident he had been taking a superfluous quantity of wine. His voice was thick, and he spoke excessively loud in order to be intelligible. There was something like a defying desperation in his tones, in the dare-devil swagger of his movement, and the almost iron pressure of his grasp upon my fingers. I subdued my own passions—nay, they were subdued—singularly so, by the resolution I had made before his entrance, and was able, therefore, to appear calm and smooth as summer water in his eyes.

"What's the matter?" I asked. "You seem excited. No evil, I trust?"

"Evil, indeed! Not much; but even if it were, I tell you,

Ned Clifford, I am just now in the mood to say, 'Evil be thou my good!' I have reason to say it; and, by the powers, it will not be said only. I will make evil my good after a fashion of my own; but how much good or how little evil, will be yet another question."

I was interested, in spite of myself, by the vehemence and unusual seriousness of my companion's manner. It somewhat harmonized with my own temper, and in a measure beguiled me into a momentary heedlessness of my particular griefs. I urged him to a more frank statement of the things that troubled him.

"Can I serve you in anything?" was the inquiry which concluded my assurance that I was sufficiently his friend to sympathize with him in his afflictions.

"You can serve me, and I need your service. You can serve me in two respects; nay, if you do not, I know not which side to turn for service. In the first place, then, I wish a hundred dollars, and I wish it to-night. In the next place, I wish a companion—a man not easily scared, who will follow where I lead him, and take part in a 'knock down and drag out,' if it should become necessary, without asking the why and the wherefore."

"You shall have the money, Kingsley."

"Stay! Perhaps I may never pay it you again."

"I shall regret that, for I can ill afford to lose any such sum; but, even to know that would not prevent me from lending you in your need. It is enough that you are in want. You tell me you are."

"I am; but my wants are not such as a pure moralist, however strong might be his friendship, would be disposed to gratify. I shall stake that money on the roll of the dice."

"Impossible! You do not game!"

"True as a gospel! Hark you, Clifford, and save us the homily. I am a ruined man—ruined by the d——d dice and the deceptive cards. I shall pay you back the hundred dollars, but I shall have precious little after that."

"But, surely, I was not misinformed. You were rich a few years ago."

"A few months! But the case is the same. I am poor now.

My riches had wings. I am reduced to my tail-feathers; but I will flourish with these to the last. I have fallen among thieves. They have clipped my plumage—close! close! They have stripped me of everything, but some small matters which, when sold, will just suffice to get me horse or halter. Some dirty acres in Alabama, are all I absolutely have remaining of any real value. But there is one thing that I may have, if I stake boldly for it."

"You will only lose again. The hope of a gamester rises, in due degree, with the increasing lightness of his pockets."

"Do not mistake me. I hope nothing from your hundred dollars; indeed, fifty will answer. I propose to employ it only as a pretext. I expect to lose it, and lose it this very night. But it will give me an opportunity to ascertain what I have suspected—too late, indeed, to save myself—that I have been the victim of false dice and figured cards. You say you will let me have the money—will you go with me—will you see me through?"

He extended his hand as he spoke, I grasped it. He shook it with a hearty feeling, while a bright smile almost dissipated the cloud from his face.

"You are a man, Clifford; and now, would you believe it, our excellent, immaculate young friend, Mr. William Edgerton, refused me this money."

"Strange! Edgerton is not selfish—he is not mean! From *that* vice he is certainly free."

"By G–d, I don't know that! He refused me the money; refused to go with me. I saw him at eight o'clock, at his own room, where he was rigging himself out for some d——d tea-drinking; told him my straits, my losses, my object and all; and what was his plea, think you? Why, he disapproved of gambling; couldn't think of lending me a sixpence for any such purpose; and, as for going into such a suspected quarter as a gambling-house—wouldn't do it for the world! Was there ever such a puritan—such a humbug!"

I did William Edgerton only justice in my reply:—

"I've no doubt, Kingsley, that such are his real principles. He would have lent you thrice the money, freely, had not your object been avowed."

"But what a devil sort of despotism is that! Can't a friend get drunk, or game, or swagger? may he not depart from the highway, and sidle into an alley, without souring his friend's temper and making him stingy? I don't understand it at all. I'm glad, at least, to find you are of another sort of stuff."

"Nay, Kingsley, I will lend you the money—go with you, as you desire; but, understand me, I do not, no more than Edgerton, approve of this gambling."

"Tut, tut! I don't want you to preach, though I could hear you with a devilish sight better temper than him. There's a hundred things that one's friend don't approve of, but shall he desert him for all that? Leave him to be plucked, and kicked, and abandoned; and, moralizing, with a grin over his fate, say, 'I told you so!' No! no! Give me the fellow that'll stand by me—keep me out of evil, if he can, but stand by me, nevertheless, at all events; and not suffer me to be swallowed up at the last moment, when an outstretched finger might save!"

"But, am I to think, Kingsley, that my help can do this?"

"No! not exactly—it may—but if it does not, what then? I shall lose the money, but you sha'n't. But, truth to speak, Clifford, I do not propose to myself the recovery of what is lost. I know I have been the prey of sharpers. That is to say, I have every reason to believe so, and I have had a hint to that effect. I have a spice of the devil in me, accordingly—a mocking, mortifying devil, that jeers me with my d——d simplicity; and I propose to go and let the swindlers know, in a way as little circuitous as possible, that I am not blind to the fact that they have made an ass of me. There will be some satisfaction, in that. I will write myself down an ass, for their benefit, only to enjoy the satisfaction of kicking a little like one. I invite you on a kicking expedition."

I felt for my dagger in my bosom, as I answered: "Very good! Have you weapons?"

"Hickory! You see! a moderate axe-handle, that'll make its sentiments understood. You are warned; you see what you are to expect. I will not take you in. Are you ready for a scratch?"

"Allons!" I replied indifferently. The truth is, my bosom was full of a recklessness of a far more sweeping character than his own. I was in the mood for strife. It promised only the more thoroughly to prepare me for the darker trial which was before me, and which my secret soul was meditating all the while with an intense and gloomy tenacity of purpose.

CHAPTER XXVIII.

MORALS OF ENTERPRISE.

I GOT him the money he required; and we were about to set forth, when he exclaimed abruptly :—

"Put money in thy own purse, Clifford. It may be necessary to practise a little *ruse de guerre*. In playing my game, it may be important that you should seem to play one also. You have no scruples to fling the dice or flirt the cards for the nonce."

"None! But I should like to know your plans. Tell me, in the first place, your precise object."

"Simply to detect certain knaves, and save certain fools. The knaves have ruined me, and I make no lamentations; but there are others in their clutches still, quite as ignorant as myself, who may be saved before they are stripped entirely. The object is not a bad one; for the rest, trust to me. I mean no harm; a little mischief only; and, at most, a tweak of one proboscis or more. There's risk, of a certainty, as there is in sucking an egg; but you are a man! Not like that d——d milksop, who gives up his friend as soon as he gets poor, and proffers him a sermon by way of telling him—precious information, truly—that he's in a fair way to the devil. The toss of a copper for such friendship."

The humor of Kingsley tallied somewhat with my own. It had in it a spice of recklessness which pleased me. Perhaps, too, it tended somewhat to relieve and qualify the intenseness of that excitement in my brain, which sometimes rose to such a pitch as led me to apprehend madness. That I was a monomaniac has been admitted, perhaps not a moment too soon for the author's candor. The sagacity of the reader made him independent of the admission.

"Your beggar," said he, somewhat abruptly, "has the only true feeling of independence. Absolutely, I never knew till now what it was to be thoroughly indifferent to what might come to-morrow. I positively care for nothing. I am the first prince Sans Souci. That shall be my title when I get among the Cumanches. I will have a code of laws and constitution to suit my particular humor, and my chief penalties shall be inflicted upon your fellows who grunt. A sigh shall incur a week's solitary confinement; a sour look, pillory; and for a groan, the hypochondriac shall lose his head! My prime minister shall be the fellow who can longest use his tongue without losing his temper; and the man who can laugh and jest shall always have his plate at my table. Good-humored people shall have peculiar privileges. It shall be a certificate in one's favor, entitling him to so many acres, that he takes the world kindly. Such a man shall have two wives, provided he can keep them peacefully in the same house. His daughters shall have dowries from government. The prince of Sans Souci will himself provide for them."

I made some answer, half jest, half earnest, in a mood of mocking bitterness, which, perhaps, more truly accorded with the temper of both of us. He did not perceive the bitterness, however.

"You jest, but mine is not altogether jest. Half-serious glimpses of what I tell you float certainly before my eyes. Such things may happen yet, and the southwest is the world in which you are yet to see many wondrous things. The time must come when Texas shall stretch to Mexico. These miserable slaves and reptiles—mongrel Spaniards and mongrel Indians—can not very long bedevil that great country. It must fall into other hands. It must be ours; and who, when that time comes, will carry into the field more thorough claims than mine. Master of myself, fearing nothing, caring for nothing; with a gallant steed that knows my voice, and answers with whinny and pricked ears to my encouragement; with a rifle that can clip a Mexican—dollar or man—at a hundred yards, and a heart that can defy the devil over his own dish, and with but one spoon between us—and who so likely to win his principality as myself? Look to see it, Clifford; I shall be a prince in Mexico; and when you hear of the prince Sans Souci be assured you know the man. Seek me then, and ask what you will. You have *carte blanche* from this moment."

"I shall certainly keep it in mind, prince."

"Do so: laugh as you please; it is only becoming that you should laugh in the presence of Sans Souci; but do not laugh in token of irreverence. You must not be too skeptical. It does not follow because I am a dare-devil that I am a thoughtless one. I have been so, perhaps, but from this moment I go to work! I shall be fettered by fortune no longer. Thank Heaven, that is now done—gone—lost; I am free from its incumbrance! I feel myself a prince, indeed; a man, every inch of me. This night I devote as a fitting finish to my old lifeless existence.

"Hear me!" he continued; "you laugh again, Clifford—very good! Laugh on, but hear me. You shall hear more of me in time to come. I fancy I shall be a fellow of considerable importance, not in Texas simply, or in Mexico, but here—here in your own self-opinionated United States. Suppose a few things, and go along with me while I speak them. That Texas must stretch to Mexico I hold to be certain. A very few years will do that. It needs only thirty thousand more men from our southern and southwestern States, and the brave old English tongue shall arouse the best echoes in the city of Montezuma! That done, and floods of people pour in from all quarters. It needs nothing but a feeling of security and peace—a conviction that property will be tolerably safe, under a tolerably stable government—in other words, an Anglo-Saxon government—to tempt millions of discontented emigrants from all quarters of the world. Will this result have no results of its own, think you? Will the immense resources of Mexico and Texas, represented, as they then will be, by a stern, pressing, performing people, have no effect upon these states of yours? They will have the greatest; nay, they will become essential to balance your own federal weight, and keep you all in equilibrio. For look you, the first hubbub with Great Britain gives you Canada, at the expense of some of your coast-towns, a few millions of treasure, and the loss of fifty thousand men. A bad exchange for the south; for Canada will make six ponderous states, the policy and character of which will be New England all over. To balance this you will have your Florida territory,* of which two feeble states may be made. Not enough for your purposes. But the same war with England will render it necessary that your fleet should take possession of Cuba; which, after a civil apology to Spain for taking such a liberty with her possessions, and, perhaps, a few millions by way of hush-money, you carve into two more states, and, in this manner, try to bolster up your federal relations. How many of her West India islands Great Britain will be able to keep after such a war, is another problem, the solution of which will depend upon the relative strength of fleets and success of seamanship. These islands, which should of right be ours, and without which we can never be sure against any maritime power so great and so arrogant as England, once conquered by our arms, find their natural, moral, and social affinities in the southern states entirely; and, so far, contribute to strengthen you in your congressional conflicts. But these are not enough, for the simple reason that the population of states, purely agricultural, never makes that progress which is made in this respect by a commercial and manufacturing people. With the command of the gulf, the possession of an independent fleet by the Texans, the political characteristics of the states of Carolina, Georgia, Florida, Alabama, Mississippi, Louisiana, and Arkansas, must undergo certain marked changes, which can only be neutralized by the adoption, on the part of these states, of a new policy corresponding with their change of interests. How far the cultivation of cotton by Texas will lead to its abandonment in Carolina and Georgia, is a question which the next ten years must solve. That they will be compelled to abandon it is inevitable, unless they can succeed in raising the article at six cents; a probability which no cotton-planter in either of these states will be willing to contemplate now for an instant. Meanwhile, Texas is spreading herself right and left. She conquers the Cumanches, subdues the native mongrel Mexicans. Her Houstons and Lamars are succeeded by other and abler men,

* Florida, since admitted, but unhappily, as a single state.

under whose control the evils of government, which followed the sway of such small animals as the Guerreros, and the Bolivars, the Bustamentés, and Sant' Annas, are very soon eradicated; and the country, the noblest that God ever gave to man, in the hands of men, becomes a country!—a great and glorious country—stretching from the gulf to the Pacific, and providing the natural balance, which, in a few years, the southern states of this Union will inevitably need, by which alone your great confederacy will be kept together. You see, therefore, why I speed to Texas. Should I not, with my philosophy, my horse, and my rifle—not to speak of stout heart and hand—reasonably aspire to the principality of Sans Souci? Laugh, if you please, but be not irreverent. You shall have *carte blanche* then if you will have a becoming faith now, on the word of a prince I say it, It is written—Sans Souci."*

"Altissimo, excellentissimo, serenissimo!"

"Bravissimo, you improve; you will make a courtier—but mum now about my projects. We must suppress our dignities here. We are at the entrance of our hell!"

We had reached the door of a low habitation in a secluded street. The house was of wood—an ordinary hovel of two stories. A cluster of similar fabrics surrounded it, most of which, I afterward discovered—though this fact could not be conjectured by an observer from the street—were connected by blind alleys, inner courts, and chambers and passages running along the ground floors. We stopped an instant, Kingsley having his hand upon the little iron knocker, a single black ring, that worked against an ordinary iron knob.

"Before I knock," said he, in a whisper, "before I knock, Clifford, let me say that if you have any reluctance—"

"None! none! knock!"

"You will meet with some dirty rascals, and you must not only meet them with seeming civility, but as if you shared in their tastes—sought the same objects only—the getting of money—the only object which alone is clearly comprehensible by their understanding."

"Go ahead! I will see you through."

* All these speculations were written in 1840–'41. I need not remark upon those which have since been verified.

"A word more! Get yourself in play at a different table from me. You will find rogues enough around, ready to relieve you of your Mexicans. Leave me to my particular enemy; you will soon see whose shield I touch—but keep an occasional eye upon us; and all that I ask farther at your hands, should you see us by the ears, is to keep other fingers from taking hold of mine."

A heavy stroke of the knocker, followed by three light ones and a second heavy stroke, produced us an answer from within. The door unclosed, and by the light of a dim lamp, I discovered before me, as a sort of warden, a little yellow, weather-beaten, skin-dried Frenchman, whom I had frequently before seen at a fruit-shop in another part of the city. He looked at me, however, without any sign of recognition—with a blank, dull, indifferent countenance; motioned us forward in silence, and reclosing the door, sunk into a chair immediately behind it. I followed my companion through a passage which was unfathomably dark, up a flight of stairs, which led us into a sort of refreshment room. Tables were spread, with decanters, glasses, and tumblers upon them, that appeared to be in continual use. In a recess, stood that evil convenience of most American establishments, whether on land or sea, a liquor bar; its shelves crowded with bottles, all of which seemed amply full, and ready to complete the overthrow of the victim, which the other appliances of such a dwelling must already have actively begun.

"Here you may take in the Dutch courage, Clifford, should you lack the native. This, I know, is not the case with you, and yet the novelty of one's situation frequently overcomes a sensitive mind like fear. Perhaps a julep may be of use."

"None for me. I need no farther stimulant than the mere sense of *mouvement*. I take fire, like a wheel, by my own progress."

"Pretty much the same case with myself. But I have been in the habit of drinking here, of late, and too deeply. To-night, however, as I said before, ends all these habits. If there is honey in the carcass, and strength from the sleep, there is wisdom from the folly, and virtue from the vice. There is a moral as well as a physical recoil, that most certainly follows the overcharge; and really, speaking according to my sincere conviction,

I never felt myself to be a better man, than just at this moment when I am about to do that which my own sense of morality fails altogether to justify. I do not know that I make you understand my feelings; I scarcely understand them myself; but of this sort they are, and I am really persuaded that I never felt in a better disposition to be a good man and a working man than just at the close of a career which has been equally profligate and idle."

I think my companion can be understood. There seems, in fact, very little mystery in his moral progress. I understood him, but did not answer. I was not anxious to keep up the ball of conversation which he had begun with a spirit so mixed up of contradictions — so earnest yet so playful. A deep sense of shame unquestionably lurked beneath his levity; and yet I make no question that he felt in truth, and for the first time, that degree of mental hardihood of which he boasted.

He advanced through the refreshment-room, to a door which led to an apartment in an adjoining tenement. It was closed, but unfastened. The sound of voices, an occasional buzz, or a slight murmur, came to our ears from within; that of rattling dice and rolling balls was more regular and more intelligible. Kingsley laid his hand upon the latch, and looked round to me. His eye was kindled with a playful sort of malicious light. A smile of pleasant bitterness was on his lips. He said to me in a whisper: —

"Stake your money slowly. A Mexican is the lowest stake. Keep to that, and lose as little as possible. You will soon see me sufficiently busy, and I will endeavor to urge my labors forward, so as to make your purgatory a short one. I shall only wait till I feel myself cheated in the game, to begin that which I came for. See that I have fair play in *that, mon ami*, and I care very little about the other."

He lifted the latch as he concluded, and I followed him into the apartment.

CHAPTER XXIX.

THE HELL.

THE scene that opened upon us was, to me, a painfully interesting one. It was a mere hell, without any of those attractive adjuncts which, in a diseased state of popular refinement, such as exists in the fashionable atmospheres of London and Paris, provides it with decorations, and conceals its more discouraging and offensive externals. The charms of music, lovely women, gay lights, and superb drapery and furniture, were here entirely wanting. No other arts beyond the single passion for hazard, which exists, I am inclined to think, in a greater or less degree in every human breast, were here employed to beguile the young and unsuspecting mind into indulgence. The establishment into which I had fallen, seemed to presuppose an acquaintance, already formed, of the gamester with his fascinating vice. It was evidently no place to seduce the uninitiate. The passion must have been already awakened—the guardianship of the good angel lulled into indifference or slumber—before the young mind could be soon reconciled to the moral atmosphere of such a scene.

The apartment was low and dimly lighted. Groups of small tables intended for two persons were all around. In the centre of the floor were tables of larger size, which were surrounded by the followers of Pharo. Unoccupied tables, here and there, were sprinkled with cards and domino; while, as if to render the characteristics of the place complete, a vapor of smoke and a smell of beer assailed our senses as we entered.

There were not many persons present—I conjectured, at a glance, that there might be fifteen; but we heard occasional voices from an inner room, and a small door opening in the rear discovered a retreat like that we occupied, in the dim light of which I perceived moving faces and shadows, and Kingsley informed me that there were several rooms all similarly occupied with ours.

An examination of the persons around me, increased the unpleasant feelings which the place had inspired. With the exception of a few, the greater number were evidently superior to their employments. Several of them were young men like my companion—men not yet lost to sensibility, who looked up with some annoyance as they beheld Kingsley accompanied by a stranger. Two or three of the inmates were veteran gamesters. You could see *that* in their business-like nonchalance—their rigid muscles—the manner at once demure and familiar. They were evidently "*habitués de l'enfer*"—men to whom cards and dice were as absolutely necessary now, as brandy and tobacco to the drunkard. These men were always at play. Even the smallest interval found them still shuffling the cards, and looking up at every opening of the door, as if in hungering anticipation of the prey. At such periods alone might you behold any expression of anxiety in their faces. This disappeared entirely the moment that they were in possession of the victim. That imperturbable composure which distinguished them was singularly contrasted with the fidgety eagerness and nervous rapidity by which you could discover the latter; and I glanced over the operations of the two parties, as they were fairly shown in several sets about the room, with a renewed feeling of wonder how a man so truly clever and strong, in some things, as Kingsley, should allow himself to be drawn so deeply into such low snares; the tricks of which seemed so apparent, and the attractions of which, in the present instance, were obviously so inferior and low. I little knew by what inoffensive and gradual changes the human mind, having once commenced its downward progress, can hurry to the base; nor did I sufficiently allow for that love of hazard itself, in games of chance, which I have already expressed the opinion, is natural to the proper heart of man, belongs to a rational curiosity, and arises, most probably, from that highest property of his intellect, namely, the love of art and intellectual ingenuity. It would be very important to know this fact, since then, instead of the blind hostility which is entertained for sports of this description, by certain classes of moralists among us, we might so employ their ministry as to deprive them of their hurtfulness and make them permanently beneficial in the cause of good education.

Kingsley seemed to conjecture my thoughts. A smile of lofty significance expressing a feeling of mixed scorn and humility, rose upon his countenance—as if admitting his own feebleness, while insisting upon his recovered strength. A sentence which he uttered to me in a whisper, at this moment, was intended to convey some such meaning.

"It was only when thrown to the earth, Clifford, that the wrestler recovered his strength."

"That fable," I replied, "proves that he was no god, at least. Of the earth, earthy, he found strength only in his sphere. The moment he aspired above it the god crushed him. I doubt if Hercules could have derived any benefit from the same source."

"Ah! I am no Hercules, but you will also find that I am no Antæus. I fall, but I rise again, and I am not crushed. This is peculiarly the source of *human* strength."

"Better not to fall."

"Ah! you are too late from Utopia. But—"

We were interrupted; a voice at my elbow—a soft, clear, insinuating voice addressed my companion:—

"Ah, Monsieur Kingsley, I rejoice to see you."

Kingsley gave me a single look, which said everything, as he turned to meet the new-comer. The latter continued:—

"Though worsted in that last encounter, you do not despair, I see."

"No! why should I?"

"True, why? Fortune baffles skill, but what of that? She is capricious. Her despotism is feminine; and in her empire, more certainly than any other, it may be said boldly, that, with change of day there is change of doom. It is not always rain."

"Perhaps not, but we may have such a long spell of it that everything is drowned. 'It's a long lane,' says the proverb, 'that has no turn;' but a man be done up long before he gets to the turning place."

The other replied by some of the usual commonplaces by

which, in condescending language, the gamester provokes and stimulates his unconscious victim. Kingsley, however, had reached a period of experience which enabled him to estimate these phrases at their proper worth.

"You would encourage me," he said quietly, and in tones which, to the unnoteful ear, would have seemed natural enough, but which, knowing him as I did, were slightly sarcastic, and containing a deeper signification than they gave out: "but you *are* the better player. I am now convinced of that. Something there is in fortune, doubtless; my self-esteem makes me willing to admit that; and yet I do not deceive myself. You have been too much for me—you are!"

"The difference is trifling, very trifling, I suspect. A little more practice will soon reconcile that."

"Ha! ha! you forget the practice is to be paid for."

"True, but it is the base spirit only that scruples at the cost of its accomplishments."

"Surely, surely!"

"You are fresh for the encounter to-night?"

"Pleasantly put! Is the query meant for the player or his purse?"

"Good, very good! Why, truly, there is no necessary affinity between them."

"And yet the one without the other would scarcely be able to commend himself to so excellent an artist as Mr. Latour Cleveland. Clifford, let me introduce you to my *enemy;* Mr. Cleveland, my *friend.*"

In this manner was I introduced. Thus was I made acquainted with the particular individual whom it was the meditated purpose of Kingsley to expose. But, though thus marked in the language of his introduction, there was nothing in the tone or manner of my companion, at all calculated to alarm the suspicions of the other. On the contrary, there was a sort of reckless joviality in the air of *abandon*, with which he presented me and spoke. A natural curiosity moved me to examine Cleveland more closely. He was what we should call, in common speech, a very elegant young man. He was probably thirty or thirty-five years of age, tall, graceful, rather slenderish, and of particular nicety in his dress. All his clothes were disposed with the happiest precision. White kid-gloves covered his taper fingers. Withdrawn, a rich diamond blazed upon one hand, while a seal-ring, of official dimensions, with characters cut in lava, decorated the other. His movements betrayed the same nice method which distinguished the arrangement of his dress. His evolutions might all have been performed by trumpet signal, and to the sound of measured music. He was evidently one of those persons whose feelings are too little earnest, ever to affect their policy; too little warm ever to disparage the rigor of their customary play; one of those cold, nice men, who, without having a single passion at work to produce one condition of feeling higher than another, are yet the very ideals of the most narrow and concentrated selfishness. His face was thin, pale, and intelligent. His lips were thick, however—the eyes bright, like those of a snake, but side-looking, never direct, never upward, and always with a smiling shyness in their glance, in which a suspicious mind like my own would always find sufficient occasion for distrust.

Mr. Cleveland bestowed a single keen glance upon me while going through the ordeal of introduction. But his scrutiny labored under one disadvantage. His eyes did not encounter mine! One loses a great deal, if his object be the study of human nature, if he fails in this respect.

"Much pleasure in making your acquaintance, Mr. Clifford; trust, however, you will find me no worse enemy than your friend has done."

"If he find *you* no worse, he will find himself no better. He will pay for his enmity, whatever its degree, as I have done, and be wiser, by reason of his losses."

"Ah! you think too much of your ill fortunes. That is bad. It takes from your confidence and so enfeebles your skill. You should think of it less seriously. Another cast, and the tables change. You will have your revenge."

"I *will!*" said Kingsley with some emphasis, and a gravity which the other did not see. He evidently heard the words only as he had been accustomed to hear them—from the lips of young gamesters who perpetually delude themselves with hopes based upon insane expectations. A benignant smile mantled the cheeks of the gamester.

"Ah, well! I am ready; but if you think me too much for you—"

He paused. The taunt was deliberately intended. It was the customary taunt of the gamester. On the minds of half the number of young men, it would have had the desired effect —of goading vanity, and provoking the self-esteem of the conceited boy into a sort of desperation, when the powers of sense and caution become mostly suspended, and no unnecessary suspicion or watchfulness then interferes to increase the difficulty of plucking the pigeon. I read the smile on Kingsley's lip. It was brief, momentary, pleasantly contemptuous. Then, suddenly, as if he had newly recollected his policy, his countenance assumed a new expression—one more natural to the youth who has been depressed by losses, vexed at defeat, but flatters himself that the atonement is at hand. Perhaps, something of the latent purpose of his mind increased the intense bitterness in the manner and tones of my companion.

"Too much for me, Mr. Cleveland! No, no! You are willing, I see, to rob good fortune of some of her dues. You crow too soon. I have a shrewd presentiment that I shall be quite too much *for you* to-night."

A pleasant and well-satisfied smile of Cleveland answered the speaker.

"I like that," said he; "it proves two things, both of which please me. Your trifling losses have not hurt your fortunes, nor the adverse run of luck made you despond of better success hereafter. It is something of a guaranty in favor of one's performance that he is sure of himself. In such case he is equally sure of his opponent."

"Look to it, then, for I have just that sort of self-guaranty which makes me sure of mine. I shall play deeply, that I may make the most of my presentiments. . Nay, to show you how confident I am, this night restores me all that I have lost, or leaves me nothing more to lose."

The eyes of the other brightened.

"That is said like a man. I thank you for your warning. Shall we begin?"

"Ready, ay, ready!" was the response of Kingsley, as he turned to one of the tables. Quietly laying down upon it the short, heavy stick which he carried, he threw off his gloves, and rubbed his hands earnestly together, laughing the while without restraint, as if possessed suddenly of some very pleasant and ludicrous fancy.

"They laugh who win," remarked Cleveland, with something of coldness in his manner.

"Ha! ha! ha!" was the only answer of Kingsley to this remark. The other continued—and I now clearly perceived that his purpose was provocation:—

"It is certainly a pleasure to win your money, Kingsley—you bear it with so much philosophy. Nay, it seems to give you pleasure, and thus lessens the pain I should otherwise feel in receiving the fruits of my superiority."

"Ha! ha! ha!" again repeated Kingsley. "Excuse me, Mr. Cleveland. I am reminded of your remark, 'They laugh who win.' I am laughing, as it were, anticipatively. I am so certain that I shall have my revenge to-night."

Cleveland looked at him for a moment with some curiosity, then called:—

"Philip!"

He was answered by a young mulatto—a tall, good-looking fellow, who approached with a mixed air of equal deference and self-esteem, plaited frills to a most immaculately white shirt-collar, a huge bulbous breastpin in his bosom, chains and seals, and all the usual equipments of Broadway dandyism. The fellow approached us with a smile; his eyes looking alternately to Cleveland and Kingsley, and, as I fancied, with no unequivocal sneer in their expression, as they settled on the latter. A significance of another kind appeared in the look of Cleveland as he addressed him.

"Get us the pictures, Philip—the latest cuts—and bring—ay, you may bring the ivories."

In a few moments, the preliminaries being despatched, the two were seated at a table, and a couple of packs of cards were laid beside them. Kingsley drew my attention to the cards. They were of a kind that my experience had never permitted me to see before. In place of ordinary kings and queens and knaves, these figures were represented in attitudes and costumes the most indecent—such as the prolific genius of Parisian bawdry alone could conceive and delineate. It seems to be a general opinion among rogues that knavery is never wholly triumphant unless the mind is thoroughly degraded; and for this reason it is, perhaps, that establishments devoted to purposes like the present, have, in most countries, for their invariable adjuncts, the brothel and the bar-room. If they are not in the immediate tenement, they are sufficiently nigh to make the work of moral prostitution comparatively easy, in all its ramifications, with the young and inconsiderate mind. Kingsley turned over the cards, and I could see that while affecting to show me the pictures he was himself subjecting the cards to a close inspection of another kind. This object was scarcely perceptible to myself, who knew his suspicions, and could naturally conjecture his policy. It did not excite the alarm of his antagonist.

The parties sat confronting each other. Kingsley drew forth a wallet, somewhat ostentatiously, which he laid down beside him. The sight of his wallet staggered me. By its bulk I should judge it to have held thousands; yet he had assured me that he had nothing beside, the one hundred dollars which he had procured from me. My surprise increased as I saw him open the wallet, and draw from one of its pockets the identical roll which I had put into his hands. The bulk of the pocket-book seeemed scarcely to be diminished. My suspicions were beginning to be roused. I began to think that he had told me a falsehood; but he looked up at this instant, and a bright manly smile on his deep purposeful countenance, reassured me. I felt that there was some policy in the business which was not for me then to fathom. The cards were cut. A box of dice was also in the hands of Cleveland.

"Spots or pictures?" said Cleveland.

"Pictures first, I suppose," said Kingsley, "till the blood gets up. The ivories then as the most rapid. But these pictures are really so tempting. A new supply, Philip!"

"Just received, sir," said the other.

"And how shall we begin?" demanded Cleveland, drawing a handful of bills, gold, and silver, from his pocket; "yellow, white, or brown?"

It was thus, I perceived, that gold, silver, and paper money, were described.

"Shall it be child's play, or—"

"Man's, man's!" replied Kingsley, with some impatience. "I am for beginning with a cool hundred," and, to my consternation, he unfolded the roll he had of me, counted out the bills, refolded them and placed them in a saucer, where they were soon covered with a like sum by his antagonist. I was absolutely sickened, and stared aghast upon my reckless companion. He looked at me with a smile.

"To your own game, Clifford. You will find men enough for your money in either of the rooms. Should you run short, come to me."

Thus confidently did he speak; yet he had actually but the single hundred which he had so boldly staked on the first issue. I thought him lost; but he better knew his game than I. He also knew his man. The eyes of Cleveland were on the huge wallet in reserve, of which the "cool hundred" might naturally be considered a mere sample. I had not courage to wait for the result, but wandered off, with a feeling not unallied to terror, into an adjoining apartment.

CHAPTER XXX.

FALSE DICE.

Though confounded with what I had seen of the proceedings of Kingsley, I was yet willing to promote, so far as I could, the purpose for which we came. I felt too, that, unless I played, that purpose, or my own, might reasonably incur suspicion. To rove through the several rooms of a gambling-house, surveying closely the proceedings of others, without partaking, in however slight a degree, in the common business of the establishment, was neither good policy nor good manners. Unless there to play, what business had I there? Accordingly I resolved to play. But of these games I knew nothing. It was necessary to choose among them, and, without a choice I turned to one of the tables where the genius of Roulette presided. A motley group, none of whom I knew, surrounded it. I placed my dollar upon one of the spots, red or black, I know not which, and saw it, in a moment after, spooned up with twenty others by the banker. I preferred this form of play to any other, for the simple reason that it did not task my own faculties, and left me free to bestow my glances on the proceedings of my friend. But I soon discovered that the contagion of play is irresistible; and so far from putting my stake down at intervals, and with philosophic indifference, I found myself, after a little while, breathlessly eager in the results. These, after the first few turns of the machine, had ceased to be unfavorable. I was confounded to discover myself winning. Instead of one I put down two Mexicans.

"Put down ten," said one of the bystanders, a dark, sulky-looking little yellow man, who seemed a veteran at these places. "You are in luck—make the most of it."

The master of the ceremonies scowled upon the speaker; and

this determined me to obey his suggestions. I did so, and doubled the money; left my original stake and the winnings on the same spot, and doubled that also; and it was not long before, under this stimulus of success, and the novelty of my situation, I found myself as thoroughly anxious and intensely interested, as if I had gone to the place in compliance with a natural passion. I know not how long I had continued in this way, but I was still fortunate. I had doubled my stakes repeatedly, and my pockets were crammed with money.

"Stop now, if you are wise," whispered the same sulky-looking little man who had before urged me to go on more boldly, as he sidled along by me for this object; "never ride a good horse to death. There's a time to stop just as there's a time to push. You had better stop now. Stake another dollar and you lose all your winnings."

"Let the gentleman play his own game, Brinckoff. I don't see why you come here to spoil sport."

Such was the remark of the keeper of the table. He had overheard my counsellor. He felt his losses, and was angry. I saw that, and it determined me. I took the counsel of the stranger. I was the more willing to do so, as I reproached myself for my inattention to my friend. It was time to see what had been his progress, and I prepared to leave the theatre of my own success. Before doing so, I turned to my counsellor, and thus addressed him: "Your advice has made me win; I trust I will not offend a gentleman who has been so courteous, by requesting him to take my place upon a small capital."

I put twenty pieces into his hand.

"I am but a young beginner," I continued, "and I owe you for my first lesson."

"You are too good," he said, but his hand closed over the dollars. The keeper of the table renewed his murmurs of discontent as he saw me turn away.

"Ah! bah! Petit, what's the use to grumble?" demanded my representative. "Do you suppose I will give up my sport for yours? When would I get a sixpence to stake, if it were not that I was kind to young fellows just beginning? There; growl no more; the twenty Mexicans upon the red!"

The next minute my gratuity was swallowed up in the great

spoon of the banker. I was near enough to see the result. I placed another ten pieces in the hand of the unsuccessful gambler.

"Very good," said he; "very much obliged to you: but, if you please, I will do no more to-night. It's not my lucky night. I've lost every set."

"As you please — when you please."

"You are a gentleman," he said; "the sooner you go home the better. A young beginner seldom wins in the small hours."

This was said in another whisper. I thanked him for his further suggestion, and turned away, leaving him to a side squabble with the banker, who finally concluded by telling him that he never wished to see him at his table.

"The more fool you, Petit," said Brinckoff; "for the youngster that wins comes back, and he does not always win. You finish him in the end as you finished me, and what more would you have?"

The rest, and there was much more, was inaudible to me. I hurried from the place somewhat ashamed of my success. I doubt whether I should have had the like feelings had I lost. As it was, never did possession seem more cumbrous than the mixed gold, paper, and silver, with which my pockets were burdened. I gladly thought of Kingsley, to avoid thinking of myself. It was certain, I fancied, that he had not lost, else how could he have continued to play? My anxiety hurried me into the room where I had left him.

They sat together, he and Cleveland, as before. I observed that there was now an expression of anxiety — not intense, but obvious enough — upon the countenance of the latter. Philip, too, the mulatto, stood on one side, contemplating the proceedings with an air of grave doubt and uncertainty in his countenance. No such expression distinguished the face of Kingsley. Never did a light-hearted, indifferent, almost mocking spirit, shine out more clearly from any human visage. At times he chuckled as with inward satisfaction. Not unfrequently he laughed aloud, and his reckless "Ha! ha! ha!" had more than once reached and startled me in the midst of my own play, in the adjoining room. The opponents had discarded their "pictures." They were absolutely rolling dice for their stakes. I saw that the wallet of Kingsley lay untouched, and quite as full as ever, in the spot where he had first laid it down. A pile of money lay open beside him; the gold and silver pieces keeping down the paper. When he saw me approach, he laughed aloud, as he cried out:—

"Have they disburdened you, Clifford? Help yourself. I am punishing my enemy famously. I can spare it."

A green, sickly smile mantled the lips of Cleveland. He replied in low, soft tones, such as I could only partly hear; and, a moment after, he swept the stake before the two, to his own side of the table. The amount was large, but the features of Kingsley remained unaltered, while his laugh was renewed as heartily as if he really found pleasure in the loss.

"Ha! ha! ha! that is encouraging; but the end is not yet. The tug is yet to come!"

I now perceived that Kingsley took up his wallet with one hand while he spread his handkerchief on his lap with the other. Into this he drew the pile of money which he had loose before on his side of the table, and appeared to busy himself in counting into it the contents of the wallet. This he did with such adroitness, that, though I felt assured he had restored the wallet to his bosom with its bulk undiminished, yet I am equally certain that no such conclusion could have been reached by any other person. This done, he lifted the handkerchief, full as it was, and dashed it down upon the table.

"There! cover that, if you be a man!" was his speech of defiance.

"How much?" huskily demanded Cleveland.

"All!"

"Ah!"

"Yes, all. I know not the number of dollars, cents, or sixpences, but face it with your winnings: there need be no counting. It is loss of time. Stir the stuff with your fingers, and you will find it as good, and as much, as you have here to put against it. On that hangs my fate or yours. Mine for certain! I tell you, Mr. Cleveland, it is all!"

Cleveland lifted the ends of the handkerchief, as if weighing its contents; and then, without more scruple, flung into it a pile not unlike it in bulk and quality: a handful of mixed gold, paper, and silver. Kingsley grasped the dice before him, and with a single shake dashed them out upon the table.

"Six, four, two," cried Philip with a degree of excitement which did not appear in either of the active opponents. Meanwhile my heart was in my mouth. I looked on Kingsley with a sentiment of wonder. Every muscle of his face was composed into the most quiet indifference. He saw my glance, and smilingly exclaimed :—

"I trust to my star, Clifford. Sans Souci—remember!"

No time was allowed for more. The moment was a breathless one. Cleveland had taken up the dice. His manner was that of the most singular deliberation. His eyes were cast down upon the table. His lips strongly closed together; and now it was that I could see the keen, piercing look which Kingsley addressed to every movement of the gambler. I watched him also. He did not immediately throw the dice, and I was conscious of some motion which he made with his hands before he did so. What that motion was, however, I could neither have said nor conceived. But I saw a grim smile, full of intelligence, suddenly pass over Kingsley's lips. The dice descended upon the table with a sound that absolutely made me tremble.

"Five, four, six!" cried Philip, loudly, with tones of evident exultation. I felt a sense like that of suffocation, which was unrelieved even by the seemingly unnatural laughter of my companion. He did laugh, but in a manner to render less strange and unnatural that in which he had before indulged. Even as he laughed he rose and possessed himself of the dice which the other had thrown down.

"The stakes are mine," cried Cleveland, extending his hand toward the handkerchief.

"No!" said Kingsley, with a voice of thunder, and as he spoke, he handed me the kerchief of money, which I grasped instantly, and thrust with some difficulty into my bosom. This was done instinctively; I really had no thoughts of what I was doing. Had I thought at all I should most probably have refused to receive it.

"How!" exclaimed Cleveland, his face becoming suddenly pale. "The cast is mine—fifteen to twelve!"

"Ay, scoundrel, but the game I played for is mine! As for

the cast, you shall try another which you shall relish less. Do you see these?"

He showed the dice which he had gathered from the table. The gambler made an effort to snatch them from his hands.

"Try that again," said Kingsley, "and I lay this hickory over your pate, in a way that shall be a warning to it for ever."

By this time several persons from the neighboring tables and the adjoining rooms, hearing the language of strife, came rushing in. Kingsley beheld their approach without concern. There were several old gamblers among them, but the greater number were young ones.

"Gentlemen," said Kingsley, "I am very glad to see you. You come at a good time. I am about to expose a scoundrel to you."

"You shall answer for this, sir," stammered Cleveland, in equal rage and confusion.

"Answer, shall I? By Jupiter! but you shall answer too! And you shall have the privilege of a first answer, shall you?"

"Mr. Kingsley, what is the meaning of this?" was the demand of a tall, dark-featured man, who now made his appearance from an inner room, and whom I now learned, was, in fact, the proprietor of the establishment.

"Ah! Radcliffe—but before another word is wasted put your fingers into the left breeches pocket of that scoundrel there, and see what you will find."

Cleveland would have resisted. Kingsley spoke again to Radcliffe, and this time in stern language, which was evidently felt by the person to whom it was addressed.

"Radcliffe, your own credit—nay, safety—will depend upon your showing that you have no share in this rogue's practice. Search him, if you would not share his punishment."

The fellow was awed, and obeyed instantly. Himself, with three others, grappled with the culprit. He resisted strenuously, but in vain. He was searched, and from the pocket in question three dice were produced.

"Very good," said Kingsley; "now examine those dice, gentlemen, and see if you can detect one of my initials, the letter 'K,' which I scratched with a pin upon each of them."

The examination was made, and the letter was found, very

small and very faint, it is true, but still legible, upon the ace square of each of the dice.

"Very good," continued Kingsley; "and now, gentlemen, with your leave—"

He opened his hand and displayed the three dice with which Cleveland had last thrown.

"Here you see the dice with which this worthy gentleman hoped to empty my pockets. These are they which he last threw upon the table. He counted handsomely by them! I threw, just before him, with those which you have in your hand. I had contrived to mark them previously, this very evening, in order that I might know them again. Why should he put them in his pocket, and throw with these? As this question is something important, I propose to answer it to your satisfaction as well as my own; and, for this reason, I came here, as you see, prepared to make discoveries."

He drew from his pocket, while he spoke, a small saddler's hammer and steel-awl. Fixing with the sharp point of the awl in the ace spot of the dice, he struck it a single but sudden blow with the hammer, split each of the dice in turn, and disclosed to the wondering, or seemingly wondering, eyes of all around, a little globe of lead in each, inclining to the lowest numeral, and necessarily determining the roll of the dice so as to leave the lightest section uppermost.

"Here, gentlemen," continued Kingsley, "you see by what process I have lost my money. But it is not in the dice alone. Look at these cards. Do you note this trace of the finger-nail, here, and there, and there—scarcely to be seen unless it is shown to you, but clear enough to the person that made it, and is prepared to look for it. Radcliffe, your fellow, Philip, has been concerned in this business. You must dismiss him, or your visiters will dismiss you. Neither myself nor my friends will visit you again—nay, more, I denounce you to the police. Am I understood?"

Radcliffe assented without scruple, evidently not so anxious for justice as for the safety of his establishment. But it appeared that there were others in the room not so well pleased with the result. A hubbub now took place, in which three or four fellows made a rush upon Kingsley—Cleveland urging

10*

and clamoring from the rear, though without betraying much real desire to get into the conflict.

But the assailants had miscalculated their forces. The youngsters in the establishment, regarding Kingsley's development as serving the common cause, were as soon at his side as myself. The scuffle was over in an instant. One burly ruffian was prostrated by a blow from Kingsley's club; I had my share in the prostration of a second, and some two others took to their heels, assisted in their progress by a smart application from every foot and fist that happened to be convenient enough for such a service.

Bnt Cleveland alone remained. Why he had not shared the summary fate of the rest it would be difficult to say, unless it was because he had kept aloof from the active struggle to which he had egged them on. Perhaps, too, a better reason—he was reserved for some more distinguishing punishment. Why he had shown no disposition for flight himself, was answered as soon as Kingsley laid down his club, which he did with a laugh of exemplary good-nature the moment he had felled with it his first assailant. The flight of his allies left the path open between himself and Cleveland, and, suddenly darting upon him, the desperate gambler aimed a blow at his breast with a dirk which he had drawn that instant from his own. He exclaimed as he struck:—

"Here is something that escaped your search. Take this! this!"

Kingsley was just lifting up the cap, which he had worn that night, from the table to his brows. Instinctively he dashed it into the face of his assassin, and his simple evolution saved him. The next moment the fearless fellow had grappled with his enemy, torn the weapon from his grasp, and, seizing him around the body as if he had been an infant, moved with him to an open window looking out upon a neighboring court. The victim struggled, yelled for succor, but before any of us could interpose, the resolute and powerful man in whose hold he writhed and struggled vainly, with the gripe of a master, had thrust him through the opening, his heels, in their upward evolutions, shattering a dozen of the panes as he disappeared from sight below. We all concluded that he was killed. We were in an upper chamber, which I estimated to be twenty or thirty feet from the ground. I was too much shocked for speech, and rushed to the window, expecting to behold the mangled and bloody corpse of the miserable criminal beneath. The laughter of Radcliffe half reassured me.

"He will not suffer much hurt," said he; "there is something to break his fall."

I looked down, and there the unhappy wretch was seen squatting and clinging to the slippery shingles of an old stable, unhurt, some twelve feet below us, unable to reascend, and very unwilling to adopt the only alternative which the case presented— that of descending softly upon the rank bed of stable-ordure which the provident care of the gardener had raised up on every hand, the reeking fumes of which were potent enough to expel us very soon from our place of watch at the window. Of the further course of the elegant culprit we took no heed. The ludicrousness of his predicament had the effect of turning the whole adventure into merriment among those who remained in the establishment; and availing ourselves of the clamorous mirth of the parties, we made our escape from the place with a feeling, on my part, of indescribable relief.

CHAPTER XXXI.

HOW THE GAME WAS PLAYED.

"WELL, we may breathe awhile," said Kingsley, as we found ourselves once more in the pure air, and under the blue sky of midnight. "We have got through an ugly task with tolerable success. You stood by me like a man, Clifford. I need not tell you how much I thank you."

"I heartily rejoice that you are through with it, Kingsley; but I am not so sure that we can deliberately approve of everything that we may have been required by the circumstances of the case to do."

"What! you did not relish the playing? I respect your scruples, but it does not follow that it must become a habit. You played to enable a friend to get back from a knave what he lost as a fool, and to punish the knavery that he could not well hope to reform. I do not see, considering the amount of possible good which we have done, that the evil is wholly inexcusable."

"Perhaps not; but this heap of money which I have in my bosom—should you have taken it?"

"And why not? Whose should it be, if not mine?"

"You took with you but one hundred dollars. I should say you have more than a thousand here."

"I trust I have," said he coolly. "What of that? I won it fairly, and he played fairly, until the last moment when everything was at stake. His false dice were then called in—and would you have me yield to his roguery what had been the fruits of a fair conflict? No! no! friend of mine! no! no! all these things did I consider well before I took you with me to-night. I have been meditating this business for a week, from the moment when a friendly fellow hinted to me that I was the victim of knavery."

"But that wallet of money, Kingsley? You assured me that you were pennyless."

"Ah! that wallet bedevilled Mr. Latour Cleveland, as it seems to have bedevilled you. There, by the starlight, look at the contents of this precious wallet, and see how much further your eyes can pierce into the mystery of my proceedings."

He handed me the wallet, which I opened. To my great surprise, I found it stuffed with old shreds of newspaper, bits of rag, even cotton, but not a cent of money.

"There! are you satisfied? You shall have that wallet, with all its precious contents, as a keepsake from me. It will remind you of a strange scene. It will have a history for you when you are old, which you will tell with a chuckle to your children."

"Children!" I involuntarily murmured, while my voice trembled, and a tear started to my eye. That one word recalled me back, at once, to home, to my particular woes—to all that I could have wished banished for ever, even in the unwholesome stews and steams of a gaming-house. But Kingsley did not suffer me to muse over my own afflictions. He did not seem to hear the murmuring exclamation of my lips. He continued:—

"I have no mysteries from you, and you need, as well as deserve, an explanation. All shall be made clear to you. The reason of this wallet, and another matter which staggered you quite as much—my audacious bet of a cool hundred—your own disconsolate hundred—as a first stake! I have no doubt you thought me mad when you heard me."

I confessed as much. He laughed.

"As I tell you, I had studied my game beforehand, even in its smallest details. By this time, I knew something of the play of most gamblers, and of Mr. Latour Cleveland, in particular. These people do not risk themselves for trifles. They play fairly enough when the temptation is small. They cheat only when the issues are great. I am speaking now of gamesters on the big figure, not of the petty chapmen who pule over their pennies and watch the exit of a Mexican, with the feeling of one who sees the last wave of a friend's handkerchief going upon the high seas. My big wallet and my hundred-dollar bet were parts of the same system. The heavy stake at the beginning led to the inference that I had corresponding resources. My big wallet lying by me, conveniently and ostentatiously, confirmed this impression. The cunning gambler was willing that I should win awhile. His policy was to encourage me; to persuade me on and on, by gradual stimulants, till all was at stake. Well! I knew this. All was at stake finally, and I had then to call into requisition all the moral strength of which I was capable, so that eye and lip and temper should not fail me at those moments when I would need the address and agency of all.

"The task has been an irksome one; the trial absolutely painful. But I should have been ashamed, once commencing the undertaking, not to have succeeded. He, too, was not impregnable. I found out his particular weakness. He was a vain man; vain of his bearing, which he deemed aristocratic; his person, which he considered very fine. I played with these vanities. Failing to excite him on the subject of the game, I made *himself* my subject. I chattered with him freely; so as to prompt him to fancy that I was praising his style, air, appearance; anon, by some queer jibe, making him half suspicious that I was quizzing him. My frequent laughter, judiciously disposed, helped this effect; and, to a certain extent, I succeeded. He became nervous, and was excited, though you may not have seen it. I saw it in the change of his complexion, which became suddenly quite bilious. I found, too, that he could only speak with some effort, when, if you remember, before we began to play, his tongue, though deliberate, worked pat enough. I felt my power over him momently increase; and I sometimes won where he did not wish it. I do verily believe that he ceased to see the very marks which he himself had made upon the cards. Nervous agitation, on most persons, produces a degree of blindness quite as certainly as it affects the speech. Well, you saw the condition of our funds when you re-appeared. I had determined to bring the business to a close. I had marked the dice, actually before his face, while we took a spell of rest over a bottle of porter. I had scratched them quietly with a pin which I carried in my sleeve for that purpose, while he busied himself with a fidgety shuffling of the cards. My leg, thrown over one angle of the table, partly covered my operations, and I worked upon the dice in my lap. You may suppose the etching was bad enough, doing precious little credit to the art of engraving in our country. But the thing was thoroughly done, for I had worked myself into a rigorous sort of philosophic desperation which made me as cool as a cucumber. To seem to empty the contents of the wallet into my lap was my next object, and this I succeeded in, without his suspecting that my movement was a sham only. The purse thus made up, I emphatically told him was all I had—this was the truth—and then came the crisis. His trick was to be employed now or never. It was employed, but he had become so nervous, that I caught a sufficient glimpse of his proceedings. I saw the slight o'hand movement which he attempted, and—you know the rest. I regard the money as honestly mine—so far as good morals may recognise the honesty of getting money by gambling;—and thinking so, my dear Clifford, I have no scruple in begging you to share it with me. It is only fit that you, who furnished all the capital—you see I say nothing of the wallet which should, however, be priceless in our eyes—should derive at least a moiety of the profit. It is quite as much yours as mine. I beg you so to consider it."

I need not say, however, that I positively refused to accept this offer. I would take nothing but the hundred which I had lent him, and placed the handkerchief with all its contents into his hands.

"And now, Clifford, I must leave you. You have yet to learn another of my secrets. I take the rail-car at daylight in the morning. I am off for Alabama; and considering my Texan and Mexican projects, I leave you, perhaps, for ever."

"So soon?"

"Yes, everything is ready. There need be no delay. I have no wife nor children to cumber me. My trunks are already packed; my resolve made; my last business transacted.

I have some lands in Alabama which I mean to sell. This done, I am off for the great field of performance, south and southwest. You shall hear of me, perhaps may wish to hear *from* me. Here is my address, meanwhile, in Alabama. I shall advise you of my further progress, and shall esteem highly a friendly scrawl from you. If you write, do not fail to tell me what you may hear of Mr. Latour Cleveland, and how he got down from the muck-heap. Write me all about it, Clifford, and whatever else you can about our fools and knaves, for though I leave them without a tear, yet, d—n 'em, I keep 'em in my memory, if it's only for the sake of the old city whom they bedevil."

Enough of our dialogue that night. Kingsley was a fellow of every excellent and some very noble qualities. We did not sympathize in sundry respects, but I parted from him with regret; not altogether satisfied, however, that there were not some defects in that reasoning by which he justified our proceedings with the gamblers. I turned from him with a sad, sick heart. In his absence the whole feeling of my domestic doubts and difficulties rushed back upon me freshly and with redoubled force.

"Children!" I murmured mournfully, as I recalled one of his remarks; "children! children! these, indeed, were blessings; but if we only had love, truth, peace. If that damning doubt were not there!—that wild fear, that fatal, soul-petrifying suspicion!"

I groaned audibly as I traversed the streets, and it seemed as if the pavements groaned hollowly in answer beneath my hurrying footsteps. In a moment more I had absolutely forgotten the recent strife, the strange scene, the accents of my friend; all but that one.

"Children! children! These might bind her to me; might secure her erring affections; might win her to love the father, when he himself might possess no other power to tempt her to love. Ah! why has Providence denied me the blessing of a child?"

Alas! it was not probable that Julia should ever have children. This was the conviction of our physician. Her health and constitution seemed to forbid the hope; and the gloomy despair under which I suffered was increased by this reflection. Yet, even at that moment, while thus I mused and murmured, my poor wife had been unexpectedly and prematurely delivered of an infant son—a tiny creature, in whom life was but a passing gleam, as of the imperfect moonlight, and of whom death took possession in the very instant of its birth.

CHAPTER XXXII.

SUDDEN LESSON AND NEW SUSPICIONS.

WHILE I had been wasting the precious hours of midnight in a gaming-house, my poor Julia had undergone the peculiar pangs of a mother! While I had been reproaching her in my secret soul for a want of ardency and attachment, she had been giving me the highest proof that she possessed the warmest. These revelations, however, were to reach me slowly; and then, like those of Cassandra, they were destined to encounter unbelief.

Leaving Kingsley, I turned into the street where my wife's mother lived. But the house was shut up—the company gone. I had not been heedful of the progress of the hours. I looked up at the tall, white, and graceful steeple of our ancient church, which towered in serene majesty above us; but, in the imperfect light I failed to read the letters upon the dial-plate. At that moment its solemn chimes pealed forth the hour, as if especially in answer to my quest. How such sounds speak to the very soul at midnight! They seem the voice from Time himself, informing, not man alone, but Eternity, of his progress to that long night, in which his minutes, hours, days, and years, are equally to be swallowed up and forgotten.

Sweet had been those bells to me in boyhood. Sad were they to me now. I had heard them ring forth merry peals on the holydays of the nation; and peals on the day of national mourning; startling and terrifying peals in the hour of midnight danger and alarm; but never till then had they spoken with such deep and searching earnestness to the most hidden places of my soul. That "one, two, three, four," which they then struck, as they severally pronounced the thrilling monotones, seemed to convey the burden of four impressive acts in a yet unfinished tragedy. My heart beat with a feeling of anxiety, such as overcomes us, when we look for the curtain to rise which is to unfold the mysterious progress of the catastrophe.

That fifth act of mine! what was it to be? Involuntarily my lips uttered the name of William Edgerton! I started as if I had trodden upon a viper. The denouement of the drama at once grew up before my eyes. I felt the dagger in my grasp; I actually drew it from my bosom. I saw the victim before me—a smile upon his lips—a fire in his glance—an ardor, an intelligence, that looked like exulting passion; and my own eyes grew dim. I was blinded; but, even in the darkness, I struck with fatal precision. I felt the resistance, I heard the groan and the falling body; and my hair rose, with a cold, moist life of its own, upon my clammy and shrinking temples.

I recovered from the delusion. My dagger had been piercing the empty air; but the feeling and the horror in my soul were not less real because the deed had been one of fancy only. The foregone conclusion was in my mind, and I well knew that fate would yet bring the victim to the altar.

I know not how I reached my dwelling, but when there I was soon brought to a sober condition of the senses. I found everything in commotion. Mrs. Delaney, late Clifford, was there, busy in my wife's chamber, while her husband, surly with such an interruption to his domestic felicity, even at the threshold, was below, kicking his heels in solemn disquietude in the parlor. The servants had been despatched to bring her and to seek me, in the first moments of my wife's danger. She had consciousness enough for that, and Mrs. Delaney had summoned the physician. He too—the excellent old man, who had assisted us in our clandestine marriage—he too was there; sad, troubled, and regarding me with looks of apprehension and rebuke which seemed to ask why I was abroad at that late hour, leaving my wife under such circumstances. I could not meet his glance with a manly eye. They brought me the dead infant—poor atom of mortality—no longer mortal; but I turned away from the spectacle. I dared not look upon it. It was the form of a perished hope, ended in a dream! And such a dream! The physician gave me a brief explanation of the condition of things.

"Your wife is very ill. It is difficult to say what will happen. Make up your mind for the worst. She has fever—has been delirious. But she sleeps now under the effect of some medicine I have given her. She will not sleep long; and everything will depend upon her wakening. She must be kept very quiet."

I asked if he could conjecture what should bring about such an event. "Though delicate, Julia was not out of health. She had been well during the evening when I left her."

"You have left her long. This is a late hour, Mr. Clifford, for a young husband to be out. Nothing but matter of necessity could excuse——"

I interrupted him with some gravity:—

"Suppose then it was a matter of necessity—of seeming necessity, at least."

He observed my emotion.

"Do not be angry with me. I assisted your dear wife into the world, Clifford. I would not see her hurried out of it. She is like a child of my own; I feel for her as such."

I said something apologetic, I know not what, and renewed my question.

"She has been alarmed or excited, perhaps; possibly has fallen while ascending the stair. A very slight accident will sometimes suffice to produce such a result with a constitution such as hers. She needs great watchfulness, Clifford; close attention, much solicitude. She needs and deserves it, Clifford."

I saw that the old man suspected me of indifference and neglect. Alas! whatever might be my faults in reference to my wife, indifference was not among them. What he had said, however, smote me to the heart. I felt like a culprit. I dared not meet his eye when, at daylight, he took his departure, promising to return in a few hours.

My excellent mother-in-law was more capable and copious in her details. From her I learned that Julia, though anxious to depart for some time before, had waited for my return until the last of her guests were about to retire. Among these happened to be "Mr. William Edgerton!"

"He offered his carriage, but Julia put off accepting for a long time, saying you would soon return. But at last he pressed her so, and seeing everybody else gone, she concluded to go, and Mr. Delaney helped her into the carriage, and Mr. Edgerton got in too, to see her home; and off they drove, and it was not an hour after, when Becky (the servant-girl) came to rout us up, saying that her mistress was dying. I hurried on my clothes, and Delaney—dear good man—he was just as quick; and off we came, and sure enough, we found her in a bad way, and nobody with her but the servants; and I sent off after you, and after the doctor; and he just came in time to help her; but she went on wofully; was very lightheaded; talked a great deal about you; and about Mr. Edgerton; I suppose because he had just been seeing her home; but didn't seem to know and doesn't know to this moment what has happened to her."

I have shortened very considerably the long story which Mrs. Delaney made of it. Rambling as it was—full of nonsense—with constant references to her "dear, good man," and her party, the company, herself, her fashion, and frivolities—there was yet something to sting and trouble me at the core of her narration. Edgerton and my wife linger to the last—Edgerton rides home with her—he and she in the carriage, alone, at midnight;—and then this catastrophe, which the doctor thought was a natural consequence of some excitement or alarm.

These facts wrought like madness in my brain. Then, too, in her delirium she raves of *him!* Is not that significant? True, it comes from the lips of that malicious old woman! she, who had already hinted to me that my wife—her daughter—was likely to be as faithless to me as she had been to herself; still, it is significant, even if it be only the invention of this old woman. It showed what she conjectured—what she thought to be a natural result of those practices which had prompted her suspicions as well as my own.

How hot was the iron-pressure upon my brain—how keen and scorching was that fiery arrow in my soul, when I took my place of watch beside the unconscious form of my wife, God alone can know. If I am criminal—if I have erred with wildest error—surely I have struggled with deepest misery. I have been misled by wo, not temptation! Sore has been my struggle, sore my suffering, even in the moment of my greatest fault and folly. Sore!—how sore!

CHAPTER XXXIII.

STILL THE CLOUD.

For three days and nights did I watch beside the sick bed of my wife. In all this time her fate continued doubtful. I doubt if any anxiety or attention could have exceeded mine; as it was clear to myself that, in spite of jealousy and suspicion, my love for her remained without diminution. Yet this watch was not maintained without some trials far more severe and searching than those which it produced upon the body. Her mind, wandering and purposeless, yet spoke to mine, and renewed all its racking doubts, and exaggerated all its nameless fears. Her veins burned with fever. She was fitfully delirious. Words fell from her at spasmodic moments — strange, incoherent words, but all full of meaning in my ears. I sat beside the bed on one hand, while, on one occasion, her mother occupied a seat upon that opposite. The eyes of my wife opened upon both of us — turned from me, convulsively, with an expression, as I thought, of disgust, then closed — while her lips, taking up their language, poured forth a torrent of threats and reproaches.

I can not repeat her words. They rang in my ears, understood, indeed, but so wildly and thrillingly, that I should find it a vain task to endeavor to remember them. She spoke of persecution, annoyance, beyond propriety, beyond her powers of endurance. She threatened me — for I assumed myself to be the object of her denunciation — with the wrath of some one capable to punish — nay, to rescue her, if need be, by violence, from the clutches of her tyrant. Then followed another change in her course of speech. She no longer threatened or denounced. She derided. Words of bitter scorn and loathing contempt issued from those bright, red, burning, and always beautiful lips, which I had never supposed could have given forth such utterance, even if her spirit could have been supposed capable of conceiving it. Keen was the irony which she expressed—irony, which so well applied to my demerits in one great respect, that I could not help making the personal application.

"How manly and generous," she proceeded, "was this sort of persecution of one so unprotected, so dependent, so placed, that she must even be silent, and endure without speech or complaint, in the dread of dangers which, however, would not light upon her head. Oh, brave as generous!" she exclaimed, with a burst of tremendous delirium, terminating in a shriek; "oh, brave as generous!—scarcely lion-like, however, for the noble beast rushes upon his victim. He does not prowl, and skulk, and sneak, watching, cat-like, crouching and base, in stealth and darkness. Very noble, but mousing spirit! Beware! Do I not know you now! Fear you not that I will show your baseness, and declare the truth, and guide other eyes to your stealthy practice? Beware! Do not drive me into madness!"

Thus she raved. My conscience applied these stinging words of scorn, which seemed particularly fitted to the mean suspicious watch which I had kept upon her. I could have no thought that they were meant for any other ears than my own, and the crimson flush upon my cheeks was the involuntary acknowledgment which my soul made of the demerits of my unmanly conduct. I fancied that Julia had detected my espionage, and that her language had this object in reference only. But there were other words; and, passing with unexpected transition from the language of dislike and scorn, she now indulged in that of love—language timidly suggestive of love, as if its utterance were restrained by bashfulness, as if it dreaded to be heard. Then a deep sigh followed, as if from the bottom of her heart, succeeded by convulsive sobs, at last ending in a gushing flood of tears.

For the space of half an hour I had been an attentive but suffering listener to this wild raving. My pangs followed every sentence from her lips, believing, as I did, that they were reproachful of myself, and associated with a now unrestrained expression of passion for another. Gradually I had ceased, in the deep interest which I felt, to be conscious that Mrs. Delaney was present. I leaned across the couch; I bent my ear down toward the lips of the speaker, eager to drink up every feeble sound which might help to elucidate my doubts, and subdue or confirm my suspicions. Then, as the accumulating conviction forced itself, embodied and sharp, like a knife, into my soul, I groaned aloud, and my teeth were gnashed together in the bitterness of my emotion! In that moment I caught the keen gray eyes of my mother-in-law fixed upon me, with a jibing expression, which spoke volumes of mockery. They seemed to say, "Ah! you have it now! The truth is forced upon you at last! You can parry it no longer. I see the iron in your soul. I behold and enjoy your contortions!"

Fiend language! She was something of a fiend! I started from the bedside, and just then a flood of tears came to the relief of my wife, and lessened the excitement of her brain. The tears relieved her. The paroxysm passed away. She turned her eyes upon me, and closed them involuntarily, while a deep crimson tint passed over her cheek, a blush, which seemed to me to confirm substantially the tenor of that language in which, while delirious, she had so constantly indulged. It did not lessen the seeming shame and dislike which her countenance appeared at once to embody, that a soft sweet smile was upon her lips at the same moment, and she extended to me her hand with an air of confidence which staggered and surprised me.

"What is the matter, dear husband? And you here, mother? Have I been sick? Can it be?"

"Hush!" said the mother. "You have been sick ever since the night of my marriage."

"Ah!" she exclaimed with an air of anxiety and pain, while pressing her hand upon her eyes, "Ah! that night!"

A shudder shook her frame as she uttered this simple and short sentence. Simple and short as it was, it seemed to possess a strange signification. That it was associated in her mind with some circumstances of peculiar import, was sufficiently obvious. What were these circumstances? Ah! that question! I ran over in my thought, in a single instant, all that array of events, on that fatal night, which could, by any possibility, distress me, and confirm my suspicions. That waltz with Edgerton—that long conference between them—that lonely ride together from the home of Mrs. Delaney, in a close carriage—and the subsequent disaster—her unconscious ravings, and the strong, strange language which she employed, clearly full of meaning as it was, but in which I could discover one meaning only! all these topics of doubt and agitation passed through my brain in consecutive order, and with a compact arrangement which seemed as conclusive as any final issue. I said nothing; but what I might have said, was written in my face. Julia regarded me with a gaze of painful anxiety. What she read in my looks must have been troublously impressive. Her cheeks grew paler as she looked. Her eyes wandered from me vacantly, and I could see her thin soft lips quivering faintly like rose-leaves which an envious breeze has half separated from the parent-flower. Mrs. Delaney watched our mutual faces, and I left the room to avoid her scrutiny. I only re-entered it with the physician. He administered medicine to my wife.

"She will do very well now, I think," he said to me when leaving the house; "but she requires to be treated very tenderly. All causes of excitement must be kept from her. She needs soothing, great care, watchful anxiety. Clifford, above all, you should leave her as little as possible. This old woman, her mother, is no fit companion for her—scarcely a pleasant one. I do not mean to reproach you; ascribe what I say to a real desire to serve and make you happy; but let me tell you that Mrs. Delaney has intimated to me that you neglect your wife, that you leave her very much at night: and she further intimates, what I feel assured can not well be the case, that you have fallen into other and much more evil habits."

"The hag!"

"She is all that, and loves you no better now than before. Still, it is well to deprive such people of their scandal-mongering, of the meat for it at least. I trust, Clifford, for your own sake, that you were absent of necessity on Wednesday night."

"It will be enough for me to think so, sir," was my reply.

"Surely, if you *do* think so; but I am too old a man, and too old a friend of your own and wife's family, to justify you in taking exception to what I say. I hope you do not neglect this dear child, for she is one too sweet, too good, too gentle, Clifford, to be subjected to hard usage and neglect. I think her one of earth's angels—a meek creature, who would never think or do wrong, but would rather suffer than complain. I sincerely hope, for your own sake, as well as hers, that you truly estimate her worth."

I could not answer the good old man, though I was angry with him. My conscience deprived me of the just power to give utterance to my anger. I was silent, and he forbore any further reference to the subject. Shortly after he took his leave, and I re-ascended the stairs. Wearing slippers, I made little noise, and at the door of my wife's chamber I caught a sentence from the lips of Mrs. Delaney, which made me forget everything that the doctor had been saying.

"But Julia, there must have been some accident—something must have happened. Did your foot slip? perhaps, in getting out of the carriage, or in going up stairs, or——. There must have been something to frighten you, or hurt you. What was it?"

I paused; my heart rose like a swelling, struggling mass in the gorge of my throat. I listened for the reply. A deep sigh followed; and then I heard a reluctant, faint utterance of the single word, "Nothing!"

"Nothing?" repeated the old lady. "Surely, Julia, there was something. Recollect yourself. You know you rode home with Mr. Edgerton. It was past one o'clock——"

"No more—no more, mother. There was nothing—nothing that I recollect. I know nothing of what happened. Hardly know where I am now."

I felt a momentary pang that I had lingered at the entrance. Besides, there was no possibility that she would have revealed anything to the inquisitive old woman. Perhaps, had this been probable, I should not have felt the scruple and the pang. The very questions of Mrs. Delaney were as fully productive of evil in my mind, as if Julia had answered decisively on every topic. I entered the room, and Mrs. Delaney, after some little lingering, took her departure, with a promise to return again soon. I paced the chamber with eyes bent upon the floor.

"Come to me, Edward—come sit beside me." Such were the gentle words of entreaty which my wife addressed to me. Gentle words, and so spoken—so sweetly, so frankly, as if from the very sacredest chamber of her heart. Could it be that guilt also harbored in that very heart—that it was the language of cunning on her lips—the cunning of the serpent? Ah! how can we think that with serpent-like cunning, there should be dove-like guilelessness? My soul revolted at the idea. The sounds of the poor girl's voice sounded like hissing in my ears. I sat beside her as she requested, and almost started, as I felt her fingers playing with the hair upon my temples.

"You are cold to me, dear husband; ah! be not cold. I have narrowly escaped from death. So they tell me—so I feel! Be not cold to me. Let me not think that I am burdensome to you."

"Why should you think so, Julia?"

"Ah! your words answer your question, and speak for me. They are so few—they have no warmth in them; and then, you leave me so much, dear husband—why, why do you leave me?"

"You do not miss me much, Julia."

"Do I not! ah! you do me wrong. I miss nothing else but you. I have all that I had when we were first married—all but my husband!"

"Do not deceive yourself, Julia; these fine speeches do not deceive me. I am afraid that the love of woman is a very light thing. It yields readily to the wind. It does not keep in one direction long, any more than the vane on the house-top."

"You do *not* think so, Edward. Such is not *my* love. Alas! I know not how to make it known to you, husband, if it be not already known; and yet it seems to me that you do not know it, or, if you do, that you do not care much about it. You seem to care very little whether I love you or not."

I exclaimed bitterly, and with the energy of deep feeling.

"Care little! *I* care little whether you love me or no! Psha! Julia, you must think me a fool!"

It did seem to me a sort of mockery, knowing my feelings as *I* did—knowing that all my folly and suffering came from the very intensity of my passion—that I should be reproached, by its object, with indifference! I forgot, that, as a cover for my suspicion, I had been striving with all the industry of art to put on the appearance of indifference. I did not give myself sufficient credit for the degree of success with which I had labored, or I might have suddenly arrived at the gratifying conclusion, that, while I was impressed and suffering with the pangs of jealousy, my wife was trembling with fear that she had for ever lost my affections. My language, the natural utterance of my real feelings, was not true to the character I had assumed. It filled the countenance of the suffering woman with consternation. She shrunk from me in terror. Her hand was withdrawn from my neck, as she tremulously replied:—

"Oh, do not speak to me in such tones. Do not look so harshly upon me. What have I done?"

"Ay! ay!" I muttered, turning away.

She caught my hand.

"Do not go—do not leave me, and with such a look! Oh! husband, I may not live long. I feel that I have had a very narrow escape within these few days past. Do not kill me with cruel looks; with words, that, if cruel from you, would sooner kill than the knife in savage hands. Oh! tell me in what have I offended? What is it you think? For what am I to blame? What do you doubt—suspect?"

These questions were asked hurriedly, apprehensively, with a look of vague terror, her cheeks whitening as she spoke, her eyes darting wildly into mine, and her lips remaining parted after she had spoken.

"Ah!" I exclaimed, keenly watching her. Her glance sunk beneath my gaze. I put my hand upon her own.

"What do I suspect? What should I suspect? Ha!"—Here I arrested myself. My ardent anxiety to know the truth, led me to forget my caution; to exhibit a degree of eagerness, which might have proved that I did suspect and seriously. To exhibit the possession of jealousy was to place her upon her guard—such was the suggestion of that miserable policy, by which I had been governed—and defeat the impression of that feeling of perfect security and indifference, which I had been so long striving to awaken. I recovered myself, with this thought, in season to re-assume this appearance.

"Your mind still wanders, Julia. What should I suspect? and whom? You do not suppose me to be of a suspicious nature, do you?"

"Not altogether—not always—no! But, of course, there is nothing to suspect. I do not know what I say. I believe I do wander."

This reply was also spoken hurriedly, but with an obvious effort at composure. The eagerness with which she seized upon my words, insisting upon the absence of any cause of suspicion, and ascribing to her late delirium, the tacit admissions which her look and language had made, I need not say, contributed to strengthen my suspicions, and to confirm all the previous conjectures of my jealous spirit.

"Be quiet," I said with an air of *sang froid.* "Do not worry yourself in this manner. You need sleep. Try for it, while I leave you."

"Do not leave me; sit beside me, dear Edward. I will sleep so much better when you are beside me."

"Indeed!"

"Yes, believe me. Ah! that I could always keep you beside me!"

"What! you are for a new honeymoon?" I said this in *a tone* of merriment, which Heaven knows, I little felt.

"Do not speak of it so lightly, Edward. It is too serious a matter. Ah! that you would always remain with me; that you would never leave me."

"Pshaw! What sickly tenderness is this! Why, how could I earn my bread or yours?"

"I do not mean that you should neglect your business, but that when business is over, you should give me all your time as you used to. Remember, how pleasantly we passed the evenings after our marriage. Ah! how could you forget?"

"I do not, Julia."

"But you do not care for them. We spend no such evenings now!"

"No! but it is no fault of mine!" I said gloomily; then, interrupting her answer, as if dreading that she might utter some simple but true remark, which might refute the interpretation which my words conveyed, that the fault was hers, I enjoined silence upon her.

"You scarcely speak in your right mind yet, Julia. Be quiet, therefore, and try to sleep."

"Well, if you will sit beside me."

"I will do so, since you wish for it; but where's the need?"

"Ah! do not ask the need, if you still love me," was all she said, and looked at me with such eyes — so tearful, bright, so sad, soliciting — that, though I did not less doubt, I could no longer deny. I resumed the seat beside her. She again placed her fingers in my hair, and in a little while sunk into a profound slumber, only broken by an occasional sob, which subsided into a sigh.

Were she guilty — such was the momentary suggestion of the good angel — could she sleep thus? — thus quietly, confidingly, beside the man she had wronged — her fingers still paddling in his hair — her sleeping eyes still turning in the direction of his face?

To the clear, open mind, the suggestion would have had the force of a conclusive argument; but mine was no longer a clear, open mind. I had the disease of the blind heart upon me, and all things came out upon my vision as through a glass, darkly. The evil one at my elbow jeered when the good angel spoke.

"Fool! does she not see that she can blind you still!" Then, in the vanity and vexation of my spirit, I mused upon it further, and said to myself: — "Ay, but she will find, ere many days, that I am no longer to be blinded!" The scales were never thicker upon my sight than when I boasted in this foolish wise.

CHAPTER XXXIV.

A FATHER'S GRIEFS.

SHE continued to improve, but slowly. Her organization was always very delicate. Her frame was becoming thin, almost to meagreness; and this last disaster, whatever might be its cause, had contributed still more to weaken a constitution which education and nature had never prepared for much hard encounter. But, though I saw these proofs of feebleness—of a feebleness that might have occasioned reasonable apprehensions of premature decay, and possibly very rapid decline—there were little circumstances constantly occurring—looks shown, words spoken—which kept up the irritation of my soul, and prevented me from doing justice to her enfeebled condition. My sympathies were absorbed in my suspicions. My heart was the debateable land of self. The blind passion which enslaved it, I need scarce say, was of a nature so potent, that it could easily impregnate, with its own color, all the objects of its survey. Seen through the eyes of suspicion, there is no truth, no virtue; the smile is that of the snake; the tear, that of the crocodile; the assurance, that of the traitor. There is no act, look, word, of the suspected object, however innocent, which, to the diseased mind of jealousy, does not suggest conjectures and arguments, all conclusive or confirmatory of its doubts and fears. It is not necessary to say that I shrunk from Julia's endearment, requited her smiles with indifference; and, though I did not avoid her presence—I could not, in the few days when her case was doubtful—yet exhibited, in all respects, the conduct of one who was in a sort of Coventry.

But one fact may be stated—one of many—which seemed to

give a sanction to my suspicions, will help to justify my course, and which, at the time, was terribly conclusive, to my reason, of the things which I feared. She spoke audibly the name of Edgerton, twice, thrice, while she slept beside me, in tones very faint, it is true, but still distinct enough. The faintness of her utterance, gave the tones an emphasis of tenderness which perhaps was unintended. Twice, thrice, that fatal name; and then, what a sigh from the full volume of a surcharged heart. Let any one conceive my situation—with my feelings, intense on all subjects—my suspicions already so thoroughly awakened; and then fancy what they must have been on hearing that utterance; from the unguarded lips of slumber; from the wife lying beside him; and of the name of him on whom suspicion already rested. I hung over the sleeper, breathless, almost gasping, finally, in the effort to contain my breath—in the hope to hear something, however slight, which was to confirm finally, or finally end my doubts. I heard no more; but did more seem to be necessary? What jealous heart had not found this sufficiently conclusive? And that deep-drawn sigh, sobbing, as of a heart breaking with the deferred hope, and the dream of youth baffled at one sweeping, severing blow.

I rose. I could no longer subdue my emotions to the necessary degree of watchfulness. I trod the chamber till daylight. Then, I dressed myself and went out into the street. I had no distinct object. A vague persuasion only, that I must do something—that something must be done—that, in short, it was necessary to force this exhausting drama to its fit conclusion. Of course William Edgerton was my object. As yet, how to bring about the issue, was a problem which my mind was not prepared to solve. Whether I was to stab or shoot him; whether we were to go through the tedious processes of the duel; to undergo the fatigue of preliminaries, or to shorten them by sudden rencounter; these were topics which filled my thoughts confusedly; upon which I had no clear conviction; not because I did not attempt to fix upon a course, but from a sheer inability to think at all. My whole brain was on fire; a chaotic mass, such as rushes up from the unstopped vents of the volcano—fire, stones, and lava—but dense smoke enveloping the whole.

In this frame of mind I hurried through the streets. The shops were yet unopened. The sun was just about to rise. There was a humming sound, like that of distant waters murmuring along the shore, which filled my ears; but otherwise everything was silent. Sleep had not withdrawn with night from his stealthy watch upon the household. It seemed to me that I alone could not sleep. Even guilt—if my wife were really guilty—even guilt could sleep. I left her sleeping, and how sweetly! as if the dream which had made her sob and sigh, had been succeeded by others, that made all smiles again. I could not sleep, and yet, who, but a few months before, had been possessed of such fair prospects of peace and prosperity? Fortune held forth sufficient promise; fame—so far as fame can be accorded by a small community—had done something toward giving me an honorable repute; and love—had not love been seemingly as liberal and prompt as ever young passions could have desired? I was making money; I was getting reputation; the only woman whom I had ever loved or sought, was mine; and mine, too, in spite of opposition and discouragements which would have chilled the ardor of half the lovers in the world. And yet I was not happy. It takes so small an amount of annoyance to produce misery in the heart of self-esteem, when united with suspicion, that it was scarcely possible that I should be happy. Such a man has a taste for self-torture; as one troubled with an irritating humor, is never at rest, unless he is tearing the flesh into a sore; he may then rest as he may.

I took the way to my office. It was not often that I went thither before breakfast. But William Edgerton had been in the habit of doing so. He lived in the neighborhood, and his father had taught him this habit during the period when he was employed in studying the profession. It might be that I should find him there on the present occasion. Such was my notion. What farther thought I had I know not; but a vague suggestion that, in that quiet hour—there—without eye to see, or hand to interpose, I might drag from his heart the fearful secret—I might compel confession, take my vengeance, and rid myself finally of that cruel agony which was making me its miserable puppet. Crude, wild notions these, but very natural.

I turned the corner of the street. The window of my office was open. "He is then there," I muttered to myself; and my teeth clutched each other closely. I buttoned my coat. My heart was swelling. I looked around me, and up to the windows. The street was very silent—the grave not more so. I strode rapidly across, threw open the door of the office which stood ajar, and beheld, not the person whom I sought, but his venerable father.

The sight of that white-headed old man filled me with a sense of shame and degradation. What had he not done for me? How great his assistance, how kind his regards, how liberal his offices. He had rescued me from the bondage of poverty. He had put forth the hand of help, with a manly grasp of succor at the very moment when it was most needed; had helped to make me what I was; and, for all these, I had come to put to death his only son. A revulsion of feeling took place within my bosom. These thoughts were instantaneous—a sort of lightning-flash from the moral world of thought. I stood abashed; brought to my senses in an instant, and was scarcely able to conceal my discomfiture and confusion. I stood before him with the feeling, and must have worn the look, of a culprit. Fortunately, he did not perceive my confusion. Poor old man! Cares of his own—cares of a father, too completely occupied his mind, to suffer his senses to discharge their duties with freedom.

"I am glad to see you, Clifford, though I did not expect it. Young men of the present day are not apt to rise so early."

"I must confess, sir, it is not my habit."

"Better if it were. The present generation, it seems to me, may be considered more fortunate, in some respects, than the past, though they are scarcely wiser. They seem to me exempt from such necessities as encountered their fathers. Their tasks are fewer—their labor is lighter——"

"Are their cares the lighter in consequence?" I demanded.

"That is the question," he replied. "For myself, I think not. They grow gray the sooner. They have fewer tasks, but heavier troubles. They live better in some respects. They have luxuries which, in my day, youth were scarcely permitted to enjoy; and which, indeed, were not often enjoyed by age.

But they have little peace:—and, look at the bankruptcies of our city. They are without number—they produce no shame—do not seem to affect the credit of the parties; and, certainly, in no respect diminish their expenditures. They live as if the present day were the last they had to live; and living thus, they must live dishonestly. It is inevitable. The moral sense is certainly in a much lower condition in our country, than I have ever known it. What can be the reason?"

"The facility of procuring money, perhaps. Money is the most dangerous of human possessions."

"There can be none other. Clifford!"

"Sir."

"I change the subject abruptly. Have you seen my son lately, Clifford?"

The question was solemnly, suddenly spoken. It staggered me. What could it mean? That there was a meaning in it—a deep meaning—was unquestionable. But of what nature? Did the venerable man suspect my secret—could he by any chance conjecture my purpose? It is one quality of a mind not exactly satisfied of the propriety of its proceedings, to be suspicious of all things and persons—to fancy that the consciousness which distresses itself, is also the consciousness of its neighbors. Hence the blush upon the cheek—the faltering accents—the tremulousness of limb, and feebleness of movement. For a moment after the old man spoke—troubled with this consciousness, I could not answer. But my self-esteem came to my relief—nay, it had sufficed to conceal my disquiet. My looks were subdued to a seeming calm—my voice was unbroken, while I answered:—

"I have seen him within a few days, sir—a few nights ago we were at Mrs. Delaney's party. But why the question, sir?—what troubles you?"

"Strange that you have not seen! Did you not remark the alteration in his appearance?"

"I must confess, sir, I did not; but, perhaps, I did not remark him closely among the crowd."

"He is altered—terribly altered, Clifford. It is very strange that you have not seen it. It is visible to myself—his mother—all the family, and some of its friends. We tremble for his life. He is a mere skeleton — moves without life or animation, feebly — his cheeks are pale and thin, his lips white, and his eyes have an appearance which, beyond anything besides, distresses me — either lifelessly dull, or suddenly flushed up with an expression of wildness, which occurs so suddenly as to distress us with the worst apprehensions of his sanity."

"Indeed, sir!" I exclaimed with natural surprise.

"So it appears to us, his mother and myself, though, as it has escaped your eyes, I trust that we have exaggerated it. That we have not imagined all of it, however, we have other proofs to show. His manner is changed of late, and most of his habits. The change is only within the last six months; so suddenly made that it has been forced upon our sight. Once so frank, he is now reserved and shrinking to the last degree; speaks little; is reluctant to converse; and, I am compelled to believe, not only avoids my glance, but fears it."

"It is very strange that he should do so, sir. I can think of no reason why he should avoid *your* glance. Can you, sir? Have you any suspicions?"

"I have."

"Ha! have you indeed?"

The old man drew his chair closer to me, and, putting his hand on mine, with eyes in which the tears, big, slow-gathering, began to fill — trickling at length, one by one, through the venerable furrows of his cheeks — he replied in faltering accents:—

"A terrible suspicion, Clifford. I am afraid he drinks; that he frequents gambling-houses; that, in short, he is about to be lost to us, body and soul, for ever."

Deep and touching was the groan that followed from that old man's bosom. I hastened to relieve him.

"I am sure, sir, that you do your son great injustice. I cannot conceive it possible that he should have fallen into these habits."

"He is out nightly — late — till near daylight. But two hours ago he returned home. Let me confess to you, Clifford, what I should be loath to confess to anybody else. I followed him last night. He took the path to the suburbs, and I kept him in sight almost till he reached your dwelling. Then I lost him.

He moved too rapidly then for my old limbs, and disappeared among those groves of wild orange that fill your neighborhood. I searched them as closely as I could in the imperfect starlight, but could see nothing of him. I am told that there are gambling-houses, notorious enough, in the suburbs just beyond you. I fear that he found shelter in these—that he finds shelter in them nightly."

I scarcely breathed while listening to the unhappy father's narrative. There was one portion of it to which I need not refer the reader, as calculated to confirm my own previous convictions. I struggled with my feelings, however, in respect for his. I kept them down and spoke.

"In this one fact, Mr. Edgerton, I see nothing to alarm you. Your son may have been engaged far more innocently than you imagine. He is young—you know too well the practices of young men. As for the drinking he is perhaps the very last person whom I should suspect of excess. I have always thought his temperance unquestionable."

"Until recently, I should have had no fears myself. But connecting one fact with another—his absence all night, nightly—the stealthiness with which he departs from home after the family has retired—the stealthiness with which he returns just before day—his visible agitation when addressed—and, oh Clifford! worst of all signs, the shrinking of his eye beneath mine and his mother's—the fear to meet, and the effort to avoid us—these are the signs which most pain me, and excite my apprehensions. But look at his face and figure also. The haggard misery of the one, sign of sleeplessness and late watching—the attenuated feebleness of the other, showing the effects of some practices, no matter of what particular sort, which are undermining his constitution, and rapidly tending to destroy him. If you but look in his eye as I have done, marking its wildness, its wandering, its sensible expression of shame—you can hardly fail to think with me that something is morally wrong. He is guilty——"

"He is guilty!"

I echoed the words of the father, involuntarily. They struck the chord of conviction in my own soul, and seemed to me the language of a judgment.

"Ha! You know it, then?" cried the old man. "Speak! Tell me, Clifford—what is his folly? What is the particular guilt and shame into which he has fallen?"

I knew not that I had spoken until I heard these words. The agitation of the father was greatly increased. Truly, his sorrows were sad to look upon. I answered him:—

"I simply echoed your words, sir—I am ignorant, as I said before; and, indeed, I may venture, I think, with perfect safety, to assure you that gaming and drink have nothing to do with his appearance and deportment. I should rather suspect him of some improper—*some guilty connection*——"

I felt that, in the utterance of these words, I too had become excited. My voice did not rise, but I knew that it had acquired an intenseness which I as quickly endeavored to suppress. But the father had already beheld the expression in my face, and perhaps the sudden change in my tones grated harshly upon his ear. I could see that his looks became more eager and inquiring. I could note a greater degree of apprehension and anxiety in his eyes. I subdued myself, though not without some effort.

"William Edgerton may be erring, sir—that I do not deny, for I have seen too little of him of late to say anything of his proceedings; but I am very confident when I say that excess in liquor can not be a vice of his; and as for gaming, I should fancy that he was the last person in the world likely to be tempted to the indulgence of such a practice."

The father shook his head mournfully.

"Why this shame?—this fear? Besides, Clifford, what we know of our son makes us equally sure that women have nothing to do with his excesses. But these conjectures help us nothing. Clifford, I must look to you."

"What can I do for you, sir?"

"He is my son, my only son—the care of many sad, sleepless hours. It was his mother's hope that he would be our solace in the weary and the sad ones. You can not understand yet how much the parent lives in the child—how many of his hopes settle there. William has already disappointed us in our ambition. He will be nothing that we hoped him to be; but of this I complain not. But that he should become base, Clifford;

a night-prowler in the streets; a hanger-on of stews and gaming-houses; a brawler at an alehouse bar; a man to skulk through life and society; down-looking in his father's sight; despised in that of the community—oh! these are the cruel, the dreadful apprehensions!"

"But you know not that he is any of these."

"True; but there is something grievously wrong when the son dares not meet the eye of a parent with manly fearlessness; when he looks without joyance at the face of a mother, and shrinks from her endearments as if he felt that he deserved them not. William Edgerton is miserable; that is evident enough. Now, misery does not always imply guilt; but in his case, what else should it imply? He has had no misfortunes. He is independent; he is beloved by his parents, and by his friends; he has had no denial of the affections; in short, there is no way of accounting for his conduct or appearance, but by the supposition that he has fallen into vicious habits. Whatever these habits are, they are killing him. He is a mere skeleton; his whole appearance is that of a man running a rapid course of dissipation which can only advance in shame, and terminate in death. Clifford, if I have ever served you in the hour of your need, serve me in this of mine. Save my son for me. Bring him back from his folly; restore him, if you can, to peace and purity. See him, will you not? Seek him out; see him; probe his secret; and tell me what can be done to rescue him before it be too late."

"Really, Mr. Edgerton, you confound me. What can I do?"

"I know not. Everything, perhaps! I confess I can not counsel you. I can not even suggest how you should begin. You must judge for yourself. You must think and make your approaches according to your own judgment. Remember, that it is not in his behalf only. Think of the father, the mother! our hope, our all is at stake, I speak to you in the language of a child, Clifford. I am a child in this. This boy has been the apple of our eyes. It is our sight for which I seek your help. I know your good sense and sagacity. I know that you can trace out his secret when I should fail. My feelings would blind me to the truth. They might lead me to use language which would drive him from me. I leave it all to you. I know not who else can do for me half so well in a matter of this sort. Will you undertake it?"

Could I refuse? This question was discussed in all its bearings, in a few lightning-like progresses of thought. I felt all its difficulties—anticipated the annoyances to which it would subject me, and the degree of self-forbearance which it would necessarily require; yet, when I looked on the noble old gentleman who sat beside me—his gray hairs, his pleading looks, the recollection of the deep debt of gratitude which I owed him—I put my hand in his; I could resist no longer.

"I will try!" was the brief answer which I made him.

"God bless, God speed you!" he exclaimed, squeezing my hand with a pressure that said everything, and we separated; he for his family, and I for that new task which I had undertaken. How different from my previous purpose! I was now to seek to save the person whom I had set forth that morning with the purpose (if I had any purpose) to destroy. What a volume made up of contradictions and inconsistencies, strangely bound together, is the moral world of man!

CHAPTER XXXV.

APPLICATION OF "THE QUESTION."

But how to save him? How to approach him? How to keep down my own sense of wrong, my own feeling of misery, while representing the wishes and the feelings of that good old man—that venerable father? These were questions to afflict, to confound me! Still, I was committed; I must do what I had promised; undertake it at least; and the conviction that such a task was to be the severest trial of my manliness, was a conviction that necessarily helped to strengthen me to go through with it like a man.

What I had heard from Mr. Edgerton in relation to his son, though new, and somewhat surprising to myself, had not altered, in any respect, my impressions on the subject of his conduct toward, or with, my wife. Indeed, it rather served to confirm them. I could have told the old man, that, in losing all traces of his son in the neighborhood of my dwelling the night when he pursued him, he had the most conclusive proofs that he had gone to no gaming-houses. But where did he go? That was a question for myself. Had he entered my premises, and hidden himself amidst the foliage where I had myself so often harbored, while my object had been the secret inspection of my household? Could it be that he had loitered there during the last few nights of my wife's illness, in the vain hope of seeing me take my departure? This was the conclusion which I reached, and with it came the next thought that he would revisit the spot again that night. Ha! that thought! "Let him come!" I muttered to myself. "I will endeavor to be in readiness!"

But, surely, the father was grievously in error; his parental fear, alone, had certainly drawn the picture of his son's reduced and miserable condition. I had seen nothing of this. I had observed that he was shy, incommunicative—seeking to avoid me, as, according to their showing, he had striven to avoid his parents. So far our experience had been the same. But I had totally failed to perceive the marks of suffering or of sin which the vivid feelings of the father on this subject had insisted were so apparent. I had seen in Edgerton only the false friend, the traitor, stealing like a serpent to my bower, to beguile from my side the only object which made it dear to me. I could see in him only the exulting seducer, confident in his ability, artful in his endeavors, winning in his accomplishments, and striving, with practised industry of libertinism, in the prosecution of his cruel schemes. I could see the grace of his bearing, the ease of his manner, the symmetry of his person, the neatness of his costume, the superiority of his dancing, the insinuation of his address. I could see these only! That he looked miserable—that he was thin to meagreness, I had not seen.

Yet, even were it so, what could this prove, as the father had conclusively shown, but guilt. Poverty could not trouble him—he had never been an unrequited lover. He had gone along the stream of society, indifferent to the lures of beauty, and with a bark that had always appeared studiously to keep aloof from the shores or shoals of matrimony. If he was miserable, his misery could only come from misconduct, not from misfortune. It was a misery engendered by guilt, and what was that guilt? I *knew* that he did not drink; and was not his course in regard to Kingsley, as narrated by that person on the night when we went to the gaming-house together—was not that sufficient to show that he was no gamester, unless he happened to be one of the most bare faced of all canting hypocrites, which I could not believe him to be. What remained, but that my calculations were right? It was guilt that was sinking him, body and soul, so that his eye no longer dared to look upward—so that his ear shrunk from the sounds of those voices which, even in the language of kindness, were still speaking to him in the severest language of rebuke. And whom did that guilt concern more completely than myself?

Say that the father was to lose his son, his only son—what was my loss, what was my shame! and upon whom should the curse most fully and finally fall, if not upon the wrong-doer, though it so happened that the ruin of the guilty brought with it overthrow to the innocent scarcely less complete!

The extent of that guilt of Edgerton?

On this point all was a wilderness, vague, inconclusive, confused and crowded within my understanding. I believed that he had approached my wife with evil designs—I believed, without a doubt, that he had passed the boundaries of propriety in his intercourse with her; but I believed not that she had fallen! No! I had an instinctive confidence in her purity, that rendered it apparently impossible that she should lapse into the grossness of illicit love. What, then, was my fear? That she did love him, though, struggling with the tendency of her heart, she had not yielded in the struggle. I believed that his grace, beauty, and accomplishments—his persevering attention—his similar tastes—had succeeded in making an impression upon her soul which had effectually eradicated mine. I believed that his attentions were sweet to her—that she had not the strength to reject them; and, though she may have proved herself too virtuous to yield, she had not been sufficiently strong to repulse him with virtuous resentment.

That Edgerton had not succeeded, did not lessen *his* offence. The attempt was an indignity that demanded atonement—that justified punishment equally severe with that which should have followed a successful prosecution of his purpose. Women are by nature weak. They are not to be tempted. He who, knowing their weakness, attempts their overthrow by that medium, is equally cowardly and criminal. I could not doubt that he had made this attempt; but now it seemed necessary that I should suspend my indignation, in obedience with what appeared to be a paramount duty. A selfish reasoning now suggested compliance with this duty as a mean for procuring better intelligence than I already possessed. I need not say that the doubt was the pain in my bosom. I felt, in the words of the cold devil Iago, those "damned minutes" of him "who dotes, yet doubts, suspects, yet strongly loves."

The shapeless character of my fears and suspicions did not

by any means lessen their force and volume. On the contrary, it caused them to loom out through the hazy atmosphere of the imagination, assuming aspects more huge and terrible, in consequence of their very indistinctness; as the phantom shapes along the mountains of the Brocken, gathering and scowling in the morning or the evening twilight. To obtain more precise knowledge — to be able to subject to grasp and measure the uncertain phantoms which I feared — was, if not to reduce their proportions, at least to rid me of that excruciating suspense, in determining what to do, which was the natural result of my present ignorance.

With some painstaking, I was enabled to find and force an interview with Edgerton that very day. He made an effort to elude me;—such an effort as he could make without allowing his object to be seen. But I was not to be baffled. Having once determined upon my course, I was a puritan in the inveteracy with which I persevered in it. But it required no small struggle to approach the criminal, and so utterly to subdue my own sense of wrong, my suspicions and my hostility, as to keep in sight no more than the wishes and fears of the father. I have already boasted of my strength in some respects, even while exposing my weaknesses in others. That I could persuade Edgerton and my wife, equally, of my indifference, even at the moment when I was most agonized by my doubts of their purity, is a sufficient proof that I possessed a certain sort of strength. It was a moral strength, too, which could conceal the pangs inflicted by the vulture, even when it was preying upon the vitals of the best affections and the dearest hopes of the heart. It was necessary that I should put all this strength in requisition, as well to do what was required by the father, as to pierce, with keen eye, and considerate question, to the secret soul of the witness. I must assume the blandest manner of our youthful friendship: I must say kind things, and say them with a certain frank unconsciousness. I must use the language of a good fellow — a sworn companion — who is anxious to do justice to my friend's father, and yet had no notion that my friend himself was doing the smallest thing to justify the unmeasured fears of the fond old man. Such was my cue at first. I am not so sure that I pursued it to the end; but of this hereafter.

My attention having been specially drawn to the personal appearance of William Edgerton, I was surprised, if not absolutely shocked, to see that the father had scarcely exaggerated the misery of his condition. He was the mere shadow of his former self. His limbs, only a year before, had been rounded even to plumpness. They were now sharp and angular. His skin was pale, his looks haggard; and that apprehensive shrinking of the eye, which had called forth the most keen expressions of fear and suspicion from the father's lips, was the prominent characteristic which commanded my attention during our brief interview. His eye, after the first encounter, no longer rose to mine. Keenly did I watch his face, though for an instant only. A sudden hectic flush mantled its paleness. I could perceive a nervous muscular movement about his mouth, and he slightly started when I spoke.

"Edgerton," I said, with tones of good-humored reproach, "there's no finding you now-a-days. You have the invisible cap. What do you do with yourself? As for law, that seems destined to be a mourner so far as you are concerned. She sits like a widow in her weeds. You have abandoned her: do you mean to abandon your friends also?"

He answered, with a faint attempt to smile:—

"No; I have been to see you often, but you are never at home."

"Ah! I did not hear of it. But if you really wished to see a husband who has survived the honeymoon, I suspect that home is about the last place where you should seek for him. Julia did the honors, I trust?"

His eye stole upward, met mine, and sunk once more upon the floor. He answered faintly:—

"Yes, but I have not seen her for some days."

"Not since Mother Delaney's party, I believe?"

The color came again into his cheeks, but instantly after was succeeded by a deadly paleness.

"What a bore these parties are! and such parties as those of Mrs. Delaney are particularly annoying to me. Why the d—l couldn't the old tabby halter her hobby without calling in her neighbors to witness the painful spectacle? You were there, I think?"

"Yes."

"I left early. I got heartily sick. You know I never like such places; and, as soon as they began dancing, I took advantage of the fuss and fiddle to steal off. It was unfortunate I did so, for Julia was taken sick, and has had a narrow chance for it. I thought I should have lost her."

All this was spoken in tones of the coolest imaginable indifference. Edgerton was evidently surprised. He looked up with some curiosity in his glance, and more confidence; and, with accents that slightly faltered, he asked:—

"Is she well again? I trust she is better now."

"Yes!" I answered, with the same *sang-froid.* "But I've had a serious business of watching through the last three nights. Her peril was extreme. She lost her little one."

A visible shudder went through his frame.

"Tired to death of the walls of the house, which seems a dungeon to me, I dashed out this morning, at daylight, as soon as I found I could safely leave her; and, strolling down to the office, who should I find there but your father, perched at the desk, and seemingly inclined to resume all his former practice?"

"Indeed! my father—so early? What could be the matter? Did he tell you?"

"Yes, i'faith, he is in tribulation about you. He fancies you are in a fair way to destruction. You can't conceive what he fancies. It seems, according to his account, that you are a night-stalker. He dwells at large upon your nightly absences from home, and then about your appearance, which, to say truth, is very wretched. You scarcely look like the same man, Edgerton. Have you been sick? What's the matter with you?"

"I am *not* altogether well," he said, evasively.

"Yes, but mere indisposition would never produce such a change, in so short a period, in any man! Your father is disposed to ascribe it to other causes."

"Ah! what does he think?"

I fancied there was mingled curiosity and trepidation in this inquiry.

"He suspects you of gaming and drinking; but I assured him, very confidently, that such was not the case. On one of these heads I could speak confidently, for I met Kingsley the other night—the night of Mother Delaney's party—who was hot and heavy against you because you refused to lend him money for such purposes. I was more indulgent, lent him the money, went with him to the house, and returned home with a pocket full of specie, sufficient to set up a small banking-operation of my own."

"You! can it be possible?"

"True; and no such dull way of spending an evening either. I got home in the small hours, and found Julia delirious. I haven't had such a fright for a stolen pleasure, Heaven knows when. There was the doctor, and there my eternal mother-in-law, and my poor little wife as near the grave as could be! But the circumstance of refusing the money to Kingsley, knowing his object, made me confident that gaming was not the cause of your night-stalking, and so I told the old gentleman."

"And what did he say?"

"Shook his head mournfully, and reasoned in this manner: 'He has no pecuniary necessities, has no oppressive toils, and has never had any disappointment of heart. There is nothing to make him behave so, and look so, but guilt—GUILT!'"

I repeated the last word with an entire change in the tone of my voice. Light, lively, and playful before, I spoke that single word with a stern solemnity, and, bending toward him, my eye keenly traversed the mazes of his countenance.

"*He has it!*" I thought to myself, as his head drooped forward, and his whole frame shuddered momentarily.

"But"—here my tones again became lively and playful—I even laughed—"I told the old man that I fancied I could hit the nail more certainly on the head. In short, I said I could pretty positively say what was the cause of your conduct and condition."

"Ah!" and, as he uttered this monosyllable, he made a feeble effort to rise from his seat, but sunk back, and again fixed his eye upon the floor in visible emotion.

"Yes! I told him—was I not right?—that a woman was at the bottom of it all!"

He started to his feet. His face was averted from me.

"Ha! was I not right? I knew it! I saw through it from

the first; and, though I did not tell the old man *that,* I was pretty sure that you were trespassing upon your neighbor's grounds. Ha! what say you? Was I not right? Were you not stealing to forbidden places—playing the snake, on a small scale, in some blind man's Eden? Ha! ha! what say you to that? I am right, am I not? eh?"

I clapped him on the shoulder as I spoke. His face had been half averted from me while I was speaking; but now it turned upon me, and his glance met mine, teeming with inquisitive horror.

"No! no! you are not right!" he faltered out; "it is not so. Nothing is the matter with me! I am quite well—quite! I will see my father, and set him right."

"Do so," I said, coolly and indifferently—"do so; tell him what you please: but you can't change my conviction that you're after some pretty woman, and probably poaching on some neighbor's territory. Come, make me your confidante, Edgerton. Let us know the history of your misfortune. Is the lady pliant? I should judge so, since you continue to spend so many nights away from home. Come, make a clean breast of it. Out with your secret! I have always been your friend. *We could not betray each other, I think!*"

"You are quite mistaken," he said, with the effort of one who is half strangled. "There is nothing in it; I assure you, you were never more mistaken."

"Pshaw, Edgerton! you may blind papa, but you can not blind me. Keep your secret, if you please, but, if you provoke me, I will trace it out; I will unkennel you. If I do not show the sitting hare in a fortnight, by the course of the hunter, tell me I am none myself."

His consternation increased, but I did not allow it to disarm me. I probed him keenly, and in such a manner as to make him wince with apprehension at every word which I uttered. Morally, William Edgerton was a brave man. Guilt alone made him a coward. It actually gave me pain, after a while, to behold his wretched imbecility. He hung upon my utterance with the trembling suspense of one whose eye has become enchained with the fascinating gaze of the serpent. I put my questions and comments home to him, on the assumption that he was playing the traitor with another's wife; though taking care, all the while, that my manner should be that of one who has no sort of apprehensions on his own score. My deportment and tone tallied well with the practised indifference which had distinguished my previous overt conduct. It deceived him on that head; but the truth, like a sharp knife, was no less keen in penetrating to his soul; and, preserving my coolness and directness, with that singular tenacity of purpose which I could maintain in spite of my own sufferings—and keep them still unsuspected—I did not scruple to impel the sharp iron into every sensitive place within his bosom.

He writhed visibly before me. His struggles did not please me, but I sought to produce them simply because they seemed so many proofs confirming the truth of my conjectures. The fiend in my own soul kept whispering, "He has it!"—and a fatal spell, not unlike that which riveted his attention to the language which tore and vexed him, urged me to continue it, until at length the sting became too keen for his endurance. In very desperation, he broke away from the fetters of that fascination of terror which had held him for one mortal hour to the spot.

"No more! no more!" he exclaimed, with an uncontrollable burst of emotion. "You torture me! I can stand it no longer! There is nothing in your conjecture! There is no reason for your suspicions! She is—"

"She? Ah!"

I could not suppress the involuntary exclamation. The truth seemed to be at hand. I was premature. My utterance brought him to his senses. He stopped, looked at me wildly for an instant, his eyes dilated almost to bursting. He seemed suddenly to be conscious that the secrets of his soul—its dark, uncommissioned secrets—were about to force themselves into sight and speech; and unable, perhaps, to arrest them in any other way, he darted headlong from my presence.

CHAPTER XXXVI.

MEDITATED EXILE.

WITH his departure sunk the spirit which had sustained me. I had not gone through that scene willingly; I had suffered quite as many pangs as himself. I had made my own misery, though disguised under the supposed condition of another, the subject of my own mockery; and if I succeeded in driving the iron into *his* soul, the other end of the shaft was all the while working in mine! His flight was an equal relief to both of us. The stern spirit left me from that moment. My agony found relief, momentary though it was, in a sudden gush of tears. My hot, heavy head sank upon my palms, and I groaned in unreserved homage to the never-slumbering genius of pain—that genius which alone is universal—which adopts us from the cradle—which distinguishes our birth by our tears, hallows the sentiment of grief to us from the beginning, and maintains the fountains which supply its sorrows to the end. The lamb skips, the calf leaps, the fawn bounds, the bird chirps, the young colt frisks; all things but man enjoy life from its very dawn. He alone is feeble, suffering. His superior pangs and sorrows are the first proofs of his singular and superior destiny.

Bitter was the gush of tears that rolled from the surcharged fountains of my heart; bitter, but free—flowing to my relief, at the moment when my head seemed likely to burst with a volcanic volume within it, and when a blistering arrow seemed slowly to traverse, to and fro, the most sore and shrinking passages of my soul. Had not Edgerton fled, I could not have sustained it much longer. My passions would have hurled aside my judgment, and mocked that small policy under which

I acted. I felt that they were about to speak, and rejoiced that he fled. Had he remained, I should most probably have poured forth all my suspicion, all my hate; dragged by violence from his lips the confession of his wrong, and from his heart the last atonement for it.

At first I reproached myself that I had not done so. I accused myself of tameness—the dishonorable tameness of submitting to indignity—the last of all indignities—and of conferring calmly, even good-humoredly, with the wrong-doer. But cooler moments came. A brief interval sufficed—helped by the flood of tears which rushed, hot and scalding, from my eyes—to subdue the angry spirit. I remembered my pledges to the father; my unspeakable obligations to him; and when I again recollected that my convictions had not assailed the purity of my wife, and, at most, had questioned her affections only, my forbearance seemed justified.

But could the matter rest where it was? Impossible! What was to be done? It was clear enough that the only thing that could be done, for the relief of all parties, was to be done by myself. Edgerton was suffering from a guilty pursuit. That pursuit, if still urged, might be successful, if not so at present. The constant drip of the water will wear away the stone; and if my wife could submit to impertinent advances without declaring them to her husband, the work of seduction was already half done. To listen is, in half the number of cases, to fall. I must save her; I had not the courage to put her from me. Believing that she was still safe, I resolved, through the excess of that love which was yet the predominant passion in my soul, in spite of all its contradictions, to keep her so, if human wit could avail, and human energy carry its desires into successful completion.

To do this, there was but one process. That was flight. I must leave this city—this country. By doing so, I remove my wife from temptation, remove the temptation from the unhappy young man whom it is destroying; and thus, though by a sacrifice of my own comforts and interests, repay the debt of gratitude to my benefactor in the only effective manner. It called for no small exercise of moral courage and forbearance—no small benevolence—to come to this conclusion. It must be understood that my professional business was becoming particularly profitable. I was rising in my profession. My clients daily increased in number; my acquaintance daily increased in value. Besides, I loved my birthplace — thrice-hallowed — the only region in my eyes —

> "The spot most worthy loving
> Of all beneath the sky."

But the sacrifice was to be made; and my imagination immediately grew active for my compensation, by describing a woodland home — a spot, remote from the crowd, where I should carry my household gods, and set them up for my exclusive and uninvaded worship. The whole world-wide West was open to me. A virgin land, rich in natural wealth and splendor, it held forth the prospect of a fair field and no favor to every new-comer. There it is not possible to keep in thraldom the fearless heart and the active intellect. There, no petty circle of society can fetter the energies or enfeeble the endeavors. No mocking, stale conventionalities can usurp the place of natural laws, and put genius and talent into the accursed strait-jacket of routine! Thither will I go. I remembered the late conference with my friend Kingsley, and the whole course of my reasoning on the subject of my removal was despatched in half an hour. "I will go to Alabama."

Such was my resolution. I was the man to make sudden resolutions. This, however, reasoned upon with the utmost circumspection, seemed the very best that I could make. My wife, yet pure, was rescued from the danger that threatened her; I was saved the necessity of taking a life so dear to my benefactor; and the unhappy young man himself — the victim to a blind passion — having no longer in his sight the temptation which misled him, would be left free to return to better thoughts, and the accustomed habits of business and society. I had concluded upon my course in the brief interval which followed my interview with William Edgerton and my return home.

The next day I saw his father. I communicated the assurance of the son, and renewed my own, that neither drunkenness nor gaming was his vice. What it was that afflicted him

I did not pretend to know, but I ascribed it to want of employment; a morbid, unenergetic temperament; the fact that he was independent, and had no rough necessities to make him estimate the true nature and the objects of life; and, at the close, quietly suggested that possibly there was some affair of the heart which contributed also to his suffering. I did not deny that his looks were wretched, but I stoutly assured the old man that his parental fears exaggerated their wretchedness. We had much other talk on the subject. When we were about to separate for the day, I declared my own determination in this manner:—

"I have just decided on a step, Mr. Edgerton, which perhaps will somewhat contribute to the improvement of your son, by imposing some additional tasks upon him. I am about to emigrate for the southwest."

"You, Clifford? Impossible! What puts that into your head?"

It was something difficult to furnish any good reason for such a movement. The only obvious reason spoke loudly for my remaining where I was.

"This is unaccountable," said he. "You are doing here as few young men have done before you. Your business increasing—your income already good—surely, Clifford, you have not thought upon the matter—you are not resolved."

I could plead little other than a truant disposition for my proceeding, but I soon convinced him that I was resolved. He seemed very much troubled; betrayed the most flattering concern in my interests; and, renewing his argument for my stay, renewed also his warmest professions of service."

"I had hoped," he said, "to have seen you and William, closely united, pursuing the one path equally and successfully together. I shall have no hopes of him if you leave us."

"The probability is, sir, that he will do better with the whole responsibility of the office thrown upon him."

"No! no!" said the old man, mournfully. "I have no hope of him. There seems to me a curse upon wealth always—that follows and clings to it, and never leaves it, till it works out the ruin of all the proprietors. See the number of our young men, springing from nothing, that make everything out of it—rise to eminence and power—get fortune as if it were a mere sport to command and to secure it; while, on the other hand, look at the heirs of our proud families. Profligate, reckless, abandoned; as if, reasoning from the supposed wealth of their parents, they fancied that there were no responsibilities of their own. I saw this danger from the beginning. I have striven to train up my son in the paths of duty and constant employment; and yet—but complaint is idle. The consciousness of having tried my best to have and make it otherwise is, nevertheless, a consolation. When do you think to go?"

"In a week or two at farthest. I have but to rid myself of my impediments."

"Always prompt; but it is best. Once resolved, action is the moral law. Still, I wish I could delay you. I still think you are committing a great error. I can not understand it. You have established yourself. This is not easy anywhere. You will find it difficult in a new country, and among strangers."

"Nay, sir, more easy there than anywhere else. If a man has anything in him, strangers and a new country are the proper influences to bring it out. Friends and an old community keep it down, suppress, strangle it. This is the misfortune of your son. He has family, friends—resources which defeat all the operations of moral courage, and prevent independence. Necessity is the moral lever. Do you forget the saying of one of the wise men? 'If you wish your son to become a man, strip him naked and send him among strangers'—in other words, throw him upon his own resources, and let him take care of himself. The not doing this is the source of that misfortune which only now you deplored as so commonly following the condition of the select and wealthy. I do not fear the struggle in a new country. It will end in my gaining my level, be that high or low. Nothing, in such a region, can keep a man from that."

"Ay, but the roughness of those new countries—the absence of refinement—the absolute want of polish and delicacy."

"The roughness will not offend me, if it is manly. The world is full of it. To be anything, a man must not have too nice a stomach. Such a stomach will make him recoil from sights of misery and misfortune; and he who recoils from such sights, will be the last to relieve, to repair them. But while I admit the roughness and the want of polish among these frontier men, I deny the want of delicacy. Their habits are rude and simple, perhaps, but their tastes are pure and unaffected, and their hearts in the right place. They have strong affections; and strong affections, properly balanced, are the true sources of the better sort of delicacy. All other is merely conventional, and consists of forms and phrases, which are very apt to keep us from the thing itself which they are intended to represent. Give me these frank men and women of the frontier, while my own feelings are yet strong and earnest. Here, I am perpetually annoyed by the struggle to subdue within the social limits the expression of that nature which is for ever boiling up within me, and the utterance of which is neither more nor less than the heart's utterance of the faith and hope which are in it. We are told of those nice preachers who 'never mention hell to ears polite.' They are the preachers of your highly-refined, sentimental society. Whatever hell may be, they are the very teachers that, by their mincing forbearance, conduct the poor soul that relies on them into its jaws. It is a sort of lie not to use the properest language to express our thoughts, but rather so to falsify our thoughts by a sort of lack-a-daisaical phraseology which deprives them of all their virility. A nation or community is in a bad way for truth, when there is a tacit understanding among their members to deal in the diminutives of a language, and forbear the calling of things by their right names. An Englishman, wishing to designate something which is graceful, pleasing, delicate, or fine, uses the word 'nice' —more fitly applied to bon-bons or beefsteaks, according to the stomach of the speaker. An energetic form of speech is rated, in fashionable society, as particularly vulgar. In our larger American cities, where they have much pretension but little character, a leg must not be spoken of as such. You may say 'limb,' but not 'leg.' The word 'woman'—one of the sweetest in the language—is supposed to disparage the female to whom it is applied. She must be called a 'lady,' forsooth; and this word, originally intended to pacify an aristocratic vanity, has become the ordinary appellative of every member of that gross family which, in the language of Shakspere, is only fit to 'suckle fools and chronicle small beer.' I shall be more free, and feel more honest in that rough world of the west; a region in which the dilettantism, such as it is, of our Atlantic cities, is always very prompt to sneer at and disparage; but I look to see the day, even in our time, when that west shall be, not merely an empire herself, but the nursing mother of great empires. There shall be a genius born in that vast, wide world—a rough, unlicked genius it may be, but one whose words shall fall upon the hills like thunder, and descend into the valleys like a settled, heavy rain, which shall irrigate them all with a new life. Perhaps—"

I need not pursue this. I throw it upon paper with no deliberation. It streams from me like the rest. Its tone was somewhat derived from those peculiar, sad feelings, and that pang-provoking course of thought, which it has been the purpose of this narrative to embody. In the expression of digressive but earnest notions like these, I could momentarily divert myself from deeper and more painful emotions. I had really gone through a great trial: I say a great trial—always assuming human indulgence for that disease of the blind heart which led me where I found myself, which makes me what I am. I did not feel lightly the pang of parting with my birthplace. I did not esteem lightly the sacrifice of business, comfort, and distinction which I was making; and of that greater cause of suffering, supposed or real, of the falling off in my wife's affection, the agony is already in part recorded. It may be permitted to me, perhaps, under these circumstances—with the additional knowledge, which I yet suppressed, that these sacrifices were to be made, and these sufferings endured, partly that the son might be saved—to speak with some unreserved warmth of tone to the venerable and worthy sire. He little knew how much of my determination to remove from my country was due to my regard for him. I felt assured that, if I remained, two things must happen. William Edgerton would persevere in his madness, and I should murder him in his perseverance! I banished myself in regard for that old man, and in some measure to requite his benefactions, that I might be spared this necessity.

When, the next day, I sought William Edgerton himself, and declared my novel determination, he turned pale as death. I could see that his lips quivered. I watched him closely. He was evidently racked by an emotion which was more obvious from the necessity he was under of suppressing it. With considerable difficulty he ventured to ask my reasons for this strange step, and with averted countenance repeated those which his father had proffered against my doing so. I could see that he fain would have urged his suggestions more vehemently if he dared. But the conviction that his wishes were the fathers to his arguments was conclusive to render him careful that his expostulations should not put on a show of earnestness. I must do William Edgerton the justice to say that guilt was not his familiar. He could not play the part of the practised hypocrite. He had no powers of artifice. He could not wear the flowers upon his breast, having the volcano within it. Professionally, he could be no *roué*. He could seem no other than he was. Conscious of guilt, which he had not the moral strength to counteract and overthrow, he had not, at the same time, the art necessary for its concealment. He could use no smooth, subtle blandishments. His cheek and eye would tell the story of his mind, though it strove to make a false presentment. I do him the further justice to believe that a great part of his misery arose from this consciousness of his doing wrong, rather than from the difficulties in the way of his success. I believe that, even were he successful in the prosecution of his illicit purposes, he would not have looked or felt a jot less miserable. I felt, while we conferred together, that my departure was perhaps the best measure for his relief. While I mused upon his character and condition, my anger yielded in part to commiseration. I remembered the morning-time of our boyhood — when we stood up for conflict with our young enemies, side by side — obeyed the same rallying-cry, recognised the same objects, and were a sort of David and Jonathan to one another. Those days! — they soothed and softened me while I recalled them. My tone became less keen, my language less tinctured with sarcasm, when I thought of these things; and I thought of our separation without thinking of its cause.

"I leave you, Edgerton, with one regret — not that we part, for life is full of partings, and the strong mind must be reconciled with them, or it is nothing — but that I leave you so unlike your former self. I wish I could do something for you."

I gave him my hand as as I spoke. He did not grasp—he rather shrunk from it. An uncontrollable burst of feeling seemed suddenly to gush from him as he spoke:—

"Take no heed of me, Clifford—I am not worthy of *your* thought."

"Ha! What do you mean?"

He spoke hastily, in manifest discomfiture:—

"I am worthy of no man's thought."

"Pshaw! you are a hypochondriac."

"Would it were that!—But you go!—when?"

"In a week, perhaps."

"So soon? So very soon? Do you—do you carry your family with you at once?"

There was great effort to speak this significant inquiry. I perceived that. I perceived that his eyes were on the ground while it was made. The question was offensive to me. It had a strange and painful significance. It recalled the whole cause, the bitter cause of my resolve for exile; and I could not control the altered tones of my voice in answering, which I did with some causticity of feeling, which necessarily entered into my utterance.

"Family, surely! My wife only! No great charge, I'm thinking, and her health needs an early change. Would you have me leave *her?* I have no other family, you know!"

The dialogue, carried on with restraint before, was shortened by this; and, after a few business remarks, which were necessary to our office concerns, he pleaded an engagement to get away. He left me with some soreness upon my mind, which formed its expression in a brief soliloquy.

"You would have the path made even freer than before, would you? It does not content you, these long morning meditations—these pretended labors of the painting-room, the suspicious husband withdrawn, and the wife, neither scorning nor consenting, willing to believe in that devotion to the art which is properly a devotion to herself? These are not sufficient opportunities, eh? There were more room for landscape, if this Othello were in Alabama—pitching his stakes, and building his log-cabin for the reception of that divinity, that finds the worship very sufficient where she is! We shall disappoint you, Mr. Edgerton!—Ah! could I but know all! Could I be sure that she did love him! Could I be sure that she did not! That is the curse—that doubt!—Will it remain so? No! no! Once removed—once in those forest regions, it can not be that she will repine for anything. She *must* love me then—she will feel anew the first fond passion. She will forget these passing fancies. They *will* pass! She is young. The image will haunt her no longer—at least, it will no longer haunt me!"

So I spoke, but I was not so sure of that last. The doubt did not trouble me, however. Sufficient for the day is the evil thereof. But I had another test yet to try. I wished to see how Julia would receive the communication of my purpose. As yet she knew nothing of my contemplated departure. "It will surprise her," I thought to myself. "In that surprise she will show how much our removal will distress her!"

But when I made known to her my intention, the surprise was all my own. The communication did not seemed to distress her at all. Surprise her it did, but the surprise seemed a pleasant one. It spoke out in a sudden flashing of the eye, a gentle smiling of the mouth, which was equally unexpected and grateful to my heart.

"I am delighted with the idea!" she exclaimed, putting her arms about my neck. "I think we shall be so happy there. I long to get away from this place."

"Indeed! But are you serious?"

"To be sure."

"I was apprehensive it might distress you."

"Oh! no! no! I have been dull and tired here, for a long while; and I thought, when you told me that Mr. Kingsley had gone to Alabama, how delightful it would be if we could go too."

"But you never told me that."

"No."

"Nor even looked it, Julia."

"Surely not—I should have been loath to have you think, while your business was so prosperous, and you seemed so well satisfied here, that I had any discontent."

"I satisfied!" I said this rather to myself than her.

"Yes, were you not? I had no reason to think otherwise. Nay, I feared you were too well satisfied, for I have seen so little of you of late. I'm sure I wished we were anywhere, so that you could find your home more to your liking."

"And have such notions really filled your brain, Julia?"

"Really."

"And you have found me a stranger—you have missed me?"

"Ah! do you not know it, Edward?"

"You shall have no need to reproach me hereafter. We will go to Alabama, and live wholly for one another. I shall leave you in business time only, and hurry back as soon as I can."

"Ah, promise me that?"

"I do!"

"We shall be so happy then. Then we shall take our old rambles, Edward, though in new regions, and I will resume the pencil, if you wish it."

This was said timidly.

"To be sure I wish it. But why do you say 'resume'? Have you not been painting all along?"

"No! I have scarcely smeared canvass in the last two months."

"But you have been sketching?"

"No!"

"What employed you then in the studio? How have you passed your mornings?"

This inquiry was made abruptly, but it did not disturb her. Her answer was strangely satisfactory.

"I have scarcely looked in upon the studio in all that time."

I longed to ask what Edgerton had done with himself, and whether he had been suffered to employ himself alone, in his morning visits, but my tongue faltered—I somehow dared not. Still, it was something to have her assurance that she had not found her attractions in that apartment in which my jealous fancy had assumed that she took particular delight. She had spoken with the calmness of innocence, and I was too happy to believe her. I put my arms about her waist.

"Yes, we will renew the old habits, for I suppose that business there will be less pressing, less exacting, than I have found it here. We will take our long walks, Julia, and make up for lost time in new sketches. You have thought me a truant, Julia —neglectful hitherto! Have you not?"

"Ah, Edward!"—Her eyes filled with tears, but a smile, like a rainbow, made them bright.

"Say, did you not?"

"Do not be angry with me if I confess I thought you very much altered in some respects. I was fearful I had vexed you."

"You shall have no more reason to fear. We shall be the babes in the wood together. I am sure we shall be quite happy, left to ourselves. No doubts, no fears—nothing but love. And you are really willing to go?"

"Willing! I wish it! I can get ready in a day."

"You have but a week. But, have you no reluctance? Is there nothing that you regret to leave? Speak freely, Julia. Your mother, your friends—would you not prefer to remain with them?"

She placed her hands on my shoulders, laid her head close to my bosom and murmured—how softly, how sweetly—in the touching language of the Scripture damsel.

"Entreat me not to leave thee, or to refrain from following after thee; for whither thou goest, I will go, and where thou lodgest, I will lodge. Thy people shall be my people, and thy God my God!"

I folded her with tremulous but deep joy in my embrace; and in that sweet moment of peace, I wondered that I ever should have questioned the faith of such a woman.

CHAPTER XXXVII.

"AND STILL THE BITTER IN THE CUP OF JOY."

ONCE more I had sunshine. The clouds seemed to depart as suddenly as they had risen, and that same rejoicing and rosy light which had encircled the brow of manhood at its dawn—long shrouded, seemingly lost for ever, and swallowed up in darkness—came out as softly and quietly in the maturer day, as if its sweet serene had never known even momentary obscuration.

Love, verily, is the purple light of youth. If it abides, blessing and blessed, with the unsophisticated heart, youth never leaves us. Gray brows make not age—the feeble step, the wrinkled visage, these indicate the progress of time, but not the passage of youth. Happy hearts keep us in perpetual spring, and the glow of childhood without its weaknesses is ours to the final limit of seventy. The sense of desolation, the pang of denial, the baffled hope, and the defrauded love, these constitute the only age that should ever give the heart a pang. I can fancy a good man advancing through all the mortal stages from seventeen to seventy-five, and crowned by the sympathies of corresponsive affections, simply going on from youth to youth, ending at last in youth's perfect immortality!

The hope of this—not so much a hope as an instinct—is the faith of our boyhood. The boy, as the father of the man, transmits this hope to riper years; but if the experience of the day correspond not with the promise of the dawn, how rapidly old age comes upon us! White hairs, lean cheeks, withered muscles, feeble steps, and that dull, dead feeling about the heart—that utter abandonment of cheer—which would be despair, were it not for a certain blunted sensibility—a sort of drowsy indifference to all things that the day brings forth, which, as it takes from life the excitement of every passion, leaves it free from the sting of any. Yet, were not the tempest better than the calm? Who would not prefer to be driven before the treacherous hurricane of the blue gulf, than to linger midway on its shoreless waters, and behold their growing stagnation from day to day? The apathy of the passions is the most terrible form in which age makes its approaches.

With an earnest, sanguine temperament, such as mine, there is little danger of such apathy, The danger is not from lethargy but madness. I had escaped this danger. It was surprising, even to myself, how suddenly my spirits had arisen from the pressure that had kept them down. In a moment, as it were, that mocking troop of fears and sorrows which environed me, took their departure. It seemed that it was only necessary for me to know that I was about to lose the presence of William Edgerton to find this relief.

And yet, how idle! With an intense *egoïsme*, such as mine, I should conjure up an Edgerton in the deepest valleys of our country. We have our gods and devils in our own hearts. The nature of the deities we worship depends upon our own. In a savage state, the Deity is savage, and expects bloody sacrifices; with the progress of civilization his attributes incline to mercy. The advent of Jesus Christ indicated the advance of the Hebrews to a higher sense of the human nature. It was the advent of the popular principle, which has been advancing steadily ever since and keeping due pace with the progress of Christian education. The people were rising at the expense of the despotism which had kept them down. It does not affect the truth of this to show that the polish of the Jewish nation was lessened at this period. Nay, rather proves it, since the diffusion of a truth or a power must always lessen its intensity. In teaching, for the first time, the doctrine of the soul's immortality, the Savior laid the foundation of popular rights, in the elevation of the common humanity — since he thus showed the equal importance, in the sight of God, of every soul that had ever taken shape beneath his hands.

The demon which had vexed and tortured me was a demon of my own soliciting — of my own creation. But, I knew not this. I congratulated myself on escaping from him. Blind fancy!—I little knew the insidious pertinacity of this demon—this demon of the blind heart. I little knew the nature of his existence, and how much he drew his nutriment from the recesses of my own nature. He could spare, or seem to spare, the victim of whom he was so sure; and by a sort of levity, in no ways unaccountable, since we see it in the play of cat with mouse, could indulge with temporary liberty, the poor captive of whom he was at any moment certain. I congratulated myself on my escape; but I was not so well pleased with the congratulations of others. I was doomed to endure those of my exemplary mother-in-law, Mrs. Delaney. That woman had her devil—a worse devil, though not more troublesome, I think, than mine. She said to me, when she heard of my purpose of removal: "You are right to remove. It is only prudent. Pity you had not gone some months ago."

I read her meaning, where her language was ambiguous, in her sharp, leering eyes—full of significance—an expression of mysterious intelligence, which, mingled with a slight, sinister smile upon her lips, for a moment, brought a renewal of all my tortures and suspicions. She saw the annoyance which I felt, and strove to increase it. I know not—I will not repeat—the occasional innuendos which she allowed herself to utter in the brief space of a twenty minutes' interview. It is enough to say that nothing could be more evident than her desire to vex me with the worst pangs which a man can know, even though her success in the attempt was to be attained at the expense of her daughter's peace of mind and reputation. I do not believe that she ever hinted to another, what she clearly enough insinuated as a cause of fear to me. Her purpose was to goad me to madness, and in her witless malice, I do believe she was utterly unconscious of the evil that might accrue to the child of her own womb from her base and cruel suggestions. I wished to get from her these suggestions in a more distinct form. I wished at the same time, to deprive her of the pleasure of seeing that I understood her. I restrained myself accordingly, though the vulture was then again at my vitals.

"What do you mean, Mrs. Delaney? Why is it a pity that I hadn't gone months ago?"

"Oh! that's enough for me to know. I have my reasons."

"But, will you not suffer me to know them? I am conscious of no evil that has arisen from my not going sooner."

"Indeed! Well, if you are not, I can only say you're not so keen-sighted a lawyer as I thought you were. That's all."

"If you think I would have made out better, got more practice, and made more money in Alabama, that, I must tell you, has been long since my own opinion."

"No! I don't mean that—it has no regard to business and money-making—what I mean."

"Ah! what can it have regard to? You make me curious, Mrs. Delaney."

"Well, that may be; but I'm not going to satisfy your curiosity. I thought you had seen enough for yourself. I'm sure you're the only one that has not seen."

"Upon my soul, Mrs. Delaney, you are quite a mystery."

"Oh! am I?"

"I can't dive into such depths. I'm ignorant."

"Tell those that know you no better. But you can't blind me. I know that you know—and more than that, I can guess what's carrying you to Alabama. It's not law business, I know that."

I was vexed enough, as may be supposed, at this malicious pertinacity, but I kept down my struggling gorge with a resolution which I had been compelled often enough to exercise before; and quietly ended the interview by taking my hat and departure, as I said:—

"You are certainly a very sagacious lady, Mrs. Delaney; but I must leave you, and wait your own time to make these mysterious revelations. My respects to Mr. Delaney. Good morning."

"Oh, good morning; but let me tell you, Mr. Clifford, if you don't see, it's not because you can't. Other people can see without trying."

The Jezabel!

My preparations were soon completed. I worked with the spirit of enthusiasm—I had so many motives to be active; and, subordinate among these, but still important, I should get out of the reach of this very woman. I could not beat her myself, but I wished her husband might do it, and not to anticipate my own story, he did so in less than three months after. He was the man too, to perform such a labor with unction and emphasis. A vigorous man with muscles like bolt-ropes, and limbs that would have been respectable in the days of Goliah. I met him on leaving the steps of Mrs. Delaney's lodgings, and—thinking of the marital office I wished him to perform—I was rejoiced to discover that he was generously drunk—in the proper spirit for such deeds in the flesh.

He seized my hand with quite a burst of enthusiasm, swore I was a likely fellow, and somehow he had a liking for me.

"Though, to be sure, my dear fellow, it's not Mrs. Delaney that loves any bone in your skin. She's a lady that, like most of the dear creatures, has a way of her own for thinking. She does her own thinking, and what can a woman know about such a business. It's to please her that I sit by and say nothing; and a wife must be permitted some indulgence while the moon lasts, which the poets tell us, is made out of honey: but it's never a long moon in these days, and a small cloud soon puts an end to it. Wait till that time, Mr. Clifford, and I'll put her into a way of thinking, that'll please you and myself much better."

I thanked him for his good opinion, and civilly wished him—as it was a matter which seemed to promise him so much satisfaction—that the duration of the honeymoon should be as short as possible. He thanked me affectionately—grasped my hand with the squeeze of a blacksmith, and entreated that I should go back and take a drink of punch with him. As an earnest of what he could give me, he pulled a handful of lemons from his pocket which he had bought from a shop by the way. I need not say I expressed my gratitude, though I declined his invitation. I then told him I was about to remove to Alabama, and he immediately proposed to go along with me. I reminded him that he was just married, and it would be expected of him that he would see the honeymoon out.

"Ah, faith!" he replied, "and there's sense in what you say; it must be done, I suppose; but devil a bit, to my thinking, does any moon last a month in this climate; and the first cloudy weather, d'ye see, and I'm after you."

It was difficult to escape from the generous embraces of my ardent father-in-law; and the whole street witnessed them.

That afternoon I spent in part with the Edgertons. I went soon after my own dinner and found the family at theirs. William Edgerton was present. The old man insisted that I should take a seat at the table and join them in a bottle of wine, which I did. It was a family, bearing apparently all the elements within itself of a happiness the most perfect and profound. Particularly an amiable family. Yet there was no insipidity. The father has already been made known; the son should be by this time; the mother was one of those strong-minded, simple women, whose mind may be expressed by its most striking characteristic—independence. She had that most obvious trait of aristocratic breeding, a quiet, indefinable, easy dignity—a seemingly natural quality, easy itself, that puts everybody at ease, and yet neither in itself nor in others suffered the slightest approach to be made to unbecoming familiarity. A sensible, gentlewoman—literally gentle—yet so calm, so firm, you would have supposed she had never known one emotion calculated to stir the sweet, glass-like placidity of her deportment.

And yet, amidst all this calm placidity, with an eye looking benevolence, and a considerateness that took note of your smallest want, she sustained the pangs of one yearning for her first born; dissatisfied and disappointed in his career, and apprehensive for his fate. The family was no longer happy. The worm was busy in all their hearts. They treated me kindly, but it was obvious that they were suffering. A visible constraint chilled and baffled conversation; and I could see the deepening anxieties which clouded the face of the mother, whenever her eye wandered in the direction of her son. This it did, in spite, I am convinced, of her endeavors to prevent it.

I, too, could now look in the same quarter. My feelings were less bitter than they were, and William Edgerton shared in the change. I did not the less believe him to have done wrong, but, in the renewed conviction of my wife's purity, I could forgive him, and almost think he was sufficiently punished in entertaining affections which were without hope. Punished he was, whether by hopelessness or guilt, and punished terribly. I could see a difference for the worse in his appearance since I had last conferred with him. He was haggard and spiritless to the last degree. He had few words while we sat at table, and these were spoken only after great effort; and, regarding him now with less temper than before, it seemed to me that his parents had not exaggerated the estimate which they had formed of his miserable appearance. He looked very much like one, who had abandoned himself to nightly dissipation, and those excesses of mind and body, which sap from both the saving and elevating substance. I did not wonder that the old man ascribed his condition to the bottle and the gaming-table. But that I knew better, such would most probably have been my own conclusion.

The conversation was not general — confined chiefly to Mr. Edgerton the elder and myself. Mrs. Edgerton remained awhile after the cloth had been withdrawn, joining occasionally in what was said, and finally left us, though with still a lingering, and a last look toward her son, which clearly told where her heart was. William Edgerton followed her, after a brief interval, and I saw no more of him, though I remained for more than an hour. He had said but little. It was with some evident effort, that he had succeeded in uttering some general observation on the subject of the Alabama prairies — those beautiful "gardens of the desert,"

"For which the speech of England has no name."

My removal had been the leading topic of our discourse, and when I declared my intention to start on the very next day, and that the present was a farewell visit, the emotion of the son visibly increased. Soon after he left the room. When I was alone with the father, he took occasion to renew his offer of service, and, in such a manner, as to take from the offer its tone of service. He seemed rather to ask a favor than to suggest one. Money he could spare — the repayment should be at my own leisure — and my bond would be preferable, he was pleased to say, to that of any one he knew. I thanked him with becoming feelings, though, for the present, I declined his assistance. I pledged myself, however, should circumstances make it necessary for me to seek a loan, to turn, in the first instance, to him. He had been emphatically my friend — *the* friend, sole, singular

—never fluctuating in his regards, and never stopping to calculate the exact measure of my deserts. I felt that I could not too much forbear in reference to the son, having in view the generous friendship of the father.

That day, and the night which followed it, was a long period with me. I had to see many acquaintances, and attend to a thousand small matters. I was on my feet the whole day, and even when the night came I had no rest. I was in the city till near eleven o'clock. When I got home I found that my wife had done her share of the tasks. She had completed her preparations. Our luggage was all ready for removal. To her I had assigned the labor of packing up her pictures, her materials for painting, her clothes, and such other matters as she desired to carry with us, to our new place of abode. The rest was to be sold by a friend after our departure, and the proceeds remitted. I knew I should need them all. Most of our baggage was to be sent by water. We travelled in a private carriage, and consequently, could take little. Julia, unlike most women, was willing to believe with me that impediments are the true name for much luggage; and, with a most unfeminine habit, she could limit herself without reluctance to the merest necessities. We had no bandboxes, baskets, or extra bundles, to be stuffed here and there, filling holes and corners, and crowding every space, which should be yielded entirely to the limbs of the traveller. Though sensitive and delicate in a great degree, she had yet that masculine sense which teaches that, in the fewness of our wants lies our truest source of independence; and she could make herself ready for taking stage or steamboat in quite as short a time as myself.

Her day's work had exhausted her. She retired, and when I went up to the chamber, she already seemed to sleep. I could not. Fatigue, which had produced exhaustion, had baffled sleep. Extreme weariness becomes too much like a pain to yield readily to repose. The moment that exercise benumbs the frame, makes the limbs ache, the difficulty increases of securing slumber. I felt weary, but I was restless also. I felt that it would be vain for me to go to bed. Accordingly, I placed myself beside the window, and looked out meditatingly upon the broad lake which lay before our dwelling.

The night was very calm and beautiful. The waters from the lake were falling. Tide was going out, and the murmuring clack of a distant sawmill added a strange sweetness to the hour, and mingled harmoniously with the mysterious goings on of midnight. The starlight, not brilliant, was yet very soft and touching. Isolated and small clouds, like dismembered ravens' wings, flitted lightly along the edge of the western horizon, shooting out at intervals brief, brilliant flashes of lightning. There was a flickering breeze that played with the shrubbery beneath my window, making a slight stir that did not break the quiet of the scene, and gave a graceful movement to the slender stems as they waved to and fro beneath its pressure. A noble pride of India* rose directly before my eyes to the south—its branches stretching almost from within touch of the dwelling, over the fence of a neighbor. The whole scene was fairy-like. I should find it indescribable. It soothed my feelings. I had been the victim of a long and painful moral conflict. At length I had a glimmering of repose. Events, in the last few days—small events which, in themselves denoted nothing—had yet spoken peace to my feelings. My heart was in that dreamy state of languor, such as the body enjoys under the gradually growing power of the anodyne, in which the breath of the summer wind brings a language of luxury, and the most imperfect sights and sounds in nature minister to a capacity of enjoyment, which is not the less intoxicating and sweet because it is subdued. I mused upon my own heart, upon the heart which I so much loved and had so much distrusted—upon life, its strange visions, delusive hopes, and the sweet efficacy of mere shadows in promoting one's happiness at last. Then came, by natural degrees, the thought of that strange mysterious union of light and darkness—life and death—the shadows that we are; the substances that we are yet to be. The future!—still it rose before me—but the darkness upon it alone showed me it was there. It did not offend me, however, for my heart was glowing in a present starlight. It was the hour of hopes rather than of fears; and in the mere

* China tree; the melia azedaracha of botanists. A tree peculiar to the south, of singular beauty, and held in high esteem as a shade-tree.

prospect of transition to the new—such is the elastic nature of youth—I had agreed to forget every pang whether of idea or fact, which had vexed and tortured me in the perished past. My musings were all tender yet joyful—they partook of that "joy of grief" of which the bard of Fingal tells us. I felt a big tear gathering in my eye, I knew not wherefore. I felt my heart growing feeble, with the same delight which one would feel at suddenly recovering a great treasure which had been supposed for ever lost. I fancied that I had recovered my treasure, and I rose quietly, went to the bed where Julia lay sleeping peacefully, and kissed her pale but lovely cheeks. She started, but did not waken—a gentle sigh escaped her lips, and they murmured with some indistinct syllables which I failed to distinguish. At that moment the notes of a flute rose softly from the grove without.

CHAPTER XXXVIII.

RENEWED AGONIES.

In that same moment my pangs were all renewed ; my repose of mind departed ; once more my heart was on fire, my spirit filled with vague doubts, grief, and commotion. The soft, sweet, preluding note of the player had touched a chord in my soul as utterly different from that which it expressed, as could by any possibility be conceived. Heart and hope were instantly paralyzed. Fear and its train, its haunting spectres of suspicion, took possession of the undefended citadel, and established guard upon its deserted outposts. I tottered to the window which I had left—I shrouded myself in the folds of the curtain, and as the strains rose, renewed and regular, I struggled to keep in my breath, listening eagerly, as if the complaining instrument could actually give utterance to the cruel mystery which I equally dreaded and desired to hear.

The air which was played was such as I had never heard before. Indeed, it could scarcely be called an air. It was the most capricious burden of mournfulness that had ever had its utterance from wo. Fancy a mute—one bereft of the divine faculty of speech, by human, not divine ministration. Fancy such a being endowed with the loftiest desires, moved by the acutest sensibilities, having already felt the pleasures of life, yet doomed to a denial of utterance, denied the language of complaint, and striving, struggling through the imperfect organs of his voice to give a name to the agony which works within him. That flute seemed to me to moan, and sob, and shiver, with some such painful mode of expression as would be permitted to the " half made-up" mortal of whom I have spoken. Its broken tones, striving and struggling, almost rising at times into a shriek, seemed of all things to complain of its own voicelessness.

And yet it had its melody — melody, to me, of the most vexing power. I should have called the strain a soliloquizing one. It certainly did not seem addressed to any ears. It wanted the continuance of apostrophe. It was capricious. Sometimes the burden fell off suddenly — broken — wholly interrupted — as if the vents had been all simultaneously and suddenly stopped. Anon, it rose again — soul-piercing if not loud — so abruptly, and with an utterance so utterly gone with wo, that you felt sure the poor heart must break with the next breath that came from the laboring and inefficient lungs. A "dying fall" succeeding, seemed to afford temporary relief. It seemed as if tears must have fallen upon the instrument, Its language grew more methodical, more subdued, but not less touching. I fancied, I felt, that, entering into the soul of the musician, I could give the very words to the sentiment which his instrument vainly strove to speak. What else but despair and utter self-abandonment was in that broken language? The full heart over-burdened, breaking, to find a vent for the feelings which it had no longer power to contain. And yet, content to break, breaking with a melancholy sort of triumph which seemed to say—

"Such a death has its own sweetness; love sanctifies the pang to its victim. It is a sort of martyrdom. He who loves truly, though he loves hopelessly, has not utterly loved in vain. The devoted heart finds a joy in the offering, though the Deity withholds his acceptance — though a sudden gust from heaven scatters abroad the rich fruits which the devotee has placed upon the despised and dishonored altar."

Such, I fancied, was the proud language of that melancholy music. Had I been other than I was — nay, had I listened to the burden under other circumstances and in another place — I should most probably have felt nothing but sympathy for the musician. As it was, I can not describe my feelings. All my racking doubts and miseries returned. The tone of triumph which the strain conveyed wrought upon me like an indignity. It seemed to denote that "foregone conclusion" which had been my cause of apprehension so long. Could it be then that Julia was really guilty? Could she have given William Edgerton so much encouragement that triumph and exultation should still mingle with his farewell accents of despair? Ah! what fantasies preyed upon my soul; haunted the smallest movements of my mind; conjured up its spectres, and gave bitterness to its every beverage! When I thought thus of Julia, I rose cautiously from my seat, approached the bed where she was lying, and gazed steadily, though with the wildest thrill of emotion, into her face. I verily believe had she not been sleeping at that moment—sleeping beyond question—she would have shared the fate of

> "The gentle lady wedded to the Moor."

I was in the mood for desperate things.

But she slept—her cheek upon her arm—pale, but oh! how beautiful! and looking, oh! how pure! Her breathing was as tranquil and regular as that of an infant. I felt, while I gazed, that hers must be the purity of an infant also. I turned from beholding her, as the renewed notes of the musician once more ascended to the chamber. I again took my seat at the window and concealed myself behind the curtain. Here I had been concealed but a few moments, when I heard a rustling in the branches of the tree. Meanwhile, the music again ceased. I peered cautiously from behind the drapery, and fancied I beheld a dark object in the tree. It might be one of its branches, but I had not been struck by it before. I waited in breathless watchfulness. I saw it move. Its shape was that of a man. An exulting feeling of violence filled my breast. I rose stealthily, went into the dressing-room, and took up one of my pistols which lay on the toilet, and which I had that afternoon prepared with a travelling charge.

"A brace of bullets," I muttered to myself, "will bring out another sort of music from this rare bird."

With this murderous purpose I concealed myself once more behind the curtain. The figure was sufficiently distinct for aim. The window was not more than twelve or fourteen paces from the tree. My nerves were now as steady as if I had been about to perform the most ordinary action. What then prevented me? What stayed my arm? A single thought—a momentary recollection of an event which had taken place in my boyhood.

What a providence that it should have occurred to me at that particular moment. The circumstance was this.

When first sent to school I had been frequently taken at advantage by a bigger boy. He had twice my strength—he took a strong dislike for me—perhaps, because I was unwilling to pay him that deference, which, as school-bully, he extorted from all others;—and he drubbed me accordingly, whenever an opportunity occurred. My resistance was vain, and only stimulated him to increased brutality. One day he was lying upon the grass, beneath an oak which stood in the centre of a common on which we usually played. It happened that I drew near him unperceived. In approaching him I had no purpose of assault or violence. But the circumstance of my nearing him without being seen, suggested to my mind a sudden thought of revenging all my previous injuries. I felt bitterness and hate enough, had I possessed the strength, to have slain a dozen. I do not know that I had any design to slay him—to revenge myself was certainly my wish. Of death probably I had no idea. I looked about me for the agent of my vengeance. A pile of old brick which had formed the foundations of a dwelling which had stood on the spot, and which had been burned, conveniently presented itself to my eye. I possessed myself of as large a fragment as my little hand could grasp; I secured a second as a dernier resort. Slowly and slily—I may add, basely—I approached him from behind, levelled the brick at his head, and saw the blood fly an instant after the contact. He was stunned by the blow, staggered up, however, with his eyes blinded by blood, and moved after me like a drunken man. I receded slowly, lifting the remaining fragment which I held, intending, if he approached me, to repeat the blow.

On a sudden he fell forward sprawling. Then I thought him dead, and for the first time the dreadful consciousness of my crime in its true character, came to my mind. I can not describe the agony of fear and horror which filled my soul. He did not die, but he was severely hurt.

The recollection of that event—of what I then suffered—came to me involuntarily, as I was about to perform a second similar crime. I shuddered with the recollection of the past, and shrunk, under the equal force of shame and conscience, from the performance of a deed which, otherwise, I should probably have committed in the brief time which I employed for reflection. With a feeling of nervous horror I put the weapon aside, and sinking once more into the chair beside the window I bore with what fortitude I might, the renewal of the accursed but touching strains that vexed me.

William Edgerton was a master of the flute. Often before, when we were the best friends, had I listened with delight, while he compelled it into discourse of music wild and somewhat incoherent still: his present performance had now attained more continuousness and character. It was still mournful, but its sorrows rose and fell naturally, in compliance with the laws of art. I listened till I could listen no longer. Human patience must have its limits. My wife still slept. I descended the stairs, opened the door with as much cautiousness as possible, and prepared to grapple the musician and haul him into the light.

It might be Edgerton or not. I was morally sure it was. By grappling with him, in such a situation, I should bring the affair to a final issue, though it might not be a murderous one. But of that I did not think; I went forward to do something; what that something was to be, it was left for time and chance to determine. But, suddenly, as I opened the door, the music ceased. Stepping into the yard, I heard the sound as of a falling body. I naturally concluded that he had heard the opening of the door, and had suffered himself to drop down to the ground. I took for granted that he had descended on the opposite side of the yard and within the enclosure of a neighbor. I leaped the fence, hurried to the tree, traversed the grounds, and found nobody. I returned, reached my own premises, and found the gate open which opened upon the street. He had gone then in that direction. I turned into the street, posted with all speed to the corner of the square, and met only the watchman. I asked, but he had seen nobody. The street was perfectly quiet. I returned, reascended to my chamber, found Julia now awake, and evidently much agitated. She had arisen in my absence, and was only about to re-enter the bed when I rushed up stairs.

What was I to think? What fear? I was too conscious of

the suspicious nature of my thoughts and fears to suffer myself to ask any questions—and she, unhappily for both of us—she said nothing. Had she but spoken—had she but uttered the natural inquiry—"Did you hear that strange music, husband?"—how much easier had been her extrication. But she was silent, and I was again let loose upon a wide sea of fears and doubts and damnable apprehensions. Once more, and now with a feeling which would not have made me forbear the use of any weapon, however deadly, I re-examined my own enclosure, but in vain. The horrible thought which possessed me was that he had even penetrated the dwelling while I was seeking him in the street; that they had met; and how was I to know the degree of tenderness which had marked their meeting and given sweetness to their adieus!

CHAPTER XXXIX.

THE NEW HOME.

With these revived suspicions, half stifled, but still struggling in my bosom, did I commence my journey for the West. My arrangements were comprehensive, but simple. I had procured a second-hand travelling carriage and fine pair of horses from an acquaintance, at a very moderate price—a price which, I well knew, I should easily get for them again on reaching my place of destination. I was my own driver. I had no money to spare in purchasing what might be dispensed with. A single trunk contained all the necessary luggage of my wife and self. What was not absolutely needed by the wayside was sent on by water. This included my books, desks, Julia's painting materials, and such other articles of the household, as were of cost and not bulky. I had previously written—as I may have stated already—to my friend Kingsley. He was to procure me temporary lodgings in the town of M——. I left much to his judgment and experience. He had once before been in Alabama and having interests there, had made himself familiar with everything in that region, necessary to be known. I put myself very much in his hands. I was too anxious to get away to urge any difficulties or make any troublesome requisitions. He was simply to procure me an abiding-place in some private family—if possible in the suburbs—until I should be able to look about me. Economy was insisted upon. I had precious little money to spare, and even the spoils of my one night's visit to the gaming-house, were of no small help in sustaining me in my determination to remove. I had not applied them previously. I confess to a feeling of shame when I was compelled by necessity at last to use them. I had saved something already from my professional income, and I procured an advance on my furniture which was left for sale. I had calculated my expenses in removing and for one year's residence in M——, and was prepared, so far as poor human foresight may prepare itself, to keep want from our doors at least for that period. I trusted to good fortune, my own resources, and the notorious fact that, at that day, there were few able lawyers in M——, to secure me an early and valuable practice. I carried with me letters from the best men in the community I had left. But I carried with me what was of more value than any letters, even though they be written in gold. I carried with me methodical habits and an energy of character which would maintain my resolution, and bear me through, to a safe conclusion, in any plan which I should contemplate. Industry and perseverance are the giants that cast down forests, drain swamps, level mountains, and create empires. I flattered myself that with these I had other and crowning qualities of intellect and culture. Perhaps it may be admitted that I had. But of what avail were all when coupled with the blind heart? Enough—I must not anticipate.

Filled with the exciting fancies engendered by the affair of the last night, I commenced my journey. The day was a fine one; the sun cheery and bright without being oppressive; and soon, gliding through the broad avenues, lined with noblest trees, which conducted us from the city to the forests, we had the pleasant carol of birds, and the lively chirp of hopping insects.

I was always a lover of the woods; green shady dells, and winding walks amidst crowding foliage. I cared little for mere flowers. A garden was never a desire in my mind. I could be pleased to see and to smell, but I had no passion for its objects. But the trees—the big, venerable oaks, like patriarchs and priests; the lofty and swaggering pines in their green helmets, like warriors of the feudal ages—these were forms that I could worship. I may say, I loved trees with a real passion. Flowers, and the taste for flowers seemed to me always petty; but my instincts led me to behold a speaking and most impressive grandeur, in these old lords of the forest, that had been the first, rising from the mighty mother, to attest the wondrous strength of her resources, and the teeming glories of her womb.

Now, however, they did not fill my soul with earnest reachings, as had ever been the case before. They soothed me somewhat, but the eyes of my mind were turned within. They looked only at the prostration of that miserable heart which was torturing itself with vague, wild doubts — guessing and conjecturing with an agonizing pain, and without the least hope of profit. I could not drive from my thoughts, the vexing circumstances of the last night in the city; and, for the first day of our journey, the hours moved with oppressive slowness. Objects which I had formerly loved to contemplate and always found sweet and refreshing, now gave me little pleasure and exacted little of my attention; and I reached our stopping-place for the night with a sense of weariness and stupor which no mere fatigue of body, I well knew, could ever have occasioned.

But this could not last. The elasticity of my nature, joined with the absence of that one person whom I had now learned to regard as my evil genius, soon enabled me to shake off the oppressive doubts and sadness which fettered and enfeebled me. Once more I began to behold the forests with all the eyes of former delight and affection, and I was conscious, after the progress of a day or two, of periods in which I entirely lost sight of William Edgerton and all my suspicions in the sweet warmth of a fresh and pleasing contemplation.

Something of this — nay, perhaps, the most of it, was due to my wife herself. There was a change in her air and manner which sensibly affected my heart. I had treated her coldly at first, but she had not perceived it; at least she had not suffered it to influence her conduct; and I was equally pleased and surprised to behold in her language, looks, and deportment, a degree of life and buoyant animation, which reminded me of the very champagne exuberance and spirit of her youth. Her eyes flashed with a sense of freedom. Her voice sounded with the silvery clearness of one, who, long pent up in the limits of a dungeon, uses the first moment of escape into the forests to delight himself with song. She seemed to have just thrown off a miserable burden; — and, as for any grief — any sign of regret at leaving home and ties from which she would not willingly part — there was not the slightest appearance of any such feeling in her mind, look, or manner. Kindly, considerately, and sweetly, and with a cheery smile in her eyes, and a springing vigor in the accents of her voice, she strove to enliven the way and to expel the gloom which she soon perceived had fastened itself upon my soul. Her own cares, if she had any, seemed to be very slight, and were utterly lost in mine. She spoke of our new abiding-place with a hearty confidence; that it would be at once a home of prosperity and peace; and, altogether convinced me for the time that the sacrifice must be comparatively very small, which she had made on leaving her birth-place. I very soon wondered that I should have fancied that William Edgerton was ever more to her than the friend of her husband.

Our journey was slow but not tedious. Had our progress been only half so rapid, I should have been satisfied. It was love alone that my heart wanted. I craved for nothing but the just requital of my own passion. I had no complaint, no affliction, when I could persuade myself that I had not thrown away my affections upon the ungrateful and undeserving. Assured now of the love of the beloved one, all the intense devotion of my soul was re-awakened; and the deepest shadows of the forest, gloomy and desolate as they were, along the waste tracts of Georgia and Alabama—in that earlier day—enlivened by the satisfied spirit within, seemed no more than so many places of retreat, where security and peace, combining in behalf of Love, had given him an exclusive sovereignty.

The rude countryman encountered us, and his face beamed with cheerfulness and good humor. The song of the black softened the toils of labor, in the unfinished clearings; and even the wild red man, shooting suddenly from out the sylvan covert, wore in his visage of habitual gravity, an air of resignation which took all harshness from his uncouth features.

Such, under the tuition of well-satisfied hearts, was our mutual experience of the long journey which we had taken when we reached the end of it. This we did in perfect safety. We found our friend, Kingsley, prepared for and awaiting us. He had procured us pleasant apartments in a neat cottage in the suburbs, where we were almost to ourselves. Our landlady was an ancient widow, without a family. She occupied but a single apartment in her house, and left the use of the rest to her lodgers. This was an arrangement with which I was particularly gratified. Her cottage lay half way up on the side of a hill which was crowned with thick clumps of the noblest trees. Long, winding, narrow foot-paths, carried us picturesquely to the summit, where we had a bird's-eye view of the town below, the river beyond—now darting out from the woods and now hiding securely beneath their umbrage—and fair, smooth, lawn-looking fields, which glowed at the proper season with the myriad green and white plumes of corn and cotton. At the foot of the cottage lay a delightful shrubbery, which almost covered it up from sight. It was altogether such a retreat as a hermit would desire. It reminded me somewhat of the lovely spot which we had left. A pleasant walk of a mile lay between it and the town where I proposed to practice, and this furnished a necessity for a certain degree of exercise, which, being unavoidable, was of the most valuable kind. Altogether, Kingsley had executed his commission with a taste and diligence which left me nothing to complain of.

He was delighted at my coming.

"You are nearer to me now," he said; "will be nearer at least when I get to Texas; and I do not despair to see you making tracks after me when I go there."

"But when go you?"

"Not soon. I am in some trouble here. I am pleading and being impleaded. You are just come in season to take up the cudgels for me. My landrights are disputed—my titles. You will have something of a lawsuit to begin upon at your earliest leisure."

"Indeed! but what's the business?"

He gave me a statement of his affairs, placed his papers in my hands, and I found myself, on inspecting them, engaged in a controversy which was likely to give me the opportunity which I desired, of appearing soon in cases of equal intricacy and interest. Kingsley had some ten thousand dollars in land, the greater part of which was involved in questions of title and preemption, presenting some complex features, and likely to occasion bad blood among certain trespassers whom it became our first duty to oust if possible. I was associated with a spirited young lawyer of the place; a youth of great natural talent, keen, quick intellect, much readiness of resource, yet little experience and less reading. Like the great mass of our western men, however, he was a man to improve. He had no self-conceit—did not delude himself with the idea that he knew as much as his neighbor; and, consequently, was pretty certain to increase in wisdom with increase of years. He had few prejudices to get over, and though he knew his strength, he also knew his weakness. He felt the instinct of natural talent, but he did not deceive himself on the subject of his deficient knowledge. He was willing to learn whenever he could find a teacher. His name was Wharton. I took to him at once. He was an ardent, manly fellow—frank as a boy—could laugh and weep in the same hour, and yet was as firm in his principles, as if he could neither laugh nor weep. As an acquaintance he was an acquisition.

Kingsley was delighted to see me, though somewhat wondering that I should give up the practice at home, where I was doing so well, to break ground in a region where I was utterly unknown. He gave me little trouble, however, in accounting to him for this movement. It was not difficult to persuade him—nay, he soon persuaded himself—that something of my present course was due to his own counsel and suggestion. To a man, like himself, to whom mere transition was pleasure, it needed no argument to show that my resolve was right.

"Who the d—l," he exclaimed, "would like always to be in the same place? Such a person is a mere cipher. We establish an intellectual superiority when we show ourselves superior to place. A genuine man is always a citizen of the world. It is your vegetable man that can not go far without grumbling, finding fault with all he sees, talking of comforts and such small matters, and longing to get home again. Such a man puts me in mind of every member of the cow family that I ever knew. He is never at peace with himself or the world, but always groaning and thrusting out his horns, until he can get back to his old range, and revel in his native marsh, joint-grass, and cane-tops. Englishmen are very much of this breed. They go abroad, grumble as they go, and if they can not carry their cane-tops with them, afflict the whole world with their lamentations. I take it for granted, Clifford, that this step to Alabama, is simply a step toward Texas. Your next will be to New Orleans, and then, presto, we shall see you on the Sabine."

"I hope not," said my wife. "You have got us into such comfortable quarters here, Mr. Kingsley, that I hope you will do nothing to tempt my husband farther. Go farther and fare worse, you know. Let well enough alone."

"Oh, I beseech you!—two proverbs at a time will be fatal to one or other of us. Perhaps both. But he can not fare worse by going to Texas."

"He will do well enough here."

"Perhaps."

"Recover your lands, for example, as a beginning."

"Ah! now you would bribe me. That is certainly a suggestion to make me keep my tongue, at least until the verdict is rendered. 'Till then, you know, I shall make no permanent remove myself."

"But do you mean to go before the trial?" I asked.

"Yes, for a couple of months or so. I should only get into some squabble with my opponents by remaining here; and I may be preparing for all of us by going in season. I will look out for a township, Mrs. Clifford, on the edge of some beautiful prairie, and near some beautiful river. Your husband has a passion for water prospects, I can tell you, and would become a misanthrope without them. I am doubtful if he will be happy, indeed, if not within telescope distance from the sea itself. I don't think that a river will altogether satisfy him."

"Oh yes, *this* must;" and as she spoke she pointed to the fair glassy surface of the Alabama, as it stretched away, at intervals, in broad glimpses before our eyes.

"Well, we shall see; but I will make my preparations, nevertheless, precisely as if he were not likely to be content. I have formed to myself a plan for all of you. I must make a dear little colony of our own in Texas. We shall have a nest of the sweetest little cottages, each with its neat little garden. In the centre we shall have a neat little playground for our neat little children; on the hill a neat little church; in the grove a neat little library; on the river a neat little barge; and over this neat little empire, you, Lady Clifford, shall be the neat little empress."

"Dear me! what a neat little establishment!"

"It shall be all that, I assure you; and it shall have other advantages. You shall have a kingdom free from taxes and wars. There shall be no law-givers but yourself. We shall have no elections except when we elect our wives, and the women shall be the only voters then. We shall have no customhouses—everything shall be free of duty;—we shall have no banks—everything shall be free of charge;—we shall have no parson, for shall we not be sinless?"

"But what will you do with the neat little church?"

"Oh! that we shall keep merely to remind us of what is necessary in less fortunate communities."

"Very good; but how, if you have no parsons, will you perform the marriage ceremony?"

"That shall be a natural operation of government. The voters having given their suffrages, you shall determine and declare with whom the majority lies, and give a certificate to that effect. The first choice will lie with the damsel having the highest number of votes; the second with the next; and so on to the end of the chapter; and then elections are to take place annually among the unmarried—the ladies being the privileged class as I said before. You will keep a record of these events, the names of parties, and so forth; and this record shall be proof, conclusive to conviction, against any party falling off from his or her duties."

"Quite a system. I do not deny that our sex will have some new privileges by this arrangement."

"Unquestionably. But you have not heard all. We shall have no doctors, for we shall have no diseases in the beautiful world to which I shall carry you. We shall have no lawyers, for we shall have no wrangling."

"Indeed; but what is my husband to do then?"

"Why, he is your husband. What should he do? He takes rank from you. You are queen, you know. He will have no need of law."

"There's reason in that; but how will you prevent wrangling where there are men and women?"

"Oh, by giving the women their own way. The government

is a despotism—you are queen—surely you will make no further objection to so admirable a system?"

In good-humored chat like this, in which our landlady, Mrs. Porterfield—a lady who, though fully sixty-five years of age, was yet of a cheery and chatty disposition—took considerable part, our first evening passed away. Though fatigued, we sat up until a tolerably late hour, enlivened by the frank spirit of our friend, Kingsley, and inspired by the natural feeling of curiosity which our change of situation inspired. It was midnight before we solicited the aid of sleep.

CHAPTER XL.

THE BLACK DOG ONCE MORE UPON THE SCENE.

THE next day was devoted to an examination of our premises and the neighborhood. The result of this examination was such as to render us better satisfied with the change that we had made. We were still young enough to be sensible to the loveliness of novelty. Everything wore that purple light which the eye of youth confers upon the object. And then there was repose. That harassing strife of the "blind heart" was at rest. I had no more suspicions; and my wife looked and spoke as if she had never had either doubts of me, or fears of herself, within her bosom. I was happiness itself, when, by the unreserved ease and gayety of her deportment she persuaded me that she suffered no regrets. I little fancied how much the change in my wife's manner had arisen from the involuntary change which had been going on in mine. I now looked the love which I felt; and she felt, in the improvement of my looks, the renewal of that fond passion which I had never ceased to feel, but which I had only too much ceased to show while suffering from the "blind heart." She resumed her old amusements with new industry. Our little parlor received constant accessions of new pictures. All our leisure was employed in exploring the scenery of the neighborhood; and not a bit of forest, or patch of hill, or streak of rivulet or stream, to which the genius of art could lend loveliness, but she picked up, in these happy rambles, and worked into fitting places upon our cottage walls.

Our good old hostess became attached to us. She virtually surrendered the management of the household to my wife. She was old and quite infirm; and was frequently confined for days to her chamber; which must have been a solitary place enough before our coming. My wife became a companion to her in these periods of painful seclusion, and thus provided her with a luxury which had been long denied her. Under these circumstances we had very much our own way. The old lady had few associates, and these were generally very worthy people. They soon became our associates also, and under the influence of better feelings than had governed me for a long time past, I now found myself in a condition of comfort, cheerfulness, and peace, which I fancied I had forfeited for ever.

Two weeks after our arrival, Kingsley took his departure for Texas, on a visit. He proposed to be absent two months. His object, as he had described it before, in some pleasant exaggerations, was to select some favorable spots for purchase, which should combine as nearly as possible the three prime requisites of salubrity, fertility, and beauty. His object was to speculate; "and this was to be done," he said, "at an early hour of the day." "The Spanish proverb," he was wont to say, "which regulates the eating of oranges, is not a bad rule to govern a man in making his speculations. Speculations (oranges) are gold at morning, silver at noon, and lead at night. It is your wise man," he added, "who buys and sells early; your merely sensible man who does so at midday; while your dunce, waiting for an increased appetite at evening, swallows nothing but lead."

I was in some respects a very fortunate man. If I had been a wise one! It has been seen that I was singularly successful in business at my first beginning in my native city. I had not been long in the town of M——, before I began to congratulate myself on the prospect of like fortune attending me there. The affairs of Kingsley brought me into contact with several men of business. My letters of introduction made me acquainted with many more; not simply of the town, but of the neighboring country. My ardency of temper was particularly suited to a frank, confiding people, such as are most of the southwestern men; and one or two accidental circumstances yielded me professional occupation long before I expected to find it. I had occasion to appear in court at an early day, and succeeded in making a favorable impression upon my hearers. To be a good speaker, in the south and southwest, is to be everything. Eloquence implies wisdom—at least all the wisdom which is supposed to be necessary in making lawyers and law-makers—a precious small modicum of a material by no means precious. I was supposed to have the gift of the gab in moderate perfection, and my hearers were indulgent. My name obtained circulation, and, in a short time, I discovered that, in a professional as well as personal point of view, I had no reason to regret the change of residence which I had made. Business began to flow in upon me. Applications reached me from adjoining counties, and though my fees, like the cases which I was employed in, were of moderate amount, they promised to be frequent, while my clients generally were very substantial persons.

It will not need that I should dwell farther on these topics. It will be sufficient to show that, in worldly respects, I was as likely to prosper in my new as in my past abode. In social respects I had still more reason to be gratified. The days went by with me as smoothly as with Thalaba. My wife was all that I could wish. She was the very Julia whom I had married. Nay, she was something more—something better. Her health improved, and with it her spirits. She evidently had no regrets. A sigh never escaped her. Her content and cheerfulness were wonderful. She had none of that vague, vain yearning which the feeble feel, called "home-sickness." She convinced me that I was her home—the only home that she desired. It was evident that she thought less of our ancient city than I did myself. I am sure that if either of us, at any moment, felt a desire to look upon it again, the person was myself. I maintained a correspondence with the place—received the newspapers, groped over them with persevering industry—nay—missed not the advertisements, and was disappointed and a discontent on those days when the mail failed. My wife had no such appetite. She sometimes read the papers, but she appeared to have no curiosity; and, with the exception of an occasional letter which she received from her mother, she had no intercourse whatever with her former home.

All this was calculated to satisfy me. But this was not all. If gentleness, sweetness, cheerfulness, and a sleepless consideration of one's wants and feelings, could convince any mortal of the love of another — I must have been satisfied. We resumed most of the habits which began with our marriage, but which had been so long discontinued. We rose with the sun, and went abroad after his example. Like him we rose to the hill-tops, and then descended into the valleys. We grew familiar with the deepest shades of wood and forest while the dewdrops were yet beading the bosoms of the wild flowers; and we followed the meandering course of the Alabama, long before the smoking steamer vexed it with her flashing paddles. My professional toils from breakfast to dinner-time — for this interval I studiously gave to my office, even if I had little to do there — occasioned the only interregnum which I knew in the positive pleasures which I enjoyed. In the afternoon our enjoyments were renewed. Our cottage was so sweetly secluded, that we did not need to go far in order to find the Elysian grove which we desired. At the top of our hill we were surrounded by a natural temple of proud pines — guarding the spot from any but that sort of divine and religious light which streams through the painted windows of the ancient cathedral. The gay glances of the sun came gliding through the foliage in drops, and lay upon the grass in little pale, fanciful gleams, most like eyes of fairies peeping upward from its velvety tufts. Here we read together from the poets — sometimes Julia sung, even while sketching. Not unfrequently, Mrs. Porterfield came with us, and, at such times, our business was to detect distant glimpses of barge, or steamboat, as they successively darted into sight, along such of the glittering patches of the Alabama as were revealed to us in its downward progress through the woods.

Our evenings were such as hallow and make the luxury of cottage life — evenings yielded up to cheerfulness, to content and harmony. Between music, and poetry, and painting, my heart was subdued to the sweetest refinements of love. Without the immorality, we had the very atmosphere of a Sybarite indulgence. I was enfeebled by the excess of sweets; and the happiness which I felt expressed itself in signs. These denoted my presentiments. My apprehensions were my sole cause of doubt and sorrow. How could such enjoyments last? Was it possible, with any, that they should last? Was it possible that they should last with me? I should have been mad to think it.

But, in the sweet delirium which their possession inspired, I almost forgot the past. The soul of man is the most elastic thing in nature. Those harassing tortures of the heart which I had been suffering for months—those weary days of exhausting doubt—those long nights of torturing suspicion—the shame and the fear, the sting of jealousy, and the suffering—I had almost forgotten in the absorbing pleasures of my new existence. If I remembered them it was only to smile; if I thought of William Edgerton it was only to pity;—and, as for Julia, deep was the crimson shadow upon my cheek, whenever the reproachful memory reminded me of the tortures which I had inflicted upon her gentle heart while laboring under the tortures of my own—when I thought of the unmanly espionage which I had maintained over conduct which I now felt to be irreproachable.

But, just at the moment when I thus thought and felt—when I no longer suffered and no longer inflicted pain—when my wife was not only virtue in my sight, but love, and beauty, and grace, and meekness—all that was good and all that was dear besides;—when my sky was without a cloud, and the evening star shone through the blue sky upon the green tops of our cottage trees, with the serene lustre of a May-divinity—just then a thunderbolt fell upon my dwelling, and blackened the scene for ever.

I had now been three months a resident in M——, and never had I been more happy—never less apprehensive on the score of my happiness—when I received a letter from my venerable friend and patron, the father of William Edgerton.

"My son," he wrote, "is no better than when you left us. We have every reason to believe him worse. He has a cough, he is very thin, and there is a flushed spot upon his cheek which seems to his mother and myself the indubitable sign of vital decay. His frame is very feeble, and our physician advises travel. Under this counsel he set off with a favorite servant on Wednesday of last week. He will make easy stages through Tennessee to the Ohio, will descend into Mississippi, and return home by way of Alabama. He contemplates paying you a brief visit. I need not say, dear Clifford, how grateful I shall be for any kindness which you can show to my poor boy. His mother particularly invokes it. I should not have deemed it necessary to say so much, but would have preferred leaving it to William to make his own communication, were it not that she so particularly desires it. It may be well to add, that on one subject we are both very much relieved. We now have reason to believe that our apprehensions on the score of his morals were without foundation. It is our present belief that he neither gamed nor drank. This is a consolation, dear Clifford, though it brings us no nigher to our wish. It is something to believe that the object of our love is not worthless; though it adds to the pang that we should feel in the event of losing him. Our parting would be less easy. For my own part, I have little hope that his journey will do him any material benefit. It may prolong his days, but can not, I fear, have any more decided influence upon his disease. His mother, however, is more sanguine, and it is perhaps well that she should be so. I know that when William reaches your neighborhood, you will make it as cheerful and pleasant to him as possible. The talent of your young and sweet wife — her endowments in painting and music — have always been a great solace to him. His tastes you know are very much like hers. I trust she will exercise them, and be happy in ministering to the comfort of one, who will not, I fear, trespass very long upon any earthly ministry. My dear Clifford, I know that you will do your utmost in behalf of your earliest friend, and I will waste no more words in unnecessary solicitation."

Such was the important portion of the letter. In an instant, as I read it, I saw, with the instinct of jealousy, the annihilation of all my hopes of happiness. All my dreams were in the dust — all my fancies scattered — my schemes and temples overthrown. Bitter was the pang I felt on reading this letter. It said more — much more — in the very language of solicitation, which the good old father professed to believe unnecessary. He poured forth the language of a father's grief and entreaty. I felt for the venerable man — the true friend — in spite of my own miserable apprehensions. I felt for him, but what could I do? What would he have me do? I had no house in which to receive his son. He would lodge, perhaps, for a time, in the community. It could not be supposed that he would remain long. The letter of the father spoke only of a brief visit. Our neighborhood had no repute, as a place of resort, for consumptive patients. I consoled myself with the reflection that William Edgerton could, on no pretence, linger more than a week or two among us. I will treat him kindly — give him the freedom of the house while he remains. A dying man, if so he be, must have reached a due sense of his situation, and will not be likely to trespass upon the rights of another. His passions must be subdued by this time. Ah! but will not his condition be more likely to inspire sympathy?

The fiend of the blind heart prompted that last suggestion. It was the only one that I remembered. When I returned home that day to dinner, I mentioned, as if casually, the letter I had received, and the contents. My eye narrowly watched that of my wife while I spoke. Hers sunk beneath my glance. Her cheeks were suddenly flushed — then, as suddenly, grew pale, and I observed, that, though she appeared to eat, but few morsels of food were carried into her mouth that day. She soon left the table, and, pleading headache declined joining me in our usual evening rambles.

CHAPTER XLI.

TRIAL—THE WOMAN GROWS STRONG.

Thus, then, I was once more at sea, rudderless—not yet companionless—perhaps, soon to be so. My relapse was as sudden as my thought. It seemed as if every past misery of doubt and suspicion were at once revived within me. All my day-dreams vanished in an instant. William Edgerton would again behold—would again seek—my wife. They must meet; I owed that to the father; and, whatever the condition of the son might be, it was evident that his feelings toward her must be the same as ever; else, why should he seek her out?—why pursue our footsteps and haunt my peace? I must receive him and treat him kindly for the father's sake; but that one bitter thought, that he was pursuing us, the deadly enemy to my peace—and now, evidently, a wilful one—gave venom to the bitter feeling with which I had so long regarded his attentions.

It was evident, too, whatever may have been its occasion, that the knowledge of his coming awakened strange emotions in the bosom of my wife. That blush—that sudden paleness of the cheek—what was their language? I fain would have struggled against the conviction, that it denoted a guilty consciousness of the past—a guilty feeling of the future. But the mocking demon of the blind heart forced the assurance upon me. What was to be done? Ah! what? This was the question, and there was no variation in the reply which my jealous spirit made. There was but one refuge. I must pursue the same insidious policy as before. I must resort to the same subterfuge, meet them with the same smiles, disguise once more the true features of my soul; seem to shut my eyes, and afford them the same opportunities as before, in the torturing hope (fear ?) that I should finally detect them in some guilty folly which would be sufficient to justify the final punishment. I must put on the aspect of indifference, the better to pursue the vocation of the spy.

Base necessity, but still, as I then fancied, a necessity not the less. Ah! was I not a thing to be pitied? Was ever any case more pitiable than mine? I ask not this question with any hope that an answer may be found to justify my conduct. It is not the less pitiable—nay, it is more—that no such answer can be found. My folly is not the less a thing of pity, because it is also a thing of scorn. That was the pity—and yet, I was most severely tried. Deep were my sufferings! Strong was that demon within me—I care not how engendered, whether by the fault and folly of others, or by my own—still it was strong. If I was guilty—base, blind—was I not also suffering? Never did I inflict on the bosom of Julia Clifford, so deep a pang as I daily—nay, hourly, inflicted upon my own. She was a victim, true—but was I less so! But she was innocently a victim, therefore, less a sufferer, whatever her sufferings, than me! Let none condemn or curse me, till they have asked what curse I have already undergone. I live!—they will say. Ah! me! They must ask what is the value of life, not to themselves, but to a crushed, a blasted heart, like mine! But I hurry forward with my pangs rather than my story.

Instantly, a barrier seemed to rise up between Julia Clifford and myself. She had her consciousness, evidently, no less than I. What was *that* consciousness? Ah! could I have guessed *that*, there would have been no barrier—all might have been peace again. But a destiny was at work which forbade it all; and we strove ignorantly with one another and against ourselves. There was a barrier between us, which our mutual blindness of heart made daily thicker, and higher, and less liable to overthrow. A coldness overspread my manner. I made it a sort of shelter. The guise of indifference is one of the most convenient for hiding other and darker feelings. Already we ceased to ramble by river and through wood. Already the pencil was discarded. We could no longer enjoy the things which so lately made us happy, because we no longer entertained the same confidence in one another. Without this confidence there is no communion sweet. And all this had been the work of that letter. The name of William Edgerton had done it all—his name and threatened visit!

But—and I read the letter again and again—it would be some time before he might be expected. The route, as laid down for him by his father, was a protracted one. "Through Georgia, Tennessee, Mississippi, then homeward, by way of Alabama." "He can not be here in less than six weeks. He must travel slowly. He must make frequent rests."

And there was a further thought—a hope—which, though it filled my mind, I did not venture to express in words. "He may perish on his route: if he be so feeble, it is by no means improbable!"

At all events, I had six weeks' respite—perhaps more. Such was my small consolation then. But even this was false. In less than a week from that time, William Edgerton stood at the door of our cottage!

Instead of going into Tennessee, he had shot straight forward, through Georgia, into Alabama.

Though surprised, I was not confounded by his presence. Under the policy which I had resolved upon, I received him with the usual professions of kindness, and a manner as nearly warm and natural as the exercise of habitual art could make it. He certainly did look very miserable. His features wore an expression of uniform despair. They brightened up, when he beheld my wife, as the cloud brightens suddenly beneath the moonlight. His eyes were riveted upon her. He was almost speechless, but he advanced and took her hand, which I observed was scarcely extended to him. He sat the evening with us, and a chilly, dull evening it was. He himself spoke little—my wife less; and the conversation, such as it was, was carried on chiefly between old Mrs. Porterfield and myself. But I could see that Edgerton employed his eyes in a manner which fully compensated for the silence of his tongue. They were seldom withdrawn from the quarter of the apartment in which my wife sat. When withdrawn, it was but for an instant, and they soon again reverted to the spot. He had certainly acquired a degree of boldness, which, in this respect, he had not before possessed. I keenly analyzed his looks without provoking his attention. It was not possible for me to mistake the unreserved admiration that his glance expressed. There was a strange spiritual expression in his eyes, which was painful to the spectator. It was that fearful sign which the soul invariably makes when it begins to exert itself at the expense of the shell which contains it. It was the sign of death already written. But he might linger for months. His cough did not seem to me oppressive. The flush was not so obvious upon his cheek. Perhaps, looking through the medium of my peculiar feelings, his condition was not half so apparent as his designs. At least, I felt my sympathies in his behalf—small as they were before—become feebler with every moment of his stay that night.

"Edgerton does not appear to me to look so badly," I said to Julia, after his departure for the evening.

"I don't know," she answered; "he looks very pale and miserable."

"Quite interesting!" I added, with a smile which might have been a sneer.

"Painfully so. He can not last very long—his cough is very troublesome."

"Indeed! I scarcely heard it. He is certainly a very fine-looking fellow still, consumption or no consumption."

She was silent.

"A very graceful fellow; very generous and with accomplishments such as are possessed by few. I have often envied him his person and accomplishments."

"You?" she exclaimed, with something like an expression of incredulity.

"Yes!—that is to say, when I was a youth, and when I thought more of commending myself to your eyes, than of anything besides."

"Ah!" she replied with an assuring smile, "you never needed qualities other than your own to commend yourself to me."

"Pleasant hypocrite! And yet, Julia, would you not be better pleased if I could draw and color, and talk landscape with you by the hour?"

"No! I have never thought of your doing anything of the kind."

"Like begets liking."

"It may be, but I do not think so. I do not think we love people so much for what they can do, as for what they are."

"Ah, Julia, that is a great mistake. It is a law in morals, that the qualities of men should depend upon their performances. What a man is, results from what he does, and so we judge of persons. Edgerton is a noble fellow; his tastes are very fine. I suspect he can form as correct an opinion of a fine picture as any one — perhaps, paint it as finely."

She was silent.

"Do you not think so, Julia?"

"I think he paints very well for an amateur."

"He is certainly a man of exquisite taste in most matters of taste and elegance. I have always thought his manners particularly easy and dignified. His carriage is at once manly and graceful; and his dancing — do you not think he dances with admirable flexibility?"

"Really, Edward, I can scarcely regard dancing as a manly accomplishment. It is necessary that a gentleman should dance, perhaps, but it appears to me that he should do so simply because it is necessary; and to pass through the measure without ostentation or offence should be his simple object."

"These are not usually the opinions of ladies, Julia."

"They are mine, however."

"You are not sure. You will think otherwise to-morrow. At all events, I think there can be little doubt that Edgerton is one of the best dancers in the circle we have left; he has the happiest taste in painting and poetry; and a more noble gentleman and true friend does not exist anywhere. I know not to whom I could more freely confide life, wealth, and honor, than to him."

She was silent. I fancied there was something like distress apparent in her countenance. I continued: —

"There is one thing, Julia, about which I am not altogether satisfied."

"Ah!" with much anxiety; "what is that?"

"I owe so much to his father, that, in his present condition, I fancy we ought to receive him in our house. We should not let him go among strangers, exposed to the noise and neglect of a hotel."

There was some abruptness in her answer :—

"I do not see how you can bring him here. You forget that we are mere lodgers ourselves; indebted for our accommodation to the kindness of a lady upon whom we should have no right to press other lodgers. Such an arrangement would crowd the house, and make all parties uncomfortable. Besides, I suppose Mr. Edgerton will scarcely remain long enough in M—— to make it of much importance where he lodges, and when he finds the tavern uncomfortable he will take his departure."

"But should he get sick at the tavern?"

"Such a chance would follow him wherever he went. That is the risk which every man incurs when he goes abroad. He has a servant with him—no doubt a favorite servant."

"Should he get sick, Julia, even a favorite servant will not be enough. It will be our duty to make other provision for him. I owe his father much; the old man evidently expects much from me by his last letter. I owe the son much. He has been a true friend to me. I must do for him as if he were a brother, and should he get sick, Julia, you must be his nurse."

"Impossible, Mr. Clifford!" she replied, with unwonted energy, while a deep, dark flush settled over her otherwise placid features, which were now not merely discomposed but ruffled. "It is impossible that I should be what you require. Suffer me, in this case, to determine my duties for myself. Do for *your friend* what you think proper. You can provide a nurse, and secure by money, the best attendance in the town. I do not think that I can do better service than a hundred others whom you may procure; and you will permit me to say, without seeking to displease you, that I will not attempt it."

I was not displeased at what she said, but it was not my policy to admit this. With an air almost of indignation, I replied:

"And you would leave my friend to perish?"

"I trust he will not perish—I sincerely trust he will continue in health while he remains here. I implore you, dear husband, to make no requisition such as this. I can not serve your friend in this capacity. I pray that he may not need it."

"But should he?"

"I can not serve him."

"Julia, you are a cold-hearted woman—you do not love me."

"Cold-hearted, Edward, cold-hearted? Not love you, Edward?—Oh, surely, you can not mean it. No! no! you can not!"

She threw herself into my arms, clasped me fondly in hers, and the warm tears from her eyes gushed into my bosom.

"Love me, love my dog—at least my friend!" I exclaimed, in austere accents, but without repulsing her. I could not repulse her. I had not strength to put her from me. The embrace was too dear; and the energy with which she rejected a suggestion in which I proposed only to try and test her, made her doubly dear at that moment to my bosom. Alas! how, in the attempt to torture others, do we torture ourselves! If I afflicted Julia in this scene, I am very sure that my own sufferings were more intense. One thing alone would have made them so. The *one* quality of evil, of the bad spirit which mingled in with *my* feelings, and did not trouble *hers*. But, just then I did not think her innocent altogether. I still had my doubts that her resistance to my wishes was simply meant to conceal that tendency in her own, the exposure of which she had naturally every reason to dread. The demon of the blind heart, though baffled for awhile, was still busy. Alas! he was not always to be baffled.

CHAPTER XLII.

CROSS PURPOSES.

WEEKS passed and still William Edgerton was a resident of M——, and a constant guest at our little cottage. He had, in this time, effectually broken up the harmony and banished the peace which had previously prevailed there. The unhappy young man pursued the same insane course of conduct which had been productive of so much bitterness and trouble to us all before; and, under the influence of my evil demon, I adopted the same blind policy which had already been so fruitful of misery to myself and wife. I gave them constant opportunities together. I found my associates, and pursued my pastimes—pastimes indeed—away from home. Poetry and song were given up—we no longer wandered by the river-side, and upon the green heights of our sacred hill. My evenings were consumed in dreary rambles, alone with my own evil thoughts, and miserable fancies, or consumed with yellow-eyed watching, from porch or tree, upon those privacies of the suspected lovers, in which I had so shamefully indulged before. I felt the baseness of this vocation, but I had not the strength to give it up. I know there is no extenuation for it. I know that it was base! base! base! It is a point of conscience with me, not only to declare the truth, but to call things by the truest and most characteristic names. Let me do my understanding the justice to say that, even when I practised the meanness, I was not ignorant—not insensible of its character. It was the strength only—the courage to do right, and to forbear the wrong—in which I was deficient. It was the blind heart, not the unknowing head to which the shame was attributable, though the pang fell not unequally upon heart and head.

Meanwhile, Kingsley returned from Texas. He became my principal companion. We strolled together in my leisure hours by day. We sat and smoked together in his chamber by night. My blind fortitude may be estimated, when the reader is told that Kingsley professed to find me a very agreeable companion. He complimented me on my liveliness, my wit, my humor, and what not—and this, too, when I was all the while meditating, with the acutest feeling of apprehension, upon the very last wrong which the spirit of man is found willing to endure;—when I believed that the ruin of my house was at hand; when I believed that the ruin of my heart and hope had already taken place:—and when, hungering only for the necessary degree of proof which justice required before conviction, I was laying my gins and snares with the view to detecting the offenders, and consummating the last terrible but necessary work of vengeance! But Kingsley did not confine himself altogether to the language of compliment.

"Good fellow and good companion as you are, Clifford—and loath as I should be to give up these pleasant evenings, still I think you very wrong in one respect. You neglect your wife."

"Ha! ha! what an idea! You are not serious?"

"As a judge."

"Psha! She does not miss me."

"Perhaps not," he answered gravely—"but for your own sake if not for hers, it seems to me you should pursue a more domestic course."

"What mean you?"

"You leave your wife too much to herself!—nay—let me be frank—not too much to herself, for there would be little danger in that, but too much with that fellow Edgerton."

"What? You would not have me jealous, Kingsley?"

"No! Only prudent."

"You dislike Edgerton, Kingsley."

"I do! I frankly confess it. I think he wants manliness of character, and such a man always lacks sincerity. But I do not speak of him. I should utter the same opinion with respect to any other man, in similar circumstances. A wife is a dependent creature—apt to be weak!—If young, she is susceptible

— equally susceptible to the attentions of another and to the neglect of her husband. I do not say that such is the case with your wife. Far from it. I esteem her very much as a remarkable woman. But women were intended to be dependents. Most of them are governed by sensibilities rather than by principles. Impulse leads them and misleads. The wife finds herself neglected by the very man who, in particular, owes her duty. She finds herself entertained, served, watched, tended with sleepless solicitude, by another; one, not wanting either in personal charms and accomplishments, and having similar tastes and talents. What should be the result of this? Will she not become indifferent where she finds indifference — devoted where she finds devotion? A cunning fellow, like Edgerton, may, under these circumstances, rob a man of his wife's affections. Mark me, I do not say that he will do anything positively dishonorable, at least in the world's acceptation of the term. I do not intimate — I would not willingly believe — that she would submit to anything of the sort. I speak of the affections, not of the virtues. There is shame to the man in his wife's dishonor; but the misfortune of losing her affections is neither more nor less than the suffering without the shame. Look to it. I do not wish to prejudice your mind against Edgerton. Far from it. I have forborne to speak hitherto because I knew that my own mind was prejudiced against him. Even now I say nothing against *him*. What I say has reference to your conduct only. I do not think Edgerton a bad man. I think him a weak one. Weak as a woman — governed, like her, by impulse rather than by principle — easily led away — incapable of resisting where his affections are concerned — repenting soon, and sinning, in the same way, as fast as he repents. He is weak, very weak — washy-weak — he wants stamina, and, wanting that, wants principle!"

"Strange enough, if you should be right! How do you reconcile this opinion with his refusal to lend you money to game upon? He was governed in that by principle."

"Not a bit of it! He was governed by habit. He knew nothing of gambling — had heard his father always preaching against it — it was not a temptation with him. His tastes were of another sort. He could not be tried in that way. The very fact that he was susceptible, in particular, to the charms of female society, saved him from the passion for gaming, as it would save him from the passion for drink. But the very tastes that saved him from one passion make him particularly susceptible to another. He can stand the temptation of play, but not that of women. Let him be tried *there*, and he falls! his principle would not save him—would not be worth a straw to a drowning man."

"You underrate—undervalue Edgerton. He has always been a true, generous friend of mine."

"Be it so! with that I have nothing to do. But friendship has its limits which it can not pass. Were Edgerton truly your friend, he would advise you as I have done. Nay, a proper sense of friendship and of delicacy would have kept him from paying that degree of attention to the wife which must be an hourly commentary on the neglect of her husband. I confess to you it was this very fact that made me resolve to speak to you."

"I thank you, my dear fellow, but I have nothing to fear. Poor Edgerton is dying—music and painting are his solace—they minister to his most active tastes. As for Julia, she is immaculate."

"I distrust neither; but you should not throw away your pearl, because you think it can not suffer stain."

"I do not throw it away."

"You do not sufficiently cherish it."

"What would you have me do—wear it constantly in my bosom?"

"No! not exactly that; but at least wear nothing else there so frequently or so closely as that."

"I do not. I fancy I am a very good husband. You shall not put me out of humor, Kingsley, either with my wife or myself. You shall not make me jealous. I am no Othello—I have no visitations of the moon."

And I laughed—laughed while speaking thus—though the keen pang was writhing at that moment like a burning arrow through my brain.

"I have no wish to make you jealous, Clifford, and I very much admire your superiority and strength. I congratulate you on your singular freedom from this unhappy passion. But you may become too confident. You may lose your wife's affections by your neglect, when you might not lose them by treachery."

"You are grown a croaker, Kingsley, and I will leave you. I will go home. I will show you what a good husband I am, or can become."

"That's right; but smoke another cigar before you go."

"There it is!" I exclaimed, laughingly. "You blow hot and cold. You would have me go and stay."

"Take the cigar, at least, and smoke it as you go. My advice is good, and that it is honest you may infer from my reluctance to part with you. I will see you at the office at nine in the morning. There is some prospect of a compromise with Jeffords about the tract in Dallas, and he is to meet Wharton and myself at your law-shop to-morrow. It is important to make an arrangement with Jeffords—his example will be felt by Brownsell and Gibbon. We may escape a long-winded lawsuit, after all, to your great discomfiture and my gain. But you do not hear me!"

"Yes, yes, every word—you spoke of Jeffords, and Wharton, and Gibbon—yes, I heard you."

"Now I know that you did not hear me—not understandingly, at least. I should not be surprised if I have made you jealous. You look wild, *mon ami!*"

"Jealous, indeed! what nonsense!" and I prepared to depart when I had thus spoken.

"Well, at nine you must meet us at the office. My business must not suffer because you are jealous."

"Come, no more of that, Kingsley!"

"By heavens, you are touched."

He laughed merrily. I laughed also, but with a choking effort which almost cost me a convulsion as I left the tavern. The sport of Kingsley was my death. What he had said previously sunk deep into my soul. Not rightly—not as it should have sunk—showing me the folly of my own course without assuming, as I did, the inevitable wilfulness of the course of others; but actually confirming me in my fears—nay, making them grow hideous as *things* and substantive convictions. It seemed to me, from what Kingsley said, that I was already dishonored

—that the world already knew my shame; and that he, as my friend, had only employed an ambiguous language to soften the sting and the shock which his revelations must necessarily occasion. With this new notion, which occurred to me after leaving the house, I instantly returned to it. It required a strong effort to seem deliberate in what I spoke.

"Kingsley," I said, "perhaps I did not pay sufficient heed to your observations. Do you mean to convey to my mind the idea that people think Edgerton too familiar with my wife? Do you mean to say that such a notion is abroad? That there is anything wrong?"

"By no means."

"Ah! then there is nothing in it. I see no reason for suspicion. I am not a jealous man; but it becomes necessary when one's neighbors find occasion to look into one's business, to look a little into it one's self."

"One must not wait for that," said Kingsley; "but where is your cigar?"

The question confused me. I had dropped it in the agitation of my feelings, without being conscious of its loss.

"Take another," said he, with a smile, "and let your cares end in smoke as you wend homeward. My most profound thoughts come from my cigar. To that I look for my philosophy, my friendship, my love—almost my religion. A cigar is a brain-comforter, verily. You should smoke more, Clifford. You will grow better, wiser—*cooler*."

"I take your cigar and counsel together," was my reply. "The one shall reconcile me to the other. *Bon repos!*" And so I left him.

I was not likely to have *bon repos* myself. I was troubled. Kingsley suspects me of being jealous. Such an idea was very mortifying. This is another weakness of the suspicious nature. It loathes above all things to be suspected of jealousy. I hurried home, vexed with my want of coolness—doubly vexed at the belief that other eyes than my own were witnesses of the attentions of Edgerton to my wife.

I stopped at the entrance of our cottage. *He* was there as usual. Mrs. Porterfield was not present. The candle was burning dimly. He sat upon the sofa. Julia was seated upon a chair at a little distance. Her features wore an expression of exceeding gravity. His were pale and sad, but his eyes burnt with an eager intensity that betrayed the passionate feeling in his heart. Thus they sat—she looking partly upon the floor—he looking at her. I observed them for more than ten minutes, and in all that time I do not believe they exchanged two sentences.

"Surely," I thought, "this must be a singularly sufficing passion which can enjoy itself in this manner without the help of language."

Of course, this reflection increased the strength of my suspicions. I became impatient, and entered the cottage. The eyes of Julia seemed to brighten at my appearance, but they were also full of sadness. Edgerton soon after rose and took his departure. I believe, if I had stayed away till midnight, he would have lingered until that time; but I also believe that if I had returned two hours before, he would have gone as soon. His passion for the wife seemed to produce an antipathy to the husband, quite as naturally as that which grew up in my bosom in regard to him. When he was gone, my wife approached me, almost vehemently exclaiming—

"Why, why do you leave me thus, Clifford? Surely you can not love me."

"Indeed I do; but I was with Kingsley. I had business, and did not suppose you would miss me."

"Why suppose otherwise, Edward? I do miss you. I beg that you will not leave me thus again."

"What do you mean? You are singularly earnest, Julia. What has happened? What has offended you? Was not Edgerton with you all the evening?"

My questions, coupled with my manner, which had been somewhat excited, seemed to alarm her. She replied hurriedly:—

"Nothing has happened! nothing has offended me! But I feel that you should not leave me thus. It does not look well. It looks as if you did not love me."

"Ah! but when you *know* that I do!"

"I do not know it. Oh, show me that you do, Edward. Stay with me as you did at first—when we first came here—

when we were first married. Then we were so—so happy!"

"You would not say that you are not happy now?"

"I am not! I do not see you as I wish—when I wish! You leave me so often—leave me to strangers, and seem so indifferent. Oh! Edward, do not let me think that you care for me no longer."

"Strangers! Why, how you talk!—Good old Mrs. Porterfield seems to me like my own grandmother, and Edgerton has been my friend——"

Did I really hear her say the single word,

"Friend!" and with such an accent! The sound was a very slight one—it may have been my fancy only;—and she turned away a moment after. What could it mean? I was bewildered. I followed her to the chamber. I endeavored to renew the subject in such a manner as not to offend her suspicions, but she seemed to have taken the alarm. She answered me in monosyllables only, and without satisfying the curiosity which that single word, doubtfully uttered, had so singularly awakened.

"Only love me—love me, Edward, and keep with me, and I will not complain. But if you leave me—if you neglect me —I am desolate!"

CHAPTER XLIII.

ACCIDENT AND MORE AGONIES.

THERE was something very unaccountable in all this. I say unaccountable, with the distinct understanding that it was unaccountable only to that obtuse condition of mind which is produced by the demon of the blind heart. My difficulties of judging were only temporary, however. The sinister spirit made his whisper conclusive in the end.

"This vehemence," it suggested, "which is so unwonted with her, is evidently unnatural. It is affected for an object. What is that object? It is the ordinary one with persons in the wrong, who always affect one extreme of feeling when they would conceal another. She fears that you will suspect that she is very well satisfied in your absence; accordingly she strives to convince you that she was never so dissatisfied. Of course you can not believe that a man so well endowed as Edgerton, so graceful, having such fine tastes and accomplishments, can prove other than an agreeable companion! What then should be your belief?"

There was a devilish ingenuity in this sort of perversion. It had its effect. I believed it; and believing it, revolted, with a feeling of hate and horror, at the supposed loathsome hypocrisy of that fond embrace, and those earnest pleadings, which, in the moment of their first display, had seemed so precious to my soul. In the morning, when I was setting forth from home, she put her arm on my shoulder:—

"Come home soon, Edward, and let us go together on the hill. Let nobody know. Surely we shall be company enough for each other. I will sketch you a view of the river while you read Wordsworth to me."

"Now," whispered my demon in my ears, "that is ingenious. Let nobody know; as if, having a friend in the neighborhood—on a visit—he sick and in bad spirits—you should propose to yourself a pleasure trip of any kind without inviting him to partake of it? She knows *that* to be out of the question, and that you must ask Edgerton if you resolve to go yourself."

Such was the artful suggestion of my familiar. My resolve—still recognising the cruel policy by which I had been so long governed—was instantly taken. This was to invite Edgerton and Kingsley both.

"I will give them every opportunity. While Kingsley and myself ramble together, well leave this devoted pair to their own cogitations, taking care, however, to see what comes of them."

I promised Julia to be home in season, but said nothing of my intention to ask the gentlemen. She thanked me with a look and smile, which, had I not seen all things through eyes of the most jaundiced green, would have seemed to me that of an angel, expressive only of the truest love.

"Ah! could I but believe!" was the bitter self-murmur of my soul, as I left the threshold.

On my way through the town I stopped at the postoffice to get letters, and received one from Mrs. Delaney—late Clifford—my wife's exemplary mother, addressed to Julia. I then proceeded to Edgerton's lodgings. He was not yet up, and I saw him in his chamber. His flute lay upon the toilet. Seeing it, I recalled, with all its original vexing bitterness, the scene which took place the night previous to my departure from my late home. And when I looked on Edgerton—saw with what effort he spoke, and how timidly he expressed himself—how reluctant were his eyes to meet the gaze of mine—his guilt seemed equally fresh and unequivocal. I marked him out, involuntarily, as my victim. I felt assured, even while conveying to him the complimentary invitation which I bore, that my hand was commissioned to do the work of death upon his limbs. Strange and fascinating conviction! But I did not contemplate this necessity with any pleasure. No! I would have prayed—I did pray—that the task might be spared me. If I thought of it at all, it was as the agent of a necessity which I could not countervail. The fates had me in their keeping. I was the blind instrument obeying the inflexible will, against which

"Reluctant nature strives in vain."

I felt then, most truly, though I deceived myself, that I had no power, though every disposition, to save and to spare. I conveyed my invitation as a message from my wife.

"Edgerton, my wife has planned a little ramble for this afternoon. She wishes to show you some of the beauties of landscape in our new abode. She commissions me to ask you to join us."

"Ah! did *she?*" he demanded eagerly, with a slight emphasis on the last word.

"Ay, did she! Will you come?"

"Certainly—with pleasure!"

He need not have said so much. The pleasure spoke in his bright eyes—in the tremulous hurry of his utterance. I turned away from him, lest I should betray the angry feeling which disturbed me. He did not seek to arrest my departure. He had few words. It was sufficiently evident that he shrunk from my glance and trembled in my presence. How far otherwise, in the days of our mutual innocence—in our days of boyhood—when his face seemed clear like that of a pure, perfect star, shining out in the blue serene of night, unconscious of a cloud.

Kingsley was already at my office when I reached it, and soon after came Mr. Wharton, followed by two of our opponents. We were engaged with them the better part of the morning. When the business hours were consumed, our transactions remained unfinished, and another meeting was appointed for the ensuing day. I invited Wharton as well as Kingsley to join us in our afternoon rambles, which they both promised to do. I went home something sooner to make preparations, and only recollected, on seeing Julia, that I had thrown the letter from her mother, with other papers, into my desk. When I told her of the letter, her countenance changed to a death-like paleness which instantly attracted my notice.

"What is the matter—are you sick, Julia?"

"No! nothing. But the letter—where is it?"

"I threw it on my table, or in my desk, with other papers, to have them out of the way; and hurrying home sooner than usual, forgot to bring it with me. I suppose there's nothing in it of any importance?"

"No, nothing, I suppose," she answered faintly.

I told her what I had done with respect to our guests.

"I am very sorry," she answered, "that you have done so. I do not feel like company, and wished to have you all to myself."

"Oh, selfish; but of this I will believe moderately! As for company, with the exception of Wharton, they are old friends; and it would not do to take a pleasure ramble, with poor Edgerton here, and not make him a party."

There was an earnest intensity of gaze, almost amounting to a painful stare, in Julia's eyes, as I said these words. She really seemed distressed.

"But really, Edward, our pleasure ramble is not such a one as would make it a duty to invite your friends. How difficult it seems for you to understand me. Could not we two stroll a piece into the woods without having witnesses?"

"Why, is that all? Why then should you have made a formal appointment for such a purpose? Could we not have gone as before—without premeditation?"

The question puzzled her. She looked anxious. Had she answered with sincerity—with truth—and could I have believed her to have been sincere, how easy would it have been to have settled our difficulties. Had she said—"I really wish to avoid Mr. Edgerton, whose presence annoys me—who will be sure to come—when you are sure to be gone—and whom I have particular reasons to wish not to meet—not to see."

This, which might be the truth, she did not dare to speak. She had her reasons for her apprehension. This, which was reasonable enough, I could not conjecture; for the demon of the blind heart was too busy in suggesting other conjectures. It was evident enough that she had secret motives for her course, which she did not venture to reveal to me; and nothing could be more natural, in the diseased state of my mind, than that I should give the worst colorings to these motives in the conjectures which I made upon them. We were destined to play at cross-purposes much longer, and with more serious issues.

Our friends came, and we set forth in the pleasant part of the afternoon. We ascended our hill, and resting awhile upon the summit, surveyed the prospect from that position. Then I conducted the party through some of our woodland walks, which Julia and myself had explored together. But I soon gave up the part of cicerone to Wharton, who was to the "*manor born.*" He was a native of the neighborhood, boasted that he knew every "bosky dell of this wild wood" and certainly conducted us to glimpses of prettiest heights, and groves, and far vistas, where the light seemed to glide before us in an embodied gray form, that stole away, and peeped backward upon us from long allies of the darkest and most solemn-sighted pines.

'But there is a finer spot just below us," he said—"a creek that is like no other that I have ever met with in the neighborhood. It is formed by the Alabama—is as deep in some places, and so narrow, at times, that a spry lad can easily leap across it."

"Is it far?"

"No—a mile only."

"But your wife may be fatigued, Clifford?" was the suggestion of Kingsley. She certainly looked so; but I answered for her, and insisted otherwise. I met her glance as I spoke, but, though she looked dissatisfaction, her lips expressed none. I could easily conjecture that she felt none. She was walking with Edgerton—and while all eyes watched the scenery, he watched her alone. I hurried forward with Kingsley, but he immediately fell behind, loitered on very slowly, and left Wharton and myself to proceed together. I could comprehend the meaning of this. My demon made his suggestion.

"Kingsley suspects them—he sees what you are unwilling to see—he is not so willing to leave them together."

We reached the stream, and wandered along its banks. It had some unusual characteristics. It was sometimes a creek, deep and narrow, but clear; a few steps farther and it became what, in the speech of the country, is called a branch; shallow, purling soft over a sand-bed, limpid yellow, and with a playful prattle that put one in mind of the songs of thoughtless children, humming idly as they go. The shrubbery along its edges seemed to follow its changes. Where the bluffs were high, the foliage was dense and the trees large. The places where its waters shallowed, were only dotted with shrub trees and wild vines, which sometimes clambered across the stream and wedded the opposing branches, in bonds as hard to break as those of matrimony. The waters were sinuous, and therefore slow. They seemed only to glide along, like some glittering serpent, who trails at leisure his silvery garments through the woods, quietly and slow, as if he had no sort of apprehension.

When we had reached a higher spot of bluff than the rest, Wharton, who was an active rather than an athletic man, challenged me to follow him. He made the leap having little space to spare. I had not done such a thing for some years. But my boyhood had been one of daring. The school in which I had grown up had given me bodily hardihood and elasticity; at all events I could not brook defiance in such a matter, and, with moderate effort, succeeded in making a longer stride. I looked back at this moment and saw Julia, still closely attended by Edgerton, just about emerging into view from a thick copse that skirted the foot of a small hill over which our course had brought us. I could not distinguish their features. They were, however, close together. Kingsley was on their right, a little in advance of them, but still walking slowly. I pointed my finger toward a shallow and narrow part of the stream as that which they would find it most easy to cross. A tree had been felled at the designated point, and just below it, in consequence of the obstructions which its limbs presented to the easy passage of the water, several sand bars had been made, by which, stepping from one to the other, one might cross dryshod even without the aid of the tree. Kingsley repeated my signal to those behind him, and led the way. I went on with Wharton, without again looking behind me.

But few minutes had elapsed after this, when I heard Julia scream in sudden terror. I looked round, but the foliage had thickened behind me, and I could no longer see the parties. I bounded backward, with no enviable feelings. My apprehensions for my wife's safety made me forgetful of my suspicions. I reached the spot in time to discover the cause of her alarm.

She was in the midst of the stream, standing upon one of the sandflats, steadying herself with difficulty, while she supported the whole form of William Edgerton, who lay, seemingly lifeless, and half buried in one of the sluices of water which ran between the sandrifts. I had just time to see this, and to feel all the pangs of my jealousy renewed, when Kingsley rushed into the water to his rescue. He lifted him out to the banks as if he had been an infant, and laid him on the shore. I went to the relief of Julia, who, trembling like a leaf, fainted in my arms the moment she felt herself in safety.

The whole affair was at that time unaccountable to me. It necessarily served to increase my pangs. Had I not seen her with my own eyes tenderly supporting the fainting frame of the man whom I believed to be my rival — whom I believed she loved? Had I not heard her scream of terror announcing her interest in his fate — her apprehensions for his safety? His danger had made her forgetful of her caution — such was the assurance of my demon — and in the fullne s of her heart her voice found utterance. Besides, how was I to know what endearments — what fond pressure of palms — had been passing between them, making them heedless of their course, and consequently, making them liable to the accident which had occurred. For, it must be remembered, that the general impression was that Edgerton's foot had slipped, and, falling into the stream while endeavoring to assist Julia, he had nearly pulled her in after him. His fainting afterward we ascribed to the same nervous weakness which had induced that of Julia. On this head, however, Kingsley was better informed. He told me, in a subsequent conversation, that he had narrowly observed the parties — that, until the moment before he fell, the hands of the two had not met — that then, Edgerton offered his to assist my wife over the stream, and scarcely had their fingers touched, when Edgerton sank down, like a stone, seemingly lifeless, and falling into the water only after he had become insensible.

All was confusion. Mine, however, was not confusion. It was commotion — commotion which I yet suppressed — a volcano smothered, but smothered only for a time, and ready to break forth with superior fury in consequence of the restraint put upon it. This one event, with the impressive spectacle of the parties in such close juxtaposition, seemed almost to render every previous suspicion conclusive.

Julia was soon recovered; but the swoon of Edgerton was of much longer duration. We sprinkled him with water, subjected him to fanning and friction, and at length aroused him. His mind seemed to wander at his first consciousness—he murmured incoherently. One or two broken sentences, however, which he spoke, were not without significance in my ears.

"Closer! closer! leave me not now—not yet."

I bent over him to catch the words. Kingsley, as if he feared the utterance of anything more, pushed me away, and addressing Edgerton sternly, asked him if he felt pain.

"What hurts you, Mr. Edgerton? Where is your pain?"

The harsh and very loud tones which he employed, had the effect which I have no doubt he intended. The other came to complete consciousness in a moment.

"Pain!" said he—"no! I feel no pain. I feel feeble only."

And he strove to rise from the ground as he spoke.

"Do not attempt it," said Kingsley—"you are not able. Wharton, my good fellow, will you run back to town, and bring a carriage?"

"It will not need," said Edgerton, striving again to rise, and staggering up with difficulty.

"It will need. You must not overtask yourself. The walk is a long one before us."

Meantime, Wharton was already on his way. It was a tedious interval which followed, before his return with the carriage, which found considerable difficulty in picking a track through the woods. Julia, after recovery, had wandered off about a hundred yards from the party. She betrayed no concern—no uneasiness—made no inquiries after Edgerton, of whose condition she knew nothing—and, by this very course, convinced me that she was conscious of too deep an interest in his fate to trust her lips in referring to it. All that she said to me was, that "she had been so terrified on seeing him fall, that she did not even know that she had screamed."

"Natural enough!" said my demon. "Had she been able to have controlled her utterance, she would have taken precious good care to have maintained the silence of the grave. But her feelings were too strong for her policy."

And I took this reasoning for gospel.

The carriage came. Edgerton was put into it, but Julia positively refused to ride. She insisted that she was perfectly equal to the walk and walk she would. I was pleased with this determination, but not willing to appear pleased. I expostulated with her even angrily, but found her incorrigible. Chagrin and disappointment were obvious enough on the face of William Edgerton.

I took my seat beside him, and left Kingsley and Wharton to escort my wife home. We had scarcely got in motion before a rash determination seized my mind.

"You must go home with me, Edgerton. It will not do, while you are in this feeble state, to remain at a public tavern."

He said something very faintly about crowding and inconveniencing us.

"Pshaw—room enough—and Julia can be your nurse."

His eyes closed, he sunk back in the carriage, and a deep sigh escaped him. I fancied that he had a second time fainted; but I soon discovered that his faintness was simply the sudden sense of an overcoming pleasure. I knit my teeth spasmodically together; I cursed him in the bitterness of my heart, but said nothing. It was a feeling of desperation that had prompted the rash resolution which I had taken.

"At least," I muttered to myself, "it will bring these damning doubts to a final trial. If they have been fools heretofore, opportunity will serve to madden them. We shall see—we shall know all very soon;—and then!—"

Ay, then!

CHAPTER XLIV.

THE DAMNING LETTER.

MRS. PORTERFIELD, good old lady, half blind, half deaf, infirm and gouty, but very good natured, easily complied with my request to accommodate my friend. My friend!—She soon put one of her bed-rooms in order, and Edgerton was in quiet possession of it sometime before the pedestrians came home. When my wife was told of what I had done, she was perfectly aghast. Her air of chagrin was well put on and excellently worn. But she said nothing. Kingsley wore a face of unusual gravity.

"You are either the most wilful or the most indifferent husband in the world," was his whispered remark to me as he bade me good night, refusing to remain for supper.

I said something to my wife about tending Edgerton—seeing to his wants—nursing him if he remained unwell, and so forth. She looked at me with a face of intense sadness, but made no reply.

"She is too happy for speech," said my demon; "and such faces are easily made for such an occasion."

I went in to Edgerton after a brief space; I found him feeble, complaining of chill. His hands felt feverish. I advised quiet and sent off for a physician. I sat with him until the physician came, but I observed that my presence seemed irksome to him. He answered me in monosyllables only; his eyes, meanwhile, being averted, his countenance that of one excessively weary and impatient for release. The physician prescribed and left him, as I did myself. I thought he needed repose and desired to be alone. To my great surprise he followed me in less than half an hour into the supper-room, where he stubbornly sat out the evening. He refused to take the physic prescribed for him and really did not now appear to need it. His eyes were lighted up with unusual animation, his cheeks had an improved color, and without engaging very actively in the conversation, what he said was said with a degree of spirit quite uncommon with him during the latter days of our intimacy.

Mr. Wharton spent the evening with us, and the ball of talk was chiefly sustained by him and myself. My wife said little, nothing save when spoken to, and wore a countenance of greater gravity than ever. It seemed that Edgerton made some effort to avoid any particularity in his manner, yet seldom did I turn my eyes without detecting his in keen examination of my wife's countenance. At such times, his glance usually fell to the ground, but toward the close of evening, he almost seemed to despise observation, or — which was more probable — was not conscious of it — for his gaze became fixed with a religious earnestness, which no look of mine could possibly divert or unfix. He solicited my wife to play on the guitar, but she declined, until requested by Mrs. Porterfield, when she took up the instrument passively, and sung to it one of those ordinary negro-songs which are now so shockingly popular. I was surprised at this, for I well knew that she heartily detested the taste and spirit in which such things were conceived. Under the tuition of my demon, I immediately assumed this to be another proof of the decline of her delicacy. And yet, though I did not think of this at the time, she might have employed the coarse effusion simply as an antidote against the predominance of a morbid sentimentalism. There is a moment in the history of the heart's suffering, when the smallest utterance of the lips, or movement of the form, or expression of the eye, is prompted by some prevailing policy — some motive which the excited sensibilities deem of importance to their desires.

She retired soon. Her departure was followed by that of Edgerton first, and next of Wharton. Mrs. Porterfield had already gone. I was alone at the entrance of our cottage. Not alone! My demon was with me — suggestive of his pangs as ever — full of subtlety, and filling me with the darkest imaginings. The destroyer of my peace was in my dwelling. My wife may or may not be innocent. Happy for her if she is, but how can that be known? It mattered little to me in the excited mood which possessed me. Let any man fancy, as I did, that one, partaking of his hospitality, lying in the chamber which adjoined his own, yet meditated the last injury in the power of man to inflict against the peace and honor of his protector. Let him fancy this, and then ask what would be his own feelings—what his course?

Still, there is a sentiment of justice which is natural to every bosom with whom education has not been utter perversion. I believed much against Edgerton; I suspected my wife; I had seen much to offend my affections; much to alarm my fears; yet I *knew* nothing which was conclusive. That last event, the occurrence of the afternoon, seemed to prove not that the two were guilty, but that my wife loved the man who meditated guilt. This belief, doubtful so long, and against which I had really striven, seemed now to be concluded. I had heard her scream; I had seen her tenderly sustaining his form; I had felt her emotions, when, the danger being over, her feminine nature gained the ascendancy and she fainted in my arms. I could no longer doubt, that if she was still pure in mind, she was no longer insensible to a passion which must lessen that purity with every added moment of its permitted exercise. Still, even with this conviction, something more was necessary to justify me in what I designed. There must be no doubt. I must see. I must have sufficient proof, for, as my vengeance shall be unsparing, my provocation must be complete. That it might be so I had brought Edgerton into the house. Something more was necessary. Time and opportunity must be allowed him. This I insisted on, though, more than once, as I walked under the dark whispering groves which girdled our cottage, and caught a glimpse of the light in Edgerton's chamber, my demon urged me to go in and strangle him. I had strength to resist this suggestion, but the struggle was a long one.

I did not soon retire to rest. When I did, I still remained sleepless. But Julia slept. In her sleep she threw herself on my bosom, and seemed to cling about and clasp me as if with some fear of separation. Had I not fancied that this close embrace was meant for another than myself, I had been more indulgent to the occasional moanings of distress that escaped her lips. But, thinking as I did, I forced her from me, and in doing so she wakened.

"Edward," she exclaimed on wakening, "is it you?"

"Who should it be?" I demanded—all my suspicions renewed by her question.

"I am so glad. I have had such a dream. Oh! Edward, I dreamed that you were killing me!"

"Ha! what could have occasioned such a dream?"

My demon suggested, at this moment, that her dream had been occasioned by a consciousness of what her guilty fancies deserved. But she replied promptly:—

"Nay, I know not. It was the strangest fancy. I thought that you pursued me along the river—that my foot slipped and I fell among the bushes, where you caught me, and it was just when you were strangling me that I wakened."

"Your dream was occasioned by the affair of the afternoon. Was nobody present but ourselves?"

"Yes—there was a man at a little distance beyond us, and he seemed to be running from you also."

"A man! who was he?"

"I don't know exactly—his back was turned, but it seemed as if it was Mr. Edgerton."

"Ha! Mr. Edgerton!"

A deep silence followed. She had spoken her reply firmly, but so slowly as to convince me of the mental reluctance which she felt in uttering this part of the dream. When the imagination is excited, how small are the events that confirm its ascendency, and stimulate its progress. This dream seemed to me as significant as any of the signs that informed the ancient augurs. It bore me irresistibly forward in the direction of my previous thoughts. I began to see the path—dark, dismal—perhaps bloody—which lay before me. I began to feel the deed, already in my soul, which destiny was about to require me to perform. A crime, half meditated, is already half committed. This is the danger of brooding upon the precipice of evil thoughts. A moment's dizziness—a single plunge—and all is over!

I doubt whether Julia slept much the remainder of the night. I know that I did not. She had her consciousness as well as mine. *That* I now know. The question—"was her consciousness a guilty one?" That was the only question which remained for me!

The next morning I saw Edgerton. He looked quite as well as on the previous night, but professed to feel otherwise—declined coming forth to breakfast, and begged me to send the physician to him on my way to the office. I immediately conjectured that this was mere practice, for he had not taken the medicine which had been prescribed.

He must keep sick to keep *here*," said my demon. "He can have no pretext, otherwise, to stay!"

When I was about to leave the house Julia followed me to the door.

"Don't forget to bring mother's letter with you," was her parting direction. I had not been half an hour at the office before a little servant-girl, who tended in the house, came to me with a message from her, requesting that the letter might be sent by her.

This earnestness struck me with surprise. I remembered the expression in my wife's face the day before when I told her the letter had been received. I now recalled to mind the fact, that, on no occasion, had she ever shown me any of her mother's letters; though nothing surely would have seemed more natural, as she knew how keen was my anxiety to hear at all times from the old maternal city.

My suspicions began to warm, and I resolved upon another act of baseness in obedience to the counsel of my evil spirit. I pretended to look awhile for the letter, but finally dismissed the girl, saying that I had mislaid it, but would bring it home with me when I came to dinner. The moment she had gone I examined this precious document. It was sealed with one of those gum wafers which are stuck on the outside of the envelope. In turning it over, as if everything was prepared to gratify my wish, I discovered that one section of the wafer had nearly parted from the paper. To the upper section of the fold it adhered closely. To the lower it was scarcely attached at all, and seemed never to have been as well fastened as the upper.

The temptation was irresistible. A very slight effort enabled me to complete the separation without soiling the paper or fracturing the seal. This was all done within my desk, the leaf of the desk being raised and resting upon my head. In this position I could easily close the desk, in the event of any intrusion, without suffering the intruder to see in what I had been engaged. Thus guarded I proceeded to read the precious epistle, which I found very much what I should have expected from such a woman. It said a great deal about her neighbors and her neighbors' dresses; and how her dear Delaney was sometimes "obstropolous," though in the end a mighty good man; and much more over which I hurried with all the rapidity of disgust. But there was matter that made me linger. One or two sentences thrown into the postscript contained a volume. I read, with lifted hair and a convulsed bosom, the following passage:—

"Delaney tells me that Bill Edgerton has gone to travel. He says to Tennessee. But I know better. I know he can't keep from you, let him try his best. But be on your guard, Julia. Don't let him get too free. Your husband's a jealous man, and if he was once to dream of the truth, he'd just as leave shoot him as look at him. I thought at one time he'd have guessed the truth before. So far you've played your cards nicely, but that was when I was by you, to tell you how. I feel quite ticklish when I think of you, and remember you've got nobody now to consult with. All I can say is, keep close. It would be the most terrible thing if Clifford should find out or even suspect. He wouldn't spare either of you. It's better for a woman in this country to drag on and be wretched, than to expose herself to shame, for no one cares for her after that. Be sure and burn this the moment you've read it. I would not have it seen for the world. I only write it as a matter of duty, for I can't forget that I'm your mother, though I must say, Julia, there were times when you have not acted the part of a daughter."

Precious, voluminous postscript! Considerate mother! "Be on your guard, Julia. Don't let him get too free!" Prudent, motherly counsel! "You've played your cards nicely." Nice lady! "I feel quite ticklish!" Elegant sensibilities!

Enough! The evil was done. Here was another piece of

damning testimony, indirect but conclusive, to show that I was bedevilled. I refolded the letter, but I could not place my lips to the wafer. The very letter seemed to breathe of poison. Faugh! I put it from me, went to the basin, and wetting the end of my finger, sufficiently softened the gum to make it more effectually fasten the letter than when I had received it. This done, I proceeded to the business of the day with what appetite was left me.

CHAPTER XLV.

VERGE OF THE PRECIPICE.

I DO not know how I got through with the business of that day. Even in my weakness I was possessed of a singular degree of strength. I saw Kingsley, Wharton, and all of the parties whom we met the day before. We came to a final decision on the subject of Kingsley's claims; I took down the heads of several papers which were to be drawn up; the terms of sale and transfer, bounds and characteristics of the land to be conveyed; and engaged in the discussion of the various topics which were involved in these transactions, with as keen a sense of business, I suspect, as any among them. The habit of suppressing my feelings availed me sufficiently under the present circumstances. Kingsley said nothing on the subject of yesterday's adventure, nor was I in the mood to refer to it. With some effort I was cheerful; spoke freely of indifferent topics, and pleased myself with the idea of my own firmness, while persuading my hearers of my good humor and my legal ability. I do not deny that I paid for these proofs of stoicism. Who does not? There is no such thing as suppressing passions which are already in action — at least, there is no such thing as suppressing them long. If the summer tempest keeps off to-day it will come to-morrow, and its force and volume is always in due proportion to the delay in its utterance. The solitudes of the forest heard my groans and agonies when man did not — and the venom which I kept from my lips, overflowed and poisoned the very sources of life and happiness within my heart.

I gave the letter to Julia without a word. She did not look

at me while extending the hand to receive it, and hurried to her chamber without breaking the seal. I watched her departing form with a vague, painful emotion of inquiry, such as would possess the bosom of one, looking on a dear object, with whom he felt that a disruption was hourly threatened of every earthly tie. That day she ate no dinner. Her brow was clouded throughout the meal. Edgerton was present, seemingly as well as at his first arrival. I had learned casually from Mrs. Porterfield that he had been in our little parlor all the morning; while another remark from the good old lady gave me a new idea of the employment of my wife.

"This writing," said she, addressing the latter, "does your eyes no good. Indeed they look as if you had been crying over your task."

"What writing?" I asked, looking at Julia, She blushed, but said nothing, and the blush passed off, leaving the sadness more distinct than ever.

"Oh, she has been writing whole sheets for the last two mornings. I went in this morning to bring her out to assist me in entertaining Mr. Edgerton, who looked so lonesome; and I do assure you I thought at first, from the quantity of writing, that you had given her some of your law-papers to do. The table was covered with it."

"Indeed!" said I—"this must be looked into. It will not do for the wife to take the husband's business from him. It looks mischievous, Mrs. Porterfield—there's something wrong about it."

"Indeed there must be, Mr. Clifford, for only see how very sad it makes her. I declare, she looks this last few weeks like a very different woman. She does nothing now but mope. When she first came here she seemed to me so cheerful and happy."

All this was so much additional wormwood to my bitter. The change in Julia, which had even struck this blind old lady, corresponded exactly with the date of Edgerton's arrival. When I saw the earnest tenderness in his countenance as he watched her, while Mrs. Porterfield was speaking, I ceased to feel any sympathy for the intense sadness which I yet could not but see in hers. I turned away, and leaving the table soon after, went to our chamber, but the traces of writing were no longer to be seen. The voluminous manuscripts had all been carefully removed. I was about to leave the chamber when Julia met me at the door.

"Come back; sit with me," she said. "Why do you go off in such a hurry always? Once it was not so, Edward."

"What! are you for the honeymoon again?"

"Do not smile so, and speak so irreverently!" she said, with a reproachful earnestness that certainly seemed to me very strange, thinking of her as I did. My evil spirit was silent. He lacked readiness to account for it. But he was not unadroit, and moved me to change the ground.

"But what long writing is this, Julia?"

"Ah! you are curious?"

"Scarcely."

"*Tell* me that you are?"

"What! at the expense of truth?"

"No! but to gratify my desire. I hoped you were; but, curious or not, it is for you."

"Let me see it, then."

"Not yet; it is not ready."

"What! shall there be more of it?"

"Yes, a good deal."

"Indeed! but why take this labor? Why not tell me what you have to say?"

"I wish I could, but I can not. You do not encourage me."

"What encouragement do you wish to speak to your husband?"

"Oh, much! Stay with me, dear husband."

"That will keep you from your writing."

"Ah! perhaps it will render it unnecessary."

"At all events it will keep me from mine;" and I prepared to go. She put her hand upon my shoulder—looked into my eyes pleadingly—hers were dewy wet—and spoke:—

"Do not go—stay with me, dear husband, do stay. Stay only for half an hour."

Why did I not stay? I should ask that question of myself in vain. When the heart grows perverse, it acquires a taste for wilfulness. I, myself, longed to stay; could I have been persuaded that she certainly desired it, I should have found my sweetest pleasure in remaining. But there was the rub—that doubt! all that she said, looked, did, seemed, through the medium of the blind heart, to be fraudulent.

"She would disguise her anxiety, that you should be gone. Leave her, and in twenty minutes she and Edgerton will be together."

Such was the whisper of my demon. I did leave her. I went forth for an hour into the woods—returned suddenly and found them together! They were playing chess, Mrs. Porterfield, with all her spectacles, watching the game. I did not ask, and did not know, till afterward, that the express solicitation of the old lady had drawn her from her chamber, and placed her at the table. The conjecture of the evil spirit proved so far correct, and this increased my confidence in his whispers. Alas! how readily do we yield our faith to the spirit of hate! how slow to believe the pure and gentle assurances of love!

Three days passed after this fashion. Edgerton no longer expressed indisposition, yet he made no offer to depart. I took care that neither word nor action should remind him of his trespass. I gave the parties every opportunity, and exhibited the manner of an indifference which was free from all disquiet—all suspicion. The sadness, meanwhile, increased upon the countenance of Julia. She gazed at me in particular with a look of earnestness amounting to distress. This I ascribed to the strength of her passions. There was even at moments a harshness in her tones when addressing me now, which was unusual to her. I found some reason for this, equally unfavorable to her fidelity. After dinner I said to Edgerton:—

"You are scarcely strong enough for a bout at the bottle. I take wine with Kingsley this afternoon. He has commissioned me to ask you."

"I dare not venture, but that should not keep you away."

"It will not," I said indifferently.

"Thank him for me, if you please, but tell him it will not do for one so much an invalid as myself."

"Very good!" and I left him, and joined Kingsley. The business of this friend being now in a fair train for final adjustment, he was preparing for his return to Texas. He had not been at my lodgings since Edgerton's arrival in M——, but we had seen each other, nevertheless, almost every day at his or at my office. Our afternoon was rather merry than cheerful. Heaven knows I was in no mood to be a *bon compagnon*, but I took sufficient pains that Kingsley should not suspect I had any reasons for being otherwise. I had my jest—I emptied my bottle—I said my good things, and seemed to say them without effort. Kingsley, always cheerful and strong-minded, was in his best vein, and mingling wit and reflection happily together, maintained the ball of conversation with equal ease and felicity. He had the happy knack of saying happy things quietly—of waiting for, and returning the ball, without running after it. At another time, I should have been content simply to have provoked him. Now, I was quite too miserable not to seek employment; and to disguise feelings, which I should have been ashamed to expose, I contrived to take the lead and almost grew voluble in the frequency of my utterance. Perhaps, if Kingsley failed in any respect as a philosopher, it was in forbearing to look with sufficient keenness of observation into the heart of his neighbor. He evidently did not see into mine. He was deceived by my manner. He credited all my fun to good faith, and gravely pronounced me to be a fortunate fellow.

"How?" I demanded with a momentary cessation of the jest. His gravity and—to me—the strange error in such an observation—excited my curiosity.

"In your freedom from jealousy."

"Oh! that, eh? But why should I be jealous?"

"It is not exactly why a man should be jealous—but why, knowing what men are, usually, that you are not. Nine men in ten would be so under your circumstances?"

"How, what circumstances?"

"With Edgerton in your house—evidently fond of your wife, you leave them utterly to themselves. You bring him into your house unnecessarily, and give him every opportunity. I still think you risk everything imprudently. You may pay for it."

I felt a strange sickness at my heart. I felt that the flame was beginning to boil up within me. The perilous turning-point of passion—the crisis of strength and endurance—was at hand.

My eyes settled gloomily upon the table. I was silent longer than usual. I felt *that*, and looked up. The keen glance of Kingsley was upon me. It would not do to suffer him to read my feelings. I replied with some precipitation:—

"I see, Kingsley, you are not cured of your prejudices against Edgerton."

"I am not—I have seen nothing to cure me. But my prejudice against him, has nothing to do with my opinion of your prudence. Were it any other man, the case would be the same."

"Well, but I do not think it so clear that Edgerton loves my wife more than is natural and proper."

"Of the naturalness of his love I say nothing—perhaps, nothing could be more natural. But that he does love her, and loves her as no married woman should be loved, by another than her husband, is clear enough."

"Suppose, then, it be as you say! So long as he does nothing improperly, there is nothing to be said. There is no evil."

"Ah, but there is evil. There is danger."

"How? I do not see."

"Suppose your wife makes the same discovery which other persons have made? Suppose she finds out that Edgerton loves her?"

"Well—what then?"

"She can not remain uninfluenced by it. It will affect her feelings sensibly in some way. No creature in the world can remain insensible to the attachment of another."

"Indeed! Why, agreeable to that doctrine, there could be no security from principle. There could be no virtue certain—nay, not even love."

"Do not mistake me. When I say *she* would be influenced—I do not mean to say that she would be so influenced as to requite the illicit sentiment. Far from it. But she must pity or she must scorn. She may despise or she may deplore. In either case her feelings would be aroused, and in either case would produce uneasiness if not unhappiness. I *know*, Clifford, that your wife perceives the passion of Edgerton—I am confident, also, that it has influenced her feelings. What may be the sentiment produced by this influence I do not pretend to say. I would not insinuate that it is more than would be natural to the breast of any virtuous woman. She may pity or she may scorn—she may despise or she may deplore. I know not. But, in either case, I regard your bringing Edgerton into the house and conferring upon him so many opportunities, as being calculated either to make yourself or your wife miserable. In either event you have done wrong. Look to it—remedy it as soon as you can."

My face burned like fire. My eyes were fixed upon the table. I dared not look upon my companion. When I spoke, I felt a choking difficulty in my utterance which compelled me to speak loud to be understood, and which yet left my speech thick, husky, and unnatural.

"Say no more, Kingsley. What you have said disturbs me. Nay, I acknowledge, I have been disturbed before. Perhaps, indeed, I know more than yourself. Time will show. At all events, be sure of one thing. These opportunities, if what you say be true, afford an ordeal through which it is necessary that the parties should now go—if it be only to afford the necessary degree of relief to my mind. Enough has been seen to excite suspicion—enough has been done, you yourself think, to awaken the feelings of my wife. Those feelings must now be tried. Opportunity will do this. She must go through the trial. I am not blind as you suppose. Nay, I am watchful, and I tell you, Kingsley, that the time approaches when all my doubts must cease one way or the other."

"But I still think, Clifford—" he began.

"No more, Kingsley. I tell you, matters must go on. Edgerton can now only be driven from my house by my wife. If she expels him, I shall be too happy not to forgive him. But if she makes it necessary that the expulsion shall be effected by my hands, and with violence—God have mercy upon both of them, for I shall not. Good night!"

"But why will you go? Stay awhile longer. Be not rash—do nothing precipitately, Clifford."

I smiled bitterly in replying:—

"You need not fear me. Have I not proved myself patient—patient until you pronounced me cold and indifferent? Why should you suppose that, having waited and forborne so long,

I should be guilty of rashness now? No, Kingsley! My wife is very dear to me—how dear I will not say; I will be deliberate for her sake—for my own. I will be sure, very sure—quite sure;—but, once sure!—Good night."

Kingsley followed me to the door. His last injunctions exhorted me to forbearance and deliberation. I silenced them by a significant repetition of the single words, "Good night—good night!" and hurried, with every feeling of anxiety and jealousy awakened, in the direction of my cottage.

CHAPTER XLVI.

THE UNBRIDLED MADNESS.

THE night did not promise to be a good one. The clouds were scudding wildly from east to west. The air was moist and chill. There was no light from moon or stars, and I strode with difficulty, though still rapidly, through the unpaved streets. I was singularly and painfully excited by the conversation with Kingsley. My own experience before, had prepared me to become so, with the slightest additional provocation. Facts were rapidly accumulating to confirm my fears, and lessen my doubts. That dark, meaning letter of Mrs. Delaney! The adventure in the streamlet.—The scream—the look—the secrecy.! What a history seemed to be compressed in these few topics.

I hurried forward—I was now among the trees. I had almost to grope my way, it was so dark. I was helped forward by some governing instincts. My fiend was busy all the while. I fancied, now, that there was something exulting in his tone. But he drove me forward without forbearance. I felt that these clouds in the sky—this gloom and excitement in my heart—were not for nothing. Every gust of wind brought to me some whisper of fear; and there seemed a constant murmur among the trees—one burden—whose incessant utterance was only shame and wo. How completely the agony of one's spirit sheds its tone of horror upon the surrounding world. How the flowers wither as our hearts wither—how sickly grows sunlight and moonlight, in our despair—how lonely and utter sad is the breath of winds, when our bosoms are about to be laid bare of hope and sustenance by the brooding tempest of our sorrows.

I had a terrible prescience of some dreadful experience which awaited me as I drove forward. Obstructions of tree and shrub, and tangled vines, encountered me, but did not long arrest, and I really felt them not. I put them aside without a consciousness.

At length a glimmering light informed me I was near the cottage. I could see the heavy dark masses of foliage that crowded before the entrance. The light was in the parlor. There was also one in the room of Mrs. Porterfield. Ours, which was on the same floor with hers, was in darkness. I never experienced sensations more like those of a drunken man than when, working my way cautiously among the trees, I approached the window. The glasses were down, possibly in consequence of the violence of the gust. But there was one thing unusual. The curtains were also down at both windows. These curtains were half-curtains only. They fell from the upper edge of the lower sash, and were simply meant to protect the inmates from the casual glance of persons in front. The house was on an elevation of two or three feet from the ground. It was impossible to see into the apartment unless I could raise myself at least that much above my own stature. I looked around me for a stump, bench, block — anything; but there was nothing, or in the darkness I failed to find it. To clamber up against the side of the house would have disturbed the inmates. I ascended a tree, and buried within its leaves, looked directly into the apartment.

They were together! alone!—at the eternal chess! Julia sat upon the sofa. Edgerton in front of her. A small table stood between them. I had arrived at an opportune moment. Julia's hand was extended to the board. I saw the very piece it rested upon. It was the white queen; but, just at that moment — nothing could be more clearly visible — the hand of Edgerton was laid upon hers. She instantly withdrew it, and looked upward. Her face was the color of carnation — flushed — so said my demon, with the overwhelming passions in her breast. The next moment the table was thrust aside — the chess-men tumbled upon the floor, and Edgerton kneeling before my wife had grasped her about the waist, and was dragging her to his knee.

I saw no more. A sudden darkness passed over my eyes. A keen, quick, thrilling pang went through my whole frame, and I fell from the tree, upon the earth below, in utter unconsciousness.

CHAPTER XLVII.

FATAL SILENCE.

STRANGE and cruel destiny! When everything depended upon my firmness, I was overwhelmed by feebleness. It seemed as if I had not before believed that this terrible moment of confirmation would come. And yet, if anybody could have been prepared for such a discovery, I should have been. I had brooded over it for months. A thousand times had my imagination pictured it to me in the most vivid and fearful aspect. I fancied that I should have been steeled by conviction against every other feeling but that of vengeance. But in reality, my hope was so sanguine, my love for Julia so fervent, I did not, amidst all my fears, really believe that such a thing could ever prove true. All my boasted planning and preparation, and espionage, had only deceived myself. I believed, at worst, that Julia might be brought to love William Edgerton, but that he would presume to give utterance to his love, and that she would submit to listen, was not truly within my belief. I had not been prepared for this, however much, in my last interview with Kingsley, I had professed myself to be.

But had she submitted? That was still a question. I had seen nothing beyond what I have stated. His audacious hand had rested upon hers—his impious arm had encircled her waist, and then my blindness and darkness followed. I was struck as completely senseless, and fell from the tree with as little seeming life, as if a sudden bullet had traversed my heart.

In this state I lay. How long I know not—it must have been for several hours. I was brought to consciousness by a sense of cold. I was benumbed — a steady rain was falling, and from the condition of my clothes, which were completely saturated, must have been falling for some time previous. I rose with pain and difficulty to my feet. I was still as one stunned and stupified, by one of those extremes of suffering for which the overcharged heart can find no sufficient or sufficiently rapid method of relief. When I rose, the light was no longer in the parlor. The parties were withdrawn.

Horrible thought! That I should have failed at that trying moment. I knew everything — I knew nothing. It was still possible that Julia had repulsed him. I had seen *his* audacity only — was it followed by *her* guilt? How shall that be known? I could answer this question as Kingsley would have answered it.

"If your wife be honest, she must now reveal the truth. She can no longer forbear. The proceeding of Edgerton has been too decided, and she shares his guilt if she longer keeps it secret. The wife who submits to this form of insult, without seeking protection where alone it may be found, clearly shows that the offence is grateful to her — that she deems it no insult."

That, then, shall be the test! So I determined. Edgerton must be punished. There is no escape. But for her — if she does not seek the earliest occasion to reveal the truth, she is guilty beyond doubt — doomed beyond redemption.

I entered the house with difficulty. I was as feeble as if I had been under the hands of the physician for weeks. A light was burning on the staircase. I took it and went into the parlor, which I narrowly examined. There were no remaining proofs of the late disorder. The table was set against the wall. The chess-men were all gathered up, and neatly put away in the box, which stood upon the mantel.

"There is proof of coolness and deliberation here!" I muttered to myself, as I took my way up-stairs. When I entered my chamber, I felt a pang, the fore-runner of a spasm. I had been for several years afflicted with these spasms, in great or small degree. They marked every singular mental excitement under which I labored. It was no doubt one of these spasms which had seized and overpowered me while I sat within the tree. Never before had I suffered from one so severe; but the violence of this was naturally due to the extreme of agony — as sudden as it was terrible—which seized upon my soul. My physician had provided me with a remedy against these attacks to which I was accustomed to resort. This, though a potent remedy, was also a potent poison. It was a medicine called the hydrocyanic or prussic acid. Five minims was a dose, but two drops were death. I went to the medicine-case which stood beneath the head of the bed, with the view to getting out the vial; but my wife started up eagerly as I approached, and with trembling accents, demanded what was the matter. She saw me covered with mud and soaking with water. I told her that I had got wet coming homeward and had slipped down the hill.

"Why did you stay so late—why not come home sooner, dear husband?"

"Hypocrite!" I muttered while stooping down for the chest.

"You are sick—you have your spasms!" she now said, rising from the bed and offering to measure the medicine. This she had repeatedly done before; but I was not now willing to trust her. Doubts of her fidelity led to other doubts.

"If she is prepared to dishonor, she is prepared to destroy you!" said my familiar.

This suggestion seized upon my brain, and while I measured out the minims, the busy fiend reminded me that I grasped the bane as well as the antidote in my hand. A stern, a terrible image of retributive justice presented itself before my thoughts. The feeling of an awful necessity grew strong within me. "Shall the adulterer alone perish? Shall the adultress escape?" The fiend answered with tremulous but stern passion—"She shall surely die!"

"If she reveals not the truth in season," I said in my secret soul; "if she claims not protection at my hands against the adulterer, she shall share his fate!" and with this resolve, even at the moment when I was measuring the antidote for myself, I resolved that the same vial should furnish the bane for her!

The medicine relieved me, though not with the same promptness as usual. I looked at the watch and found it two o'clock. My wife begged me to come to bed, but that was impossible. I proceeded to change my garments. By the time that I had finished, the rain ceased, the stars came out, the morning promised to be clear. I determined to set forth from my office. I had no particular purpose; but I felt that I could not meditate where she was. She continually spoke to me — always tenderly and with great earnestness. I pleaded my spasms as a reason for not lying down. But I lingered. I was as unwilling to go as to stay. I longed to hear her narrative; and, once or twice, I fancied that she wished to tell me something. But she did not. I waited till near daylight, in order that she should have every opportunity, but she said little beyond making professions of love, and imploring me to come to bed.

In sheer despair, at last, I went out, taking my pistol-case, unperceived by her, under my arm. I went to my office where I locked it up. There I seated myself, brooding in a very whirlwind of thought, until after daylight.

When the sun had risen, I went to a man in the neighborhood who hired out vehicles. I ordered a close carriage to be at my door by a certain hour, immediately after breakfast. I then despatched a note to Kingsley, saying briefly that Edgerton and myself would call for him at nine. I then returned home. My wife had arisen, but had not left the chamber. She pleaded headache and indisposition, and declined coming out to breakfast. She seemed very sad and unhappy, not to say greatly disquieted — appearances which I naturally attributed to guilt. For — still she said nothing. I lingered near her on various small pretences in the hope to hear her speak. I even made several approaches which, I fancied, might tend to provoke the wished-for revelation. Indeed, it was wished for as ardently as ever soul wished for the permission to live — prayed for as sincerely as the dying man prays for respite, and the temporary remission of his doom.

In vain! My wife said little, and nothing to the purpose. The moments became seriously short. Could she have anything to say? Was it possible that, being innocent, she should still lock up the guilty secret in her bosom? She could not be innocent to do so! This conclusion seemed inevitable. In order that she should have no plea of discouragement, I spoke to her with great tenderness of manner, with a more than usual display of feeling. It was no mere show. I felt all that I said and looked. I knew that a trying and terrible event was at hand

—an event painful to us both—and all my love for her revived with tenfold earnestness. Oh! how I longed to take her into my arms, and warn her tenderly of the consequences of her error; but this, of course, was impossible. But, short of this, I did everything that I thought likely to induce her confidence. I talked familiarly to her, and fondly, with an effort at childlike simplicity and earnestness, in the hope that, by thus renewing the dearest relations of ease and happiness between us, she should be beguiled into her former trusting readiness of speech. She met my fondnesses with equal fondness. It seemed to give her particular pleasure that I should be thus fond. In her embrace, requiting mine, she clung to me; and her tears dropping warm upon my hands, were yet attended by smiles of the most hearty delight. A thousand times she renewed the assurances of her love and attachment—nay, she even went so far as tenderly to upbraid me that our moments of endearment were so few;—yet, in spite of all this, she still forbore the *one only* subject. She still said nothing; and as I knew how much she *could* say and ought to say, which she did not say, I could not resist the conviction that her tears were those of the crocodile, and her assurances of love the glozing commonplaces of the harlot.

In silence she suffered me to leave her for the breakfast-table. She looked, it is true—but what had I to do with looks, however earnest and devoted? I went from her slowly. When on the stairs, fancying I had heard her voice, I returned, but she had not called me. She was still silent. Full of sadness I left her, counting slowly and sadly every step which I took from her presence.

Edgerton was already at table. He looked very wretched. I observed him closely. His eye shrunk from the encounter of mine. His looks answered sufficiently for his guilt. I said to him:—

"I have to ride out a little ways in the country this morning, and count upon your company. I trust you feel well enough to go with me? Indeed, it will do you good."

Of course, my language and manner were stripped of everything that might alarm his fears. He hesitated, but complied. The carriage was at the door before we had finished breakfast;

and with no other object than simply to afford her another opportunity for the desired revelation, I once more went up to my wife's chamber. Here I lingered fully ten minutes, affecting to search for a paper in trunks where I knew it could not be found. While thus engaged I spoke to her frequently and fondly. She did not need the impulse to make her revelation, except in her own heart. The occasion was unemployed. She suffered me once more to depart in silence; and this time I felt as if the word of utter and inevitable wo had been spoken. The hour had gone by for ever. I could no longer resist the conviction of her shameless guilt. All her sighs and tears, professions of love and devotion, the fond tenacity of her embrace, the deep-seated earnestness and significance in her looks — all went for nothing in her failure to utter the one only, and all-important communication.

Let no woman, on any pretext, however specious, deceive herself with the fatal error, that she can safely harbor, unspoken to her husband, the secret of any insult, or base approach, of another to herself!

CHAPTER XLVIII.

TOO LATE!

EDGERTON announced himself to be in readiness, and, at the same time, declared his intention to withdraw at once from our hospitality and return to his old lodging-house. He had already given instructions to his servant for the removal of his things.

"What!" I said with a feeling of irony, which did not make itself apparent in my speech—"you are tired of our hospitality, Edgerton? We have not treated you well, I am afraid."

"Yes," he muttered faintly, "too well. I have every reason to be gratified and grateful. No reason to complain."

He forced himself to say something more by way of acknowledgment; but to this I gave little heed. We drove first to Kingsley's, and took him up; then, to my office, where I got out, and, entering the office, wrapped up my pistol-case carefully in a newspaper, so that the contents might not be conjectured, and bringing it forth, thrust it into the boot of the carriage.

"What have you got there?" demanded Kingsley.

"Something for digestion," was my reply. "We may be kept late."

"You are wise enough to be a traveller," said Kingsley; and without further words we drove on. I fancied that when I put the case into the vehicle, Edgerton looked somewhat suspicious. That he was uneasy was evident enough. He could not well be otherwise. The consciousness of guilt was enough to make him so; and then there was but little present sympathy between himself and Kingsley.

I had already given the driver instructions. He carried us into the loneliest spot of woods some four miles from M——, and in a direction very far from the beaten track.

"What brings you into this quarter?" demanded Kingsley. "What business have you here?"

"We stop here," I said as the carriage drove up. "I have some land to choose and measure here. Shall we alight, gentlemen?"

I took the pistol-case in my hands and led the way. They followed me. The carriage remained. We went on together several hundred yards until I fancied we should be quite safe from interruption. We were in a dense forest. At a little distance was a small stretch of tolerably open pine land, which seemed to answer the usual purposes. Here I paused and confronted them.

"Mr. Kingsley," I said without further preliminaries, "I have taken the liberty of bringing you here, as the most honorable man I know, in order that you should witness the adjustment of an affair of honor between Mr. Edgerton and myself."

As I spoke I unrolled the pistol-case. Edgerton grew pale as death, but remained silent. Kingsley was evidently astonished, but not so much so as to forbear the obvious answer.

"How! an affair of honor? Is this inevitable—necessary, Clifford?"

"Absolutely!"

"In no way to be adjusted?"

"In but one! This man has dishonored me in the dearest relations of my household."

"Ha! can it be?"

"Too true! There is no help for it now. I am dealing with him still as a man of honor. I should have been justified in shooting him down like a dog—as one shoots down the reptile that crawls to the cradle of his children. I give him an equal chance for life."

"It is only what I feared!" said Kingsley, looking at Edgerton as he spoke.

The latter had staggered back against a tree. Big drops of

sweat stood upon his brows. His head hung down. Still he was silent. I gave the weapons to Kingsley, who proceeded to charge them.

"I will not fight you, Clifford!" exclaimed the criminal with husky accents.

"You must!"

"I can not—I dare not—I will not! You may shoot me down where I stand. I have wronged you. I dare not lift weapon at your breast."

"Wretch! say not this!" I answered. "You must make the atonement."

"Be it so! Shoot me! You are right! I am ready to die."

"No, William Edgerton, no! You must not refuse me the only atonement you can make. You must not couple that atonement with a sting. Hear me! You have violated the rites of hospitality, the laws of honor and of manhood, and grossly abused all the obligations of friendship. These offences would amply justify me in taking your life without scruple, and without exposing my own to any hazard. But my soul revolts at this. I remember the past—our boyhood together—and the parental kindness of your venerated parent. These deprive me of a portion of that bitterness which would otherwise have moved me to destroy you. Take the pistol. If life is nothing to you, it is as little to me now. Use the privilege which I give you, and I shall be satisfied with the event."

He shook his head while he repeated:—

"No! I can not. Say no more, Clifford. I deserve death!"

I clapped the pistol to his head. He folded his arms, lifted his eyes, and regarded me more steadily than he had done for months before. Kingsley struck up my arm, as I was cocking the weapon.

"He must die!" I exclaimed fiercely.

"Yes, that is certain!" replied the other. "But I am not willing that I should be brought here as the witness to a murder. If he will fight you, I will see you through. If he will not fight you, there needs no witness to your shooting him. You have no right, Clifford, to require this of me."

"You are not a coward, William Edgerton?"

"Coward!" he exclaimed, and his form rose to its fullest

height, and his eye flashed out the fires of a manhood, which of late he had not often shown.

"Coward! No! Do I not tell you shoot? I do not fear death. Nay, let me say to you, Clifford, I long for it. Life has been a long torture to me—is still a torture. It can not now be otherwise. Take it—you will see me smile in the death agony."

"Hear me William Edgerton, and submit to my will. You know not half your wrong. You drove me from my home—my birthplace. When I was about to sacrifice you for your previous invasion of my peace in C——, I looked on your old father, I heard the story of his disappointment—his sorrows—and you were the cause. I determined to spare you—to banish myself rather, in order to avoid the necessity of taking your life. You were not satisfied with having wrought this result. You have pursued me to the woods, where my cottage once more began to blossom with the fruits of peace and love. You trample upon its peace—you renew your indignities and perfidies here. You drive me to desperation and fill my habitation with disgrace. Will you deny me then what I ask? Will you refuse me the atonement—any atonement—which I may demand?"

"No, Clifford!" he replied, after a pause in which he seemed subdued with shame and remorse. "You shall have it as you wish. I will fight you. I am all that you declare. I am guilty of the wrong you urge against me. I knew not, till now, that I had been the cause of your flight from C——. Had I known that!"

Kingsley offered him the pistol.

"No!" he said, putting it aside. "Not now! I will give you this atonement this afternoon. At this moment I can not. I must write. I must make another atonement. Your claim for justice, Clifford, must not preclude my settlement of the claims of others."

"Mine must have preference!"

"It shall! The atonement which I propose to make shall be one of repentance. You would not deny me the melancholy privilege of saying a few last words to my wretched parents?"

"No! no! no!"

"I thank you, Clifford. Come for me at four to my lodgings—bring Mr. Kingsley with you. You will find me ready to atone, and to save you every unnecessary pang in doing so."

This ended our conference. Kingsley rode home with him, while, throwing myself upon the ground, I surrendered myself to such meditations as were natural to the moods which governed me. They were dark and dismal enough. Edgerton had avowed his guilt. Could there be any doubt on the subject of my wife's? He had made no sort of qualification in his avowal of guilt, which might acquit her. He had evidently made his confession with the belief that I was already in possession of the whole truth. One hope alone remained—that my wife's voluntary declaration would still be forthcoming. To that I clung as the drowning man to his last plank. When Kingsley and Edgerton first left me, I had resolved to waste the hours in the woods and not to return home until after my final meeting in the afternoon with the latter. It might be that I should not return home then, and in such an event I was not unwilling that my wife should still live, the miserable thing which she had made herself. But, with the still fond hope that she might speak, and speak in season, I now resolved to return at the usual dinner hour; and, timing myself accordingly, I prolonged my wanderings through the woods until noon. I then set forward, and reached the cottage a little sooner than I had expected.

I found Julia in bed. She complained of headache and fever. She had already taken medicine—I sat beside her. I spoke to her in the tenderest language. I felt, at the moment when I feared to lose her for ever, that I could love nothing half so well. I spoke to her with as much freedom as fondness; and, momently expecting her to make the necessary revelation, I hung upon her slightest words, and hung upon them only to be disappointed.

The dinner hour came. The meal was finished. I returned to the chamber, and once more resumed my place beside her on the couch. I strove to inspire her with confidence—to awaken her sensibilities—to beguile her to the desired utterance, but in vain. Of course I could give no hint whatsoever of the knowledge which I had obtained. After that, her confession would have been no longer voluntary, and could no longer have been credited.

Time sped—too rapidly as I thought. Though anxious for vengeance, I loved her too fondly not to desire to delay the minutes in the earnest expectation that she would speak at last. She did not. The hour approached of my meeting with Edgerton; and then I felt that Edgerton was not the only criminal.

Mrs. Porterfield just then brought in some warm tea, and placed it on the table at the bed head. After a few moments' delay, she left us alone together. The eyes of my wife were averted. The vial of prussic acid stood on the same table with the tea. I rose from the couch, interposed my person between it and the table—and, taking up the poison, deliberately poured three drops into the beverage. I never did anything more firmly. Yet I was not the less miserable, because I was most firm. My nerve was that of the executioner who carries out a just judgment. This done, I put the vial into my pocket. Julia then spoke to me. I turned to her with eagerness. I was prepared to cast the vessel of tea from the window. It was my hope that she was about to speak, though late, the necessary truths. But she only called to me to know if I had been to my office during the morning.

"Not since nine o'clock," was my answer. "Why?"

"Nothing. But are you going to your office now, dear husband?"

"Not directly. I shall possibly be there in the course of the afternoon. What do you wish? Why do you ask?"

"Oh, nothing," she replied; "but I will tell you to-morrow why I ask."

"To-morrow!—tell me now, if it be anything of moment. Now! now is the appointed time!" The serious language of Scripture became natural to me in the agonizing situation in which I stood.

"No! no! to-morrow will do. I will not gratify your curiosity. You are too curious, husband;" and she turned from me, smiling, upon the couch.

I felt that what she might tell me to-morrow could have nothing to do with the affair between herself and Edgerton.

That could be no object for jest and merriment. I turned from her slowly, with a feeling at my heart which was not exactly madness—for I knew then what I was doing—but it was just the feeling to make me doubtful how long I should be secure from madness.

"To-morrow will not do," I muttered to myself as I descended the stairs. "Too late!—too late!"

CHAPTER XLIX.

SUICIDE.

FROM the cottage I proceeded to Kingsley's. He was in readiness, and waiting me. We drove directly to Edgerton's lodging-house, the appointed hour of four being at hand. Kingsley only alighted from the carriage, and entered the dwelling. He was absent several minutes. When he returned, he returned alone.

"Edgerton is either asleep or has gone out. His room-door is locked. The landlord called and knocked, but received no answer. He lacks manliness, and I suspect has fled. The steamboat went at two."

"Impossible!" I exclaimed, leaping from the carriage. "I know Edgerton better. I can not think he would fly, after the solemn pledge he gave me."

"You have only thought too well of him always," said the other, as we entered the house.

"Let us go to the room together," I said to the landlord. "I fear something wrong."

"Well, so do I," responded the publican. "The poor gentleman has been looking very badly, and sometimes gets into a strange wild taking, and then he goes along seeing nobody. Only last Saturday I said to my old woman, as how I thought everything warn't altogether right *here*,"—and the licensed sinner touched his head with his fore-finger, himself looking the very picture of well-satisfied sagacity. We said nothing, but leaving the eloquence to him, followed him up to Edgerton's chamber. I struck the door thrice with the butt end of my whip, then called his name, but without receiving any answer.

Endeavoring to look through the key-hole, I discovered the key on the inside, and within the lock. I then immediately conjectured the truth. William Edgerton had committed suicide.

And so it was. We burst the door, and found him suspended by a silk handkerchief to a beam that traversed the apartment. He had raised himself upon a chair, which he had kicked over after the knot had been adjusted. Such a proceeding evinced the most determined resolution.

We took him down with all despatch, but life had already been long extinct. He must have been hanging two hours. His face was perfectly livid—his eyeballs dilated—his mouth distorted—but the neck remained unbroken. He had died by suffocation. I pass over the ordinary proceedings—the consternation, the clamor, the attendance of the grave-looking gentlemen with lancet and lotion. They did a great deal, of course, in doing nothing. Nothing could be done. Then followed the "crowner's" inquest. A paper, addressed to the landlord, was submitted to them, and formed the burden of their report.

"I die by my own hands," said this document, "that I may lose the sense of pain, bodily and mental. I die at peace with the world. It has never wronged me. I am the source of my own sorrows, as I am the cause of my own death. I will not say that I die sane. I am doubtful on that head. I am sure that I have been the victim of a sort of madness for a very long time. This has led me to do wrong, and to meditate wrong—has made me guilty of many things, which, in my better moments of mind and body, I should have shrunk from in horror. I write this that nobody may be suspected of sharing in a deed the blame of which must rest on my head only."

Then followed certain apologies to the landlord for having made his house the scene of an event so shocking. The same paper also conveyed certain presents of personal stuff to the same person, with thanks for his courtesy and attention. An adequate sum of money, paying his bill, and the expenses of his funeral, was left in his purse, upon the paper.

Kingsley assumed the final direction of these affairs; and having seen everything in a fair way for the funeral, which was appointed to take place the next morning, he hurried me away to his lodging-house.

CHAPTER L.

CONFESSION OF EDGERTON.

WHEN within his chamber, he carefully fastened the door and placed a packet in my hands.

"This is addressed to you," he said. "I found it on the table with other papers, and seeing the address, and fearing that if the jury laid eyes on it, they might insist on knowing its contents, I thrust it into my pocket and said nothing about it there. Read it at your leisure, while I smoke a cigar below."

He left me, and I opened the seal with a sense of misgiving and apprehension for which I could not easily account. The outer packet was addressed to myself. But the envelope contained several other papers, one of which was addressed to his father; another—a small billet, unsealed—bore the name of my wife upon it.

"That," I inly muttered, "she shall never read!"

An instant after, I trembled with a convulsive horror, as the demon who had whispered in my ears so long, seemed to say, in mocking accents:—

"Shall not! Ha! ha! She can not! can not!" and then the fiend seemed to chuckle, and I remembered the insuppressible anguish of Othello's apostrophe, to make all its eloquence my own. I murmured audibly:—

> "My wife! my wife! What wife?—I have no wife!
> Oh, insupportable—oh, heavy hour!"

My eyes were blinded. My face sunk down upon the table, and a cold shiver shook my frame as if I had an ague. But I recovered myself when I remembered the wrongs I had endured—her guilt and the guilt of Edgerton. I clutched the papers—brushed the big drops from my forehead, and read as follows:—

"Clifford, I save you guiltless of my death. You would be less happy were my blood upon your hands, for, though I deserve to die by them, I know your nature too well to believe that you would enjoy any malignant satisfaction at the performance of so sad a duty. Still, I know that this is no atonement. I have simply ceased from persecuting you and the angelic woman, your wife. But how shall I atone for the tortures and annoyances of the past, inflicted upon you both? Never! never! I perish without hope of forgiveness, though, here, alone with God, in the extreme of mortal humility, I pray for it!

"Perhaps, you know all. From what escaped you this morning, it would seem so. You knew of my madness when in C——; you know that it pursued you here. Nothing then remains for me to tell. I might simply say all is true; but that, in the confession of my guilt and folly, each particular act of sin demands its own avowal, as it must be followed by its own bitter agony and groan.

"My passion for your wife began soon after your marriage. Until then I had never known her. You will acquit me of any deliberate design to win her affections. I strove, as well as I could, to suppress my own. But my education did not fit me for such a struggle. The indulgence of fond parents had gratified all my wishes, and taught me to expect their gratification. I could not subdue my passions even when they were unaccompanied by any hopes. Without knowing my own feelings, I approached your wife. Our tastes were similar, and these furnished the legitimate excuse for frequently bringing us together. The friendly liberality of your disposition enlarged the privileges of the acquaintance, and, without meaning it at first, I abused them. I sought your dwelling at unsuitable periods. Unconsciously, I did so, just at those periods when you were most likely to be absent. I first knew that my course was wrong, by discovering the unwillingness which I felt to encounter you. This taught me to know the true nature of my sentiments, but without enforcing the necessity of subduing them. I did not seek to subdue them long. I yielded myself up, with the recklessness of insanity, to a passion whose very sweetness had the effect to madden.

"My fondness for your wife was increased by pity. You

neglected her. I was at first indignant and hated you accordingly. But I became glad of your neglect for two reasons. It gave me the opportunities for seeing her which I desired; and I felt persuaded with a vain folly, that nothing could be more natural than that she would make a comparison, favorable of course to myself, between my constant solicitude and attention and your ungenerous abandonment. But I was mistaken. The steady virtue of the wife revenged the wrong which, without deliberately intending it, I practised against the husband. When my attentions became apparent, she received me with marked coolness and reserve; and finally ceased to frequent the *atelier*, which, while art alone was my object, yielded, I think, an equal and legitimate pleasure to us both.

"I saw and felt the change, but had not the courage to discontinue my persecutions. My passion, and the tenacity with which it enforced its claims, seemed to increase with every difficulty and denial. The strangeness of your habits facilitated mine. Almost nightly I visited your house, and though I could not but see that the reserve of your wife now rose into something like hauteur, yet my infatuation was so great that I began to fancy this appearance to be merely such a disguise as Prudence assumes in order to conceal its weaknesses, and discourage the invader whom it can no longer baffle. With this impression I hurried on to the commission of an offence, the results of which, though they did not quell my desires, had the effect of terrifying them, for some time at least, into partial submission. Would to God, for all our sakes, that their submission had been final!

"You remember the ball at Mrs. Delaney's marriage? I waltzed once with your wife that evening. She refused to waltz a second time. The privileges of this intoxicating dance are such as could be afforded by no other practice in social communion—the lady still preserving the reputation of virtue. I need not say with what delight I employed these privileges. The pressure of her arm and waist maddened me; and when the hour grew late, and you did not appear, Mrs. Delaney counselled me to tender my carriage for the purpose of conveying her home. I did so;—it was refused; but, through the urgent suggestions of her mother, it was finally accepted. I assisted her to the carriage, immediately followed, and took my place beside her. She was evidently annoyed, and drew herself up with a degree of lofty reserve, which, under other cirumstances, and had I been less excited than I was, by the events of the evening, would have discouraged my presumption. It did not. I proceeded to renew those liberties which I had taken during the dance. I passed my arm about her waist. She repulsed me with indignation, and insisted upon my setting her down where we were, in the unfrequented street, at midnight. This I refused. She threatened me with your anger; and when, still deceiving myself on the subject of her real feelings, I proceeded to other liberties, she dashed her hand through the windows of the coach, and cried aloud for succor. This alarmed me. I promised her forbearance, and finally set her down, very much agitated, at the entrance of your dwelling. She refused my assistance to the house, but fell to the ground before reaching it. That night her miscarriage ensued, and my passions for a season were awed into inactivity, if not silence.

"Still, I could not account for her forbearance to reveal everything to you. You were still kind and affectionate to me as ever. I very well knew that had she disclosed the secret, you were not the man to submit to such an indignity as that of which I had been guilty. It seems—so I infer from what you said this morning—that you knew it all. If you did, your forbearance was equally unexpected and merciful. Believing that she had kept my secret, my next conclusion was inevitable. 'She is not altogether insensible to the passion she inspires. Her strength is in her virtues alone. Her sympathies are clearly mine!' These conclusions emboldened me. I haunted your house nightly with music. Sheltered beneath your trees, I poured forth the most plaintive strains which I could extort from my flute. Passion increased the effect of art. I strove at no regular tunes; I played as the mood prompted; and felt myself, not unfrequently, weeping over my own strange, irregular melodies.

"Your sudden determination to remove prevented the renewal of my persecutions. I need not say how miserable I was made, and how much I was confounded by such a determination. Explained by yourself this morning, it is now easily understood;

but, ignorant then of the discoveries you had made — ignorant of your merciful forbearance toward my unhappy parents — for I can regard your forbearance with respect to myself as arising only from your consideration of them — it was unaccountable that you should give up the prospect of fortune and honors, which success, in every department of your business, seemed certainly to secure you.

"The last night — the eve of your departure from C——, I resumed my place among the trees before your dwelling. Here I played and wandered with an eye ever fixed upon your windows. While I gazed, I caught the glimpse of a figure that buried itself hurriedly behind the folds of a curtain. I could suppose it to be one person only. I never thought of you. Urged by a feeling of desperation, which took little heed of consequences, I clambered up into the branches of a pride of India, which brought me within twenty feet of the window. I distinctly beheld the curtain ruffled by the sudden motion of some one behind it. I was about to speak — to say — no matter what. The act would have been madness, and such, doubtless, would have been the language. I fortunately did not speak. A few moments only had elapsed after this, when I heard a few brief words, spoken in *her* voice, from the same window. The words were few, and spoken in tones which denoted the great agitation of the speaker. These apprized me of my danger.

"'Fly, madman, for your life! My husband is on the stairs.'

"Her person was apparent. Her words could not be mistaken though spoken in faint, feeble accents. At the same moment I heard the lower door of the dwelling unclose, and without knowing what I did or designed, I dropped from the tree to the ground. To my great relief, you did not perceive me. I was fortunately close to the fence, and in the deepest shadow of the tree. You hurried by, within five steps of me, and jumped the fence, evidently thinking to find me in the next enclosure. Breathing freely and thankfully after this escape, I fled immediately to the little boat in which I usually made my approaches to your habitation on such occasions; and was in the middle of the lake, and out of sight, long before you had given over your fruitless pursuit. The next day you left the city, and I remained, the wasted and wasting monument of passions which had been as profitlessly as they were criminally exercised.

"You were gone;—you had borne with you the object of my devotion; but the passion remained and burnt with no less frenzy than before. You were not blind to the effect of this frenzy upon my health and constitution. You saw that I was consuming with a nameless disease. Perhaps you knew the cause and the name, and your departure may have been prompted by a sentiment of pity for myself, in addition to that which you felt for my unhappy parents. If this be so — and it seems probable — it adds something to the agony of life — it will assist me in the work of atonement — it will better reconcile me to the momentary struggle of death.

"My ill health increased with the absence of the only object for whom health was now desirable. To see her again — to the last — for I now knew that that last could not be very remote —was the great desire of my mind. Besides, strange to say, a latent hope was continually rising and trembling in my soul. I still fancied that I had a place in the affections of your wife. You will naturally ask on what this hope was founded. I answer, on the supposition that she had concealed from you the truth on the subject of my presumptuous assault upon her; and on those words of warning by which she had counselled me to fly from your pursuit on that last night before you left the city. These may not be very good reasons for such a hope, but the faith of the devotee needs but slight supply of aliment; and the fanaticism of a flame like mine needs even less. A whisper, a look, a smile — nay, even a frown — has many a time prompted stronger convictions than this, in wiser heads, and firmer hearts than mine.

"My father counselled me to travel, and I was only too glad to obey his suggestions. He prescribed the route, but I deceived him. Once on the road, I knew but one route that could do me good, or at least afford me pleasure. I pursued the object of my long devotion. Here your conduct again led me astray. I found you still neglectful of your wife. Still, you received me as if I had been a brother, and thus convinced me that Julia had kept my secret. In keeping it thus long I now fancied it had become hers. I renewed my devotions, but with as little profit as before. She maintained the most rigid distance, and I grew nervous and feeble in consequence of the protracted homage which I paid, and the excitement which followed from this homage. You had a proof of this nervousness and excitement in the incident which occurred while crossing the streamlet. I extended her my hand to assist her over, and scarcely had her fingers touched mine, when I felt a convulsion, and sunk, fainting and hopelessly into the stream.* Conscious of nothing besides, I was yet conscious of her screams. This tender interest in my fate increased my madness. It led to a subsequent exhibition of it which at length fully opened my eyes to the enormity of my offence.

"You blindly as I then thought, took me to your dwelling as if I had been a brother. Ah! why? If I was mad, Clifford, your madness was not less than mine. It was the blindest madness if not the worst. The progress of my insanity was now more rapid than ever. I fancied that I perceived signs of something more than coldness between yourself and wife. I fancied that you frowned upon her; and in the grave, sad, speaking looks which she addressed to you, I thought I read the language of dislike and defiance. My own attentions to her were redoubled whenever an opportunity was afforded me; but this was not often. I saw as little of her while living in your cottage as I had seen before, and, but for the good old lady, Mrs. Porterfield, I should probably have been even less blessed by her presence. She perceived my dullness, and feeble health, and dreaming no ill, insisted that your wife should assist in beguiling me of my weariness. She set us down frequently at chess, and loved to look on and watch the progress of the game.

"She did not always watch, and last night, while we played together, in a paroxysm of madness, I proceeded to those liberties which I suppose provoked her to make the revelation which she had so long forborne. My impious hands put aside the board, my arms encircled her waist; while, kneeling beside her, I endeavored to drag her into my embrace. She repulsed me; smote me to her feet with her open palm; and spurning me

* An incident somewhat similar to this occurs in the Life of Petrarch, as given by Mrs. Dobson, but the precise facts are not remembered, and I have not the volume by me.

where I lay grovelling, retired to her chamber. I know not what I said—I know not what she answered—yet the tones of her voice, sharp with horror and indignation, are even now ringing in my ears!

"Clifford, I have finished this painful narration. I have cursed your home with bitterness, yet I pray you not to curse me! Let me implore you to ask for merciful forbearance from her, to whom I feel I have been such a sore annoyance—too happy if I have not been also a curse to her. What I have written is the truth—sadly felt—solemnly spoken—God alone being present while I write, while death lingers upon the threshold impatient till I shall end. I leave a brief sentence, which you may or may not, deliver to your wife. You will send the letter to my father. You will see me buried in some holy enclosure; and if you can, you will bury with my unconscious form, the long strifes of feeling which I have made you endure, and the just anger which I have awakened in your bosom. Farewell!—and may the presiding spirit of your home hereafter, be peace and love!"

CHAPTER LI.

DOUBTS — SUMMONS.

The billet which was addressed to my wife was in the following language :—

"Lady, on the verge of the grave, having sincerely repented of the offence I have given you, I implore you to pity and to pardon. A sense of guilt and shame weighs me down to earth. You can not apply a harsher judgment to my conduct than I feel it deserves; but I am crushed already. You will not trample the prostrate. In a few hours my body will be buried in the dust. My soul is already there. But, though writhing, I do not curse; and still loving, I yet repent. In my last moments I implore you to forgive! forgive! forgive!"

This was all, and I considered the two documents with keen and conflicting feelings. There was an earnestness—a sincerity about them, which I could not altogether discredit. He had freely avowed his own errors; but he had not spoken for hers. I did not dare to admit the impression which he evidently wished to convey of her entire innocence, not only from the practices, but the very thoughts of guilt. It is in compliance with a point of honor that the professed libertine yet endeavors to excuse and save the partner of his wantonness. In this light I regarded all those parts of his narrative which went to extenuate her conduct. There was one part of her conduct, indeed, which, as it exceeded his ability to account for, was beyond his ability to excuse—namely, her strange concealment of his insolence. This was the grand fault which, it appeared to me, was conclusive of all the rest. It was now my policy to believe in this fault wholly. If I did not, where was I? what was my condition?—my misery?

I sat brooding, with these documents open before me on the table, when Kingsley tapped at the door. I bade him enter, and put the papers in his hands. He read them in silence, laid them down without a word, and looked me with a grave composure in the face.

"What do you think of it?" I demanded.

"That he speaks the truth," he replied.

"Yes, no doubt — so far as he himself is concerned."

"I should think it all true."

"Indeed! I think not."

"Why do you doubt, and what?"

"I doubt those portions in which he insists upon my wife's integrity."

"Wherefore?"

"There are many reasons; the principal of which is her singular concealment of the truth. She suffers a strange man to offend her virtue with the most atrocious familiarities, and says nothing to her husband, who, alone, could have redressed the wrong and remedied the impertinence."

"That certainly is a staggering fact."

"According to his own admission, she warns him to fly from the wrath of her husband, to which his audacity had exposed him — warns him, in her night-dress, and from the window of her chamber."

"True, true! I had forgotten that."

"Look at all the circumstances. He haunts the house — according to his own showing, persecutes her with attentions, which are so marked, that, when he finds her husband ignorant of them, leads him to the conclusion — which is natural — that they are not displeasing to the wife. He avails himself of the privileges of the waltz, at the marriage of Mrs. Delaney, to gratify his lustful anticipations. He presses her arm and waist with his d——d fingers. Rides home with her, and, according to his story, takes other liberties, which she baffles and sets aside. But, mark the truth. Though she requires him to set her down in the street — though she makes terms for his forbearance — a wife making terms with a libertine — yet he evidently sees her into the house, and when she is taken sick, hurries for the mother and the physician. He tells just enough of the story to convict himself, but suppresses everything which may convict her. How know I that this resistance in the carriage was more than a sham? How know I that he did not attend her in the house? That they did not dabble together on their way through the dark piazza — along the stairs? — Nay, what proof is there that he did not find his way, with polluting purpose, into the very chamber? — that chamber, from which, not three weeks after, she bade him fly to avoid my wrath! What makes her so precious of his life — the life of one who pursues her with lust and dishonor — if she does not burn with like passions? But there is more."

Here I told him of the letter of Mrs. Delaney, in which that permanent beldame counsels her daughter, less against the passion itself, than against the imprudent exhibition of it. It was clear that the mother had seen what had escaped my eyes. It was clear that the mother was convinced of the attachment of the daughter for this man. Now, the attachment being shown, what followed from the concealment of the indignities to which Edgerton had subjected her, but that she was pleased with them, and did not feel them to be such. These indignities are persevered in — are frequently repeated. Our footsteps are followed from one country to another. The husband's hours of absence are noted. His departure is the invariable signal for them to meet. They meet. His hands paddle with hers; his arms grasp her waist. True, we are told by him, that she resists; but it is natural that he should make this declaration. Its truth is combated by the fact that, of these insults, *she* says nothing. That fact is everything. That one fact involves all the rest. The woman who conceals such a history, shares in its guilt.

Kingsley assented to these conclusions.

"Yet," he said, "there is an air of truthfulness about these papers — this narrative — that I should be pleased to believe, even if I could not; — that I should believe for your sake, Clifford, if for no other reason. Honestly, after all you have said and shown — with all the unexplained and perhaps unexplainable particulars before me, making the appearances so much against her — I can not think your wife guilty. I should be sorry to think so."

"I should now be sorry to think otherwise," I said huskily. I thought of that poisonous draught. I thought with many misgivings, and trembled where I sat.

"You surprise me to hear you speak so. Surely, Clifford, you love your wife?"

"Love her!" I exclaimed; I could say no more. My sobs choked my utterance.

"Nay, do not give up," he said tenderly. "Be a man. All will go well yet. The facts are anything but conclusive. These papers have a realness about them, which have their weight against any suspicions, however strong. Remember, these are the declarations of a dying man! Surely, all minor considerations of policy would give way at such a moment to the all-important necessity of speaking the truth. Besides, there is one consideration alone, to which we have made no reference, which yet seems to me full of weight and value. Edgerton could scarcely have been successful in his designs upon your wife. He was in fact dying of the disappointment of his passions. They could not have been gratified. Success takes an exulting aspect. He was always miserable and wo-begone — always desponding, sad, unhappy, from the first moment when this passion began, to the last."

"Guilt, guilt, nothing but guilt!"

"No, Clifford, no!—The guilt that works so terribly upon conscience as to produce such effects upon the frame, inevitably leads to repentance. Now, we find that Edgerton pursued his object until he was detected."

I shook my head.

"Do not steel yourself against probabilities, my dear fellow," said Kingsley.

"Proofs against probabilities always!"

"No! none of these are proofs except the papers you have in your hands, and the imperfect events which you witnessed. I am so much an admirer of your wife myself, that I am ready to believe this statement against the rest; and to believe that, however strange may have been her conduct in some respects, it will yet be explained in a manner which shall acquit her of misconduct. Believe me, Clifford, think with me——"

"No! no! I can not—dare not! She is a——"

"Do not! Do not! No harsh words, even were it so! She has been your wife. She should still be sacred in your eyes, as one who has slept upon your bosom."

"A traitress all the while, dreaming of the embraces of another."

"Clifford, what can this mean? You are singularly inveterate."

"Should I not be so? Am I not lost—abandoned—wrecked on the high seas of my hope—my fortunes scattered to the winds—my wealth, the jewel which I prized beyond all beside, which was worth the whole, gone down, swallowed up, and the black abyss closed over it for ever?"

"We are not sure of this."

"I am!"

"No! no!"

"I am! Though she be innocent, who shall rid me of the doubt, the fear, the ineradicable suspicion! *That* blackens all my sunlight; *that* poisons all my peace. I can never know delight. Nay, though you proved her innocent, it is now too late. Kingsley, by this time I have no wife!"

"Ha! Surely, Clifford, you have not——"

"Hark! Some one knocks! Again!—again!—I understand it. I know what it means. They are looking for me. She is dead or dying. I tell you it is quite in vain that you should argue. Above all, do not seek to prove her innocent."

The knocking without increased. He seized my arm as I was going forward, and prevented me.

"Compose yourself," he said, thrusting me into a chair. "Remain here till I return. I will see what is wanted."

But I followed him, and reached the door almost as soon as himself. It was as I expected. I had been sent for. My wife was dangerously ill. Such was the tenor of the message. More I could not learn. The servant had been an hour in search of me. Had sought me at the office and in other places which I had been accustomed to frequent; and I felt that after so long a delay, there was no longer need for haste. Still, I was about to depart with hasty footsteps. The servant was already dismissed. Kingsley grasped my arm.

"I will go along with you," he said; and as we went, he spoke, in low accents, to the following effect:—

"I know not what you have done, Clifford; and there is no need that I should know. Keep your secret. I do not think the worse of you that you have been maddened to crime. Let the same desperation nerve you now to sufficient composure. Beware of what you say, lest these people suspect you."

"And what if they do? Think you, Kingsley, that I fear? No! no! Life has nothing now. I lost fear, and hope, and everything in her."

"But may she not live?"

"No, I think not; the poison is most deadly. Though, even if she lives, my loss would not be less. She ceased to live for me the moment that she began to live for another!"

CHAPTER LII.

DEATH.

NOTHING more was said until we reached the cottage. Mrs. Porterfield and the physician met us at the entrance. We had come too late!

She was dead. They had found her so when they despatched the servant in quest of me; but they were not certain of the fact, and the servant was instructed to say she was only very ill. The physician was called in as soon as possible; but had declared himself, as soon as he came, unable to do anything for her. He had bled her; and, before our arrival, had already pronounced upon her disease. It was apoplexy!

"Apoplexy!" I exclaimed involuntarily. Kingsley gave me a look.

"Yes, sir, apoplexy," continued the learned gentleman. "She must have had several fits. It is evident that she was conscious after the first, for she appears to have endeavored to reach the door. She was found at the entrance, lying upon the floor. When I saw her, she must have been lifeless a good hour."*

He added sundry reasons, derived from her appearance, which he assured us were conclusive on this subject; but to these I gave little heed. I did not stop to listen. I hurried to the chamber, closed the door, and was alone with my victim, with my wife!

My victim!—my wife!

* The reader will be reminded of the melancholy details in the case of Miss Landon — L. E. L. — whose fate is still a mystery.

I stood above her inanimate form. How lovely in death—but, oh! how cold! I looked upon her pale, transparent cheeks and forehead, through which the blue lines of veins, that were pulseless now, gleamed out, showing the former avenues of the sweet and blessed life. I was disarmed of my anger while I gazed. I bent down beside her, took the rigid fingers of her hand in mine, and pressed my lips upon the bloodless but still beautiful forms of hers.

I remembered her youth and her beauty—the glowing promise of her mind, and the gentle temper of her heart. I remembered the dear hours of our first communion—how pure were our delights—how perfect my felicity. How we moved together as with one being only—beside the broad streams of our birthplace—under the shelter of shady pines—morning, and noon, and in the star-lighted night—never once dreaming that an hour like this would come!

And she seemed so perfect pure, as she was so perfect lovely! Never did I hear from her lips sentiment that was not—not only virtuous, but delicate and soft—not only innocent but true—not only true but fond! Alas! so to fall—so to yield herself at last! To feel the growth of rank passions—to surrender her pure soul and perfect form to the base uses of lust—to be no better than the silly harlot, that, beguiled by her eager vanity, surrenders the precious jewel in her trust, to the first cunning sharper that assails her with a smiling lie!

Oh God! how these convictions shook my frame! I had no longer strength for thought or action. I was feebler than the child, who, lost in the wood, struggles and sinks at last, through sheer exhaustion, into sobbing slumber at the foot of the unfeeling tree. I did not sob. I had no tears. But at intervals, the powers of breathing became choked, and my struggles for relief were expressed in a groan which I vainly endeavored to keep down. The sense of desolation was upon me much more strongly than that of either crime or death. I did not so much feel that she was guilty, as that I was alone! That, henceforth, I must for ever be alone. This was the terrible conviction;—and oh! how lone! To lessen its pangs, I strove to recall the fault for which she perished—to renew the recollection of those thousand small events, which, thrown together, had seemed to me mountains of rank and reeking evidence against her. But even my memory failed me in this effort. All this was a blank. The few imperfect and shadowy facts which I could recall seemed to me wholly unimportant in establishing the truth of what I sought to believe; and I shuddered with the horrible doubt that she might be innocent! If she were indeed innocent, what am I!

With the desperate earnestness of the cast-away, who strives, in mid-ocean, for the only plank which can possibly retard his doom, did I toil to re-establish in my mind that conviction of her guilt which the demon in my soul had made so certain by his assurances before. Alas! I had not only lost the wife of my bosom, but its fiend also. Vainly now did I seek to summon him back. Vainly did I call upon him to renew his arguments and proofs! He had fled—fled for ever; and I could fancy that I heard him afar off, chuckling, with hellish laughter, over the triumphant results of his malice.

I know not how long I hung over that silent speaker. Her pale, placid countenance—her bloodless lips, that still seemed to smile upon me as they had ever done before;—and that eye of speaking beauty—only half closed—oh! what conclusive assurances did they seem to give of that innocence which it now seemed the worst impiety to doubt! I would have given worlds—alas! how impotent is such a speech! Death sets his seal upon hope, and love, and endeavor; and the regrets of that childish precipitation which has obeyed the laws of passion only, are only so many mocking memorials of the blind heart, that jaundiced the face of truth, and distorted all the aspects of the beautiful.

Once more I laughed—a vain hysterical laugh—the expression of my conviction that I was self-doomed and desperate; and, writhing beside the inanimate angel whom I then would have recalled, though with all her guilt—assuming all of it to have been true—to the arms that wantonly cast her off for ever—I grasped the cold senseless limbs in my embrace, and placed the drooping head once more upon the bosom where it could not long remain! What a weight! The pulsation in my own heart ceased, and, with a shudder, I released the chilling form from my grasp, and found strength barely to compose the limbs once more in the bed beside me.

I pass over the usual and unnecessary details. There was a show of inquiry of course; but the one word of the learned young gentleman in black silenced any further examination. It was shown to the inquest by Mrs. Porterfield that my wife had been sick—that she was suddenly found dead. The physician furnished the next necessary fact. I was not examined at all. I stood by in silence. I heard the verdict—"Death by apoplexy"—with a smile. I was not unwilling to state the truth. Had I been called upon I should have done so. At first I was about to proffer my testimony, but a single sentence from the lips of Kingsley, when I declared to him my purpose, silenced me:—

"If you are not afraid to declare your own act, you should at least scruple to denounce her shame! She died your wife. Let that seal your tongue. The shame would be shared between you! You could only justify your crime by exposing hers!"

With the stern strength of desperation I stood above the grave, and heard the heavy clod ring hollowly upon the coffin. And there closed two lives in one. My hopes were buried there as effectually as her unconscious form.

Life is not breath simply. Not the capacity to move, and breathe, to act, eat, drink, sleep, and say, "Thank God! we have ate, drank, and slept!" The life of humanity consists in hope, love, and labor. In the capacity to desire, to affect, and to struggle. I had now nothing for which I could hope, nothing to love, nothing to struggle for!

Yes! life has something more:—endurance! This is a part of the allotment. The conviction of this renewed my strength. But it was the strength of desolation! I had taken courage from despair!

CHAPTER LIII.

REVELATION—THE LETTER OF JULIA.

It must be remembered, that, in all this time — amidst all my agonies — my feelings of destitution and despair — I had few or no doubts of the guilt of Julia Clifford. My sufferings arose from the love which I had felt — the defeat of my hopes and fortune — the long struggle of conflicting feelings, mortified pride, and disappointed enjoyment. Excited by the melancholy spectacle before me — beholding the form of her, once so beautiful — still so beautiful — whom I had loved with such an absorbing passion — whom I could not cease to love — suddenly cut off from life — her voice, which was so musical, suddenly hushed for ever — the tides of her heart suddenly stopped — and all the sweet waters of hope dried up in her bosom, and turned into bitterness and blight in mine — the force of my feelings got the better of my reason, and cruel and oppressive doubts of the justness of her doom overpowered my soul. But, with the subsiding of my emotions, under the stern feeling of resolve which came to my relief, and which my course of education enabled me to maintain, my persuasions of her guilt were resumed, and I naturally recurred to the conclusions which had originally justified me to myself, in inflicting the awful punishment of death upon her. But I was soon to be deprived of this justification — to be subjected to the terrible recoil of all my feelings of justice, love, honor and manliness, in the new and overwhelming conviction, not only that I had been premature, but that she was innocent!—innocent, equally of thought and deed, which could incur the reproach of impurity, or the punishment of guilt.

Three days had elapsed after her burial, when I re-opened and re-appeared in my office. I did not re-open it with any intention to resume my business. That was impossible in a place, where, at every movement, the grave of my victim rose, always green, in my sight. My purpose was to put my papers in order, transfer them to other parties, dispose of my effects, and depart with Kingsley to the new countries, of which he had succeeded in impressing upon me some of his own opinions. Not that these furnished for me any attractions. I was not persuaded by any customary arguments held out to the ambitious and the enterprising. It was a matter of small moment to me where I went, so that I left the present scene of my misery and overthrow. In determining to accompany him to Texas, no part of my resolve was influenced by the richness of its soil, or the greatness of its probable destinies. These, though important in the eyes of my friend, were as nothing in mine. In taking that route my object was simply, *to go with him.* He had sympathized with me, after a rough fashion of his own, the sincerity of which was more dear to me than the roughness was repulsive. He had witnessed my cares—he knew my guilt and my griefs—this knowledge endeared him to me more strongly than ever, and made him now more necessary to my affections than any other living object.

I re-opened my office and resumed my customary seat at the table. But I sat only to ruminate upon things and thoughts which, following the track of memory, diverted my sight as well as my mind, from all present objects. I saw nothing before me, except vaguely, and in a sort of shadow. I had a hazy outline of books against the wall; and a glimmering show of papers and bundles upon the table. I sat thus for some time, lost in painful and humiliating revery. Suddenly I caught a glimpse of a packet on the table, which I did not recollect to have seen before. It bore my name. I shuddered to behold it, for it was in the handwriting of my wife. This, then, was the writing upon which she had been secretly engaged, for so many days, and of which Mrs. Porterfield had given me the first intimation. I remembered the words of Julia when she assured me that it was intended for me—when she playfully challenged my curiosity, and implored me to acknowledge an anxiety to know the contents. The pleading tenderness of her speech and manner now rose vividly to my recollection. It touched me more now — now that the irrevocable step had been taken — far more than it ever could have affected me then. Then, indeed, I remained unaffected save by the caprice of my evil genius. The demon of the blind heart was then uppermost. In vain now did I summon him to my relief. Where was he? Why did he not come?

I took up the packet with trembling fingers. My nerves almost failed me. My heart shrank and sank with painful presentiments. What could this writing mean? Of what had *Julia Clifford* to write? Her whole world's experience was contained, and acquired, in my household. The only portion of this experience which she might suppose unknown to me was her intercourse with Edgerton. The conclusion then was natural that this writing related to this matter; but, if natural, why had I not conjectured it before? Why, when I first heard of it, had the conclusion not forced itself upon me as directly as it did now? Alas! it was clear to me now that I was then blind; and with this clearness of sight my doubts increased; but they were doubts of myself, rather than doubts of her.

It required an effort before I could recover myself sufficiently to break the seal of the packet. First, however, I rose and reclosed the office. Whatever might be the contents of the paper, to me it was the language of a voice from the grave. It contained the last words of one I never more should hear. The words of one whom I had loved as I could never love again. It was due to her, and to my own heart, that she should be heard in secret; — that her words — whether in reproach or repentance — whether in love or scorn — should fall upon mine ear without witness, in a silence as solemn as was that desolate feeling which now sat, like a spectre, brooding among the ruins of my heart.

My pulses almost ceased to beat—my respiration was impeded — my eyes swam — my senses reeled in dismay and confusion —as I read the following epistle. Too late! too late! Blind, blind heart! And still I was not mad!— No! no!— that would have been a mercy which I did not merit!— that would have been forgetfulness — utter oblivion of the wo which I can never cease to feel.

THE LAST LETTER OF JULIA.

"HUSBAND, DEAR HUSBAND!

"I write to you in fear and trembling. I have striven to speak to you, more than once, but my tongue and strength have failed me. What I have to tell you is so strange and offensive, and will be to you so startling, that you will find it hard to believe me; and yet, dear husband, there is not a syllable of it which is not true! If I knew that I were to die to-morrow I could with perfect safety and confidence make the same confession which I make now. But I do not wish you to take what I say on trust; look into the matter yourself—not precipitately—above all, not angrily—and you will see that I say nothing here which the circumstances will not prove. Indeed, my wonder is that so much of it has remained unknown to you already.

"Husband, Mr. Edgerton deceives you—he has all along deceived you—he is neither your friend nor mine. I would call him rather the most dangerous enemy; for he comes by stealth, and abuses confidence, and, like the snake in the fable, seeks to sting the very hand that has warmed him. I know how much this will startle you, for I know how much you think of him, and love him, and how many are the obligations which you owe to his father. But hear me to the end, and you will be convinced, as I have been, that, so far from your seeking his society and permitting his intimacy in our household, you would be justified in the adoption of very harsh measures for his expulsion—at least, it would become your duty to inform him that you can no longer suffer his visits.

"To begin, then, dear husband, Mr. Edgerton has been bold enough to speak to me in such language, as was insulting in him to utter, and equally painful and humiliating for me to hear. He has done this, not once, nor twice, nor thrice, but many times. You will ask why I have not informed you of this before; but I had several reasons for forbearing to do so, which I will relate in the proper places. I fancied that I could effectually repel insult of this sort without making you a party to it, for I feared the violence of your temper, and dreaded that the consequences might be bloodshed. I am only prompted to take a different course now, as I find that I was mistaken in this impression — and perceive that there is no hope of a remedy against the impertinence but by appealing to you for protection.

"It was not long after our marriage before the attentions of Mr. Edgerton became so particular as to annoy me; and I consulted my mother on the subject, but she assured me that such were customary, and so long as you were satisfied I had no reason to be otherwise. I was not quite content with this assurance, but did not know what other course to take, and there was nothing in the conduct of Mr. Edgerton so very marked and offensive as to justify me in making any communication to you. What offended me in his bearing was his fixed and continued watchfulness — the great earnestness of his looks — the subdued tones of his voice when he spoke to me, almost falling to a whisper, and the unusual style of his language, which seemed to address itself to such feelings only as do not belong to the common topics of discourse. The frequency of his visits to the studio afforded him opportunities for indulging in these practices; and your strange indifference to his approaches, and your equally strange and most unkind abandonment of my society for that of others, increased these opportunities, of which he scrupled not to take constant advantage. I soon perceived that he sought the house only at the periods when you were absent. He seemed always to know when this was the case; and I noted the fact, particularly, that, if, on such occasions, you happened to arrive unexpectedly, he never remained long afterward, but took his departure with an abruptness that, it seemed wonderful to me you should not have perceived. Conduct so strange as this annoyed rather than alarmed me; and it made me feel wretched, perhaps, beyond any necessity for it, when I found myself delivered up, as it were, to such persecution, by the very person whose duty it was to preserve me, and whose own presence, which would have been an effectual protection, was so dear to me always. Do not suppose, dear Edward, that I mean to reproach you. I do not know what may have been your duties abroad, and the trials which drew you so much from home, and from the eyes of a wife who knows no dearer object of contemplation than the form of her husband. Men in business, I know, have a thousand troubles out of doors, which a generous sensibility makes them studious never to bring home with them; and, knowing this, I determined to think lovingly of you always—to believe anything rather than that you would willingly neglect me;—and, by the careful exercise of my thoughts and affections, as they should properly be exercised, so to protect my own dignity and your honor, as to spare you any trouble or risk in asserting them, and, at the same time, to save both from reproach.

"But, though I think I maintained the most rigid reserve, as well of looks as of language, this unhappy young man continued his persecutions. In order to avoid him, I abandoned my usual labors in the studio. From the moment when I saw that he was disposed to abuse the privileges of friendship, I yielded that apartment entirely to him, and invariably declined seeing him when he visited the house in the mornings. But I could not do this at evening; and this became finally a most severe trial, for it so happened, that you now adopted a habit which left him entirely unrestrained, unless in the manner of his reception by myself. You now seldom remained at home of an evening, and thus deprived me of that natural protector whose presence would have spared me much pain with which I will not distress you. Ah! dearest husband, why did you leave me on such occasions? Why did you abandon me to the two-fold affliction of combating the approaches of impertinence, at the very moment when I was suffering from the dreadful apprehension that I no longer possessed those charms which had won me the affections of a husband. Forgive me! My purpose is not to reproach, but to entreat you.

"I need not pass over the long period through which this persecution continued. Your indifference seemed to me to give stimulus to the perseverance of this young man. Numberless little circumstances combined to make me think that, from this cause, indeed, he drew something like encouragement for his audacious hopes. The strength of your friendship for him blinded you to attentions which, it seemed to me, every eye must have seen but yours. I grew more and more alarmed; and a second time consulted with my mother. Her written answer you will find, marked No. 1, with the rest of the enclosures in this envelope. She laughed at my apprehensions, in sisted that Mr. Edgerton had not transcended the customary privileges, and intimated, very plainly as you will see, that a wife can suffer nothing from the admiration of a person, not her husband, however undisguised this admiration may be — provided she herself shows none in return ;— an opinion with which I could not concur, for the conclusive reason that, whatever the world may think on such a subject, the object of admiration, if she has any true sensibilities, must herself suffer annoyance, as I did, from the special designation which attends such peculiar and marked attention as that to which I was subjected. My mother took much pains, verbally and in writing, as the within letters will show you, to relieve me from the feeling of disquiet under which I suffered, but without effect; and I was further painfully afflicted by the impression, which her general tone of thought forced upon me, that her sense of propriety was so loose and uncertain that I could place no future reliance upon her counsels in relation to this or any kindred subject. Ah, Edward! little can you guess how lonely and desolate I felt, when, unable any longer to refer to her, I still did not dare to look to you.

"One opinion of hers, however, had very much alarmed me. You will find it expressed in the letter marked No. 3, in this collection. When I complained to her of the approaches of Mr. Edgerton, and declared my purpose of appealing to you if they were continued, she earnestly and expressly exhorted me against any such proceeding. She assured me that such a step would only lead to violence and bloodshed — reminded me of your sudden anger — your previous duel — and insisted that nothing more was necessary to check the impertinence than my own firmness and dignity. Perhaps this would have been enough, were it always practicable to maintain the reserve and coldness which was proper to effect this object; and, indeed, I could not but perceive that the effect was produced in considerable degree by this course. Mr. Edgerton visited the house less frequently; grew less impressive in his manner, and much more humble, until that painful and humiliating night of my mother's marriage. That night he asked me to dance with him. I declined; but afterward he came to me accompanied by my mother. She whispered in my ears that I was harsh in my refusal, and called my attention to his wretched appearance. Had I reflected upon it then, as I did afterward, this very allusion would have been sufficient to have determined me not to consent;—but I was led away by her suggestions of pity, and stood up with him for a cotillion. But the music changed, the set was altered, and the Spanish dance was substituted in its place. In the course of this dance, I could not deceive myself as to the degree of presumption which my partner displayed; and, but for the appearance of the thing, and because I did not wish to throw the room into disorder, I would have stopped and taken my seat long before it was over. When I did take my seat, I found myself still attended by him, and it was with difficulty that I succeeded finally in defeating his perseverance, by throwing myself into the midst of a set of elderly ladies, where he could no longer distinguish me with his attentions. In the meantime you had left the room. You had deserted me. Ah! Clifford, to what annoyance did your absence expose me that night! To that absence, do we owe that I lost the only dear pledge of love that God had ever vouchsafed us—and you know how greatly my own life was perilled. Think not, dearest, that I speak this to reproach you; and yet —could you have remained!—could you have loved, and longed to be and remain with me, as most surely did I long for your presence only and always—ah! how much sweeter had been our joys—how more pure our happiness—our faith—with now—perhaps, even now—the dear angel whom we then lost, living and smiling beneath our eyes, and linking our mutual hearts more and more firmly together than before!

"That night, when it became impossible to remain longer without trespassing—when all the other guests had gone—I consented to be taken home in Mr. Edgerton's carriage. Had I dreamed that Mr. Edgerton was to have been my companion, I should have remained all night before I would have gone with him, knowing what I knew, and feeling the mortification which I felt. But my mother assured me that I was to have the carriage to myself—it was she who had procured it;—and it was not until I was seated, and beheld him enter, that I had the least apprehension of such an intrusion. Edward! it is with a feeling almost amounting to horror, that I am constrained to think that my mother not only knew of his intention to accompany me, but that she herself suggested it. This, I say to *you!* You will find the reasons for my suspicions in the letters which I enclose. It is a dreadful suspicion—at the expense of one's own mother! I dare not believe in the dark malice which it implies.—I strive to think that she meant and fancied only some pleasant mischief.

"I shudder to declare the rest! This man, your friend—he whom you sheltered in your bosom, and trusted beyond all others—whom you have now taken into your house with a blindness that looks more like a delusion of witchcraft than of friendship—this impious man, I say, dared to wrap me in his embrace—dared to press his lips upon mine!

"My cheek even now burns as I write, and I must lay down the pen because of my trembling. I struggled from his grasp—I broke the window by my side, and cried for help from the wayfarers. I cried for you! But you did not answer! Oh, husband! where were you? Why, why did you expose me to such indignities?

"He was alarmed. He promised me forbearance; and, convulsed with fright and fear, I found myself within our enclosure, I knew not how; but before I reached the cottage I became insensible, and knew nothing more until the pangs of labor subdued the more lasting pains of thought and recollection.

"You resolved to leave our home—to go abroad among strangers, and Oh! how I rejoiced at your resolution. It seemed to promise me happiness; at least it promised me rescue and relief. I should at all events be free from the persecution of this man. I dreaded the consequences, either to you or to himself, of the exposure of his insolence. I had resolved on making it; and only hesitated, day by day, as my mother dwelt upon the dangers which would follow. And when you determined on removal, it seemed to me the most fortunate providence, as it promised to spare me the necessity of making this painful revelation at all. Surely, I thought, and my mother said, as this will put an effectual stop to his presumption, there will be no need to narrate what is already past. The only motive in telling it at all would be to prevent, not to punish: if the prevention is effected by other means, it is charity only to forbear the relation of matters which would breed hatred, and probably provoke strife. This made me silent; and, full of new hope—the hope that having discarded all your old associates and removed from all your old haunts, you would become mine entirely—I felt a new strength in my frame, a new life in my breast, and a glow upon my cheeks as within my soul, which seemed a guaranty for a long and happy term of that love which had begun in my bosom with the first moments of its childish consciousness and confidence.

"But one painful scene and hour I was yet compelled to endure the night before our departure. Mr. Edgerton came to play his flute under our window. I say Mr. Edgerton, but it was only by a sort of instinct that I fixed upon him as the musician. Perhaps it was because I knew not what other person to suspect. Frequently, before this night, had I heard this music; but on this occasion he seemed to have approached more nearly to the dwelling; and, indeed, I finally discovered that he was actually beneath the China-tree that stood on the south front of the cottage. I was asleep when the music began. He must have been playing for some time before I awakened. How I was awakened I know not; but something disturbed me, and I then saw you about to leave the room stealthily. I heard your feet upon the stairs, and in the next moment I discovered one of your pistols lying upon the window-sill, just beneath my eyes. This alarmed me; a thousand apprehensions rushed into my brain; all the suggestions of strife and bloodshed which my mother had ever told me, filled my mind; and without knowing exactly what I did or said, I called out to the musician to fly with all possible speed. He did so; and after a delay which was to me one of the most cruel apprehension, you returned in safety. Whether you suspected, and what, I could not conjecture; but if you had any suspicions of me, you did not seem to entertain any of him, for you spoke of him afterward with the same warm tone of friendship as before.

"That something in my conduct had not pleased you, I could see from your deportment as we travelled the next morning. You were sad, and very silent and abstracted. This disappeared, however, and, day by day, my happiness, my hope, my confidence in you, in myself, in all things, increased—and I felt assured of realizing that perfect idea of felicity which I proposed to myself from the moment when you declared your purpose to emigrate. Were we not happy, husband—so happy at M——, for weeks, for months—always, morning, noon, and night—until the reappearance of this false friend of yours? Then, it seemed to me as if everything changed. Then, that other friend of yours—who, though he never treated me with aught but respect, I yet can call no friend of mine—Mr. Kingsley, drew you away again from your home—carried you with him to his haunts—detained you late and long, by night and day—and I was left once more exposed to the free and frequent familiarity of Mr. Edgerton. He renewed his former habits; his looks were more presuming, and his attentions more direct and loathsome than ever. More than once I strove to speak with you on this hateful subject; but it was so shocking, and you were so fond of him, and I still had my fears! At length, moved by compassion, you brought him to our house. Blind and devoted to him—with a blindness and devotion beyond that which the noblest friendship would deserve, but which renders tenfold more hateful the dishonest and treacherous person upon whom it is thrown away—you command me to meet him with kindness—to tend his bed of sickness—to soothe his moments of sadness and despondency—to expose myself to his insolence!

"Husband! my soul revolts at this charge! I have disobeyed it and you; and I must justify myself in this my disobedience. I must at length declare the truth. I have striven to do so in the preceding narrative. This narrative I began when you brought this false friend into our dwelling. He must leave it. You must command his departure. Do not think me moved by any unhappy or unbecoming prejudices against him. My antipathies have arisen solely from his presumption and misconduct. I esteemed him—nay, I even liked him—before. I liked his taste for the arts, his amiable manners, his love of music and poetry, and all those graces of the superior mind and education, which dignify humanity, and indicate its probable destinies. But when he showed me how false he was to a friendship so free and confiding as was yours—when he abused my eyes and ears with expressions unbecoming in him, and insulting and ungenerous to me—I loathed and spurned him! While he is in your house I will strive and treat him civilly, but do not tax me further. For your sake I have borne much; for the sake of peace, and to avoid strife and crime, I have been silent—perhaps too long. The strange, improper letters of my mother, which I enclose, almost make me tremble to think that I have paid but too much deference to her opinion. But, in the expulsion of this miserable man from your dwelling, there needs no violence, there needs no crime! A word will overwhelm him with shame. Remember, dear husband, that he is feeble and sick; it is probable he has not long to live. Perform your painful duty privily, and with all the forbearance which is consistent with a proper firmness. In truth, he has done us no real harm. Let us remember *that!* If anything, he has only made me love you the more, by showing so strongly how generous is the nature which he has so infamously abused. Once more, dear husband, do no violence. Let not our future days be embittered by any recollections of the present. Command, compel his departure, and come home to me, and keep with me always. "Your own true wife,

"JULIA CLIFFORD."

"*Postcript.*—I had closed this letter yesterday, thinking to send it to your office in the afternoon. I had hoped that there would be nothing more;—but last night, this madman—for such I must believe him to be—committed another outrage upon my person! He has a second time seized me in his arms and endeavored to grasp me in his embrace. O husband!—why, why do you thus expose me? Do you indeed love me? I sometimes tremble with a fear lest you do not. But I dare not think so. Yet, if you do, why am I thus exposed—thus deserted—thus left to a companionship which is equally loathsome to me and dishonoring to you? I implore you to open your eyes—to believe me, and discard this false friend from your dwelling and your confidence. But, oh, be merciful, dear husband! Strike no sudden blow! Send him forth with scorn but remember his feebleness, his family, and spare his life. I send this by Emma. Let no one see the letters of my mother, but burn them instantly. "Your own "JULIA."

And this was the writing which had employed her time for days before the sad catastrophe! And it was for this reason that she asked, with so much earnestness, if I had been to my office on the day when I drove Edgerton out into the woods for the adjustment of our issue? No wonder that she was anxious at that moment. How much depended upon that simple and ordinary proceeding. Had I but gone that day to my office as usual! ......

There were no longer doubts. There could be none. There was now no mystery. It was all clear. The most ambiguous portions of her conduct had been as easily and simply explained as the rest. But it availed nothing! The blow had fallen. I was an accursed man — truly accursed, and miserably desolate.

I still sat, stolid, seemingly, as the insensible chair which sustained me, when Kingsley came in. He took the papers from my unresisting hands. He read them in silence. I heard but one sentence from his lips, and it came from them unconsciously:—

"Poor, poor girl!"

I looked round and started to my feet. The tears were on his manly cheeks. I had shed none. My eyes were dry! The fountains of tears seemed shut up, arid and thirsty.

"I must make atonement!" I exclaimed. "I must deliver myself up to justice!"

"This is madness," said he, seizing my arm as I was about to leave the room.

"No: retribution only! I have destroyed her. I must make the only atonement which is in my power. I must die!"

"What you design is none," he said solemnly. "Your death will atone nothing. It is by living only that you can atone!"

"How?"

"By repentance! This is the grand—the only sovereign atonement which the spirit of man can ever make. There is no other mode provided in nature. The laws, which would take your life, would deprive you of the means of atonement. This is due to God; it can be performed only by living and suffering. Life is a duty because it is an ordeal. You must preserve life, as a sacred trust, for this reason. Even if you were a felon—one wilfully resolving and coldly executing crime—you were yet bound to preserve life! Throw it away, and though you comply with the demand of social laws, you forfeit the only chance of making atonement to those which are far superior. Rather pray that life may be spared you. It was with this merciful purpose that God not only permitted Cain to live, but commanded that none should slay him. You must live for this!"

"Yet I slew *her!*"

He did with me as he pleased. Three days after beheld us on our way to the rich empire of Texas—its plains, rich but barren—unstocked, wild—running to waste with its tangled weeds—needing, imploring the vigorous hand of cultivation. Even such, at that moment, was my heart! Rich in fertile affections, yet gone to waste; waiting, craving, praying for the hand of the cultivator!—Yet who now was that cultivator?

To this question the words of Kingsley, which were those of truth and wisdom, were a sufficient answer; and evermore an echo arose as from the bottom of my soul; and my lips repeated it to my own ears only; and but one word was spoken; and that word was—"ATONEMENT!"

THE END.

www.ingramcontent.com/pod-product-compliance
Lightning Source LLC
LaVergne TN
LVHW040755070826
844660LV00025B/1152